A LOT LIKE CHRISTMAS

FESTIVE HOLIDAY READING COLLECTION

MELISSA HILL

Copyright © Little Blue Books 2019

The right of Melissa Hill to be identified as the Author of the Work has been asserted by her in accordance with the Copyright, Designs and Patents Act 1988.

All rights reserved. No part of this publication may be reproduced, stored in a retrieval system, or transmitted, in any form or by any means without the prior written permission of the author. You must not circulate this book in any format.

All characters in this publication are fictitious and any resemblance to real persons, living or dead is purely coincidental.

A LOT LIKE CHRISTMAS

(THE HOLIDAY SWITCH)

CHAPTER 1

It was unbelievable how a couple of snow flurries could make everyone in Boston suddenly forget how to drive, Ally Walker mused, frustrated as she sat in the back of the taxi winging its way to the airport.

Granted, it wasn't often they made it all the way till December without any significant accumulations. But none of that especially mattered right now. All she could think about was making her flight.

"Outta the way!" her cab driver remonstrated as the car in front stopped suddenly at the airport terminal's no stopping zone.

Ally scooted towards the edge of the back seat in an attempt to see out of the windshield. "You know what ... this is good. I can walk the rest of the way."

The driver pulled up to the curb, and tapping her phone to pay him, (adding a nice holiday tip) she exited the car quickly and hopped round back to grab her stuff from the trunk. Extending the pull handle of her carry-on suitcase, she was off and running into the terminal building, not even letting her three inch pumps slow her down.

Using her free hand to pull her trench coat tighter around her body and her wool sheath dress, Ally attempted to create a barrier against the bitter cold. And questioned what she could have been thinking this morning not wearing pantyhose while bitter snow flurries pelted her bare legs.

Inside, she made it to the security line in quick time. After years of practice, Ally could do this in her sleep. Which was fortunate because after a non-stop work day that began at 5am this morning, she *felt* half asleep.

"Come on, come on," she muttered impatiently as she waited for the airline app to load so she could pull up her digital boarding pass.

But with 'no reservation found' displaying onscreen, Ally reluctantly gave up her place in the line to call her assistant.

"Walters Tech," Mel answered, in her most professional and chipper voice.

"It's me," Ally greeted, trying not to make herself sound too demanding, but time was of the essence. "Why can't I check in for my flight?"

"You know you're not with your usual, right? They don't fly into your friend's location. I thought I'd mentioned that. "

Ally winced. She hated changes of plan.

"I didn't know that. Text me the info? Maybe if I run to the gate I can still make it."

"Yeah you're cutting it kinda close, considering…"

"I had to make a stop by my apartment on the way," Ally explained, glancing at the garment bag laid carefully on top of her luggage, sequins sparkling brightly through the plastic covering.

She'd fallen instantly in love with the dress nearly four years ago when she happened to pass by it in a department store window and threw caution to the wind, purchasing it without any particular occasion in mind.

Since then the gown had been sitting in her closet, just waiting for the right moment to shine. And in her suitcase was a gorgeous pair of silver heels with jewelled straps she'd purchased a week later to match.

Just in case an opportunity presented itself, which it seemed would happen this weekend, courtesy of Ally's best friend Lara's invite to the Snow Ball, a gala event being held in her Maine hometown.

A girl couldn't just wear any old shoes with *that* dress.

Ally hadn't put much else thought into packing for this particular visit though, since her friend had more clothes than Saks and she and Lara were pretty much the same size.

Lara's was by all accounts a *very* small town, so she figured most other outings while there would call for a pretty casual dress code.

Besides, the visit was just a short festive diversion from her final destination; Florida, which called for shorts, bikinis and not a whole lot else.

Ally always preferred to travel light.

"You wouldn't *believe* how crowded the airport is today," she muttered to Mel now.

Ally had flown over 100,000 miles that year, and never had to fight her way through this many people. All of them just taking their time, walking in large groups, talking, laughing, carrying huge wrapped gifts.

Didn't they know about gift cards? Or online shopping? Granted she had a couple of small things in her luggage for Lara's kids, but they barely took up any room.

Ally prided herself on travelling light.

"Two days before Christmas and you didn't expect it to be crowded?" her assistant laughed.

"Well, Christmas Eve and Day are usually quiet; that's why they're usually my favourite days to fly," she said, scowling at a man who'd almost rolled his suitcase right over her toes.

"Because most people spend those days with family, not travelling on vacation," Mel said. "Which reminds me, you're all set for your usual Clearwater Beach hotel. As soon as Christmas is done, you'll be en route to palm trees and sunshine."

Which to Ally right about now, sounded like heaven.

CHAPTER 2

She certainly wouldn't be getting any sunshine and palm trees in upstate Maine.

Looking around again at the crammed airport, Ally started to doubt whether she'd in fact made the right decision visiting Lara and her family for the holidays, rather than going straight to Florida.

But time spent with her old friend was long overdue and since she hadn't yet visited her friend's house, and rarely took time off from her tech consulting business, this time of year was a good opportunity as any.

"Thanks Mel," she said to her assistant now. "Enjoy your time off, and Merry Christmas."

Out of breath a little from running in heels, Ally scrambled to check in at the other airline's digital kiosk with only minutes to spare.

As her boarding pass printed, a sudden horror filled her when she saw the seat number printed next to her name. Not only was this the first time in recent memory she hadn't been upgraded, but to add insult to injury, they had the nerve to ask her to board in the *final* group.

Ally had been pretty much royalty on the biggest airline in the country for the last four years in a row thanks to her weekly travel schedule and copious airmiles.

SkyAir rewarded her for her loyalty by treating her like gold. She was usually the first one on the aircraft, whereupon she almost always enjoyed a complimentary upgrade to first or business class.

What would it be like to fly as a regular person again?

She barely had time to think about what lay ahead as she hurried onwards to her gate.

"Last call, boarding group #5," someone called over the loudspeaker just as she arrived. Looking around the gate, Ally saw only four other people waiting to board.

She quickly scanned her pass and wheeled her bag through, only to find the line at a standstill on the jet bridge.

No doubt the passengers already onboard were searching for overhead space or playing musical chairs with their fellow seat mates trying to secure seats next to the family members they were traveling with.

As if it would be so difficult to spend a two hour flight apart.

"Ma'am," a flight attendant approached her then. "I'm afraid we are going to have to check your luggage today."

"Excuse me?" Ally asked, in the hope she'd misheard. Her bag was TSA approved. It fit perfectly in the overhead storage compartment and was just the right size to hold her clothing, her work computer and toiletries. This lady had to be mistaken.

"Overhead storage is limited on these smaller puddle hoppers," she explained pleasantly. "Don't worry, we'll just store it beneath the hold and it will be waiting for you at the carousel on the other side."

Worry wasn't the right word. Annoyed was more like it. Though not wanting to prolong the boarding process any further, Ally reluctantly handed over her case, first grabbing her garment bag off the top.

"OK, well is there somewhere on board I could hang this maybe?" she asked.

"We only have a small area for the crew's items. We're not supposed to, but that dress is gorgeous. It would be a real shame if it got wrinkled."

"Thank you," Ally smiled gratefully, as the attendant took the garment bag and headed back out the gate.

A little bit of separation anxiety kicked in and she felt compelled to watch as her trusty suitcase and favourite dress were spirited away somewhere.

It occurred to Ally then she hadn't arranged for a bag tag, but before she had time to get the flight attendant's attention, the line started moving again and she needed to keep up.

Ally attempted one final peek behind, when the line once again stopped abruptly and she collided into a taller man in front. His plaid sports coat felt soft again her cheek and she was close enough to see the slight wear in the leather patches at the elbows.

Assuming he was older based on his style of clothing, when he turned around she was surprised to find that he was in fact, much younger - likely in his early thirties, just like her.

And cute.

"Pardon me," he apologised gently, his blue eyes laser- focused on hers and normally, the intensity of such a gaze would make Ally uncomfortable.

But this gave her time to study his face. She could see that his eyes also had specks of green, his nose was straight and his square jaw line was covered with light stubble. He looked like the kind of guy who would normally be clean shaven, but for some reason had skipped his morning shave for a day or two.

"No, my fault," she mumbled. "I wasn't paying attention."

Ally was almost sorry when he broke their eye contact as the line began to move again, leaving her to stare at the back of his head once more.

Maybe boarding last wasn't so bad after all.

CHAPTER 3

A few more minutes passed before Ally was finally able to board the aircraft and locate her seat.

The sight of the narrow, cramped coach class seat after traveling primarily in the comforts of first class was a rude awakening, and deflated her spirits yet again.

The seat appeared to be only about two feet wide, the armrests were narrow and metal and it clearly didn't have a footrest.

Even at only 5' 3" she still had to crouch down and scoot her legs sideways to fit into it. Though at least she was seated in the aisle and could possibly stretch out her legs a bit that way.

She spent the final minutes before take off on her phone trying to get through all unread work emails that had come in since she'd exited the taxi.

One was from a client confirming a conference call for the 23rd and Ally updated her calendar. She would be in Maine for that one. Lara surely had to have a spare room or some private space she could take the call from, so this shouldn't be a problem.

She made it through another seven or so emails before she heard the dreaded announcement.

"Ladies and gentleman, please switch all cellphones to flight mode, power down computers and other electronics equipment and safely stow them."

Ally harrumphed. How much more pleasant the flying experience would be if someone could figure out a way for passengers to use their phones while in flight?

Not that airlines seemed at all concerned these days with their customer's comfort. The small seat and lack of overhead storage space on this one were alone a testament to that.

Loss of productivity was certainly an inconvenience, but on the bright side at least she could use this time to unwind and read. About the only time she got the opportunity to indulge in reading just for pleasure. So at least there was that to look forward to.

A couple of minutes after take-off, the drinks cart pulled up along side Ally's seat before she even had a chance to unfasten her seat belt.

She brought her elbow in towards her body to prevent it from inadvertently being bumped with the sharp edges of the metal cart. The arm rest was way too narrow for even her elbow to comfortably rest.

"Can I get you a drink ma'am?"

Ally smiled, thinking how a chilled glass of wine would be just the thing to help her relax for the almost two hour flight. "I'll have a glass of chardonnay if you have it."

"Sure. That will be $8. Cash only."

It has been such a long time since she had flown coach that Ally had completely forgotten that drinks were extra! She reached for her purse, but already knew she didn't have any cash on her. Carrying paper these days was like lugging around a stone and chisel, outdated to say the least.

Was this airline the final frontier of the digital revolution?

"Actually, maybe just some water."

"Sure. That will be $2."

Water was no longer free either?

Frustrated, Ally leaned back into the headrest of her seat, wishing she had stopped for something before she boarded.

"You know what, I'll pass - I don't have any cash on me right now."

She swallowed, her throat already beginning to feel dry at the thought of two hours without anything to drink.

"Here, I've got it."

Ally looked up as she heard a man's voice pipe up from somewhere nearby. Across the aisle, one row behind and diagonal to her own seat was the guy with the plaid sports coat she'd bumped into while boarding.

And much to her embarrassment, he was extending a couple of dollars towards the flight attendant.

"Thank you, that's very kind," she said. "But I'm fine really."

The flight attendant hesitated a little at the guy's outstretched hand, unsure what to do.

"Please - I insist." He nodded and the attendant duly accepted on her behalf.

"Thank you," Ally smiled and took a sip from the plastic cup once it was set on her tray table, while trying to think of how to properly thank the generous stranger.

"Not a problem," he said, as the cart moved on.

"Here, let me pay you back." She tapped her phone screen, and began to pull up her mobile banking app. "If you just tell me your email address, I can Revolut it to you now."

"It's only two dollars, I think I'll survive. In fact, I have more if you really want that wine."

She chuckled. "If we hit any turbulence I may take you up on that." The man reached for his wallet once again, not seeming to pick up on her lighthearted tone. "Hey, I was just joking, honestly."

"Well, the offer is there."

"Thanks." Ally moved her gaze to the back of the seat in front, avoiding more eye contact. The feeling of being indebted to this stranger for his kind act was foreign to her.

It had been a long time since she'd wanted anything that she'd been unable to provide for herself. Even long before her mother died really.

Even during her last relationship, Ally was more often than not the one footing the bill when they went out for dinner.

"I take it you don't fly this airline often?" The helpful stranger spoke again.

"First time."

He offered a knowing smile and Ally found herself unsure of what to do next. For some reason, she didn't want their conversation to end.

"What are you reading?" she asked, noticing the book he had resting on his lap.

When he held it up, she recognised the name of a bestselling author.

"Oh, snap. I've actually just started his series; I'm almost done with the first book. I was hoping to finish it ... aw, damn." Just then she remembered her device was in her carry-on bag. The one the flight attendant had whisked away earlier.

When the stranger looked puzzled, she explained this to him.

"I just realised my e-reader is in my luggage. They made me check it."

"They took mine too. The flight's so busy I guess," he shrugged, while Ally wondered what she'd do now to pass the time.

The guy turned back to his book, but then stopped. "I can read aloud if you like. I've been told I have a voice for radio. Or is that a face."

She couldn't help but giggle at his cheesy joke. It reminded her of what Mel referred to as a 'dad joke'.

The kind of joke that would embarrass a teenager if it had been their father making it. Having grown up without a dad, Ally was never able to fully relate to the expression. The thought of a little embarrassment seemed like a small price to pay.

"Henry looks over the horizon in search of ..." He read from his book in a dramatic tone, while the passenger seated next to him shot a stern look, clearly not amused.

"Guess he's not a radio fan," Ally leaned across and whispered. "But don't worry - I'll be fine. Enjoy yours in peace. And thanks again for the water."

"No problem." He winked. "But maybe next time you should rethink your reliance on digital."

Ally smiled. She didn't have the heart to tell him that digital was not only her job, but pretty much her life.

She didn't know what she'd do without tech. As it was, missing her iPad on this flight was like missing an arm.

Instead, she turned back and closed her eyes, suddenly exhausted by her hectic day.

And before Ally knew it, she'd relaxed into a deep and peaceful slumber.

CHAPTER 4

The next thing Ally felt was someone patting her arm. Startled, she sat up in her seat and looked wildly around, trying to remember where she was.

"Must've been a nice dream," the flight attendant who'd just woken her teased, "flight's landed."

Ally scrambled to get up, only to find her neck stiff and her legs heavy. Further adding to her confusion was the fact that she seemed to be the very last person on board.

She looked around, wondering how the passenger sitting next to her in the window seat had made it past without her waking. And then instinctively she glanced at the seat across the aisle where the helpful guy had been sitting, and found herself wishing it weren't empty.

It would have been nice to thank him again before they parted ways.

Then her cheeks felt hot at the thought of him seeing her fast asleep while making his way off the plane. What if her mouth had been wide open with a line of drool down the side of her mouth? What if the altitude made her snore?

She shook her head in an attempt to rid her mind of these embarrassing thoughts.

Hopping up, she automatically opened the overhead bin out of habit to retrieve her case, forgetting that it wasn't in there. It was only when the flight attendant returned with her garment bag that she remembered she would have to wait for it at the carousel.

As she exited through to the terminal, Ally was greeted by the sound of tinny Christmas tunes in the background.

She couldn't understand for the life of her why an airport would play background music so loudly, let alone the old festive favourite that was currently blaring. A shame no one could come up with any new original holiday tunes anymore. Hearing the same songs year after year was a bit depressing.

As she approached the quiet carousel, she realised that at least one advantage to being the last person off the plane was everyone else had already picked up their stuff and she wouldn't need to fight for her spot.

Her case was the only one left on the carousel, and cut a lonely sight, wandering round and round the circuit.

Ally grabbed it by the handle and hoisted it up, noticing that it felt a little heftier than she remembered.

She really was exhausted.

As she set off to exit the terminal, she quickly powered her phone back on to figure out where she was meeting Lara, frowning a little when she realised how little battery it had left.

Her best friend answered after one ring, and she strained to hear over the background music. "Hey, I've just landed, you here?" She heard a baby crying on the other end of the line.

"Almost there sweetie," she cooed, in a tone Ally had never heard before. "Be right there!" she yelled back into the phone then, sounding much more like the Lara she knew.

Outside the building, almost as soon as the phone disconnected, Ally spied a mini van pull forward to the curb.

One hand was still on the wheel, but as soon as she spotted the messy heap of dark blonde hair pilled on top of the driver's head, she knew it was Lara.

Her friend's hair had been the first thing Ally noticed about her when they first met back in college.

She was sitting behind Lara n an art history class, and while the professor was showing slides of Hagia Sophia, she was memorised by the way her soft curls bounced each time she moved her head.

Ally had always wanted to be able to do her own hair the same way, but hers was poker straight. Her mom had been the only one who was able to get it to cooperate in any way.

One day during class, she finally decided to ask the girl how she did it. Lara was only too happy to show her, and they were pretty much inseparable the rest of college.

Ally always felt such a sense of nostalgia and joy when she remembered her carefree years as college student.

She had initially selected History as her major, since it was something she was endlessly interested in. Luckily enough, by the time she was a sophomore, her college advisor was kind enough to show her the starting salaries of various majors.

Ally's mother's declining health meant she would be on her own soon enough and she immediately switched to Computer Science, the top-paying field at the time.

Now, one hand on her luggage, the other raised in greeting, she walked towards the mini van that was stopped in the designated pick-up area.

"Riley, pick that up for your sister and she'll stop crying," she heard as she approached the van. Even with the windows rolled up, her best friend's voice was still audible.

She waited a few seconds before tapping lightly on the widow with her knuckles, hoping the noise didn't startle everyone.

"Thank you honey," Ally heard, before Lara turned around and looked out her window. She beamed and hurriedly undid her seat belt as she reached for the door handle. "Hey big city girl!" her friend exclaimed jumping from the car and throwing her arms around her. "Let me help you with your bags."

"No, don't worry, I've just got one. Pop the trunk and I'll throw it in."

Ally went to the rear of the car, peeking inside the widows at her adorable five year old godson and brand new goddaughter.

This would be her first time meeting Charlotte since she was born six months earlier. Another reason for this visit since she would get to do so while she was still a baby. Something her schedule hadn't allowed five years ago when Riley was born.

When Lara and her husband eventually did make a trip with Riley to Boston he was already walking by the time Ally got to meet him.

Opening the trunk, Ally hesitated when she saw the mountain of toys, fresh diapers and what appeared to be trash, piled almost as high as the back of the seat.

"Just throw it anywhere, don't worry - nothing back there is important," Lara called back and Ally followed her friend's instructions and hoisted the suitcase up and onto the shortest pile of the debris, once again laying her dress neatly over the top of it.

"Aunt Ally!" Riley squealed once she'd settled in to the passenger seat. It took her a few minutes to situate her feet since the floor was also littered with food wrappers.

"There you are honey. Riley you are even more handsome than the last time I saw you."

"Can I play some games on your phone?"

Lara swiped her outstretched hand past her neck, the universal gesture for 'do that and I'll kill you.'

"Sorry bud, my phone's almost dead. I need to charge it." That was actually the truth though. Ally glanced down at screen and saw she was now at 10%. Bummer.

Another downside of the different airline - there were usually charging stations in the armrests of her usual. But this one had been basic and without frills - to say the least.

"We are having a tech free Christmas," Lara supplied.

"Sounds like fun," Ally said, with as much sarcasm as possible.

"We want to spend the holidays connecting as a family without all these distractions. And it's not good for developing young brains to be so overly stimulated."

"Poor kids. My mom certainly never limited mine, and look how I turned out."

"Exactly, a cautionary tale."

Ally laughed and moved aside empty juice boxes on the car's console in an attempt to locate a phone charger.

"Lara you have got to be kidding me..." she said, holding up the end of the adapter.

"What?"

"Your phone must be at least two years old if you still use this to charge it."

"Like I have time to keep track of how old my phone is. It still works, so why would I buy a new one?"

Ally shook her head in amazement, realising she'd need to wait until she could unpack her own.

"Oh I can't believe you're finally here!" her friend enthused. "Especially on Christmas. I thought for sure you'd have made plans with Gary. How is that going?"

Ally made a face. "It's not - going I mean. According to him we were never actually dating in the first place. Really fooled me."

"Unbelieveable. Men these days."

"So what are the plans for tonight?" she asked, changing the subject. "We heading out somewhere? I checked the OpenTable app but couldn't find anything ... "

"Like for dinner?" Lara bit her lip. "With these two, restaurants are more trouble than they're worth these days."

"I can imagine. What time do they go to bed? We could head out then."

"Ha! By the time I get them both down I'm almost ready to pass out myself."

"Oh, sorry." Ally did her best to hide her disappointment. She had been looking forward to a night out with her best friend forever. Although she supposed it was foolish to think they'd be able to recreate the kind of fun they used to have in college.

"Don't be sorry, I'm sure not. I used to think bar hopping was so fun. Now it just seems empty compared to what I have now."

Lara looked into her rearview mirror at her smiling baby and fidgeting toddler in the backseat. "I've some pizza back at the house. We'll show you what real fun is."

"Great, I like pizza." As Ally looked over at her friend in her oversized sweatshirt, a Christmas elf on the front and her fuzzy black sweatpants, it was hard to remember what Lara was like before she become a mother.

How was this the same woman who used to complain at 2am when the bars would close because she didn't want to go home?

"Anyway, better to save our energies for the Snow Ball," Lara added then. "I've hired a sitter so we can go all out, hair, false eyelashes, the works. So I really hope you packed a knockout dress."

"Sure did."

"Oh we're going to have so much fun! Tomorrow is the ice maze, and then the tree lighting. You'll really like that one."

Ally swallowed hard. A bunch of people standing around in the freezing cold waiting for someone to flip the switch on a few lights didn't exactly sound like a rip-roaring time.

And the ice maze sounded very much like a kids thing.

Oh well, she'd get into the spirit of all this stuff, for Lara's sake at least.

It was a couple of days, tops. After that Ally would be chilling beneath the palm trees, pina colada in hand, Christmas a distant memory.

Heaven.

CHAPTER 5

After a forty-five minute drive through mostly woodlands, Lara turned onto a dimly lit road.

"Country living at it's finest," her friend declared.

Out of the darkness, a massive house appeared and Ally made no attempt to hide her surprise.

"Uh you didn't think to tell me you lived in a mansion?"

She was shocked enough when six years ago Lara broke the news that she was leaving Boston with her new husband Mark. The two women had done everything together, it was hard for Ally to imagine them living in different states.

Mark's grandmother had just passed and left them a house in his home town. He was also apparently the family heir to a small business, a restaurant and a few other things in the place.

Funny how Lara, the one who'd stuck with Art as her major in college, knowing she'd likely never make a lot of money and didn't care, ended up living in a house like this.

Wealth and material things never mattered to her best friend though, which is probably why Lara never told her about this place.

All these years, Ally had felt sorry for her friend living in Hicksville. But now, she felt a bit sorry for herself thinking how her entire apartment could probably fit into her friend's foyer!

Lara proceeded to pull into the wraparound driveway with trees surrounding either side, all lit by beautiful white fairy lights. A coating of fresh white snow sat on top of each tree as if it had been hand-placed by a professional decorator.

Columns surrounding the porch were decorated with alternating red and green festive garland.

It all looked like something out of a Christmas card.

"Nice isn't it? It belonged to Mark's grandmother. Way too much space for us, but it means a lot to him raising his family here."

"I'll say. It's like the McAllister's place in *Home Alone*."

Ally grabbed her bag and helped Riley out of his car seat while Lara picked up the baby carrier and headed inside.

A massive Christmas tree took up over half the entryway, and every branch had beautiful, distinctive ornaments dangling. The angel on top was pretty much level with a grand second-story staircase.

The whole effect was magnificent, truly like something out of a movie and Ally almost thought of asking Lara for a map of the place, just in case she got lost.

"Mommy, I'm hungry," Riley declared, as he threw off his coat.

"Alright, let's get the pizza in. Will you show Aunt Ally where the guest room is? I'm sure she's dying to get out of those work clothes."

Ally glanced down at her dress and pumps. She had never really thought of her outfit as 'work clothes' before. But perhaps something casual would indeed be more appropriate for pizza and playing with the kids.

She headed upstairs, struggling a little as she hefted her case up the grand, seemingly never-ending stair case.

Inside the guest room, she threw it onto the bed and undid the zipper. Then throwing the lid back, she stopped and frowned.

A beige sweater lay on top, a fancy expensive looking cashmere one that Ally couldn't recall packing.

Or *owning* for that matter.

Moving it aside, her frown deepened with what she found underneath; a bunch of books and notebooks.

Three had the same cover, with mountains in the background -

proper books. Ally didn't even own four hardcopy books, much less three of the same.

She continued to dig, hoping that whomever put these relics in her suitcase on top of her stuff, wasn't also a thief that would have taken her phone charger.

But came up empty handed, as she pushed aside a tuxedo, a pair of slippers, until finally realization dawned.

This was *not* her bag!

Yes, it was the same type and model as the one she'd taken on every trip since she founded her tech consultant business six years ago, but it definitely wasn't the one she'd boarded the plane with.

She must have grabbed it by mistake. But no, this was the only one left on the carousel, which was why she'd taken it in the first place.

Which meant that someone else had picked up hers.

They were the one who had made the mistake.

What on earth was she going to do?

CHAPTER 6

*A*lly fell backwards onto the bed as the realisation sunk in even further.

She had no laptop, no VPN, no phone charger. Let alone personal belongings, like a toothbrush or makeup or underwear even!

How was this possible? And what should she do? Once the phone on her battery died, she'd be completely cut off from the outside world.

Ally struggled to keep her breathing even, as she went to find her friend.

"Lara!" she called helplessly down the hallway. "All of my stuff is gone."

Her friend came out of the master bedroom with baby Charlotte on her hip. "What do you mean - gone?"

"I grabbed the wrong bag at the airport. Well, I mean I didn't - someone else did and I got this one instead which obviously isn't mine, so I don't have any stuff and …"

"OK calm down. I can lend you anything you need for the moment - I've got spare toiletries and we can grab the basics in town …"

"No, my stuff, work stuff. My laptop was in here and my charger and iPad … I have important calls and a couple of Zoom meetings coming up - I can't miss them."

"You'll get it all back in no time, I'm sure. Just relax. First things first, let's get you some clothes and then we can call the airline. With your status they'll probably hire a limo to hand-deliver it all back to you."

If only it had happened on my airline, Ally thought, unable to share her friend's optimism. Taking a deep breath, she followed Lara into her bedroom, doing her best to focus on the clothing options she was offering, but all she could think about was a finding a way to get her bag back.

"I know - I'll get my assistant on it. She'll be able to figure it out with the airline."

"Great idea."

Though Ally wasn't sure exactly how, since the bag she had didn't have an airline identification tag. And neither did hers. Which meant like hers, it must also have been stowed unexpectedly.

Then she groaned, remembering that Mel had officially logged off for the holidays.

Still, she was sure she wouldn't mind, and pinged her a quick text, before her phone ran out and she was *seriously* stuck.

"If you could just lend me something to wear tonight to sleep in? And maybe something for tomorrow morning at that ice maze thing just in case."

With the arm that wasn't holding her baby, Lara reached for a pair of pants draped over the arm of a rocking chair. "These are thermals. You can wear them under these jeans tomorrow. And I'll find you a sweater and some boots."

"Thanks." Ally examined the pants trying to determine if they'd fit her.

"And for tonight, take this." Lara threw her two large flannel items, a pair of decidedly unfeminine pyjamas, the kind a grandfather might wear.

Ally returned to the guest room to try on the nightclothes her friend had been kind enough to lend her. It felt strange to be wearing pyjamas when she hadn't yet eaten dinner, but the feeling of the warm flannel against her skin was too good to pass up.

She caught a glimpse of herself in the floor length mirror on the back of the door before heading down the stairs.

Despite her worries, the festive red and green and poinsettia flowered pattern made her smile at her own reflection.

Never in a million years could Ally have imagined herself wearing Christmas pjs, but something about it had almost magically made her feel better already.

CHAPTER 7

"Merry Christmas," Jake Turner called to the driver as he exited the cab in front of the chateau his family rented every year in this Maine small town for the holidays.

As a kid, having to spend Christmas so far from his friends in Boston was a total drag, but as an adult, he anticipated this break from hectic city life.

"Jakey!" his younger sister Meghan squealed and ran towards him from the doorway. She had her arms wrapped around him before he could even set his luggage down.

"Hello to you too. Did I miss anything good?"

He hated the fact that he wasn't able to join the rest of the family when they'd arrived a couple of days ago. But the holiday shopping season was a busy time for his profession.

His publisher had somehow landed a book signing at Barnes & Noble and being in desperate need of exposure (and sales), Jake was only too happy to agree.

"Just the same ole, same ole," said Meghan. "I'd much rather hear about your book signing."

He let out a big sigh.

"That bad?"

"Just wasn't quite the turnout we'd hoped."

"I'm sorry. But hey, don't worry about it. Your job is to write, theirs is to take care of sales. Your new book is amazing. If that publisher can't sell it, maybe you should just find someone else."

Even in adulthood his baby sister thought he could do no wrong.

"The business is changing now, though. According to my agent, I need to connect more with my readers. She keeps trying to get me on social media." He wrinkled his nose.

"Well, I actually agree with her on that one. You are *way* behind the times. A real techno dinosaur."

"Not behind, I just prefer my privacy. I know that kind of makes me an anomaly in our generation," he laughed.

"Hey, enough about work, hurry up and get changed out of that old man history professor vibe you've got going on," Melanie urged, her nose wrinkling at the sight of his jacket. "Everyone's here and we're just about to eat."

"Great, I'm starving. Let me just drop my stuff up and get settled in."

The chateau was rustic in the most literal sense of the word, and all of the ceilings were made of exposed dark wooden beams. Though the open fire and twinkling lights of the Christmas tree in the living area made it wonderfully welcoming and festive, especially for family gatherings.

Jake took off upstairs to his usual room, the same one he stayed in every year.

Putting his suitcase on the bench along the end of the bed, he hurried to unzip it and retrieve his slippers for starters, so he could get out of these constricting leather shoes.

But upon opening the case, Jake knew immediately that something wasn't right. He most certainly didn't pack a pair of sparkly, four inch heels. Nor a pearl-studded clutch. Or an entire department stores-worth of colourful bikinis…

What the…?

'You've got to be kidding me…"

He'd picked up the wrong bag at the airport. At the realisation, a panic ignited with such force that his heart began to beat rapidly.

Jake tried to calm himself so he could think. He quickly zipped the bag back up, almost as if he was doing something illegal, and raced back downstairs, signalling his sister out to the hallway.

"My bag - I grabbed the wrong bag at the airport," he whispered loudly to Meghan, trying her utmost to stay out of earshot of any others.

She gave him a curious look. "OK, I'm sure we can call the airline. They probably still have yours. Calm down."

"I can't calm down! Is Heidi in there?" Jake indicated the living room as he paced back and forth, his mind racing.

"No, she's in town with Mom - why? Oh, no!" Meghan suddenly realised the seriousness of the situation. "You don't mean to tell me *that* was in the…"

"It was." Jake looked around wildly. "Which is why I have to get that bag back. Now."

CHAPTER 8

A little later Ally was greeted by the most wonderful cooking smell as she entered Lara's kitchen downstairs.

Her friend stood by the quartz island in the middle of her massive gourmet kitchen, looking all the world like a culinary professional.

Besides the jaunty elf hat she was sporting, and Ally had to giggle at the sight.

Lara pulled a steaming hot flatbread pizza from the oven and set it in the middle of an impressive spread of delicious-looking salads and dips. She then drizzled olive oil out of a very fancy green bottle over the mushroom and goat cheese pizza toppings.

"Hope you're hungry..." she sang as Ally got closer.

"Starving. Though I wish you hadn't gone to so much trouble. When you said pizza in the car, I just assumed..."

"That I'd be serving you junk? Like I would do such a thing." Lara grabbed half a lemon and squeezed it over a large bowl of baby arugula, topped with freshly shaved parmesan.

"Boys dinner!" she yelled and as if on cue, her husband Mark and little Riley came racing into the kitchen and each grabbed a plate from the pile on the counter.

"Riley eats arugula? And mushrooms?" Ally asked in surprise.

"Oh yes, he's very adventurous. Grab a plate and dig in."

She tried to remember the last time she'd eaten a meal that someone else had prepared for her, and sadly couldn't.

Once everyone had a full plate, they all gathered around the kitchen table to eat together. The lights were low and soft festive tunes played in the background.

It was unbelievable warm and cosy and Ally got a sense of why her friend loved her little family so much.

This was ... wonderful.

"Aunt Ally, want to see my trains?" Riley asked when they'd finished eating.

"Sure, I'd love to."

He grabbed her by the hand and almost yanked her out of her seat in his excitement, leading her to the corner of the living area where there were almost 50 pieces of wooden train tracks on the floor, and dozens magnetic trains.

The warm glow of the fireplace lit up the family room and made it magical. Five stockings hung from the mantel, each awaiting a visit from Santa. Ally could only imagine the excitement the kids would experience on Christmas morning.

Riley sat on the floor and immediately went to work connecting the pieces of the tracks. His eyebrows furrowed as he concentrated on his design.

"Ally would you like some more wine?" Lara, ever the gracious hostess, called out from the kitchen.

"Sure - if you are."

"Ha! If I drink this late at night I'll be asleep before anyone else. But don't let that stop you."

"No no, I'm busy over here. But thank you."

In no time, Riley had built a massive circular train track, complete with a bridge and two junctures. He slid his six engine train around the corners, making whistling sounds.

Ally stood a few feet in front straddling the tracks with one leg on each side. "Tunnel!" she teased playfully, causing Riley to look up with a huge smile.

He expertly steered his cars past, ducking to fit under and screamed in delight as he passed.

"Again!" he shouted, still laughing.

This time, Ally got down with her hands and knees on either side of the tracks and just as he cleared her tunnel, she grabbed him from behind in a giant bear hug. "You forgot to pay the toll."

He erupted with laughter as she lifted him into the air and Charlotte began to giggle too, in the way only a small baby can.

She continued to play with Riley, coming up with at least twenty different tunnel challenges, until Mark announced it was time for bed.

"But Dad ..." he whined, not happy the fun was over and Ally had to stop herself from objecting also, not wanting their game to end. She was enjoying herself a lot more than she'd expected.

"Will you be here tomorrow?" Riley asked before heading upstairs.

"I sure will, and we're going to have so much fun. Tomorrow is the ice maze, right?"

"Yay!"

After, Ally insisted on cleaning up so Lara could rock Charlotte. She couldn't help but stare at the baby's sweet face as she nestled close to her mother and closed her eyes.

Lara caressed her baby's head, and Ally wondered if her wispy blonde hair felt as soft as it looked.

"I'm so glad you decided to come and spend Christmas with us," her friend said in a soft whisper.

Ally nodded, almost afraid to answer.

"It's OK, she is a very sound sleeper. Has to be, with a five year old brother."

"I know. And I can't believe this is only our second Christmas together. Remember that year, the big snow storm when I was marooned at your place?"

They'd dressed up in two of the ugliest holiday sweaters and thrown together some food from whatever was in Lara's fridge, then spent the rest of the evening talking until the early hours.

The next morning, Ally awoke to a present under the small tabletop tree in her friend's place. The tag read 'from Santa'.

She still had the fuzzy socks that were inside the perfectly wrapped package.

Her friend had always been Christmas crazy but it was only now that Ally was beginning to appreciate it.

"I promise, *this* will be a Christmas to remember," Lara said. "This town goes all out with the holiday cheer and decorations - and the ice maze. Plus the big Christmas Eve Snow Ball. Honestly, by the time I'm finished with you, you won't have time to think, much less work."

At the mention of work, Ally felt her heart deflate afresh at the realisation she was without any of her conferencing equipment.

And her phone battery was now running perilously low.

"Do you have an office I could maybe use for my meetings tomorrow?" she asked Lara.

"Yeah, we have a den, next room over. Very quiet and private. But why do you have meetings set up anyway? Who wants to work on the holidays?"

But Ally had already gone to check out the den, making a mental checklist of what she would need; phone, computer, an extra monitor, decent internet.

She sat in the large leather desk chair, powering up the desktop and ran a quick diagnostic test to determine Lara's wifi speed. Much to her surprise, it wasn't fast enough to run her mobile conferencing software, even if she did have it. It wasn't even fast enough to stream a movie.

How on earth did Lara and Mark survive?

Going back to the family room, she made a mental note to see about getting their internet speed upgraded.

It would be her gift to them for being such gracious hosts.

Ally was tempted to take out her phone and create a reminder for herself, but until she secured a charger, she had to maintain what little battery life was left.

The thought of being completely without her phone too was enough to make her panic. It was her lifeline; she'd be completely lost without it.

There was still no reply from Mel about her missing luggage, and she hoped against hope that her assistant hadn't well and truly logged off for the Christmas break.

But why wouldn't she? The last time they'd spoken, as far as Mel was concerned, Ally was all set.

Just as she was about to express these worries to Lara, she noticed her friend's eyes were closed while Charlotte curled up against her chest.

Ally stopped, in awe of the cosy maternal scene.

Then Lara's eyes flickered open. "Oops, sorry about that. she's been teething, so I'm a little behind on my sleep."

"Sounds rough. You should get to bed."

"I feel terrible though. Here you are on your first night and I'm falling asleep on you." Lara stood up, gingerly carrying a still dozing Charlotte. "Look, try to get some sleep yourself and try not to worry about the luggage thing. It'll be returned in no time. In fact, I'm sure whoever took yours is already figuring out a way to get it back."

"Hope so." Ally nodded and quietly followed upstairs in her friend's wake.

Still fuelled by the trauma of losing her suitcase and the nap she took earlier on the airplane, she wasn't ready for sleep though.

She ran through any potential options for entertainment in her mind. No iPad, laptop, just an almost-dead phone - and no TV in the guest room either.

It wasn't looking very promising.

Wandering around the bed, her gaze drifted to the suitcase and the books she had discovered earlier.

She picked up a hardback and rang a finger across the embossed author name on the front: J.T. Walker.

Never heard of him.

She flipped the book to its back cover, whereupon reviewers sang their praises for this apparent fictional masterpiece.

Huh.

Ally moved the suitcase onto the floor and crawled into bed with the book.

Perhaps a few chapters of this would be just what she needed to drift off.

CHAPTER 9

Ally awoke the following morning to the sound of footsteps. Having lived alone the last fifteen years, it was enough to rouse her from a deep sleep.

Her body begged her to close her eyes again, but the realisation of what had happened the day before awakened her quick-smart.

She had a mission to accomplish.

"Morning!" Lara greeted her over a mug of coffee.

"Please tell me you have lots more of that," Ally groaned, walking into the kitchen mid-yawn.

"A whole pot. Help yourself."

She duly grabbed a mug from the cupboard that Lara gestured towards, and filled it to the brim.

"I hope Charlotte didn't wake you last night."

"Not at all, I was just late up reading. I got stuck into a really great book."

Lara's stared at her, surprised.

Ally shrugged. "I found it in that other person's suitcase. And as crazy as it sounds, I think the owner of the suitcase might be the writer of the book."

Lara frowned. "I don't follow. Why would you think that?" she asked, while whisking pancake batter.

"It had three copies of the same book in it, plus a notebook with handwritten outlines of what I think is going to be a sequel. And he's got some nice clothes. Rich guy's clothes."

"You looked through a stranger's stuff? What else did you do, try on his clothes?"

"No, I wasn't trying to be nosy. I just thought maybe there'd be a name or a phone number in there, some way of contacting the guy."

"Good idea. Was there?"

"No. Though he must travel quite a bit, he had all of his toiletries in travel size and they had been used before." It took Ally ages to realise what a time saver it was to have a special set of travel toiletries always ready to go.

"You're like a detective. What else did you find?"

"A few really nice cashmere sweaters, a pair of slippers, some socks and a carefully folded tux even. The quality of everything was top notch too."

Lara made a face. "Sounds like what my grandpa packs when he travels."

"But if I'm right, and he is the author of the books, then I also know his name - well kinda. J.T. Walker."

"Great, well that's a good start isn't it?"

"You'd think. I googled him to see if there was maybe a social media profile, or author website I could reach him at, but there were little to no personal details at all online, just book stockists and reviews. If his clothes are that nice he must be pretty successful. So strange."

Ally wrapped her hands around her warm coffee cup and savoured a few sips, waiting for the caffeine to activate the rest of her brain so she could think of a way to contact JT Walker.

Bad wifi or not though, she'd need to use Lara's desktop computer, because thanks to that little spate of online research in the early hours to find out more about the author, her phone battery had finally given up the ghost.

Though at least she'd be able to secure a charger today. While Ally was confident her assistant would surely come up with the goods in the meantime, she was feeling a lot brighter about the prospect of getting her bag back.

Of all the things she did on a daily basis as a tech consultant, locating this J.T. Walker guy should be a piece of cake.

CHAPTER 10

Jake opened his eyes and was relieved to see the sun was finally up.

That meant he no longer had to force himself to try and sleep like he'd been doing for the last eight hours, while his mind continued to bombard him with different ways of potentially getting his bag back.

Usually, when he found himself unable to sleep, he'd use the time to write, so not having his notebook was adding injury to insult. Especially when he had a plot to outline - preferably by the end of holidays.

He'd make a stop at the general store in town for a new one though; one thing at least, that was easy to replace.

The evening before he and Meghan had racked their brains till the early hours to see if there was anything they could do to locate his bag, but to no avail.

He'd been waiting on the line for almost an hour to speak to somebody from the airline, and in the end they'd told him to lodge a lost property query and they'd get back to him.

The representative seemed bored and patently uninterested in his plight, but Jake thought, she had no real idea what was at stake here.

And it wasn't as though he could tell her either - just in case it made things worse.

Though at least there had been one spark of hope.

"Maybe the person who owns the case you took by mistake, picked up yours?" Meghan had suggested much later, after a family dinner during which Jake spent much of the time fretting. "Did you check it out - see if there's maybe any contact details in there?"

"Good idea."

Telling the others he needed an early night after the day's travel, Jake was finally able to examine the bag properly.

And mercifully, attached to the top handle, he spied that there was indeed one of those plastic inserts with a business card and - thank goodness - office phone number inside.

But having little choice but to call it a day given the late hour, he planned to call the number first thing, and with luck he'd have his bag (and it's precious contents) back in no time.

Maybe the other person hadn't even realised the mix-up yet?

But when earlier that morning he'd phoned the number for Walters Technology, the line rang out. Not especially surprising given it was so close to Christmas, but what was he going to do now?

"Morning," he greeted Meghan dully, as he entered the kitchen, looking for coffee.

He was relieved she was the only one awake at this early hour. Unlike last night, when he'd no choice but to share the news about the business card in a hush, now they could strategise freely without being overheard.

"You look well rested," she teased, raising an eyebrow.

"Yeah, a bit too much on my mind to sleep."

"Don't worry. I have a lead."

Jake almost dropped his cup.

"You do?"

"Yes, if you weren't so behind the times you could have done this yourself last night. A quick google and I found Walters Tech on social media. It took like, thirty seconds."

Meghan pulled up the page and handed her phone to her brother. From what he could make out it was a generic business page - something to do with electronics and technology, which was already pretty apparent from the company name.

"OK, this is great and all, but how is this going to help? I just tried the number, and there's no reply - presumably they're finished for the holidays."

"Yes, but the business seems like just a smaller one-man show than some big enterprise. According to this, the owner's name is Ally Walters - and *this* is Ally's personal profile," Meghan pointed out with a flourish. "She must've been travelling on the same flight, and if you have her bag, then most likely she has yours." She shrugged. "So now we just need to a way to find Ally. Makes sense actually, that a tech consultant would be carrying that weird-looking charger."

Unfamiliar electronics aside, Jake did his best to be patient, still not understanding how a social media page was going to help him get his bag back - today.

Unless they could send this ... Ally a message somehow?

Though Meghan seemed to have it all figured out. "Now, look at this," she told him, trying to remain patient with him. "See that, at the top of her page?"

Jake looked again at the screen and read a post from someone called Lara Clark which read; *Excited to be setting my high-achieving bestie a* real *challenge today! Knowing Ally she'll be out by midday.*

He frowned at his sister. "I still don't get it."

"Ally - the woman whose bag you have - is tagged in that post, linking to the ice maze."

He looked blank.

Meghan rolled her eyes. This person, Lara Clark tagged her 'bestie' Ally Walters, who it seems happens to be headed to the ice maze - right here in this town - *today*."

Jake eyes widened. "Oh wow! Good detective work."

That was surprisingly easy actually. He'd go to the ice maze this morning, find this Ally, who by now surely must have also realised the mistake, and would be only too happy to make the switch.

Out by midday...

Finally Jake's heart lifted. He'd have everything back before he knew it.

CHAPTER 11

❄

After breakfast, Ally spent most of the morning on Lara's phone to the airline, being directed from pillar to post.

But none of the four representatives she spoke with, nor indeed anyone at the airport, could shine a light on the location of her bag.

Nothing had been handed in at the terminal, and with no trackable luggage tag for the airline to trace, by the end of multiple conversations and hours on hold, she was still no closer to being reunited with her bag.

She'd also tried in vain to contact Mel, but her assistant clearly wasn't picking up email or her phone since logging off for the holidays - and certainly not from an unfamiliar landline.

While Lara was adamant Ally could borrow whatever she needed for the duration of the stay, there was still the pressing matter of the upcoming work calls, and indeed the subsequent Florida trip.

She needed to get her stuff back pronto and if it meant chasing down this J.T. person to see if he'd been to one to accidentally take her bag, so be it.

By now she was willing to try *anything*.

But first and foremost, she needed to get her phone back up and running so that she wasn't completely cut off and dependent on Lara for everything.

It was a weird feeling for Ally, being so helpless and out of control like this. But the return of her beloved phone would soon set her back on track.

Now, as she entered the town's general store, she was taken aback at the wide array of items the tiny retailer carried. Everything from hardware items, gifts, home decor, plus books and magazines. Impressive though probably necessary, given it was one of only three stores in the little town.

If you needed something, your choices were here, the grocery store, or the clothing boutique Ally hoped stocked bikinis in winter. Just in case.

But there was one category of items she wasn't seeing in this place yet, and that was electronics.

"Can I help you ma'am?" an older man greeted from behind the counter and Ally knew from Lara's description that he was the owner of the shop. A true town fixture.

"Yes, I'm in desperate need of a phone charger. Do you have one for this particular model?" she asked, showing him her device.

"Well, I haven't come across that one before, but I have a few that might work, I think." The man proceeded to pull out a large box from under the counter.

It contained six different types of chargers, sadly none of which would work, Ally realised, her spirits dropping. Hers was a brand new model and had only been on the market for a couple of weeks. Clearly the price of early adoption was steep.

She thanked the man for his time, and was just about to leave when she noticed some distinctive looking spiral-bound notebooks near the counter. They reminded her of the one in the suitcase and immediately, she thought of something.

"Hey did anyone come in to buy one of these today by any chance?" she asked, figuring it was a long shot, but what the hell...

He stopped to think. "Come to think of it, yes a little while ago actually. A couple - on their way to the ice maze apparently. He needed gloves too."

Now *this* news was music to Ally's ears. Maybe small town living wasn't as bad as she thought. And she congratulated herself on her good ole fashioned detective skills.

"Did you catch a name by any chance?"

"No didn't get that much - like I said, they were in a hurry. Definitely from out of town though, much like yourself I'd wager."

That made sense too. "Yes, I'm here to visit my friend - she recommended I come here, Lara Clark?"

The man beamed. "Of course I know Lara, and Mark too. Great couple, pillars of this community."

Ally smiled. "They are a great couple. Well, she's actually waiting for me in the car, and we're on our way to the ice maze too, so I'd better get going, but thank you so much for your help."

"No problem. Tell Lara I said hi. And little Riley too."

"I will. But I might need to pop back before tomorrow - besides a charger, I'm also in need of some Christmas gifts for Lara and her family." She sighed, reminding herself again of her current predicament. "You see, I lost my luggage en route here, and if I don't get it back soon I'm out of luck until after Christmas. My gifts, along with my clothes were in there too. About all I have left is a sparkly dress and that's not much use in this weather."

The man smiled. "Coming along to the Snow Ball then? It's a great evening, the holiday highlight of the year in this town."

Ally gulped, not having anticipated the event as that big of a deal. With luck by then she'd be reunited with her shoes too. Otherwise she was going to cut a very sorry sight tomorrow night in her sparkly dress with no accessories, or even decent underwear.

"Well, maybe I'll see you there," the shop owner continued smiling, and Ally nodded politely.

Then, before turning again to leave she thought of something. "That couple … who bought the notebooks earlier - can you tell me what either of them looked like?"

The man thought for a bit. "Well, she was maybe early thirties with long, curly hair, green jacket and grey bobble hat and very friendly like you. He was tall - lighter hair maybe? Wearing corduroy trousers. And a red knit sweater. Typical out of towner stuff." He chuckled.

"Wonderful, thank you so much." Ally headed back to the car to tell Lara what she had learned.

"Guess who could also be on the way to the ice maze?" she said, answering her own question before she even gave her friend a chance to guess. "J.T. must be in town too."

"Well, I hate to sound negative, but we do get a lot of out of towners coming to the ice maze at this time of year. Could be a needle in a haystack."

"I do know whoever bought the notebook is wearing corduroy pants, and a red sweater," Ally said, proudly filling her in on the couple's description.

Lara wrinkled her nose. "Old guy clothes. Well, at least *that* should narrow it down."

CHAPTER 12

"OK, if this is Lara, how do I find Ally at the ice maze? Or even know what she looks like?" Jake was asking, as he continued to scroll on his sister's phone.

Meghan showed him where to click for Walters Technology, and they both looked for a photo or more pertinent info about Ally, as he scrolled through various pictures of office space, computer equipment, and a few business articles.

They continued to search, hoping to find at least one picture of their mystery woman.

And while her friend had lots of personal photographs on her social media profile, there seemed none at all of Ally.

"This is obviously more of a business page," Meghan pointed out. "All her posts seem to be tagged reviews from clients. And very satisfied ones at that."

Jake began reading some of the rave reviews. Clearly this Ally was very good at what she did. Not that he understood any of the technological lingo.

All these years he had been reluctant to get involved in social media. The idea of posting pictures of his private life for all to see was enough to make his skin crawl.

But if he could make a page like this one, just about his work and perhaps interact with people at arm's length? That might not be so bad.

"Can we send her a message or anything?" he asked Meghan then. "Ask her to meet with us at the maze and maybe bring the bag?"

"We'd have to find out if she has it first. I'll send a friend request and add a little message."

'You're a genius." Jake grinned as she typed away.

He knew he should probably try to relax and just wait to see if this Ally would reply, but again it was so close to Christmas - would she even be checking business messages?

No, the idea of sitting around and not doing anything was impossible - especially considering what was at stake.

He needed to explore all options, including the ice maze.

"I'm going to head down there anyway, see if I can maybe even spot the friend there. She said out by midday right? "

"Ice Maze? Sounds like fun," another voice approaching the kitchen piped up and Jake froze, knowing who it was, but almost afraid to look and confirm his fears.

"Morning Heidi," Meghan greeted in a high voice, as an attractive blonde approached and kissed Jake on the cheek.

"What time were you thinking of heading out?" Heidi asked.

"In about like fifteen minutes or so actually, before it gets too crowded," Jake replied, in the hopes she wouldn't want to tag along. Then he'd have a lot of explaining to do.

"OK, I'll go jump in the shower first."

Before Jake could think of another excuse, his sister beat him to it.

"But I thought Mom needed you for food shopping today. You know, to help with Christmas dinner"

Jake did his best to act calm, as Heidi frowned considering. Then much to his luck, she smiled. "I'd forgotten all about that. You're right, maybe I'll just catch up with you guys later."

And as he and Meghan grabbed their coats and hurried outside to the car, Jake let out the breath he didn't realise he'd been holding.

CHAPTER 13

❄

Ally spent the entire car ride to the ice maze thinking of the best way to try and identify the guy who'd bought the notebook, assuming it was the same guy whose case she had.

If he did indeed happen to be J.T. Turner, it was a real shame that there was no author photo on those books.

A needle in a haystack for sure.

Still, as soon as Lara's minivan pulled into the parking lot, she began scanning every person they passed, looking for guy in a red sweater and corduroy trousers and a dark haired woman in a green coat.

"Ally?" Lara's mournful voice pulled her back to the present, as her friend lifted the baby out of her car seat.

"What's up?"

"I can't believe this, but Charlotte's just had an accident - a messy one, by the looks of it. I think I'm going to have to either take her home or to a restroom somewhere to change her."

Ally looked at the baby, still smiling despite the fact that she was indeed a mess, and then back at the very long line already formed at the ice maze entrance.

"Maybe we should all go - looks pretty busy here."

But the look of disappointment in Riley's eyes nearly broke her heart.

"You go on ahead, and maybe just meet us after?" Ally suggested then, grabbing Riley's hand. She was sure they'd be in and out of here in no time.

And anyway she wanted to keep an eye out for red sweater and corduroy pants guy - just in case.

"You sure you don't mind? We'll be back soon."

"Course not. They take virtual pay right?"

Lara chuckled. "This isn't DisneyWorld." She rummaged in her purse and gave Ally a couple of twenties before heading back to the car with Charlotte.

But her friend was only a few feet away when she turned back. "Look!" she urged.

Ally looked to the man her friend was pointing towards, heading their way, and immediately scrunched up her nose. He was indeed wearing the right colour combo, but he looked to be about eighty years old.

Still …

"Excuse me, are you J.T Turner?" Ally asked, when the guy neared the back of the line, feeling a bit ridiculous.

He was far too old to be the owner of the suitcase. And his pants were more olive, not green.

"What did you say?" He leaned closer, obviously a little hard of hearing.

"I'm looking for a man named J.T? Maybe an author?" she repeated, a little louder.

The man smiled, and Ally felt her heart lift a little until he spoke again. "I wish I could help you. The only J.T. I know is long gone. But if you're ever in need of a Malcom, that I could help you with," he added, with a wink.

"Thanks anyway." She grabbed Riley's hand and shuffled back up her place in the line, feeling a little stupid now.

When finally, they entered the ice maze, she glanced dubiously at the ten foot walls of ice and did a rough calculation in her head of the approximate square footage.

It had to be at least five thousand square feet.

Once they were inside, it would be almost impossible to continue her hunt for her mystery notebook guy - unless he happened to be directly in front of her in the maze.

As she and Riley headed off down the first corridor, they had two choices; right or left.

Ally peered down each of the options, trying to gauge which was correct and which would lead into a dead end. There was no way to tell. And she didn't like the odds.

"Let's go this way, Aunt Ally," Riley chose the left without any thought.

But Ally was frustrated. If she had her phone, she could've grabbed an aerial view of their current location, focused in on the ice structure, downloaded the data into a GPS and then programmed it to find the quickest route possible to the exit.

They'd be in and out in no time.

But without GPS, this was going to take forever. And if they got lost, there was no way to call for help either!

She broke out in palpitations a little at the thought of being without her trusty phone, until Riley tugged on her jacket. "Come on! It's this way."

Ally forced herself to smile through her panic; this little guy was depending on her.

He took off running and Ally caught him at the next fork, just as he was turning left. She figured this was taking them backwards though, and he was most certainly heading in the wrong direction.

"Riley? I think we went the wrong way."

Laugher filled the ice passage, as he once again turned left, causing Ally to lose all sense of direction.

"Think we're lost?" he teased.

"I know we are." This made Riley laugh even harder as he took off once again, taunting her to catch him.

And despite herself, and for the first time since she'd got here, Ally began to forget about her missing suitcase, and actually have some fun.

CHAPTER 14

❄

Jake sat in the car with his sister, feeling like a couple of detectives on a stakeout as they watched everyone enter and exit the ice maze from the parking lot.

At least they knew what Ally's friend Lara looked like, given she had so many pictures on her social media profile.

But most importantly they'd garnered from her post that she'd be here this morning with her businesswoman friend, who presumably had Jake's case.

Despite this very promising lead, he still couldn't relax - at least not until they'd successfully located the woman and gotten his luggage back.

"You know, I still can't take you seriously, dressed like that," Meghan commented, with a snicker.

Jake looked down at the outfit he'd borrowed from his father. The clothes, while old-fashioned were warm and perfectly suited for the circumstances. Ice mazes by their nature were ... icy cold.

And why his sister was focused on something so irrelevant when there was so much at stake here, was beyond him.

As they approached the entrance to the maze, the line was already stretching halfway to the parking lot.

Jake watched a small boy, patiently waiting in line holding his mother's hand. It reminded him of the very first time he'd come to this place as a child.

He could feel the kid's excitement as he marvelled at the ten foot walls made entirely of ice. Probably wondering how anyone could create such a thing, just like Jake had.

For the next few minute, he and Meghan continued to scan through everyone entering and exiting, hoping they'd be able to spot Ally's friend.

As they did so, Jake's gaze suddenly stopped on a woman with sleek mid-length brown hair.

He studied her profile, trying to figure out why she looked so familiar. Then he realised - it was the woman on the flight here, the one who didn't have any cash on her.

"Jake," his sister's voice brought him back to the present. "Why are you staring? That woman looks nothing like Lara."

"Uh I know." He looked back to where the woman from the flight was standing, to see her grab a young boy by the hand and smile down at him.

Oh she was a mom. For some reason he hadn't pictured her that way on the plane. At all.

"Look, look, I think that could be her!" Meghan exclaimed then, grabbing her brother by the arm.

He turned quickly as his sister pointed out a blond woman fitting Lara Clark's description, pushing a stroller back through the crowds at a very fast pace, only about a couple of feet away.

As he tried to follow, he did his best to avoid bumping into all the people who were headed in the opposite direction.

"Sorry," he apologised, colliding with someone, then turned once the man assured him he was fine, only to come inches from running right into someone else.

Jake felt like a complete jerk; this wasn't him. He stopped, took a deep breath and looked once again to see how far away he was from reaching Ally Walker's friend.

But she was now at the door of her mini van, effortlessly lifting her baby's car seat in, folding down the stroller and speeding away.

Clearly this Lara had somewhere to be other than the ice maze. Was there some emergency with the baby that she had to leave?

And where was her friend? Was Ally already inside? Should he maybe go inside and search?

But neither he or Meghan had any idea what she looked like….

Frustrated afresh, he resisted the urge to fall to his knees. He'd been so close too.

The idea that if he had just been fast enough to reach that woman, he might well be holding his bag right now was enough to make him want to kick himself.

And the fact that he, a writer, was considering such a cliche made him even more annoyed.

"I just can't believe we just missed her," he groaned to Meghan.

Now it felt like he was right back at square one.

Not to mention that in the meantime, there was still no return call from the airline and without his precious notebook, no way for him to finish plotting out his next book in time.

To say nothing of the most pressing loss of all.

Heidi…

Tomorrow was Christmas Eve, and this situation truly was going from bad to worse.

CHAPTER 15

Having changed Charlotte and taken the opportunity to grab a peaceful gingerbread latte while her son and Ally were in the maze, Lara returned to the parking lot, deciding to wait for them at the exit.

There was no point in dragging the baby in there now, not when she was already ornery after her diaper accident.

And knowing Ally, they would surely have made it out by now.

Sure enough, within a few minutes, the two came running through the exit.

"We made it!" Ally cried with some relief, when Lara drove over to meet them.

"See I told you!" Riley said proudly. "Mommy, you should have seen it in there. It was so hard, but I found the way. It was so much fun."

"So glad you guys enjoyed it."

"I never would have made it without you," Ally laughed and the two high-fived each other as they got back into the car.

"So, any sign of green trousers guy?" Lara asked her then.

"Nope. The man you pointed out wasn't him and I didn't see anyone else fitting that description inside. It was a long shot but …"

"Well, we can keep an eye out at the tree-lighting ceremony later.

And ... wait!" Lara added, her eyes widening suddenly. The gala. You said there was a tux in there?"

The tux - of *course!* The guy surely wouldn't have packed a tuxedo unless he was going to The Snow Ball.

Ally felt her spirits lift, as she realised that if all else failed, maybe, just maybe, she had a real shot at finding J.T. Turner.

CHAPTER 16

❄

That afternoon Lara baked peppermint fudge in the kitchen while Ally and Reilly made paper snowflakes by warmth of the fireplace, soft carols playing in the living room.

Through spending time with them all, Ally was beginning to finally understand why people traveled such great distances to enjoy the holidays with their families for the holidays.

It was so cosy and festive, it was almost enough to make her forget all about her conference calls scheduled for later that evening.

Almost.

She managed to get through them on Lara's rickety old wifi, but must to her friend's regret, the timing meant that she had to miss the tree-lighting ceremony.

While normally Ally would've jumped at the chance to forgo such a cheesy outing, she was now kinda sorry she'd scheduled any work stuff at all, she was enjoying herself so much.

Maybe now she could also understand why Mel had gone AWOL - clearly her assistant, unlike Ally, was able to leave the office behind.

But it meant that with Lara's family partaking in more festivities, she had the cosy house all to herself, and feeling a little stuffed after all the hot chocolate and peppermint fudge, from earlier, went upstairs to read more of the book, while awaiting the others' return.

In truth, the story had really grabbed her now, and she'd fallen a little bit in love with J.T. Turner's writing, especially the way he seemed so emotionally intuitive and interested in his characters.

Author or not, it kind of made her want to meet the owner of the suitcase all the more, and when Ally eventually reached the final page, she instinctively went to the case and idly looked through it again.

Weirdly drawn to feeling some way closer to the man who'd also been reading the same heartfelt words.

Then, suddenly conscious of how stalkerish it was, she deftly began zipping back up all the pockets, as if to hide evidence of her snooping.

But on one of the outside pockets (the one where she usually kept her phone charger) the zipper seemed strained.

Ally reached into the pocket to see if she could push the bulky object blocking it out of the way. Rummaging further inside, her fingers brushed up against something hard, yet velvety to the touch and curious afresh, she pulled it out.

To discover that it was a small navy blue box - a jewelry box.

Eyes widening, she tentatively opened the lid and sure enough, inside was a stunningly beautiful diamond ring.

An engagement ring...

For reasons that she couldn't quite explain, Ally's heart sank to the pit of her stomach.

The guy was obviously planning to propose to someone this Christmas.

And the realisation struck Ally then, that she really needed to get this bag back to its owner - for more reasons than one.

CHAPTER 17

As he sat with his family over dinner after the tree lighting ceremony, Jake had a fresh spring in his step.

Finally, he had a lead - a proper lead!

Despite multiple calls to the airline subsequently, he'd heard nothing at all, and after missing Ally Walker's friend at the ice maze, was seriously beginning to give up all hope of getting his bag back.

Until on the way back from the maze, he'd popped in the general store, before joining Meghan for a hot chocolate at the cafe next door.

He knew he'd go out of his mind between now and Christmas trying to figure out a way to locate his bag - and the ring - and needed to distract himself.

What better way to do that than bury himself in his writing? To say nothing of the fact that he needed to finish plotting out the new book.

So, deciding to pick up a replacement notebook from the collection he knew they carried at the general store, he chatted briefly to the friendly owner.

"Must be something in the air today, Jake," Harry the owner commented, when he placed his purchase on the countertop to pay. "That's the second one I sold today, and you're usually my best customer for these."

"You mean, only customer." He nodded distractedly, not exactly in the mood for small talk until Harry said something else. "And there was a woman in earlier too, asking if anyone had bought one."

At this Jake's ears picked up, his author brain whirring instinctively. "Seems like an odd query."

"I thought the same. You know these out of towners though, strange as they come."

Jake smiled and was about to put his wallet away when Harry's next words stopped him in his tracks.

"Wanted a charger for some futuristic phone she had - never seen anything like it."

The phone charger... the unusual one from Ally Walter's bag that even Meghan didn't recognise.

"Did she say anything about losing a charger along with her luggage?" he asked, and Harry looked up at him, surprised.

"Yes, as it happens. Some problem with the airline. Said all she had left was a dress for the Snow Ball tomorrow night."

The shoes .... suddenly all the pieces were clicking into place.

"What else did she say?" Jake pressed, thanking the heavens for small-town gossip, as Harry told him everything he could glean about the woman he was trying to find.

But most important of all, Ally Walters was heading to tomorrow night's gala.

So all Jake had to do now was arrange to connect with her at the Snow Ball, swap the bags back, and be reunited with his luggage - and the ring.

Now, as he looked across the dinner table at Heidi's pretty face shining in the candlelight, he finally allowed himself to relax.

Just in time.

CHAPTER 18

❄

On Christmas Eve, once the kids were asleep, Ally and Lara went upstairs to the master bedroom to get ready for the gala ball.

The size of the bathroom was about the same as her entire Boston apartment.

She watched as Lara looped large strands of her hair around the barrel of her curling iron. As she let them go, they fell into perfect rings.

"So are you excited about tonight?" her friend asked.

Earlier that day, Lara had gotten a call from the general store owner, passing on a message from the owner of the bag, who'd somehow managed to track her down.

They'd made arrangements to switch the cases back at tonight's event, and while Ally knew she should be thrilled about getting her stuff back, for some reason she felt … flat.

It meant that J.T. would be reunited with the ring and get to propose to some lucky woman this Christmas, while she, Ally would be reunited with … her phone charger.

"Ally, do you have a crush on this guy?" Lara's questions automatically made her cheeks redden. She looked down at the hairbrush in her hands, afraid her expression would invite even more questioning.

"What? No. Nothing like that. At all. I think maybe I've just built up a picture of him from his stuff and his writing. He just seems so ... intuitive."

As soon as the words were out of her mouth, she realised how foolish they sounded.

"I knew it! Oh this could really be the start of something you know. Maybe he's done the same with your stuff and tonight, will take one look at you and think losing his suitcase was the best thing that ever happened to him. So let's finish getting ready and get you to your Prince Charming."

Ally didn't have the heart to tell her about the ring, to say nothing of the fact that she didn't want to admit she'd been prying in the bag to that extent.

Better to let her idealistic friend enjoy her fantasy, nice and all as it was.

Lara put down the curling iron and Ally shook her head, watching her shiny curls bounce. It was exactly how her mother used to do her hair every Christmas Eve when she was a child.

She went back to her room and lifted the sparkling dress off of the hanger. Then held her breath as she slipped it on, hoping it still fit after four years waiting.

After struggling with the zipper a little, Ally went to the mirror and barely recognised her own reflection.

"Here we come! Get your cameras ready," Lara called to her husband, as Ally stood at the top of their huge staircase.

"Wow! You look ... incredible. Doesn't she look great Mark?" Lara said proudly.

She and her husband looked like proud parents standing at the bottom of the staircase as Ally descended past the twinkling Christmas tree, feeling herself almost like a fairy princess.

She smiled, doing her best to join in the excitement and despite herself, couldn't help but wonder what J.T. might say when they finally met and he caught sight of her in this dress.

Then she kicked herself for thinking the guy would say anything other than, 'thanks for my suitcase.'

Lara and her silly, romantic notions were well and truly starting to get to her.

CHAPTER 19

❄

When her friend had told Ally that Mark's family ran the town inn, she'd pictured a small bed and breakfast, maybe converted from an existing large old home with a few guest rooms.

She couldn't have imagined they in fact owned a full scale hotel, with eighteen bedrooms, a fine dining restaurant, plus a ballroom big enough to hold the entire town's population.

"This is … incredible," Ally gushed, as she climbed the massive centre staircase that lead from the lobby to the ballroom, fully bedecked in sparkling holiday finest.

Holding the hem of her dress with one hand to prevent herself from tripping, she took a quick peek to see if the shoes she had borrowed were visible as she walked.

It was kind of Lara to lend her some heels since her own were still in her bag. Though these were a bit big for her and she could already feel blisters forming on the backs of her heels.

The three made their way through the crowd at a snail's pace, stopping to talk with a few of Mark and Lara's friends.

Everyone was very cordial and polite to her, an out of towner, but once they had asked Ally an appropriate number of questions about her career and Boston, the conversation would once again turn to community or children.

And once again Ally felt herself at a loss, beginning to realise that her life was totally defined by work. She didn't belong here, and the realisation made her sad.

J.T had requested to meet at the top of the staircase at 9pm. Which was only a few minutes from now.

Ally was eager and nervous all at the same time. Though once the exchange was final, at least she'd be free to head home and put herself out of her misery.

"Hey, it's almost 9pm," Lara said then, touching her arm gently. "Are you sure you don't want Mark to just meet the guy and switch back the bags?"

"Thanks but no, I'm fine." Ally couldn't quite put her finger on it.

But for some reason this felt personal.

SHE MADE her way back out front, where there was a small table and friendly volunteers that checked everyone's tickets.

They had been kind enough to watch the suitcase and Ally did her best to smile as she grabbed it and headed back up the staircase to the meeting spot.

Feeling unaccountably alone, she just hoped he would be punctual so they could get this over and done with.

And instinctively reached into her purse to check the exact time on her phone, feeling silly yet again for relying on it when it was long dead.

She looked around and spotted a grandfather clock at the top of the stairs whereupon a loud chime announced 9pm exactly.

"Ally?" The voice from the bottom of the stairs made her breath catch in her throat a little.

And as her gaze moved down the stairs to the marble tile of the lobby floor, the first thing she spotted was her case.

The slightly worn wheels, the wonky top zipper ... how had she not noticed at the time that the other one was far too pristine to be hers?

The man holding her own picked it up in one hand and began climbing the stairs. As he climbed higher, Ally noticed first what a nice tux he had on. Obviously must've found a replacement somewhere.

And next, that Lara was wrong about J.T. being an old man.

In fact he seemed to be about the same age as she.

It was only in that moment that it finally registered; he'd called her by name. How on earth did he know her name?

Ally finally looked up at his face, and the instant she looked into his blue-green eyes, she couldn't believe it.

The guy from the flight ... The plaid sports coat, the water, him jokingly reading his book - all the memories of that brief encounter suddenly came rushing back.

"It's ... you," she gasped.

CHAPTER 20

But still, how on earth did he know her name? Then Ally felt silly, realising that she'd forgotten her business card was attached to the handle.

Which meant that it should've been easy for him to reach her before now?

But of course, she remembered then, her phone was long dead and Mel had since disappeared into the festive ether.

So how *did* he find her?

"Jake," he greeted, extending a hand. "Nice to meet you - again."

"I can't ... believe it was you all along." For some reason she felt completely tongue-tied.

"I'm so sorry I picked up your stuff by mistake. I'm sure you've missed this." He gestured towards her bag.

"I have. And same with you." She went to hand the other case to him then, then hesitated. "Actually I'm not a hundred percent sure this is yours, though. I think it belongs to a writer named J.T."

He laughed, and she wondered what he could possibly find funny about all this.

"J.T. is my author name. I take it you found my books ... and my notebook? At least I hope that's still there." He grimaced.

OK, maybe that made sense.

"It is. And don't worry; all your stuff is still inside. Although I should admit I did read a book. Sorry about that."

"Don't be. In fact, if you want to keep it, I have plenty."

Jake took his suitcase and lightly patted the outer pocket while Ally did her best to not feel a little offended.

Or deflated.

"Don't worry, the ring is still there, too."

He exhaled. "Man, you have no idea what a relief that is! My brother would've killed me."

Brother ... Her mind froze as she stopped to think what this meant. The ring belonged to his brother?

"He's planning on proposing to his girlfriend, Heidi tomorrow morning. I offered to pick up the ring at the family jeweler in Boston on the way here. To be honest, I didn't even tell him my bag was missing, but I was beginning to really worry I wouldn't find you in time."

"How did you find me?" she asked, genuinely curious.

"Well, my sister found your social media profile and we went to seek you out with your friend at the ice maze yesterday. And believe it or not, I even saw you standing in line - with a little kid."

"You saw me with Riley? But why didn't you come up and talk to us? He's Lara's son." She couldn't believe it. "Especially when I was looking for you there too. The guy at the store said..."

"Exactly. I couldn't believe it when he told me that a woman had been in looking for a charger and asking if anyone had bought a notebook. I knew it had to be you. Well, not that I knew that it was actually *you*, in that you are Ally. But I'm so glad it is."

Her eyes flickered upward, and her heart began to speed up. "You are?"

He smiled, eyes twinkling. "Yes. And I'm not sure if you've realised this yet, but this is pretty much a tech-free town. Cash only. So if you need someone to buy you a drink ..."

Ally winced a little.

"Aw I'm sorry, I guess I shouldn't have assumed," Jake said quickly, colouring.

"No, I just need to change my shoes," she admitted, reddening too.

"My feet are *killing* me. I had to borrow these from my friend and they're way too small."

She shifted from one foot to the other, trying to minimize her discomfort, while also trying to process what exactly was going on here.

The guy from the plane was J.T.

Jake.

"I'm sorry it took me so long to find you," he was saying, while Ally did her best to squat down low enough in her dress to unzip her suitcase.

She tottered a little and almost fell backwards toward the stairs, but Jake put a hand out to steady her.

"Let me."

He unzipped her bag for her, knowing the shoes were right on top.

Ally happily kicked off Lara's torturous heels, and awkwardly tried to balance on one foot as Jake set hers on the floor in front of her.

Then incredibly, he crouched down and steadied her with one hand, while using the other to hold up a shoe for her to place her foot inside.

Ally felt dizzy.

"Better?" he grinned once both sparkly sandals were duly fastened on her feet.

"So much."

Then Jake gallantly extended his elbow and Ally smiled, feeling a little like Cinderella as she placed her arm inside it.

And with the ring now safely in his inside pocket, Jake and Ally stowed their cases, and together set off back to the ballroom.

CHAPTER 21

❋

Just as they were halfway across the dance floor and heading for the bar, the lights turned low.

"Time to find that special someone and make your way onto the floor," the singer of the band announced as the opening bars of *A Lot Like Christmas* began to play.

Ally stood frozen with awkwardness, while all around men took their partners and wives by the hand.

Turning to Jake, she was certain he felt the same discomfort, but when her gaze met his, she saw him smile.

"Talk about timing. Shall we?" He gently took Ally's right hand and placed it on top of his shoulder, then took the other and placed it on his side, before wrapping his own around her waist.

Her arms felt rigid as wooden boards. What must everyone be thinking?

She looked around the room, feeling reassured then that absolutely no one else was even looking in their direction. They were all too busy with their own dance partners. So she began to relax a little and enjoy the moment.

Ally and Jake began to move slowly to the music, their bodies finding a natural pace within seconds.

Then over her shoulder she spotted Lara, whose eyes were out on stalks. She grinned and gave Ally a big thumbs up before placing her head back onto Mark's shoulder.

Copying her example, Ally did the same.

As soon as her head found a comfortable position on Jake's shoulder, a sense of almost surreal calm descended upon her. Following his lead felt so natural that she was able to completely lose herself in the moment.

And in his arms.

They continued to dance for what seemed like hours, until eventually Lara tapped her on the shoulder.

"So sorry to interrupt you two, but we really should get going. I promised the sitter."

"Oh! I totally lost track of time."

Jake stood back and still smiling, he grabbed her hand and kissed it.

"See you the day after tomorrow? I'll text you the address - now that you've got your charger back. And Merry Christmas."

Ally nodded, and once she'd collected her case and they headed back to the car, Lara could hardly wait to hear all the details.

"The day after tomorrow?" she urged. "Tell me everything!"

"Yes, Jake - J.T. - invited me to dinner with his family. And his brother's engagement celebrations."

"Amazing!" Her friend hugged her. "You guys look so perfect together. And he seems wonderful. But I thought you were leaving for Florida the day after tomorrow?"

"I think I might stay on a while longer if that's OK with you?"

"Of course - as long as you like!"

Ally smiled as gently falling snowflakes cooled her rosy cheeks. This truly was turning out to be the strangest, but perhaps the best, Christmas yet.

And she got the sense that from now on - in more ways than one - maybe she wouldn't need to travel so light.

MAGIC IN MANHATTAN

CHAPTER 1

❄

Alice walked through Central Park. She could feel the snow on the end of her tongue, and for the first time in weeks believed that things were beginning to get easier.

It was about time.

Harry had died in October. It had been six weeks from the diagnosis to the funeral. The apartment that they had spent two years setting up on the Upper East Side had not even been lived in.

She had stayed there last night for the first time in the master bedroom, the one that Harry had painted a pretty tortoiseshell green.

She could remember each and every one of the items in that bedroom, and the discussions and arguments they had had about them all.

She felt closer to him there, but the pain lay in her chest like a physical lump.

It hurt so, so bad.

The snow in the park was getting heavier, but instead of heading home she sat on a bench near the tree - their tree: the one where Harry had spontaneously kissed her during a walk here in the fall.

"I love you, Alice," was all he had said, but it had been enough.

The park was empty at this time of day and apart for a few kids building a snowman, no one had passed by.

Last night in the bedroom, she'd found the tickets for a concert in his best coat pocket.

It was to have been a surprise for her this Christmas. The Beatles were to play Carnegie Hall the following spring and Harry had been involved in setting up their tour.

"You've got to hear this group, they are the tops," he'd told her and he was right, the up and coming English band were indeed wonderful.

Just then a squirrel jumped through the snow and bounded up the tree to her left.

Alice looked up at it and realised she'd never really appreciated how beautiful the tree was. From the top, a squirrel might be able to see all the way to Staten Island. Assuming the squirrel was interested in looking.

She smiled to herself as she walked over to it.

The snow was falling harder and clinging to the bark. Alice pressed both hands into the snow, just like she and Harry had done up in the Catskill Mountains last winter.

She hugged the tree. It was nice to hug something.

As she did she noticed a small hole in the bark, one that was just large enough to fit a hand into. Alice had no idea why she did it, but she placed her hand in the hole, almost expecting to get bitten.

But instead she felt something else entirely. She pulled out a crumpled piece of paper which she quickly realised was not just a random piece of trash, but a letter.

She went back to the bench, cleared some snow and sat down to read it.

H,

I waited for you, but once again you didn't turn up. I know I said some hurtful things for which I am sorry. I was just so scared of losing you. I don't understand why you won't leave him. If you tell him about us, we could be in London soon. This was why I wanted to see you, to tell you that the company have agreed that I should spend two years in the UK office. I said yes, because it would mean that we could be together and he would be out of our lives for good.

My heart is your heart. S xxx

. . .

ALICE WAS PLEASED to see that there was still some love out there in the world. She sometimes felt that all love and hope had died with Harry.

The world went on, life moved on.

She decided to immediately put the letter back where she had found it.

There was some lucky, (if unhappily attached) person out there waiting on it.

CHAPTER 2

❄

Alice didn't return to the park for a few days.
This was going to be her first Christmas without Harry and she didn't want to spend it with her family.

So early Christmas week, she took the train to Poughkeepsie to visit her sister and then after a couple of days of trying not to argue, continued on to Albany to see her mother.

By the time she got back to the city and the park, just two days before Christmas, the snow was still lying on the ground.

Alice embraced the solitude. She loved her mother but a few days had been more than enough.

She dared to visit the tree again and after looking around to make sure she wasn't being watched, she placed her hand in the hole.

This time she pulled out two pieces of paper, one was the original letter and the other was something new.

YOU ARE BEGINNING *to worry me. It has now been three weeks since we last spoke and I don't think I can go on without a word from you. I think about you all day, I even dream about you. Please, please, get in touch.*
S. x

. . .

THAT NIGHT when Alice got back to her apartment some of Harry's work friends came round for a visit. It was good to have company and it even better to be able to talk about Harry properly, not the skating around the subject that her mother and sister seemed to indulge in.

However as the night wore on, her mind began to drift back to the letters.

She wondered who the couple were, how old they might be and why were they leaving notes for each other in a tree in Central Park?

Perhaps this was just a quick distraction for one of them but it seemed the other had invested significantly more in the relationship.

"More coffee?" asked Harry's oldest friend, Jim.

Alice shook her head.

"You seem to be somewhere else tonight, though I guess that's understandable," he added gently.

"I'm sorry," apologized Alice. "I've been to see my mother and traveling has taken a toll...."

"No need to say anything. I'll round up the rest of the guys and we'll let you be."

Jim was always her favourite of all Harry's pals. He understood, and was sensitive.

When the apartment was all hers once more, she went to the study, the one that Harry had intended to use at weekends.

Then, not entirely sure what she was doing or why, Alice started to write a note.

I am so sorry that I have taken so long to reply. He has started to get suspicious and follows me around. I know I must tell him but please give me a few more days.

She had no idea why she was doing this. Perhaps she didn't want to let 'S' down?

Or maybe she had done it for herself

CHAPTER 3

She could only hazard a guess as to when that second letter had been placed in the tree.

It might have been early morning or late at night - perhaps on the way to or from work.

So Alice took the safe option and went to the park in the early afternoon. Again, there was far fewer people around, so she removed the two letters from before and replaced it with her note.

She had to be honest and admit she was getting a thrill from all of this.

She felt excited as she crossed Columbus Circle, and as she passed several men entering the park, she wondered if any of them were 'S' on his way to the tree.

Later, Alice thought she would go back to check to see if there had been a response. She pulled out the note but she was disappointed to find it was just the one she had left.

She sat on the bench for a while, scolding herself for being so stupid, for being so childish. Then out of the corner of her eye, a figure stopped at the tree then moved on.

Alice didn't get to see the person properly but she was sure it was a man. And sure enough, when she went back to the tree her note was gone.

. . .

THE FOLLOWING MORNING the snow was beginning to melt a little so she thought she might take an early morning walk around the park.

If 'S' wasn't going to come until the afternoon, her journey would probably be fruitless.

But to her delight, there was another letter already there.

You have made me the happiest man in the world! To know you care about me and are still thinking of us being together has suddenly made me look forward to Christmas. Please tell him soon, so that we can put all of this behind us.

I love you more than I have, or will, anyone in the world. S xxxxxxx

Alice knew the letter was meant for someone else but it had been written to the author of the last letter and that was her.

She sat on the bench and tears began to flow.

This girl 'H' was far luckier and richer than she possibly realised.

She decided to head back to the apartment and write a reply.

Of course I care about you.

That was all the words she felt were necessary.

Though Alice grew worried after her note had been collected but there was no response the next day or the day after that.

In fact, there was nothing for a whole week.

CHAPTER 4

Then on a bright snowy afternoon, when she had decided to stop being so stupid and give up this silliness altogether, she found another message.

I put your note in my wallet and took it with me to London. I have found an apartment or a flat as they call it over there, one that would be ideal for the two of us. I have to start work on January 7 but it means we could have Christmas and New Year together. Would you like that?

S. xxxxxxxxx

Alice's heart sank. Was this all wrong? She was leading this poor man into believing, that the love of his life was going elope across the Atlantic with him.

What if the real 'H' decided she had made a mistake? What if the real 'H placed another letter in the tree?

What then?

Alice told herself that she should just stop this whole charade now and come clean. But first, just one more note, one final message so that she could arrange to meet S and try to explain the truth about her actions.

I would love to talk with you soon so we can discuss everything. They say it is going to snow tonight so could we meet here in the park tomorrow, Christmas Eve, by this tree? There is so much I want to say to you, to explain.

. . .

SHE WENT down at the crack of dawn to place the letter in the tree to make sure S had time to reply. When she passed by later in the day, there was another note.

What a romantic idea! Of course I'll meet you by the tree. Say 1pm and then we can go for a walk. There is so much I want to tell you as well. I will be working in London for a PR company; the same company who represent that new British group, The Beatles? There is talk that I may be working with the group directly. How exciting is that? I can't wait to see you. Until tomorrow.

CHAPTER 5

Alice sat most of the night looking out of her apartment window at the most exciting city in the world, her mind turning over the options.

The Manhattan skyline had never looked brighter and full of promise.

What should she do? Go to the tree? Sit on the bench and wait for the man to arrive as arranged?

S was sure to be disappointed and indeed annoyed that Alice had taken it upon herself to intercept the notes, but she'd been so taken by the romance and adventure of it all that she hadn't thought this through.

She just hoped that when she explained all this to him that he'd understand.

And perhaps the universe had meant for her to find the letter, and bring two lovelorn people together?

Clearly H, whoever she was, had no interest in being with S given that she hadn't responded to any of his notes.

Although on second thoughts, what if he became really angry? Then she'd end up feeling even worse and on Christmas Eve too. Suddenly she wondered whether going to this meeting was a good idea after all.

She sighed. Once again she wished Harry was here; he'd give her advice on the best course of action, would know whether or not she should just let this lie or follow her instincts.

But Harry wasn't here was he?

Alice was just getting ready to go to bed when she noticed something sitting on the bedside locker. It was the tickets to The Beatles concert that he had bought.

She smiled, realising the significance and the odd coincidence that the man she planned to meet was also connected to the group in some way.

And there and then Alice knew that her beloved was indeed pointing her in the right direction, and that whatever happened at the park tomorrow was meant to be.

In fact, it didn't even matter what happened.

She was moving on - just as her husband would have wanted.

Merry Christmas, Harry.

CHRISTMAS IN PARIS

CHAPTER 1

❋

A room full of Thompson & Jonas Associates cheered as they raised their glasses to toast the chairman's yuletide address.

It was the yearly Christmas party and everyone was dressed in festive finery as they ate the best catered food and wine the advertising agency would spring for.

It was the cheeriest time of the year, and Emily Richardson absolutely loved it.

"Merry Christmas, Tom," she said to her colleague and friend, who was already three sheets to the wind - his arm draped around his wife Bernice.

"Merry Christmas Em!" they both chorused back, silly grins on their faces.

"So what are you doing over the holidays? You're more than welcome to join us again, if you'd like," Bernice offered kindly. "Was great having you at ours last year. My brother in particular took a right fancy to you. I'm sure he'd love to see you again," she added with a wink.

"Ah you're both very kind, but believe it or not, I've got plans this year," Emily informed with a grin of her own. "I'm off to Paris."

"Paris? But you won't know anyone," Tom countered gruffly. "Don't you think this time of year should be spent with friends and family?"

"Of course, but this year, with Nan gone, I have no family in London anymore. And as much fun as I have with you guys, I'm a bit tired of being the odd one out at a table full of couples and families."

"I hear you," Tom commented, sipping on his beer.

"Oh, you shouldn't let a thing like that bother you: one of these years *you'll* be the one with a boyfriend, or who knows, maybe even a husband to accompany you," Bernice reassured her. "Though I must admit, I'm actually envious now - Christmas in Paris sounds divine."

"I've always wanted to see the city, and what better time?" Emily smiled. "The Eiffel Tower, Champs-Élysée and all the festive lights… It's going to be glorious."

"When are you leaving?"

"Friday morning," Emily raised her glass of champagne and took a long sip.

"Well, we'll miss you at ours this year, but I expect you'll have a ball on your adventures," Tom said, hiccuping a little.

"You never know what those adventures will bring either," Bernice chimed in with a wink. "Paris is the City of Love after all…"

CHAPTER 2

"Must you go?" Her best friend Sarah's voice was ringing in her ears as Emily packed her suitcase. "The boys'll really miss you."

"*You'll* miss your on-call babysitter, you mean," she countered, folding her favourite red cashmere jumper and placing it gently on top of her other stuff.

"Well that too, but seriously no one can handle my boys like you can."

The two childhood friends, who were only a year apart in age, were often mistaken for twins.

They were both average height with honey blonde hair and slender figures. Sarah had put on a little more weight after having four children, but Emily thought it suited her, and gave her more curves from her formerly athletic build.

Emily herself still had had some semblance of the swimmer's tone she'd had in her school days, though she'd softened out quite a bit since giving up the gruelling training schedule.

"Sorry but you, Jeff and the boys are just going to have to do your best without me," she joked.

"I'm really going to miss you at Christmas, though" Sarah got up from her reclined position on Emily's bed and held out her arms for a hug.

"I won't be gone *that long*," she replied, wrapping her arms around her friend and pulling her into a tight embrace. "But I *need* this trip. I need to get out of London. Explore what else is out there," she added as she released her friend and turned back to her packing.

"It's because of Nan, isn't it?" Sarah stated.

Emily's green eyes focused on the clothes that were already in her case, as she thought of her Nan.

Andrea Sutton had been ninety years old when she'd died earlier in the year.

While most didn't think she'd live that long, Emily knew she would. Her grandmother had a resilient spirit like none she'd ever encountered and one she hoped she'd passed on to her only grandchild.

"Yes," she admitted. "It is because of Nan," She took a seat on the bed, an unfolded garment still in her hands.

"I knew this trip was very spur of the moment, considering it's not long since you got the money."

Emily sighed. "I suppose I just felt the need to do *something* with the inheritance, something special to honour Nan. She always lived life to the fullest." Her gaze met Sarah's. "She was everything to me, you know?"

"I know," her friend replied with a smile.

"That's why I need to go. Nan did so much for me, but the things *she* wanted to do in life she never got to. She wanted to see Paris. She raised me on those old Gene Kelly movies, and it was her dream to go to the places she saw in movies but never got to. I feel like I owe it to her now to see every place she wanted to. It's the best way to celebrate her life that I can think of."

Sarah smiled. "Then you should go. Honour Nan," she said, pulling her friend into another hug. "I'm sure this trip will be everything she would have wanted for you, and more."

CHAPTER 3

Charles de Gaulle Airport was bustling with tourists and travellers who were headed out to visit family and friends over the holiday period.

Snow was falling as Emily stepped out of the terminal and into the chilly air.

She shivered slightly at the change in temperature, but the feeling was invigorating and the smile on her face reflected her enthusiasm as she searched for a taxi.

"Madame, you take my card?" a driver encouraged in heavily accented English, handing her a small white card.

"Thank you," she said reading his name, "Monsieur Babin."

"Maurice," he corrected cheerfully as they drove away in his cab. "I show you all the sights of Paris. You just call me, and I will be there," he said with a snap of his fingers.

"You're a tour guide too?" she mused smiling.

"In Paris, all taxi drivers are also tour guides. Didn't you know?"

"No I didn't, but thanks for telling me."

"You are staying at a lovely hotel, Madame."

"Emily."

"That's a pretty name," he replied pleasantly. "The hotel - my wife and I stayed there for our honeymoon. It's excellent, *très excellente*," he emphasised with a theatrical kiss of his fingers.

It made Emily giggle. Nan would have loved this. "Thanks for letting me know I made a good choice."

"My pleasure."

The drive to the hotel was faster than Emily had expected, though she believed Maurice may have had some car racing experience in his past, given the way he drove his taxi.

He pointed out the locations of the Air and Space Museum and the George-Valbon State Park as they drove. Maybe she'd visit them on another trip, but this time round she only wanted to see the city's more picturesque and romantic spots.

They arrived at the hotel, and Emily was delighted to find it even more magnificent in real life than it had been in the online pictures.

The white building, with gold and green accents and a planter box on every window and balcony, was dusted in patches of snow. It was like something from a film set, and the perfect place to spend Christmas week.

The lobby was just as picturesque as the exterior, and decorated in rich purple and gold, it radiated opulence and reminded her of a scene from a classic movie, where everything was so vibrant and alive and reminiscent of times gone by.

An attractive brunette greeted Emily at reception as she approached the front desk. "My name is Angelique and I'm your concierge. How may I assist you today?"

"Emily Richardson, I have a reservation," she stated as Angelique checked her computer.

"Ah yes, Miss Richardson, I see this is your first time in Paris," Angelique replied. "And you have reserved one of our finest suites. The views are spectacular," she assured. "Martin, will take your bags up," she added, indicating to the porter who was standing nearby.

"Follow me Madame," he said with a smile, taking the keys from Angelique and heading towards the elevator.

Emily followed, admiring the décor as she went. The hotel again made her feel as if she were in a movie, and the decor of the lobby extended throughout the building. It was like stepping back into a more regal time, with statues and fine art adorning every corner.

Her suite was located on the top floor. She'd wanted the best view and the suite she'd been given didn't fail. The colour scheme was gold and white, with an elegant but simply designed sitting room and a bedroom to the left. The entire suite was carpeted, and the bed visible from the living room. Emily was excited to find that it looked exactly how she'd seen it online, with the wall canopy adorning the head of the bed.

Martin deposited her bags in her room before wishing her a good day. The moment he was gone Emily walked out onto the balcony to see the view.

Even better than she'd anticipated.

The Eiffel tower stood regally ahead, the Arc de Triomphe to her right and somewhere in between was the Champs-Élysées, her intended first stop.

"I should unpack first," she mused, but knew in her heart she wasn't going to. She wanted to get out into the city and see everything. It felt as if she had waited a long time for this trip, and she wasn't about to waste a second of it.

"I'm here Nan - in Paris," she whispered, wishing her grandmother was in the room with her right now. "I hope you can see this. Isn't it beautiful?"

She turned back into the bedroom, closing the balcony door behind her as she grabbed a few things and headed out.

This was one of the few times of the year when Emily got to shake off the stress of her job and simply enjoy every day.

Her Nan had always said she needed to do better at enjoying life, so maybe it was time she started.

CHAPTER 4

The falling snow made the air crisp and hearty and brought a smile to Emily's face as she looked up and down the busy street.

She was really here. She'd really come to Paris!

She strolled to her right, her hands stuffed into the front pockets of her red padded coat. She didn't need to rush, she planned to savour every moment of just being in such a beautiful city.

She smiled to herself as she watched couples walking arm-in-arm along the avenue, some in a rush and some like her, taking it easy.

It was only a short walk, no more than a few minutes, before Emily found herself at Place Charles de Gaulle, the Arch de Triomphe standing at the centre.

It was even more breath-taking in reality than in photos or in movies, even with all the cars rushing around it. It really was beautiful but she'd have to take a better look later, because right now she had an appointment one avenue over, on the Champs-Élysées.

Trees lined both sides of the street as Emily began her stroll. It wasn't quite like what she'd seen in the movies, more familiar shops and chain stores had moved in since, replacing stylish cafés with American brandnames.

She chuckled. "I guess that American in Paris left more than he expected ..." she mused, walking away from McDonalds. She had no interest in fast food - in this city, she wanted something much more authentic.

The Renault restaurant was just that. Located along the avenue it was both modern and contemporary within a warm and welcoming atmosphere that made Emily indifferent to the fact that she was eating alone. She rarely did so, but this was a new day and she was ready for new experiences.

She was seated on one of the upstairs tiers, where all the chairs were yellow-coloured. The place had such a fun and irreverent feel, that she was sure children must love it. She decided there and then to treat herself; who cared about a few extra pounds at this time of year?

She started with avocado and shrimp tartare, followed by Milanese veal cutlet with linguine pesto, and topped everything off with a vanilla crème brûlée and two glasses of sauvignon blanc.

The meal was amazing, and she made a mental note to come there again during her trip if she had the time.

Looking down from her perch on the first floor, Emily watched other diners down below.

Some had large bags draped over chairs, no doubt full of festive trinkets to take home to decorate, or gifts ready to be wrapped. She wondered what would be the best places to find toys for the boys and gifts for Sarah and Jeff, plus maybe a little something for herself to commemorate her trip.

She was enjoying the view, slowly draining her final glass of wine, when she thought she spotted someone familiar down below.

She squinted, trying to see the face properly, but from this angle it was difficult and there were so many people.

Finally she shook her head; she was being silly. It couldn't possibly be *him*, could it?

After all, it had been at least ten years, would she still even recognise him now?

"Don't let your eyes play tricks on you," she admonished herself, draining her glass.

There was no way Patrick Wilde could be in Paris.

CHAPTER 5

The Champs-Élysées had so much to offer that Emily could hardly keep track of it all. There was so much to see on the main avenue, but also the side streets as well.

There was no way she was going to be able to take everything in on one day. The designer stores alone left her wanting more, and she hadn't even been to half of them. This was a shopper's paradise, and for the first time she was going to allow herself to enjoy it.

"I guess I'm going to have to make a repeat visit," she mused, as she looked into a boutique window. The handbags were fantastic and the designs so quintessentially French. She was *definitely* coming back to get one of those, maybe even two.

"See something you like?" a male voice said from over her shoulder.

Emily looked up, but hadn't the chance to turn around, before the speaker's reflection in the glass caught her gaze. He was tall, with carefully coiffed black hair, hazel eyes with dark rimmed glasses seated on a straight nose.

Then there was the smile, one she'd know anywhere, but still Emily couldn't believe he could actually be there.

"Patrick?" she said in disbelief, forcing herself to turn around and see for sure.

"Hello there," he replied, with the same grin. "This is a surprise."

Emily could hardly speak she was so shocked. "Yes, it is." She needed to catch her breath. "I really can't believe it's you. Were you in the Renault a little while ago too? I thought I saw someone who looked like you, but convinced myself it couldn't be."

"That was me," he chuckled. "When I saw you from up the street I wasn't sure it was you either, but I decided to take a chance. When I got closer I absolutely knew it was. You still bite your lip when you're thinking about something."

"Oh," she replied, raising a hand to her mouth unconsciously. "I suppose I do still do that."

"Glad to see everything hasn't changed," he laughed.

"But some things have. You look great! I would hardly have recognised you. You've become a real … man," she mumbled, still a bit tongue-tied.

"Are you saying I wasn't when we were together?" he teased with a raised brow.

"Ah we were both children," she defended quickly.

"We were eighteen. I'd hardly call us children," Patrick corrected, before adding wickedly. "And we certainly didn't act like it."

Emily's cheeks blushed at the inference. He was the first boy she ever really loved, and the first she'd slept with too, both reasons to never forget him.

And she hadn't, even though life had pulled them in different directions.

"Do you have time to get a coffee?" he asked, inclining his head.

"Only if I get to pick the place."

He laughed. "Typical Emily. You always liked to run the show."

She smiled. "As you said, some things haven't changed."

CHAPTER 6

his had to be a dream. She couldn't *really* be standing in a Ladurée café with Patrick Wilde. And in Paris of all places.

Every person had 'one who got away', or so she was always told. Though Patrick wasn't quite that because he hadn't gotten away as such - the choice to end their two year relationship had been mutual.

Emily had gone to university in London, and Patrick had no desire to leave their little home hamlet of Kingham in Oxfordshire.

He had a family inn and restaurant to tend to, and an ailing mother who needed his help. They'd wanted to stay together, but Patrick believed it selfish of him to ask Emily to stay when she'd been accepted to her first choice university. It was a once in a lifetime opportunity he didn't want her to give up or postpone. He wanted her success and she wanted his, but for that time his future was in their hometown.

They'd tried to stay in touch, but the hectic schedule of her life in London and his responsibilities, soon saw their communications dwindle into nothing.

A year or so later, it was over. Then Emily met someone new and started dating, and she presumed he'd done the same.

Their paths had never crossed again since, and though there had been times when she'd thought of him in fond memory, that was all that was left. Sometimes she'd wondered what might have happened if she'd made another choice, but it was something she could never know.

Yet now Patrick Wilde was there, right in front of her - in Paris - and she could hardly believe the change in him.

He had once been an athletic, broad shouldered swimmer who wore terribly thick glasses and stuttered when he was nervous, but none of that bothered her.

She found his shyness endearing and his swimming prowess formidable. Then there was his temperament. Patrick was always polite, helpful and willing to offer an encouraging word to anyone, and a lending hand.

He wasn't all shyness however; there had been a time, when they were around sixteen, when he'd got into a terrible fight with one of their schoolmates. He left the boy with a black eye and a bloody lip, but he'd deserved it in Emily's mind, having dared to speak ill of Patrick's unwell mother.

Though Emily never condoned fighting, she was very proud of him that day, and the way he'd stood up for his mother, a woman who had always treated her well.

Staring was rude, but now Emily couldn't help herself. Patrick stood at the elaborate counter, which was adorned with all manner of sweet macarons and colourful boxes that reminded her more of an elegant perfumey of times past than a delicatessen.

"Here we go," he said, as he approached her. "Something to go with our coffees. Shall we go find some place to sit?"

"Lead the way," Emily offered. "You seem to know your way around quite well."

"I should," he said with a laugh. "I've lived in the city for five years now."

Emily halted. Had she heard him right? "You *live* here - in Paris?"

"Yes," he confirmed, pushing the door open to the street and allowing her to go ahead of him. "I have a place in Gros Caillou, near Champ-de-Mars."

"I can't believe it," Emily replied, wide-eyed. "You never seemed interested in even leaving Kingham, far less crossing the Channel to move to Paris. What happened?"

"A couple of years after you left, my mother died," Patrick informed her, his expression growing momentarily sad.

"I'm so sorry to hear that. I hope …" Emily began, but the words were useless. There was no point in saying them.

"It's alright. She went peacefully in the end, which was all anyone could hope for," he continued as they walked. "After she was gone, my uncle thought it best to take me in. He didn't think I should have been left with the bills and the burden. So I sold the inn then moved to Bristol with my uncle's family. Eventually I enrolled in school and won a scholarship to study business here in Paris. Looks like those French lessons we took in school were of some use," he mused.

"You got the scholarship because you knew French?"

"And because I was in the top percentile in my class," he added mischievously.

"Then what happened?" she asked.

"My year here landed me a job with a company I interned with, and as they say the rest is history," he said with a shrug. "They put me in an apartment, gave me a car and well, that's it."

"I always knew you'd be successful," Emily said with a smile. "I'm so proud of you."

"And what of you? What have you been up to?"

"Well, after I moved to London, it was a bit of an adjustment for me," she admitted, biting her lip. "Being on my own wasn't something I was used to, and having Nan so far away was a little worrying, but she called me all the time and I called her, so it made things easier. I gave up competitive swimming for my studies, though. I just do it for exercise now."

"You - giving up the pool?"

"I could say the same of you," she countered.

"I guess we both knew we weren't going to be Olympians, so it made sense to give it up for things that would take us further."

"True."

"Where are you working in London?" he asked.

"An advertising firm, Thompson & Jonas. I've been there since graduation," she informed him. "I'm Creative Director."

"So soon?" he questioned, surprise lacing his words.

"Yes. Don't you think I could be good enough for the post?" she questioned, folding her arms across her chest.

"Of course you could. You could do anything you set your mind to Emily," he replied, giving her a familiar look.

CHAPTER 7

"You'd better believe it," she countered. "I worked my ass off interning with them from my second year, and by the time I'd graduated, they had a place for me in their Creative Department. Since then I've given up holidays, some weekends, and whatever I had to in order to get the job done. Thankfully, the company is a place that recognises you for your effort, and I was promoted a year after I started as a full-time employee. Since then I've continued to pull my weight so my bosses have given me more responsibility."

"Sounds wonderful, though very busy I'd imagine. What time do you have for your personal life?"

"Not much," Emily replied with a laugh. "I work and on the occasion when I do have time, I spend it with Sarah and her family. You remember Sarah don't you?"

"Sarah Marsh?"

"She's Sarah Cartwright now," Emily informed him. "She's been married seven years and has four boys now, all under the age of five. They live in London too."

"She must be busy," Patrick said in surprise.

"I do my best to help. When she and Jeff, her husband, need some time alone, I'm godmother and babysitter."

"And what does your boyfriend have to say about that?" Patrick questioned, taking Emily slightly by surprise, as they crossed into the park.

The snow, which had since ceased, began to fall again lightly, speckling Patrick's dark hair in white flecks.

"I don't have a boyfriend," she admitted, sipping her coffee and plunging her hand into the bag of treats he'd procured. "What's this?"

"*Noisette Chocolat,*" Patrick said in the most beautiful French she'd ever heard. "Chocolate and hazelnut macaron," he added, realising she was still lost.

"Thanks," she said, taking a bite.

"Someone hasn't been practicing their French," he teased, taking a long gulp of his coffee.

"Haven't had the chance to be honest," she admitted, between chews of the delicious morsel. It was so good it made her hum in satisfaction.

"I see you're enjoying that," Patrick mused.

"It's delicious."

"So back to this no boyfriend. Do you have a husband then?" he continued his questioning, as they began to stroll beneath the trees. A few seconds later they'd found a bench and deposited themselves upon it, while Emily enjoyed her second macaron.

"No husband," she once again confirmed. "What about you?"

"None of the above either," he admitted, shaking his head.

"But why?" He was handsome, successful, and if he had the same disposition he had when they were young, then his personality was stellar. And best of all he lived in Paris, the city of love! What woman wouldn't want him?

"Thanks, my ego need a little rubbing," he replied. He took another long drink of his coffee, then shrugged. "I suppose the women I've met have all been missing something," he divulged.

"Like what?" Emily asked, intrigued.

"Like I said just … something," he replied, his eyes meeting hers and making her heart leap. What did he mean by that? Could he be referring to her?

No, she admonished. It wasn't possible. Patrick couldn't still have feelings for her.

Could he?

Their hands met in the bag, each gripping a side of the last macaron. Patrick tugged on one end teasingly, while she made a face, his words still tumbling in her mind.

"Take it," he said, releasing the morsel.

"Thank you," she replied, promptly sinking her teeth into the delicate chocolate flavoured confection. She could feel Patrick's eyes on her, and the flush that was creeping up her chest under his scrutiny.

She was being silly, she told herself again. It couldn't be possible.

But as Emily's gaze met his full on, she found herself wondering something she hadn't in years.

What might have been…

CHAPTER 8

❄

*H*ad it all been a wonderful dream? Emily questioned as she rolled over in bed the following morning.

The sun was shining in through the hotel window, letting her know that the morning was now well into the day.

Had her meeting with Patrick Wilde been real?

She reached over to the bedside table for her phone, a small card slipping out from within the case as she opened it. There in stylised black writing, was Patrick's name, office information and mobile number, and on the back his home number.

It *had* been real.

She clutched the tiny piece of card in her hand and held it to her chest, as a flood of emotions swept through her. Could it be that she was getting a second chance with her first love? Was Tom's wife right and had the City of Love, brought love to her?

"I should call him," she said to herself, springing up in bed. "No, it would be too soon. You'd look desperate," she countered then, putting the card on her lap and looking down at it. She'd wait at least another day, which was enough time to remove any sign of desperation on her part.

It was a respectable time frame, she told herself as she hoped out of bed and headed to the bathroom to get ready for the day. Paris had lots more to offer, and she wasn't going to see it from her suite.

HALF AN HOUR later she was headed downstairs. She'd slept in so late that breakfast was more than likely over, which meant she'd have to find someplace else to eat.

She wasn't ready for lunch yet, and she had a craving for croissants or even a crêpe. She had just collected her coat when the in-room phone rang.

"Hello?" she answered, and was greeted by Angelique's distinct cadence, informing her that there was someone downstairs waiting for her, a Mr. Wilde.

Patrick - here - now?

Emily's heart felt as if it would leap from her chest the moment she heard his name. She couldn't help but think of what his presence at her hotel meant, when she'd been scolding herself for potentially acting desperate by calling him.

Her step was just a little quicker as she left her room for the elevator, informing Angelique to ensure that Patrick knew she'd be right down.

CHAPTER 9

"I just took a chance seeing if you'd be here," Patrick informed her, when she reached him. "I thought with all the sightseeing you'd planned you may have been out and about already."

"I had intended to," she admitted with an embarrassed laugh. "Unfortunately it seems my bed was more persuasive this morning."

"I get that," he chuckled. "Perhaps I can make up for it by giving you a personal tour around the city?"

"Don't you have better things to do? I know you're on holiday too, but you must've had other plans before you met me," she queried.

There was a twinkle in his eye. "Plans can change. Besides, I think this will be lots more fun."

Emily grinned and nodded.

"That's settled then. Let's go," he stated, offering her an arm. Emily took it and they headed out of the hotel.

After a few minutes she recognised the route. "We're headed to the Arc de Triomphe?"

"I thought it the best place to start our tour."

"Great, I had it on my list of places to see because I only got a glimpse yesterday," she informed him. "But do you mind stopping on the way? I'm a little hungry."

"Why didn't you say so? I know the perfect place to grab brunch," he replied, turning them back around and heading in the opposite direction.

"Where are we going now?"

"You'll see," he informed her intriguingly.

The eclectic café Patrick took her to was a sight to behold. The furniture was reminiscent of the regency era, some chairs covered in a plush velvety blue, while others in leopard print. There were white monkey statues with lightbulbs in them and a large mirror adorned half of one wall. Emily would have loved to eat outside and enjoy the alfresco dining, but it was far too chilly, so she'd have to live that dream another day.

"Pick whatever you want - my treat," Patrick stated as the menus were placed before them.

"I couldn't," Emily replied. "You're already being my free tour guide. You should get something out of all this. I'll buy this time."

He touched her hand gently. "Who said I wasn't getting something from this," he said, his soft gaze set on hers and it made Emily's stomach flip.

"OK," she acquiesced softly. "Your treat."

Was all the food so good in Paris? she wondered a few minutes later. With no breakfast she was famished and pumpkin soup was just what she needed on a chilly day, especially with delicious French roast.

"Now that you're fed and watered, we can start our tour," Patrick joked as he paid the bill.

CHAPTER 10

A few minutes later they were once again headed in the direction of the Arc de Triomphe, chatting animatedly as they went.

It must have been the conversation, because before Emily knew it they were at Place Charles de Gaulle and crossing the street to the monument.

"Its spectacular," she said, a little dazed as she stood at the foot of the structure. The memorial torch was unlit, much to her disappointment. "I thought the flame would be burning," she mumbled as she walked around the memorial, which was decorated with fresh flowers though barred by a low black chain.

"They rekindle it at six-thirty," Patrick informed her. "One of the associations of the La Flamme sous l'Arc de Triomphe veterans do it."

She looked at him in wonder. "You do seem to know a lot about this city."

He shrugged. "When I first moved here I did everything a tourist would do. Saw every sight. Then when it became home, I wanted to know more," Patrick continued, turning to look at her. "This place is a part of me now, as much as England was."

Emily went back to his side and hooked her arm in his. "It makes me a little sad," she said referring to the monument. "They don't even know his name, the man whose life they commemorate here. Makes you wonder how many more were lost and never found. Whose families never knew what happened to them, or returned with no name to mark their graves."

"War is a terrible thing but one that mankind keeps repeating," Patrick replied, laying a gentle hand on top of hers.

"Do you think we'll ever change? That there will ever be a world without fighting?"

"I doubt it. Most people gauge their happiness against the prosperity of others. When one set of people think the other has something they should, they fight for it. They fight for what they think is right. The only problem is we *all* think we're right."

Emily looked up at him quizzically.

"As long as we keep fighting over who's right and who's wrong, there will never be a world without war. All we can do is create something beautiful to help ease the pain of those wars, and celebrate the people who were lost to them."

The notion pained Emily. Her Nan was unknown to the world, important to no one but her. There was no special place to mark her life, only a headstone in a graveyard back home.

"We really need to celebrate people while they're alive," she said softy.

"I agree."

"Show me something cheerier now?" she suggested, still holding his gaze.

"It would be my pleasure," Patrick stated, taking one last look at the monument, before leading her away.

CHAPTER 11

❋

How did Patrick know just where to take her to make her smile?

The Palais Galleria, the museum of fashion, was every woman's dream. Filled with temporary collections showcasing well-known, slightly known and forgotten designers from around the world.

The exterior was inspired by Palladian architecture but known for its Beaux-Arts style. It reminded Emily of something you'd expect to find in Italy, perhaps in Rome, the preserved remnant of some ancient colonnade.

Here you could see designs that were hand-drawn by some of the most distinct and memorable designers, see their clothing draped elegantly on mannequins, or photographed in timeless memorial to the stars who'd made or worn some of the best clothing the world had ever seen.

It was a stark contrast to the Arc de Triomphe, which had left Emily a bit melancholy. Now she felt invigorated.

"Did I choose right?" Patrick asked from behind her. He was standing by a far wall watching her with some amusement.

"You absolutely did," she replied in delight, turning back to the display of Mariano Fortuny's famous Delphos gown, which was designed in 1909.

The designer was considered a liberator of the female form, and the dress before Emily was the epitome of it. Made of plain silk, and so finely pleated that it didn't even wrinkle after being rolled in a ball, it was spectacular. Emily could only imagine herself in a dress like it. She'd feel like an heiress in it.

"That would look great on you," Patrick commented, his arms folded casually over his chest.

"I'd have to win the lottery first," Emily joked.

"You always liked fashion didn't you? Even when you couldn't afford it," he commented, running his finger under the collar of her cashmere coat. "But I can see that has changed."

"I have a few nice pieces," she replied. It was true; she adored fashion; it didn't matter what, clothes, shoes or bags. She may not have had much of a social life, but she certainly dressed like someone who did.

"Let's go someplace you enjoy now," she said to Patrick, taking him by the hand and pulling him towards the exit.

"We better get a taxi if we're going where I'd like to go," he joked. "It's not exactly walking distance."

"I'm intrigued. Where to?"

"You'll see," he smiled, as they walked out to find a taxi.

CHAPTER 12

❄

"When did you become so cultured?" Emily asked, as she stood before the Louvre Palace, home of the famed museum.

It was a formidable building, which had originally been built as a fortress. Then there was the iconic modern glass pyramids which marked the main entrance.

"I *have* to get a photo of this," she commented, slightly in awe.

Patrick waylaid a passerby, the gist of the conversation Emily was just able to get. They spoke so quickly in French it was hard to get to grips with what he was saying, but she figured he was asking the gentleman to take their photograph.

He took her phone and passed it to the other man, before coming to stand behind Emily and hugging her from behind. It was strange having his arms wrapped around her again, but so warm and familiar too. He lowered his cheek beside hers and she dared a glance, marking the hue along his jaw. Suddenly she heard a snap, and realised the man had taken the photo.

"Another," Patrick requested in French, as he turned to meet her eyes. He smiled at her, a wide smile she knew matched her own, as she folded her arms over his and kept his gaze.

"Did I tell you how beautiful you look today?" he asked, as the phone snapped again.

"No," Emily replied softly.

His smile grew, his eyes boring deep into hers. "You look beautiful, Emily." He tucked her hair behind her ear as the phone snapped again.

Then the man moved to hand back the phone and just like that the spell was broken and Emily was brought, heart racing back to her surroundings.

When Patrick returned to her side she was still trying to get her heart to slow. "Shall we go in?" she asked, eager to distract herself from the thundering in her chest.

"Of course," he said, handing her phone back to her.

They started their tour in Egyptian Antiquities, where she took several shots beside the Great Sphinx of Tanis,

"It's like I've gone to Paris and Egypt all in one day," she commented as she admired the beautifully crafted sculpture, which like its Giza counterpart was missing a nose. "Could you imagine that anyone could craft such a thing?" she continued in wonder, a soft chuckle drawing her attention. "What?" she asked, turning to Patrick, who was blocking his mouth with his hand as he laughed.

"The look on your face," he replied. "You're like a child on a first trip to DisneyLand."

"Is that a bad thing?"

"Not in my book."

"Then shall we continue?"

"Lead the way," Patrick encouraged, falling in step behind her, making her stomach flip once more. She knew he was watching her, she could feel his gaze upon her and had to fight the urge to look back at him.

Her efforts failed however, and when she dared to half turn to see if she was right, she was met by those beautiful hazel eyes, staring intently at her with a mischievous smile on his face.

"See something you like?" she mustered the courage to ask.

"You know I do," he replied coolly. "The real question is, do you?"

CHAPTER 13

*E*mily suddenly felt weak all over. She didn't want to be obvious, but it was clear there was something still between them.

But what?

Was it just their reminiscing unearthing the remnants of emotions past?

Or was this something entirely new?

"Perhaps," she replied playfully, as she turned around and continued into the next room.

Here, she saw ancient jewellery and art, papyrus scrolls, more ancient artefacts and mummies. It was more than she had ever expected, and it was only the contents of one of the many rooms within the Louvre.

"Had enough yet?" Patrick asked as they existed the last exhibit.

"How does anyone ever have enough of Paris?" she replied awestruck. "I don't think I have enough room in my brain to hold everything I've seen today, and we haven't even toured the art museum yet."

"We can always come back here," he suggested. "But it's near dinnertime now and I'm hungry."

"Is it? I hadn't realised it was so late, I was so taken by everything."

"Then we can come again tomorrow, but right now I need feeding," he said, then added jokingly. "I'd hate for you to faint from hunger either."

"That happened only once!" she protested laughing. "I'd had swimming practice that day and woke up too late to get breakfast."

"I didn't say anything …" Patrick teased, eyes twinkling and Emily had to laugh at the memory. He still remembered stuff about their past that to her was long-forgotten. Or had been at least.

"Where shall we eat then?" she asked.

"The best place in town."

"Where's that?" she queried, wondering what fancy local restaurant he was about to wow her with.

He smiled enigmatically. "You'll find out when we get there."

CHAPTER 14

*E*mily stood before a vista looking out at a city twinkling in snow and lights.

It was breath-taking, almost surreal.

Paris lay at her feet, or so it seemed she thought as she gazed out from the second floor vantage point of none other than the Eiffel tower. The Jules Verne restaurant was one of five places to dine in the tower, but equally spectacular as all the others.

Every table had a great view, but the table that Patrick requested was situated beside one of the large glass walls overlooking the city.

Emily couldn't bring herself to sit just yet though. "It's like you can see all of France from here," she commented, as Patrick stood beside her.

"Not France, but definitely all of Paris," he chuckled. "I'm so glad you like it."

"Like it? I love it! I can't believe they were able to accommodate us at such short notice, especially so close to Christmas."

"Usually you'd have to wait sometimes as long as two weeks for a reservation," Patrick informed her, "but my company uses this place for business lunches a lot, so they usually find some way to accommodate us."

"So you're a man about town too?" she mused, causing him to blush slightly.

"I'm no man about town, Emily, I just happen to know the right people. *They're* the ones who are the men about town. I just work for them."

She sighed. "Could you ever have imagined that us two kids from Oxfordshire would wind up in big cities like we are now?"

"Never in a million years," he said. "I thought I'd stay in Kingham all my life, but it wasn't meant to be." He turned to her. "But I'm glad for it."

"You are?"

"I got to see you again, didn't I? All those years in England and we never saw each other. A day in Paris and here we are."

The look on his face was indescribable, and so sweet, it made her remember all the half glances and smiles across the classroom when they were in school. Were those feelings alive again? How long would they last this time? She was only going to be in the city for a long weekend, then she had to go home.

"We better take our table before they give it away," he joked then.

Emily nodded, and allowed him to escort her to their table, where he pulled out her seat and made sure she was settled before taking his.

THEIR MEAL WAS SUPERB, the best eight courses she'd ever had in her life, and the first time for it.

"That was so delicious. I wish I could rewind the night and do it all again," she mused, sipping her glass of wine.

"It was good, wasn't it?" Patrick agreed. His eyes had hovered between her and his plate the entire night, except for the moments when Emily had pulled his attention to the sights below.

She'd attempted to identify what she was seeing, and had done miserably at it. Patrick on the other hand, seemed to have all parts of the city committed to memory.

"What're you doing tomorrow night?" he asked, leaning on his elbows as he spoke.

"Nothing, actually. I suppose I'll wander around a bit more and then eat at the hotel. Why?"

"Would you like to come over to my place for dinner?"

Her heart gave a little flip. "I'd love that. Thank you."

"Not to sound like a song, but what about the day after? You'll still be here, yes?"

"Yes, but nothing planned either," she said with a smile, guessing that another invitation was imminent.

"My boss has a special Christmas party every year for us who don't have family in the city," he informed. "It's at his house in La Muette. I go by myself usually," he informed her. "And I'd rather not this year. Go by myself I mean."

"You asking me to go with you?" Emily asked, her surprise clear.

"Would you?"

"I don't know Patrick, it's a big business party with everyone you know, and your boss. What would they think if you showed up with me?" she questioned.

"They'd think that you're someone special to me," he countered. "And they'd be right."

CHAPTER 15

"Oh," she began, but he silenced her with the gentle squeeze of her hand.

"I watched you walk away from me ten years ago Emily, and it almost killed me. Did you know that?"

"No," she replied, shaking her head. "You said you were fine, that you wanted the best for me."

"I did, but I also wanted you to stay. I knew if you left and saw what was out there beyond our little town you wouldn't come back. And I was right. You didn't."

"I thought you'd moved on too …"

"I tried, but every woman I met just wasn't enough. They weren't enough, because they weren't you."

Patrick's words were so sincere that they tore at the fibres of her heart. Back then, she'd wanted to believe what he'd said when he wished her well all those years ago, but somewhere deep inside, she'd known he was lying. She'd wanted to go to London so badly that she'd ignored it.

Even when she convinced herself he'd move on, it was because she knew *she* needed to. If left to herself, Emily would have loved Patrick forever.

Perhaps that was why her other relationships had never worked out either; like him, she was looking for someone else while in the arms of another.

"When I saw you yesterday, I thought I'd finally been given my chance," he continued. "That somehow fate had returned you to me in the most unexpected of ways," he confessed. "Once I knew it really was you, I didn't hesitate this time. I was too afraid if I did you might turn away and I'd lose you again."

"Patrick…"

"Let me say this, please. I don't know by what means we found each other again here or why, but I do want to find out. I took a step towards you yesterday Emily, but now I need you to step towards me, if you're as curious and confused about this as I am."

His eyes were urging her response, but Emily wasn't sure what to say. This was unexpected.

Wonderful, but unexpected.

"I don't know if I can take that step," she admitted finally. "Your life is here, in this beautiful city," she began, turning her eyes to the twinkling lights beneath before returning them to his face. "Mine's in London, remember?"

"It's only a train journey away," he countered seriously.

Emily considered his words. "You're right, it is only a train journey away, but how long can we live with that?"

"What do you mean?"

"I mean, how long could we realistically go with a sea between us, having to trudge from one country to the other? How many times a month should we do it? Should I come to you or you to me? Only on special days, or when work will allow us? We both have demanding jobs that take up our time and energy, Patrick. How much time do you think either of us would have to dedicate to a long distance relationship?"

She could tell her questions were deflating his hopes, but she had to look at the reality of the situation.

They weren't teenagers anymore. She had a job where people depended on her, and a position she'd worked years and sleepless nights to achieve. He'd done the same. How could she ask him to leave it? How could he ask her?

"You're saying you don't feel anything for me then?" he questioned, his tone low.

"That's not it," she countered. "I do. I think I always have, but I can't ignore where we both are either."

"Can't we just see what happens?" he asked.

"I really don't know if I can do that."

"Why not?"

"Because I don't want to get my hopes up, get more attached to you, and have one of us walk away again. I know I couldn't go through that again. Could you?"

Patrick looked at her for the longest time, his silence increasing her anxiety. Finally he spoke. "No, I don't think I could either," he replied, clearly disheartened.

"Do you still want to have me over for dinner tomorrow night?" she asked unsure.

"Emily, I'd rather be with you than anyone else," Patrick said, brightening a little. "I'll pick you up at seven."

"I'll be waiting," she said smiling, but inside she wasn't sure.

Had she done the right thing?

CHAPTER 16

The next day, Emily was seriously considering cancelling their dinner to hide under the covers and order room service, but Patrick had called to confirm he'd be picking her up, and she knew she wouldn't - *couldn't* - do it, the moment she heard his voice.

The drive to his apartment was a quiet one.

They were both obviously feeling the tension from their heart to heart the night before, and Emily had no idea how to remedy it.

She couldn't take her words back, and she couldn't change the facts either. The sooner they accepted that the better, wasn't it?

Patrick's apartment was modern and fresh, the walls and cupboards all painted white, with dark wooden floors throughout. The fixtures were modern stylish, and very contemporary.

"Did you decorate this place yourself?" Emily couldn't help questioning, as she saw the colourful decorative cushions on the couch. It really was the quintessential bachelor pad.

"No," Patrick said with a chuckle. "It came already decorated when I moved in. Part of the company package."

"I wish I had such a company package," she replied, as she continued to look around, albeit somewhat furtively.

"Feel free to take a tour. I have nothing to hide," Patrick offered, as he opened a bottle of red wine and left it to breathe.

"You sure the ghosts of girlfriends past won't come out to get me?"

He chuckled. "I'm pretty sure I had those demons exorcised a long time ago."

Emily wandered around his apartment slowly, taking in every nook and cranny. He kept it exceptionally neat, which was a surprise, considering how messy his childhood bedroom used to be.

"Maybe he has a maid," she mused.

"Yep. She comes in on Mondays," his voice chimed from behind her, making her jump.

"You almost scared me to death," she admitted, with a hand to her chest.

"I wouldn't want that," he stated, stepping closer. "I'm still planning on convincing you that you and I can work."

Her heart danced a little. "Patrick, I thought I already explained –"

"Yes, you explained why you thought we couldn't work, but you haven't yet heard the reasons I think we can."

How she wanted him to be right, that there was some way they could do this, but something told her it was impossible.

Couldn't he just enjoy the time they had together here now and not worry about anything afterwards?

"I let you go too easily before. I'm going to make it difficult for you this time," he said, stepping towards her and closing the space between them.

Every synapse in Emily's brain began to fire as Patrick's hands sought her arms gently, his thumbs stroking her exposed skin as a gentle tug drew her closer.

She shouldn't let this happen. She should push him away and leave, go back to the hotel and not answer any of his calls.

There was only one problem with that though. She didn't want to, couldn't resist. Despite her protests, Emily knew she wanted what was about to happen.

His face drew closer and her heart quickened even more, until all she could hear was the sound of it drumming in her ears.

She licked her lips involuntarily in anticipation of the moment when his would meet hers, yet still she was nervous. She hadn't kissed a man in a couple of years. She hadn't kissed Patrick in over ten.

Could you forget how? Emily didn't have long to wonder though, as seconds later, she felt Patrick's mouth on hers.

His lips were gentle, asking, not demanding and Emily willingly gave in. She returned his kiss with equal tentativeness, allowing herself to relearn the feel of him after all these years.

CHAPTER 17

❄

*H*is technique had changed, grown better.
He no longer had the excited anticipation of a teenager, eager to explore and claim. Patrick's kisses had matured just like he had, and Emily found that even more irresistible.

When their lips finally parted she was breathless, and her knees just a little shaky. Thankfully he hadn't released his grip on her so the fear of falling was eliminated, though the smile on his face didn't help the situation.

"Shall we eat?" he asked then, as if nothing at all had happened.

Compose yourself Emily. It wasn't that good of a kiss.

Who was she kidding? Yes it was.

"Sure," she mumbled, stepping round him and heading back to the living room.

Sitting at the table, she discovered something else new and improved about Patrick. He could cook.

The table was laid tastefully, with matching dinnerware and cutlery. "Did this come with the flat too?"

"No, this bit is all my doing," Patrick replied. "You seem to forget that our family owned a restaurant," he reminded her.

"Touché. So what are we eating?"

He practically beamed with pride as he began to uncover the festive meal he'd prepared, course by course.

They started with the amuse bouche, a bite-sized puffed pastry filled with ham, cheese and chives, followed by pheasant wrapped in bacon with chestnut stuffing, roasted mushrooms and vegetables.

Afterwards, as was fitting in Paris, Patrick served a cheese platter with small salad, and then topped it all off with a Yule Log.

"I can believe you made everything but the log," Emily challenged, as she dabbed the corners of her mouth and set her napkin aside.

"Guilty as charged."

Emily smirked at him.

"What? I'm not a baker. I cook," he stated matter-of-factly, as he began to clear the table.

"Do you want a hand with that?"

"No, you just go and take a seat on the couch, and I'll be right with you," Patrick ordered.

"If you say so," she replied, taking her glass and walking over the couch, a spring in her step.

She made herself comfortable as she watched him continue to clear the table, before pushing up his sleeves and beginning to wash up.

It was strange, but there was something so cosy and domestic about the whole situation that she couldn't take her eyes away. When he finally settled on the couch beside her, he looked tired but was smiling.

"I did ask if you wanted help," she teased.

"I know, but you're my guest. I wasn't about to ask you to work for your dinner."

"Fair enough," she replied. "Now what?"

"Now," he said, picking up the TV remote. "We watch *Miracle on Thirty-Fourth Street,* and we fall asleep on the couch."

"Is that so?"

He grinned. "I had it all planned." He turned on the TV, the opening scene for the movie immediately appearing.

"You did plan this ..." she giggled.

"Yes I did. It's one of the things I really missed after you were gone.

Not having you for our traditional Christmas week movie-watching sessions."

"Well then," Emily replied, settling in alongside him and resting her head on his shoulder, as the movie began. "We need to make up for that."

She'd missed this too - all of it - and it felt so amazing to have it back again.

CHAPTER 18

Her stay rolled by so quickly, *too* quickly. Emily could hardly keep it all straight.

They'd spent a lot of time together at Patrick's place, watching movies and just enjoying getting to know one another again.

He'd made her entire trip to Paris a dream, but as the time came closer to ending, Emily began to dread the inevitable moment when they'd have to say goodbye.

He had done his best in the meantime to convince her that things could work, if only she'd give them a chance.

His persuasions were convincing, but not enough to surmount Emily's fears. What if they pursued a relationship and it ended, like all of her relationships before?

What if this entire thing was just the effects of the most romantic city in the world? Or worse, the lingering memories of a past they hadn't fully let go of?

"Stop thinking so much," Patrick demanded, tugging on her hand as they left her hotel. I'm not going to let you mope for your last day in Paris."

She looked at him sadly. Their last day together. It all kept coming back to the one fact. "Where're we off to now?" she asked, dismissing her own melancholy.

"Somewhere suitably Christmassy."

PARIS TRULY DID LOOK incredible at Christmastime.

The Champs-Élysée had been transformed for the season, and from the Grand Palais to the Concorde Palace the avenue was lit from top to bottom, each of the two hundred trees that lined the road bedecked in twinkling fairly lights, creating a wonderland.

"They outdo themselves every year," Patrick commented, looking down the avenue to where the Christmas markets were set up.

Emily felt like a child again, as she walked beneath the lights alongside Parisians hooked arm-in-arm, some kissing affectionately, others admiring the Christmas fair.

There were stalls in abundance, each offering their own take on festive specialities, from handmade crafts, to freshly made crêpes and sweets.

"Can we go there?" Emily asked, turning her gaze to the Ferris wheel that marked the end of the Concorde Palace.

"If you want," Patrick replied. "It's the biggest in the world, outdoes your London one even."

"Really? Actually, it does look bigger than the London Eye, even at this distance," she replied.

"You always did like going on those things," he commented.

"What can I say, I like looking at the world from a different perspective sometimes."

"That's good then, because I'm hoping you might change your view on a couple of things," he prodded gently.

"Stop it," she replied, giving him a playful shove.

"I'm not giving up. Not until you walk away."

"Can't we just enjoy now? It's my last day after all."

"That's why I'm trying so hard," he replied. "Because I don't want this to be *our* last day."

CHAPTER 19

He was wearing her down. The closer the time for her to return home, and the more time she spent with him, the less she wanted to leave.

Could it really work? Was this really their second chance? Maybe their last?

"You owe me a gift," Patrick stated out of the blue.

"What?"

"A thank you gift for showing you around the city. Come on."

They weaved through the crowd, their direction the Concorde Palace, but suddenly Patrick swerved to the right and led her down a side street.

Emily barely caught the name, Avenue Montaigne.

Like where they'd left, the avenue was illuminated in lights of all sorts of shapes, and in front of a Dior boutique was a giant chandelier. The trees were also dressed in their finest, decorated with so many lights that they seemed to be made entirely of them.

Still, she was baffled as to what Patrick could possibly want from there.

Then they stopped.

"What?" she asked, confused.

"Look up," he said, pointing up the ball of lights above their heads, some mistletoe hanging from it. Emily laughed instantly.

"Is that it - your gift?"

"It's enough, for now," Patrick replied, but didn't move.

Emily knew what he was saying, even without words.

Step towards me. Take a leap of faith. I'm right here.

Her eyes focused on the snow around their boots, and the way Patrick - her childhood sweetheart - held her fingers in his, each hooked into the other.

They'd always been bound together. In a small place like Kingham everyone knew everyone. They'd gone through every stage of school together, but only realised they loved one another when they were in their teens.

Now standing before him, in a city hundreds of miles away from all that, Emily had to make a choice.

She couldn't keep wanting him near, yet pushing him away with her words.

She stepped forward and sure enough, Patrick was waiting for her.

CHAPTER 20

The moment she moved, he pulled her in, enveloping her within the warmth of his body as his lips pressed against hers.

This kiss wasn't the gentle one from his apartment, it was a statement of everything he felt.

Love. Passion. Faithfulness. Endurance.

It was the kind of kiss that some women waited their entire lives to get and often never did.

When they parted, Emily was in tears.

"What's the matter?" he asked gently, brushing her cheek with his gloved hand. The soft fabric was like down against her skin.

"I'm happy, but so scared, all at the same time," she admitted, wrapping her arms around his waist, her head against his chest. She felt his hand against her head, stroking her hair.

"There's no need to be afraid. I'm right here, and I'm not going anywhere. I'm not letting you go, not ever again."

"What does this mean though?" she asked, through tearful smiles.

"It means some love is meant to be. Doesn't matter how many years you have to wait for it. When it's right, the time comes and everything falls into place. Just like it is for us now. Now we just have to write the rest of the story."

"Where will it lead?" she questioned.

"To a happy ending, I hope," Patrick teased softly before kissing her again.

CHAPTER 21

The following morning it was time to go home.

She'd had an amazing trip, one she would never forget.

"I don't want to leave, Nan," Emily whispered, staring off her balcony, her eyes shifting between the Eiffel tower and the Arc de Triomphe.

Paris truly was the City of Love and second chances. This weekend it had given her both.

Live your life.

The thought entered her mind without summons, a fragment of words spoken by Nan the day Emily had told her she wanted to study in London, but was afraid to leave. It was that simple to her grandmother. Live your life.

Was she living her life? Was the life she had the life she wanted? If she'd been asked the question a few days ago she would have said yes, immediately.

Now, she wasn't so sure.

The knock on the door told her it was time to check out, the porter had come for her bags and Patrick was due to pick her up out front at any moment.

"*Au revoir*, Paris," she said, turning from her window and headed towards the door.

. . .

PATRICK WAS on time as usual, and within minutes of her arrival in the lobby and the customary procedures to leave, she was seated beside him in his car, holding hands as they drove towards the airport.

The silence was unusual between them, but for some reason on this occasion, it wasn't uncomfortable, but companionable.

Emily didn't want to speak and Patrick didn't seem to feel the need to either. They were content just to be with each other.

Charles de Gaulle came into view far sooner than expected. Patrick pulled her suitcase from the boot and sent her on ahead to get checked in. She'd protested, but he'd insisted and in the end he won.

She was almost to the counter when he appeared with three bags. She looked at him curiously. "That one isn't mine."

"No," Patrick said, a small smile creeping across his face. "It's mine."

If he'd meant to shock her he'd succeeded, and she was almost too stunned to speak as excitement began bubbling inside.

"Does this mean you're coming with me ... to London?" she asked slowly, trying to keep her joy under control.

"It's only days till Christmas. I haven't taken a holiday outside of the usual in years. I told my boss there was a very special someone I needed to spend more time with, and he gave me an additional stint off."

Her smile could no longer be contained. "You have a very understanding boss."

"He was once a man in love too. He understood where I was coming from." Patrick's gaze lingered on her face as he reached for her hand. She squeezed it tightly.

She too had made a decision she had yet to tell him, and there was no better time than now.

CHAPTER 22

✳

"Well, he won't need to lose you for too long."

"Why is that?"

"Because you won't have to come to London from now on to see your 'special someone,'" she smiled.

Patrick looked completely lost, and it was a look that amused her tremendously.

They stepped up to the counter.

"I'm still waiting for you to explain," he stated as he handed over his ticket and hers.

Emily turned to him. "I made a decision."

"OK..."

"I'm going to live my life, the life I want," she said, touching her palm to his face. "That life is with you. I'm moving to be with you - in Paris."

One moment she was standing at the desk, the next she was being spun round and lifted up in Patrick's arms, as confused passengers looked on.

"You won't regret this. I promise. I swear, you'll never regret this," he was saying as he peppered her face with kisses. "Emily, I have loved you all my life and - "

"*Excusez-moi?*" the clerk droned, in an attempt to get their attention.

A flush filled Emily's face as Patrick apologised and set her down, returning to the counter. He collected their boarding passes and apologised to the passengers waiting impatiently, albeit good-humouredly, behind them.

She wouldn't let go of his hand as they moved towards the departures hall.

"So how are we going to do this?" he babbled as they walked. "What should we do first?"

"Well, first you come to London with me for Christmas. I'll have to speak to my boss when I get back after the holidays, give notice and all that. Then I'll have to see about giving up the lease on my place and finding somewhere in Paris."

"You don't have to worry about that," Patrick replied. "I know a great place you can stay," he assured her, a bright smile on his face.

She smiled, delighted. "I thought you might."

Taking a seat in front of the large circular window that framed the sky and the runway below, Emily and Patrick continued to talk excitedly about what would happen next.

All of a sudden, anything seemed possible. Everything. There was nothing they couldn't do together.

She rested her head on his shoulder. "Patrick?"

"Yes, Emily."

"Say it now," she asked, a smile tickling her lips.

"Say what?"

"That thing you started to say back at the check-in desk."

He pulled her closer. "Emily Richardson, I have loved you all my life and will love you for the rest of it. We belong together you and I; always have."

She squeezed his arm and closed her eyes, savouring the sound of his words.

"So I guess we did find our happy ending after all," she said softly. "Right here in the City of Love."

Patrick smiled. "*Absolument.*"

THE CHRISTMAS WEDDING

CHAPTER 1

❄

"Molly?" a voice called up to where the blonde twenty-eight-year-old sat gazing out the window as a dusting of snow fell softly outside.

Molly O'Brien barely noticed the noise. She was captivated by the magic of this first snow – even if it was just flurries - and which she knew would have melted away by the time she and her parents boarded the plane to Italy later that morning.

There was just something about Christmastime – the brisk cold weather, greenery around the hearth, candles and fairy lights, holly and mistletoe – that filled her with such joy she could hardly contain herself. And with everything building to an even more joyous occasion now just a couple of sleeps away, Molly was entranced.

"Love?" her mother's voice came again, this time from just down the hall.

Molly sighed and returned to the suitcase laid open on her childhood bed, folding up the last of her clothes and stuffing them in the remaining spaces.

A long packing list rested nearby. She glanced through it as her mind raced. Forgetting anything for this trip would be disastrous. She couldn't afford to be distracted or unfocused.

A gentle knock came at the door, followed by a creak as it opened. Her mother Helen stood in the doorway.

Just then, Molly was struck by the greyish streaks in her mother's blonde hair; surely they hadn't been there before. But her ever-glamorous mum was getting older. They all were.

However, despite the strands of grey and the faint lines around her lips, Molly couldn't remember a time when Helen looked better. The years agreed with her.

She smiled. "Hey, Mum."

'We're all set to go, love. Have you packed the last of it?"

Molly nodded and took her mother's arm, bringing her over to the window. "Look," she smiled. "Isn't it beautiful?"

Helen sighed. "It is, honey, yes," she said wistfully. "I remember you and Caroline sitting here as young kids for hours just watching the snow fall in winter. We could barely peel you two away for anything. Well, except maybe for a few Jammie Dodgers..."

"Feeling nostalgic?" Molly asked casually. She looked at her mother who had the same dreamy look on her face she herself had. It ran in the family apparently.

Helen shook her head. "Just a bit, maybe," she admitted. "It's hard to see your baby grow up before your eyes. And now, well I suppose I'm just wishing we could have the wedding for you that your father and I always envisioned. I always knew you would get married at this time of year with that love of Christmas of yours, but I never expected that you would do it somewhere else."

"Ah, mum," Molly replied, "we've been through all this a million times already." She was exhausted. Her parents had barely let up with their complaints since, she and her fiancé Ben had announced their intentions to get married in Rome.

Helen put her hands up defensively. "I know, I know," she responded, "and it is of *course* your wedding – yours, and Ben's."

Helen thought back to the little girl playing weddings with her best friend, Caroline. There was always a beautiful red and green bouquet, teddy bears and dolls representing friends and family - and snow boots under an old white costume.

THE CHRISTMAS WEDDING

"Mum," Molly said gently. "Look around this room. What do you see?"

Helen looked at the walls of the room that had been Molly's bedroom for most of the last three decades.

Framed posters of the Colosseum, St. Peter's Basilica, and the Trevi Fountain graced the walls.

On the bookshelves were everything from Italian phrasebooks and texts on Roman history, to tomes by Dante Alighieri and Italo Calvino.

Even the wallpaper, though a bit frayed and yellowed now, featured a watermark of the Arch of Constantine.

It was in effect, the most Italian room in all of Ireland.

"I've been dreaming of this forever," Molly continued. "A Christmas wedding in Rome has *always* been the dream. And finally it's coming true."

Molly was as in love with Italy almost as much as she was with her fiancé.

She had studied Italian literature in University College Dublin, and had even taken several Italian cooking classes for fun. While she may no longer be that little girl dressing up teddy bears and 'marrying' her best friend, she was still the woman with Italian posters, books, and maps in her bedroom.

Helen nodded. "I know, love," she said kindly. "And your dad and I want to give you the wedding of your dreams. Even if it happens to be in another country."

She had struggled to come to terms with her daughter's decision, but at this point, there was no turning back. Molly and Ben were getting married in Rome on Christmas Eve - two days from now.

"Girls!" Molly's father Paddy yelled at the two women from the foot of the stairs. "It's time we headed off."

Paddy O'Brien had also been staring out the window at the snow rolling in and wondering how long they would be stuck at Dublin airport because of it.

"We're coming now," Helen called down to him. She turned to Molly. "Ready, sweetheart?" she asked with a smile.

Molly looked through the packing list once more, nodded and pulled her stuffed suitcase off the bed.

She grinned. "Ready as I'll ever be."

CHAPTER 2

❋

"Tell me again why we couldn't fly First Class?"

Patricia Pembrey did *not* like flying steerage – and she certainly did not approve of the sort milling about in Luton Airport just then.

She made a horrified face as an elderly couple slowly walked past her, chewing gum loudly and clicking their canes against the tile floor.

"Because, mother," her son Ben said flatly, "we're going to travel like normal people for once."

He had predicted his mother was going to be a pain, but he had no idea she would be this intolerable. The complaints had started months ago and it looked like they were not ending anytime soon.

"Oh, nonsense, Ben," Patricia said coolly, adjusting the foxtail scarf over her shoulder. "We do travel like normal people, normal for our class." She stuttered, lifting her arms in frustration, "Tell him, James."

Lord James Pembrey, 15th Earl of Daventry, was nonplussed.

"I know, dear," he said pompously. His travel usually included a private boarding area at Heathrow away from the public, waitresses with endless champagne flutes, and takeoffs scheduled around his agenda.

This was too much like roughing it for his liking.

Ben shook his head, completely frustrated with his parents' inability to see past their own wants and needs.

"Look," he said, his brown eyes darting towards the fast food lines. "I'll pop over to Costa and pick us up some coffees. Will that do?"

He loved his parents, and they had given him a wonderful life filled with opportunities many only dreamed of – but they could be such woeful snobs that he sometimes wondered whether he'd been adopted.

He had been so completely different to them that when he'd gone off to university, he'd deliberately chosen not to go to Oxford or Cambridge but instead to University College Dublin – much to his parents' chagrin.

And he was glad that he had; it's where he'd met Molly.

He remembered clearly that first night he'd laid eyes on her at a social in a pub following a big rugby match.

Molly and her friend Caroline had come in, and Molly's large doe eyes met Ben's from across the crowded room.

He was normally confident, but something about her had told him that she wasn't the type that would instantly fawn over him, as so many other girls did once they found out he was bona fide English gentry.

But, unlike in the UK, that kind of thing meant little in Ireland. Part of the reason Ben had shipped out of England in the first place.

He took a deep breath and marched over to talk to her – and promptly knocked a drink off a server's tray and down the front of her top. Horrified, she'd stomped out of the pub with Caroline following at her heels. It was as awful a first encounter as any had ever been.

He counted himself lucky, then, that only two weeks later, they happened to meet again at a college party for Italian & Classical Degree students.

Ben had been invited by a mutual friend after he offered to make a pasta dish his old nanny cooked up for him and his brother every time his parents were off travelling.

Molly had made her way into the kitchen, the smell of the homemade sauce tempting her. When she saw the idiot from the bar, she'd immediately turned on her heel but Ben was faster. He grabbed her arm as she was leaving, apologising the entire way.

She'd looked at the man in the dirty apron, red sauce splattered on his cheeks, with his dark hair, deep brown eyes boring apologetically into hers, and couldn't find a reason to be angry any longer.

They'd ended up talking the whole night through, eventually watching the sun rise over campus.

As he watched her in the glow of the early morning light, the warm sunshine reflecting in her wide blue eyes, Ben knew, even at that early moment, that this was the woman he was going to marry.

On Christmas Eve five years later, he had it all planned out as he took them on a journey of their old college haunts. They'd gotten fish and chips from the chipper they'd always gone to after a night on the town, went for a drink before closing at the pub where they'd had that first run in, and eventually wandered into St Stephen's Green.

With light snowflakes swirling around them, and fairy lights shining amidst the trees above, Molly pushed her bundled-up body closer into his as they sat down on one of the benches.

As she talked about their Christmas plans for the next day, she turned to him expectantly, her eyes shining with excitement.

But Ben was not there, at least not where he had just been sitting. He was down on one knee, and pulled out a little black velvet box, his hands trembling as he searched for the words he had rehearsed for months – before promptly dropping the ring in the snow.

Ben was horrified as he squinted his eyes and searched the damp snow for the sparkling diamond once belonging to his grandmother.

But Molly only laughed and bent down, easily picking up the antique ring with its beautiful three off-centre diamonds, tears in her eyes.

She brought her red-gloved hand to his face. "Oh, you don't even have to ask," she told him, beaming. "Of course I'll marry you."

There hadn't even been a question of where - or indeed when - to get married. Winter in Rome, at Christmastime.

While Ben had suggested that Molly's family might be more comfortable with a traditional Irish ceremony at home, she wouldn't hear of it.

She also knew Ben too well – particularly, that his family's wealth and prominence embarrassed and irritated him.

Anything traditional would have been dwarfed by the excess and pomposity the Pembreys would no doubt insist on bringing to the table.

So in the end they'd both known that a small, intimate gathering at an historic church in Rome – just family and friends - was exactly what they wanted. The arrangements had taken nearly a year, though they'd had lost of help from a wedding planner in Italy to navigate the details.

And now days before Christmas, Ben found it hard to believe that here he was, ordering coffees at the airport, about to board a plane to Rome to meet his soon-to-be wife.

He grinned and thanked the barista as he picked up the coffees, leaving some change in a small jar next to the register. "Thanks - Merry Christmas."

He returned to their boarding gate to find his mother, daintily dusting off the plastic airport seat with his father's handkerchief.

"Oh, you have *got* to be joking, Mother," he said, rolling his eyes and thrusting a cup her way.

"What?" she inquired innocently. "We'll have to find a reputable dry cleaner once we have landed in Italy. I am not packing this handkerchief in our luggage."

Ben handed his father his coffee and strode away. "Ben?" his father called from behind him, "where are you going now?"

"To find a bar," he grumbled. "I need a stiff drink."

CHAPTER 3

❄

"Caroline!" Molly darted excitedly towards her best friend, her trainers nearly bouncing off the tiled floors of Rome's Da Vinci Airport.

Yes it had been a couple of months since they had last seen each other, as Caroline now lived in Cork, but by Molly's reaction, one would think it had been years.

Caroline Davison giggled and bounded in the opposite direction and the two embraced forcefully, their collective weight tilting to and fro from their exuberance, eventually causing them to almost fall over in a fit of laughing and hugs.

"Oh my God, Molly, you're getting *married*!" Caroline exclaimed, her green eyes sparkling and dark curls bouncing, as she helped her friend to her feet.

"Wait - I'm doing what?" Molly teased, a wicked smile filling her face.

"Grand. Well, we're here now, so to hell with Ben, let's find you a nice Italian Romeo!"

The two laughed hysterically as Molly's parents joined them near the baggage claim.

Helen's arms stretched out towards Caroline, embracing her in a familiar, gentle hug. Caroline gave both O'Briens a kiss on the cheek, wishing them a Happy Christmas.

"How was the flight from Dublin?" she asked.

"The flight was fine," Helen replied. "It's everything since that…"

"*Mum,*" Molly scolded.

"All your mother is saying," Paddy picked up, "is that maybe the natives could be a *bit* more helpful."

"Dad," she groaned, "Italians aren't required to speak English, you know."

"No," Paddy agreed, "but when you go to an airport cafe and order a cup of tea, they should at least have *some* idea what you mean."

"Relax, Mr O'Brien. It's nearly Christmas…though you wouldn't know it here," Caroline said, casting a dubious glance around the airport.

Unlike Cork airport from which she'd flown earlier this morning, she was surprised to find that the festive decor in Italy seemed lacking. While airports back home were usually all holly and ivy and Christmas trees, here, everything seemed a bit more subdued.

Only a few strands of fairy lights and some signs reading *Chiuso per Natale* ("Closed for Christmas") let travellers know that any sort of holiday was imminent.

But perhaps the Italians didn't make such a big deal of it? As it was Caroline's first time in the country and she knew very little about the place, she couldn't be sure.

But no doubt she would soon find out. In any case, her best friend adored the city and was looking forward to not only her wedding, but also showing everyone around.

Molly was about to speak again when a pair of hands covered her eyes and a familiar voice whispered in her ear.

"Guess who?" She grabbed the hands, turned around, and found herself face-to-face with her fiancé. She held Ben's face in her hands, stood on her tiptoes, and kissed him.

"Here comes the groom," Caroline laughed, as Ben then bent over to kiss her cheek.

"Great to see you, Car," he said. "How's life in Cork?"

"Fine as ever, Ben, how are you?"

He opened his mouth to reply, but as he did, came the sound of someone complaining on approach "...and I swear to you, James, if there is no butler service, I won't stay. I simply won't!"

"And I wouldn't hear of it, darling," Ben's father replied. He searched the crowd, finally finding his son in the mix of faces. "There you are. We've been looking for you. We have a driver waiting."

Molly shook hands awkwardly with both Patricia and James Pembrey. She'd met his parents a couple of times over the years, and was well used to their snooty behaviour.

At first, she wasn't sure what to make of them, especially considering Ben was as humble and down-to-earth as they came. Fortunately because they lived in the UK, she and Ben didn't have much to do with them.

"And you remember my parents, Paddy and Helen?" Molly said quickly, while the rest of the wedding party exchanged muted greetings.

Both sets of parents had met briefly after the engagement, but as her working class parents had little in common with English nobility, it had been somewhat ... strained.

Caroline watched the whole scene unfold as she waited at carousel belt. After a few more beats of awkward quiet amongst the families, she cleared her throat.

Molly looked to her confusedly, then added, "Oh of course! And Caroline, my best friend and bridesmaid."

Caroline smiled and approached the Pembreys. "Hello there," she greeted, beaming.

She got little in response. Instead the Pembreys, the O'Briens, and Caroline all stood there in complete silence as the conveyer belt clanked and clattered around.

"So," she said, attempting to break the ice, "who's ready for some wine tasting?"

"As long as it's not one of those so-called 'Super Tuscans,'" Patricia groused. "Never had a more overrated wine in my life."

The awkward silence resumed. Caroline smiled tightly and stared down at her feet until she was tapped on the shoulder by a small man with a wiry moustache.

"Scusi?" he said in a heavily accented voice, "You are Miss Davison, yes?"

She nodded. "I am. Can I help you?"

"Can you come with me, please?"

She followed him, perplexed.

"Signorina," the man said once they were away from the crowd, "I am afraid I have some bad news."

"What do you mean, 'bad news?'" she repeated, frowning.

"Your package," he said.

She was puzzled. "My… package?"

"No, scusi, that is not the right word," he apologised. "Sorry, my English, it is not so good. I mean, *luggage*. Your luggage – it did not arrive."

CHAPTER 4

❄

The lobby of the Hotel Marliconi was gloriously opulent, a mix of old-world wood, Italian marble and art deco stained glass.

White stone statues of women with water pitchers stood in a small fountain in the centre of the massive reception room, giving it the extravagant feel of something from a movie, while overhead a magnificent fresco depicted a classic Renaissance scene.

Additional Christmas-themed decor – a tree, nativity scene, and a few red-and-green bows dotted here and there – gave the hotel a somewhat more festive look, though Caroline couldn't help but notice again how much more subdued it was compared to the glitzier stuff back home.

Still, any Christmassy decor paled in comparison to the inherent beauty of the city itself.

Caroline was still reeling from her first sight of the Colosseum on the approach to the city of Rome from the airport. And everywhere she looked were jaw-dropping sights of Renaissance architecture and Italian grandeur.

A gigantic structure of Corinthian columns, fountains, and equestrian sculpture in the centre of the city that Molly pointed out as the Victor Emmanuel monument was awe-inspiring, as was a passing glimpse of the

Roman Forum, and the myriad Baroque fountains and pretty piazzas that gave the picturesque city an almost other-worldly feel.

Now she and Molly approached the reception desk arm-in-arm. Molly still seemed jittery, bothered by the absence of Caroline's bridesmaid dress and she thought, a little put out by the fact that her best friend seemed to be the only one in the wedding party impressed by the city sights.

On the way in the taxi, the O'Briens seemed distracted and uncomfortable, and only nodded in passing when Molly pointed out areas of interest and beauty.

For someone who loved Italy as much as her friend, and was so eager to share her great passion for the city she'd chosen as her wedding destination, it was no doubt disappointing.

She rubbed her friend's shoulders reassuringly.

"The dress will come in time, Mol," she soothed, guiding her to the front desk. "Don't worry. It's just a hiccup – nothing to worry about. It wouldn't be a wedding without a little bad luck."

Behind them, Molly's parents gazed around the hotel reception, a little taken aback.

"It's a bit ... grand, isn't it?" Helen commented.

"It is," Paddy responded. "I don't mind paying for a nice hotel, but I certainly didn't expect a palace."

At the back of the group, James and Patricia Pembrey shuffled into the lobby, followed by Ben, whose voice echoed off the marble walls as he barked into his phone.

"Mark, this is simply ridiculous," he said testily. "No – no – I don't – listen to me, I don't *care*. This is my *wedding*. You're my brother, my best man. I think it's fair of me to expect you to be here at least ... okay." He hung up the phone and shoved it back in his pocket.

"So where's Mark?" Molly asked when Ben caught up with her at reception.

He sighed. "Still back in London working on some kind of 'server issues,'" he said in an irritated voice. "He says he's 'trying' to get away, but it could be well be tomorrow night by the time he arrives." Then he

THE CHRISTMAS WEDDING

took a deep breath and put his arm around his fiancee. "Look. Let's just get everyone checked in and then we'll all go have a drink and chill out a bit, OK?"

Molly nodded, and turned back to the check in desk. The young Italian woman behind the counter had a bored, almost lackadaisical look on her face as she leaned against the back wall, gazing at her phone.

Ben threw a quick glance towards Molly and called out, "Um, excuse me?"

The woman sighed, put her phone in her pocket, and walked up to her computer.

"Buonasera," she greeted with fake cheeriness, "how can I help you today?"

"Buonasera," Molly replied with a smile. "We'd like to check into our rooms please. There should be four in total, all under the name O'Brien."

The woman typed some info into her computer, and the machine beeped. "I'm sorry," she said, "I have no rooms under that name. Would they be under another?"

"Erm, Pembrey, perhaps?" Ben offered.

She typed the letters in. This time there was no beep, but rather a chime, followed by a look of sheer confusion on the part of the clerk. "I am sorry," she said, not looking particularly apologetic, "I must speak to my manager. One moment, please."

Caroline joined them at the desk. "What's going on?" she inquired.

Molly shrugged. "Dunno," she said. "She just looked really confused and then bounded off."

A few moments later, the clerk returned with a short, bald, mustachioed manager, a grave look on his face. "Buonasera," he greeted them, "are you Signorina O'Brien?"

"I am," she nodded. Ben's parents now huddled close to them, attempting to hear what was going on. "What's the problem?" Molly asked the manager.

"It seems we have a small ... issue," he stated. "Our hotel – it is fully booked, and though we have your reservation, it seems we have sold the rooms."

Molly's jaw nearly hit the ground. "You've done *what?*" she demanded.

"It was a mistake, I assure you, Signorina, and not one that happens at this hotel often." He looked towards the staff member suspiciously, as if she personally were the one to blame.

Molly threw her hands up in the air and walked off. Ben looked to his parents – at which point James stepped in – and he darted after his fiancée.

As he went, he heard his father assume his most pompous, House of Lords voice: "Now see here, sir, this is our son's wedding, and we were assured of having four suites at this hotel. It was *guaranteed*, so do you know what you're going to do? I'll tell you what you are going to do. You will…"

BEN WAS out of earshot when he found Molly at the other end of the lobby, staring out the window towards a picturesque piazza. He went over and put a hand on her shoulder. "Molly, hon," he said consolingly, "it's going to be okay – "

"'Okay?'" she whispered, as she turned to face him. "Ben, *nothing* is okay. First, Caroline's dress doesn't get here, my parents do nothing but complain about the place, your best man isn't even sure he'll make it… and now, they can't find our room reservations. What exactly is okay?"

"That we're here in Rome to be married, like we always wanted."

"Oh, Ben," she cried, tears threatening. "I know that, but …I'm wondering if doing this at Christmas was a mistake. This has been nothing but a disaster so far – and we've only been in the city less than an hour. To say nothing of the fact that it doesn't feel very Christmassy at all."

Ben hugged her close. "Do you trust me?" he asked, a glint in his eye. She looked up at him, wiped her eyes, and nodded. "Then trust me when I say it's going to work itself out. I promise." She sniffled a bit but nodded again.

A few moments later, Patricia and James rejoined the group, along with a handsome Italian man in his late thirties with deep brown eyes, and a smile that immediately sent both Caroline's and Molly's hearts aflutter.

He went straight up to Molly and kissed her on both cheeks. "Signorina," he said, still smiling, in perfect English but with a delicious Italian inflection. "My name is Fabrizio, and I am your coordinator for your stay with us here at the Hotel Marliconi."

He turned to Ben, who held out his hand for a handshake, but Fabrizio leaned in and kissed him on both cheeks as well. "Here in Italy," he explained, "we do not shake hands usually – we are a passionate people. We enjoy intimacy."

Molly's father rolled his eyes. He leaned forward and whispered to his wife, "A handshake will be intimate enough for me, thanks very much." Helen stifled a laugh as the wedding planner introduced himself to the rest of the group.

"Firstly," Fabrizio said after his introductions, "please accept my apologies for the mix-up with your reservations. Signor Pembrey – "

James cleared his throat. "*Lord* Pembrey, actually," he corrected pompously.

" – sorry," Fabrizio apologised, with a twinkle in his eye, "*Lord* Pembrey. We are not yet very certain what happened, but rest assured, we will do everything we can to accommodate you."

Molly brightened immediately. "So we're getting our rooms then?" she asked.

The smile left Fabrizio's face. "Well," he said, immediately causing her face to fall, "that is what we hope. We unfortunately have all of our suites currently occupied. However, we can for now put you in our also beautiful Deluxe Room, and if a suite becomes available, we will of course move you there."

Molly opened her mouth to protest, but Ben took her hand and wrapped it in his.

"It's better than nothing," he said.

"*Fantastico,*" Fabrizio said enthusiastically, his smile still in place. "Now, I will call someone to help you with your bags. Perhaps you would like to bathe, relax for a bit. Can we meet at our terrazza restaurant in, say, one hour to discuss plans for your wedding?"

"Sounds good," Ben replied.

"*Eccellente!*" the Italian man grinned. "I will send up the luggage with, maybe, a bottle of wine for each of you? Will that be acceptable?"

Caroline perked up at the words she'd been waiting for. "*God* yes, please," she said. "We could *definitely* use some of that."

CHAPTER 5

❄

Patricia rubbed her damp hair with a towel, a scowl on her face.

"Dear God," she complained, "what is this made of, sandpaper?"

James lay on the bed, scanning through Italian broadcasts on the TV. "How was the water pressure, dear?"

"Awful," she frowned. "And the bathroom has some kind of… odd fragrance."

"I think they call that 'soap,' darling."

"This really is intolerable, James," Patricia replied, exasperation in her eyes. "I understood that this hotel would be acceptable to our standards."

James shook his head. "The concierge chap assured me that they're going to get this taken care of, my dear," he told her. "For now, we'll just have to… make do. Though I agree this bedlinen does seem quite garish."

NEXT DOOR, Molly and Caroline opened the bottle of wine that had been delivered to their room a few minutes before.

Molly took a long, deep sip while Caroline kicked off her shoes and put her feet up. "This really isn't so bad, is it?" she asked her.

"It's not," Molly agreed, gazing out the window at the Roman rooftops below. "But I really wanted a suite."

"Oh come on, Mol," Caroline chuckled. "When in Rome - isn't what they say?"

Her friend sighed and sipped her wine. "Is it so wrong to just want this to be perfect?" she asked after a long pause.

"Every bride wants her wedding to be perfect," Caroline said soothingly. "But it very rarely happens that *nothing* goes wrong."

"It just worries me, a little that's all. Like, is *this* how my life with Ben is going to start?"

"You mean, in one of the romantic cities in the world at Christmastime?" Molly took a large swig of her wine. "Nasty."

"Ah, you know what I mean."

"Yes," Caroline nodded – but she smiled teasingly.

"Of course I know what you mean. In your head you're been planning this perfect Italian wedding for most of your life. But you are putting too much pressure on yourself. At the end of a wedding day, is just a *day* – no matter where it is. It's going to be brilliant of course, but don't put *too* much emphasis on it."

"That's easy for you to say," Molly countered, finishing her wine, "seeing as the closest you've come to getting married was when we were four and you and Raggedy Andy were an item—"

She stopped short, realising what she'd just said. She looked over to Caroline, who stared at her, the slight tremor on her friend's lips making it that clear Molly had hurt her.

"Oh, God, Caroline," she began, "I – I don't know – I'm so sorry. That was *literally* the nastiest thing I could've said to you. What is going on with me?"

"It's fine," Caroline said softly.

"No, it's really not," Molly continued. "I'm really – "

"I know, Mol," Caroline said, a half-smile on her face. "Besides, maybe I'll meet a gorgeous, bronzed Italian while I'm here."

"Like Fabrizio?" she teased.

"Ew," Caroline replied, horrified. "He's so…"

"Charming? Handsome? *Dreamy?*"

"...cheesy, I was going to say," Caroline concluded. "The guy is every bad stereotype of every movie set in Italy ever." She finished off her own wine and poured another glass. "Why can't life just be like *Pretty Woman?*" she asked.

Molly looked at her quizzically. "You want to be a prostitute with a weirdly expressive mouth?" she asked, giggling.

"Okay, right, not *Pretty Woman* – the other one – *Runaway Bride?*"

"*Not* the best comparison," Molly said, dissolving in a fit of laughter. Then she sighed and reached for her friend, enveloping her in a tight embrace. "You know I love you, don't you?" she said. "And that I'm proud beyond belief that you're going to be bridesmaid."

"Enough of the Hollywood smaltz," Caroline berated but she was smiling. "Now, drink up. We have a lot of work to do before we meet up again with Fabio this evening."

"Fabrizio," Molly corrected. "*Fabio* is the dude on the cover of romance novels."

"Same difference," her friend grinned.

CHAPTER 6

❄

*A*t seven pm, the wedding party reconvened on the hotel's rooftop terrazza, taking in the extraordinarily beautiful cityscape.

Ancient icons such as the Colosseum, Roman Forum and Pantheon recalled Rome's time as the fearsome hub of the Roman Empire, while catacombs and clandestine churches harked back to the early days of Christianity.

Lording it over the Vatican was St Peter's Basilica, the greatest of the city's monumental basilicas, a towering masterpiece of Renaissance architecture and clearly visible from where they sat.

Paddy had at first been a bit disappointed that there was no Guinness and the only beer available was bottled Peroni, but being able to look out at such a glorious view seemed worth it.

He sat with his wife making small talk with Ben's parents whom he wasn't all that keen on.

"So," he said, a bit awkwardly, "have you been to Italy before?"

"Oh," Patricia said, with something that sounded vaguely like a combination of a forced laugh and a throat-clearing, "*many* times. We used to take Ben and Mark to the Amalfi Coast on holidays when they were little. Stopped a few times here to see the sights and take in the art and culture. But if you're to do anything in Italy, you simply *must* visit

Tuscany. The wines…" she nodded towards her half-full glass, "…are much better than *this* swill."

The awkward silence resumed until Ben's father spoke up. "So then, Paddy my good man, what is it that you do again? Forgive me - I've forgotten."

Paddy took a sip of his beer. "Well, I worked in courier delivery for a number of years, mostly delivering packages locally. DHL bought the company a few years back but I still run the delivery service - I just don't have to actually *go* on the deliveries anymore."

James sat upright. "So," he said interestedly, "you used to pull out packages from a van or something like that?"

"Well," Paddy replied, his eyes narrowing somewhat, "it was something *like* that in that the job title was *literally* pulling packages out of a van so… yes."

"I think I need another glass of wine," Patricia interjected, swallowing a large gulp from her glass and hailing the waiter.

MOLLY WAS FEELING CONSIDERABLY HAPPIER after a bath and a few glasses of chianti with Caroline.

She now sat on the hotel's beautiful rooftop terrace curled up on a wicker sofa alongside Ben, munching absentmindedly on some Italian cheeses and grapes, while Caroline relaxed nearby.

"You know," she said, "Santa Maria church is very small. Mum and Dad won't know what hit them when they see how tiny it is."

Ben snickered. "You think *your* parents will be surprised?" he asked. "Mine will simply be livid. I can hear it now: mother getting her nose in a snit, saying things like, 'Huh! It's so dusty in here,' and father with his upright disapproval, wondering where the 'right honourable gentlemen' of Italy are supposed to get married." He exhaled through his nose dramatically. "It's going to be *classic*."

Caroline, seated across from them, giggled. "You two," she smiled. "You're so… so *perfect* together. I'm just… I'm just…"

"Drunk?" Molly suggested, laughing. "We did go through that wine Fabrizio sent to the room awfully quickly."

"Speaking of which," Ben noted, looking at his watch, "where *is* Fabrizio? He's over an hour late."

"Dunno," Caroline said. "Want me to go look for him?"

"Would you mind?" Molly asked gratefully.

She patted her friend on the knee. "I'll be right back," she promised. She got up and made her way towards the lift, heading down to the lobby.

At the desk, she asked the clerk if she'd seen Fabrizio, but he apparently hadn't been around since earlier.

Annoyed, she returned to the lift but as she exited the lobby, she noticed a man sitting by the downstairs bar, flashing a big smile and flirting with the pretty young bartender.

Caroline marched over to him with a full head of steam and tapped him on the shoulder.

"Excuse me," she said, "exactly what do you think you're doing?"

Fabrizio turned to look at her and smiled. "Ah, *Bella*" he greeted energetically, "so wonderful to see you again."

"Don't give me that crap," she said sternly. "We've been waiting upstairs on you for an hour. And I find you sitting down here, drinking and – and – *flirting*?"

Fabrizio took her by the hand. "Signorina," he said, dramatically, "I did not mean to offend. But life is too short to worry about being a little late. Sometimes, we must go where the moment takes us."

Caroline pulled her hand back brusquely. "Well, buddy" she replied her voice terse, "the 'moment' had better take you up there to talk to Molly and Ben about their wedding in short order, or we're going to be finding another planner *and* another hotel."

The Italian put his hands up defensively. "Okay, okay," he said, "but tell me, Signorina… are you more upset that I am late, or more upset that I was speaking with a woman whose beauty is so inferior to yours?"

Caroline blushed slightly but didn't break her icy stare. "Don't think for a second that nonsense is going to work on *me*," she said fiercely. "I've heard all about you swarthy, Italian charmers."

Fabrizio raised an eyebrow. "Swarthy?" he repeated bemusedly.

Caroline continued without breaking stride. "You're all 'passion' and 'fire' and 'embrace your inner blah-blah-blah' for foreign women – and then when you get what you want you never speak to us again. So don't try your tricks on me, mister."

Fabrizio nodded curtly. "Yes, Signorina," he said, his face a picture. "I will no longer comment on the radiance of your beauty, which puts a sunset to shame…"

Caroline rolled her eyes. "If you're done doing… whatever it was you were doing here, I'd appreciate it if you'd come now and talk to my friend about her wedding. She could really use your help."

Fabrizio downed the last of his drink and pushed out his stool from the bar. "After you," he offered.

"Oh, no," she said sarcastically, "I insist – after *you*."

Caroline was pleased with her performance; she'd successfully done exactly what she set out to do, performing her bridesmaid duties well.

But despite herself - and feeling like a bit of an idiot for feeling that way - she couldn't help but admit that there was something about Fabrizio's smile that made her insides tingle.

CHAPTER 7

"I don't think you understand …" Molly said tersely.
They'd been discussing her plans and expectations leading up to the wedding on Christmas Eve, but Fabrizio's nonchalant attitude was now seriously rubbing her up the wrong way.

No matter what she suggested they do, the Italian gave off an air of frustrating carelessness, and resisted giving their days any structure whatsoever.

"We really want to see the sights of Rome - show the wedding guests some of this wonderful city."

"Of course, *Signorina*, of course," he responded gently, again flashing his debonair smile. "But *Roma* – she is not like other cities. She demands a certain… spontaneity. You must listen to her to see where she takes you."

Molly's father had had just about enough. He threw his napkin onto the plate in front of him – still full of small, white *calamari*, which Paddy couldn't bring himself to eat, considering the look of the tentacles – and jabbed a finger at the man sitting across from him.

"Now, listen here lad," he scolded, "I think we have been very patient so far with you. There's a lot we want to see and do while we're here, and I think we have the right to have some sort of plan. For God's sake man, this is our daughter's wedding!"

Helen put a hand on his arm, and he calmed down a bit. "What my husband is trying to say," Molly's mum began, "is that we want to make sure everything about the trip is being taken care of, and right now you aren't reassuring us that it is."

"*Signores*," Fabrizio responded apologetically, "Please, listen. All will be fine. We have the church, we have a priest – Padre Beppe, he is the best – and afterwards, we will have a wonderful dinner here on the terrazza. It is also Christmas, yes? We will drink some wine, eat some delicious Italian food, and have some fun."

Patricia cleared her throat. "I certainly hope so. In the meantime, if you would be so kind as to bring us a bottle of the '67 Conterno Monfortino, we'd like to buy a bottle for the table."

"And perhaps a few packets of crisps as well?" Molly's father added hopefully, as Patricia glared at Paddy as if he was something she'd scraped off the bottom of her shoe.

Fabrizio stood back and bowed his head. "But of course, *signores*. Would anyone like anything else? Caffe? Limoncello?"

"Could we get a pot of tea as well?" Helen inquired. "I could really go for a good strong cup right now."

"Ah," Fabrizio frowned, "I am afraid the hotel will likely not have any tea to speak of. Perhaps a caffe – erm, espresso?"

"Coffee?" Paddy gaped incredulously. "At this hour? Are you mad? We'd be up all night."

Fabrizio eyed Molly's mother. "Perhaps that is a good thing, yes?" he joked.

Caroline snorted and Molly blushed, but Paddy was not amused. "Now, see here lad ..." he insisted, evidently offended.

Fabrizio looked abashed. "I am sorry, signore," he said with a feint towards apologising, "it is only that I am, how you say, hot-blooded and your wife, she is so beautiful. I joke."

"Well, it's not amusing, nor is it appreciated," Paddy replied curtly.

Fabrizio again flashed an apologetic look towards Helen, then he turned to Caroline and winked before walking off to get the drinks.

. . .

"Well ..." said Caroline after Fabrizio was out of earshot, "He's a saucy one, isn't he?"

"Very much so," Helen agreed, sipping from a glass of still water on the table. "He just seems so... forward." She sighed and blushed a little. "Though I have to say, it's been a while since a strange man looked at me like that."

"Mum!" Molly was aghast. "Anyway," she said wickedly, "I think he's much more interested in Caroline."

Caught off-guard, Caroline began stammering. "Wha – I – I wasn't – I – that is—" She was completely flustered, and she fought down a fierce burning in her cheeks. "I don't think so," she said finally, attempting to salvage what was left of her pride.

"Methinks the lady doth protest too much," Ben teased.

"Oh come *on*," Caroline protested. "Sure, he's ... erm, good-looking... but you know how these Mediterranean men are…"

"*I* don't," Molly said with a grin. "Enlighten us, Caroline since you seem to know it all."

"I've heard the same stories you have," she sighed, looking around the table for support but not getting any. "Oh stop it, you know exactly what I'm talking about. There are stories – legends, really – about Italian men and their dashing good looks and well-cut jaw lines and *gorgeous* accents and – *ahem*—" She noticed she was getting a bit carried away and cleared her throat. "*Anyway*, they're always on the prowl, looking for a foreign girl to make their… conquest."

"Because they're Romans, and they conquer things?" Helen volunteered, with a glint in her eye. "Much like your dad over here."

"Mum!" Molly blurted, horrified afresh at her mother's brazenness, while Caroline and Ben laughed uncontrollably.

Patricia scowled. "My word," she said, disapproval dripping from her voice. "Is this *really* conversation for polite company?"

"Quite so," James agreed as Fabrizio returned with the bottle of wine. He stood up. "I think it's time we turned in for the evening, Patricia," he continued. "We've had… a very long day."

"Oh, come on, Father," Ben pleaded, "don't be that way."

"Was it something I said?" Fabrizio asked, coming back with the wine. When no one responded, or even met his eyes, he understood the implication. "Well, I will not keep bothering you. I shall see you all tomorrow then. *Buona notte.*"

He left again, leaving an air of despondent silence to settle on the rest of the group.

"You know something?" Caroline said, cutting through the rampant awkwardness. "I think I should turn in, too. We have a long day ahead of us tomorrow, and I think I've had enough wine for one night. Would you mind, Mol?"

Molly shrugged. "You're right," she said. She yawned as she got up, only now realising that, despite the abrupt way the Pembreys had exited, there might have been some truth to what they'd said, too.

And she was exhausted, and so disappointed that their Italian trip had started so badly.

Ben's parents were annoyed, her own parents out of their comfort zone, and what with the disinterested wedding planner, missing dress and best man still absent, it seemed nothing had gone right for them so far.

"Night all," she sighed, giving her parents a kiss on the cheek. "Hopefully tomorrow will be a better day."

CHAPTER 8

Ben sat back in his chair, equally deflated.
Here they were, in Molly's favourite city in the world, during her favourite time of the year to get married– and she seemed miserable.

Helen put a hand on his knee, breaking his reverie. "Don't worry about her, love," she said warmly. "She's just nervous about … well, all of it I suppose."

Ben nodded. "Yeah, I know." He smiled at his future mother-in-law and stood to leave. "I'd better turn in, too. I've got a few things I need to take care of before bedtime. Hope you understand." He shook hands with Paddy and kissed Helen on the cheek. "You two have a good night."

Once Ben was gone, Paddy turned to his wife. "So… what do you make of the Pembreys?"

Helen rolled her eyes. "*He* doesn't say much," she began, "which I suppose is a good thing. Whereas *her* …"

Paddy nodded. "I know what you mean," he agreed. "She comes off as a bit … stuck-up, doesn't she?"

"Stuck-up, pretentious, condescending… So unlike Molly. Or Ben, for that matter." She sipped her wine and sat back, gazing out at the glorious Roman skyline. "Paddy, honestly," she said sadly, "what on God's green earth are we doing here?"

"Supporting Molly," he answered. "She is young, and she's stupid, but she is wholly in love with that boy. And this city for whatever reason." He looked at the plate of *calamari* again, eyeing the tentacles suspiciously, as if they might begin to twitch and move at any second, "Despite that, we owe it to our daughter to give our love and support."

Just then, his phone buzzed, and he pulled it out to take a look.

"Well yes, of course," Helen pressed on, "but a Christmas wedding in Rome? A tiny church? These little—" she picked up a piece of *calamari*, "—*things*, with their tentacles and round heads? Bit of a disaster really …"

"What's that?" Paddy hadn't heard a thing his wife had just said. An email he had just received said that something had gone wrong with a delivery back home. His eyes narrowed towards the phone again as he began typing furiously. "Sorry love, I really have to check in with the office."

"Paddy," Helen chided, "you're in Rome. For your daughter's wedding. For God's sake, ditch the phone for the next forty eight hours at least."

"It'll just be a minute," he insisted. "I promise. I'll be right back." He stood and walked off to talk on the phone.

Helen sat in silence, gazing out over the city skyline.

She sipped her wine quietly for a few minutes, thinking. Paddy had always worked hard, but lately he'd become obsessive. Her husband simply was a workaholic. She'd held out hopes that he could put the phone away while they were here, but the indication already was that he wouldn't.

She waited nearly half an hour like that, watching the city lights from her perch on the terrazza.

When Paddy didn't return, she finished the rest of her glass and gave up, sighing deeply.

Once again, the work that was supposed to be easier now that he wasn't making the deliveries ended up being more difficult.

Helen called the lift and returned to her Roman hotel room alone.

CHAPTER 9

❄

The following morning, the sun shone brightly from the small hotel window, waking Helen from her sleep.

Paddy was already downstairs in the lobby sipping the one kind of tea he had managed to get from the kitchen.

She stretched her neck, trying to get the crook out of her neck from the lumpy mattress and quickly got dressed. She could only hope today's adventures in Rome would be nothing like the day before

The rest of the group drank their *caffè e latte* with bread and jam. Paddy could not believe that there was no eggs, rashers or sausages – bacon didn't seem to be in the Italian diet at all.

"What I wouldn't give for some black pudding," he whispered regretfully to his wife as she signed for the bill.

"I'll be hungry in an hour," Helen agreed. "Though I suppose it explains how all these Italians are so slim…"

IN THE LOBBY, the wedding party once again waited for Fabrizio to meet them.

Somewhat unsurprisingly (at least to Caroline), he was nowhere to be seen. She went up to the desk to inquire about their coordinator, but Fabrizio was absent.

Though she wasn't certain the desk clerk had fully understood her, routinely referring to their coordinator as *il capo*, which according to Caroline's iPhone translator app, meant *the boss*.

She chose to keep this from Molly and the others to avoid their stress. Instead, she asked the receptionist for some tour brochures, and arranged for a taxi to be called.

When she finally rejoined the others, she was completely armed with maps and tickets still warm from the hotel's printer.

"Okay," she said as she returned. "Turns out, Fabrizio isn't able to make it this morning, but we've got a whole itinerary here, so don't worry."

Molly opened her mouth to protest, but Caroline kept talking. "So first up, we're going to go check out the Forum of Augustus, followed by the Colosseum. After that, I suggest we get ourselves some lunch near the Piazza di Spagna, and maybe do some shopping, because why not? We're in Rome, so let's do this right. And if we're finished in time, we can go and see Santa Maria, where you two lovebirds—" she motioned towards Ben and Molly with a wide, gaping smile, "—are getting married."

The cars pulled up moments later, not giving anyone a chance to disagree with her last minute plans.

However, Ben held back a little and when they were alone, he asked Caroline intensely, "Where exactly is Fabrizio? I thought he was supposed to meet us here."

She shrugged. "Apparently, the guy is about as reliable as our reservations were," she said. "So I improvised."

"You did all this on the fly this morning?" Ben looked impressed. "That's ... incredible. Thank you."

Caroline nodded. "That's what bridesmaids are for. But listen: don't tell Molly about this, okay? She's stressed enough as it is. And with your parents and hers... well, I think you can agree that we have to make this as easy on her as possible."

CHAPTER 10

❄

Incredibly, the weather was sweltering, and not at all the festive picture postcard Molly had been hoping for.

The unseasonable December warmth meant that just in walking around the Forum of Augustus, she found herself sweating profusely, even though all she was wearing were jeans and a t-shirt.

She took a look around, perched on the steps just outside the Temple of Mars Ultor, trying to see it for the first time through her parents' eyes.

She should have felt exhilarated – but instead, she seemed oddly let down. All around were tacky shops selling postcards, shot glasses, t-shirts, official Forum of Augustus chocolates – everyone looking to make a few euros off the tourists who passed through the gates each and every day.

Whatever the Forum might once have been, whatever its relationship to what Rome once was in the days of Caesar Augustus, it just wasn't authentic anymore.

An hour and a half later, as they walked around the Colosseum, she felt little better. Here was *the* place from her posters and textbooks and Roman histories, a building of Italian antiquity that had haunted her dreams since she was a child…

"What do you think Dad?" she asked Paddy who was shuffling along behind her, looking hot and bothered in his red woollen jumper and heavy jeans.

"It's nice, but I thought it would be bigger. I suppose it's kind of a skeleton of the football stadiums back home?'" he said, decidedly unimpressed.

Ben noticed her dejected demeanour and came up behind her, wrapping his arms around her waist.

"Hey," he said, kissing her on the cheek. "Having fun?"

"Actually, no," she replied sullenly. "You know, I've adored this city since I was a little girl, and I loved it when I first came here back in college too, but whatever I'm seeing doesn't seem to at all translate to my parents. I so want them to understand why we chose this wonderful city for our wedding. "

"Yes, but what can you do only show them around?" he asked. "Maybe organise some gladiator battles? A few lions?" His eyes twinkled.

"I don't know," she replied glumly. "Maybe they have a point too. To a lot of people, this seems like just another Italian tourist site, something to be catalogued on Instagram photos and Facebook check-ins." She sighed. "Or maybe I'm just stressed or overtired or something."

Ben released his arms and took her hand in his. "Listen, Mol," he said in a low, voice. "It's not about where we are but where we're going. You and me, we're getting married in a couple of days. And I don't care if we're in Dublin or Rome, New York or New Delhi – all I want is you as my wife. This will be great because of you. And because of us. What matters isn't this," he explained, pointing to the ancient ruins surrounding them. "What matters is how we feel about each other now, and when you walk down that aisle on Christmas Eve."

Molly stood on her tiptoes and kissed Ben on the lips. "You know," she said, smiling, "you're very sweet sometimes."

"I do what I can, Mrs. Pembrey," he replied, kissing her again.

She laughed. "I'm not Mrs yet, *Lord* Pembrey."

"Ugh, don't remind me of the title. My mother does enough of that for both of us."

CHAPTER 11

❄

*A*fter leaving the Colosseum, the wedding party headed towards Piazza di Spagna.

Molly took their driver's suggestion for a classy, tasteful *ristorante* for lunch, after which they planned to break off and walk around the stores in the area – Gucci, Armani, Prada, and all the other high-end Italian designers with storefronts nearby.

Sitting next to Paddy on the way was a chore for Helen. Once again, her husband spent the whole time on his phone, spitting directions at his assistant, tapping out emails and seeming extremely stressed over what sounded like minor issues.

Bad weather in Dublin had caused a delay on a major shipment, and never once did Paddy look up from the screen, so engrossed was he in trying to fix the unfixable from afar.

A few times, Helen tried to point out some of the sights ("Look, the Opera House. "We *must* remember to come back and walk through this park while we're here"), but to no avail; Paddy was in his own little world, consumed by work as usual.

At the restaurant, Patricia and James insisted on paying, and proceeded to order the most extravagant things on the menu in highly affected (and to Molly's ear - poorly worded) Italian.

Soon, buttered quail arrived on their table, followed by spaghetti with anchovies and squid as their *primi*. The younger ones gamely kept up with the Pembreys, but Paddy and Helen found themselves once again at a loss.

"How are we supposed to eat this stuff?" Paddy whispered.

They tried to munch on what they could, but he felt a cold shudder go down his spine each time his nose even caught wind of an anchovy.

As if that weren't enough, the *secondi* course came out blazing and steaming with a smell that Helen found stomach-churning. "What on earth is that?" she asked Patricia.

"Beef cheeks," Ben's mother said reverently. "They're quite the delicacy - you'll love them."

"Actually," Helen said, "I'm not feeling very well just now…"

"Oh Mum," Molly said, "do you want us to call you a taxi or—"

"No, no," she said, "I think a bit of fresh air might do me good. Paddy, can you…?"

"Of course love," he said. They exited together, a look of disapproved consternation overtaking Patricia's face.

CHAPTER 12

❄

Outside the restaurant, Paddy was famished. "This is all mad stuff, isn't it?" he said glumly as they walked down the cobblestone street. "I'm starving."

"I don't understand why Ben's parents can't just eat normal things," Helen added. "Who in their right mind would eat a cow's cheek when you could have steak or roast?"

"The same people who order for the whole table without asking, I'd say," Paddy joked and the two of them laughed together.

They stopped at a nearby cafe and picked up a couple of cold-cut sandwiches. Without even a passing familiarity with Italian, ordering was difficult, but they were able to point at the meats that they wanted, and it did the trick.

Helen guided Paddy back towards the park she had seen on their way over in the taxi, and Paddy picked up two chocolate gelatos from a shop just outside the entrance.

She felt her heart melt along with the gelato as she walked along on Paddy's arm. It was almost like she was a teenager again, meeting him on a first date.

The park – which turned out to be the famed Pincian Hill, or *Pincio* – could not have been better for a romantic stroll. A beautiful lake surrounded by trees strung with fairy lights, sparkled in the late afternoon sunlight.

Latin columns, street lamps and statues lined the winding paths, where children giggled and played while their doting parents dashed off after them, ensuring they were never completely out of sight.

Helen sighed, taking it all in. It was perfect – exactly the kind of authentic Italian experience Molly was always taking about.

But it didn't last.

Shortly before they were supposed to rejoin the rest of the wedding party, Paddy got yet another phone call from Dublin.

"Paddy," she pleaded, "can't you just ignore it? Felicity and the others can handle it. Isn't that why you employ them in the first place?"

"I'm not just a worker anymore, love," he replied. "I'm the *manager*. If something fails, it's not just a problem for me – every one of our employees could be at risk. This is our busiest time of the year too. I have to take this. Sorry." He walked off a few paces ahead of her.

Helen sighed sadly and continued walking, watching the late winter sun cast magnificent light over the Eternal City in these glorious surrounds, all by herself.

CHAPTER 13

❄

When that evening, the group returned to the Hotel Marliconi, they were greeted by a familiar form with ruffled hair and a winning smile.

Fabrizio was standing by reception and grinning at them.

Caroline was not amused. "Stay here," she told the rest of them. She marched over to the Italian, her jaw set and determined. "Where in God's name have *you* been all day?" she demanded.

"Ah, Signorina Caroline," he said, letting the word roll round on his tongue, "how has your day been so far?"

"How – has – our – day – been?"

"Yes, that is what I asked," he replied pleasantly.

"*I* planned the whole day, Fabrizio," she exploded, jabbing a finger towards his chest. "I did it to keep the bride that *you're* supposed to be working for, sane. I arranged *every*thing. And you helped with *nothing*. I have been improvising all day, because *you* - Mr Wedding Planner can't do your job."

"Ah, signorina," he soothed laconically, "you really must relax. I am sorry you thought I would be here today. I did not mean for you to have such difficulty."

"That's the point, you absolute *arse*," she continued yelling. "Molly and Ben are *paying* for a service, and you're not providing it. I'd fire you right here and now if it was up to me, but I don't have any say in the matter."

"Signorina – Caroline – please, allow me to make it up to you." Fabrizio put his hand around her shoulder. "If you'll go up to the terraza…"

"We've already *done* that. I'm not waiting up there again all night expecting to hear plans, only for you to sit at the bar flirting."

"Please. Come with me. And bring the others, too. I will go now – meet me up there as soon as you can, yes?"

Caroline sighed angrily. "I swear to God, Fabrizio, if this turns into another one of your 'let's-meet-ups' where we wait for an hour for you to show your face…"

"I promise you, it will not," he said solemnly. Then he bowed and headed upstairs without another word.

Caroline gathered the others and headed to the lift.

On the way up, she was stuck with the endless prattle of Patricia Pembrey, who was having a very one-sided conversation with Helen O'Brien.

"Yes, the Dolce & Gabbana store was fine, but Prada was incredibly disappointing. 'So many shoes, so little time,' I thought, but really, it was about fifty variations on the same shoe. And the handbags? Pssh. Nothing worth mentioning. Now, of *course* I walked out with a new pair," she slapped a shopping bag, "but I wasn't particularly impressed, at any rate. Now Gucci, on the other hand, was something special. I simply *had* to pick up a few scarfs, and then a shirt to go with them and before I knew it, I was so weighed down with clothes that I could hardly move! It was—"

The ding of the lift cut Patricia off, much to the others' relief.

They exited and were immediately shocked: there, in front of them was a table set up with seven places, along with twinkling wine glasses, and that perfect late evening view of St. Peter's Basilica below.

Candles on the table and fairy lights strung overhead completed the scene of romantic Italian serenity.

"Did you…?" Ben asked Caroline, pointing at the table.

She shook her head. "No, I – I had no idea," she said in wonder, glancing over at a beaming Fabrizio, who held out a chair for Molly.

"Come, come," he said. "Pembreys, O'Briens, and the beautiful Signorina Caroline, come! Sit! Eat!"

He pointed at the salad set out in little bowls on the table. "Here we have salad with lettuce, onion, green pepper, tomatoes, and crumbled gorgonzola cheese. We will pair this with a sweet vermouth *aperitivo*. Please, enjoy."

Caroline couldn't believe it. She had been raging at Fabrizio all day long, but here, he had outdone himself. This was beautiful, and she could tell by Molly's face that it was a lot more like her Italian dream.

When she saw him head back to the kitchen, she excused herself and followed him. "Fabrizio," she called when she was far enough away that the others couldn't hear her.

He turned and smiled. "Ah, Signorina Caroline. Is there something not to your liking?"

She shook her head. "No, I have to say… I did not expect this at all. The lights, the food, the wine, the view… It's fantastic. Molly and Ben are thrilled. But I have to know… when I was yelling at you before, downstairs, why didn't you tell me you had this planned?"

His smile grew wider. "Because then, I wouldn't have the opportunity to speak with you now," he said, laying the charm on even more thickly.

Caroline blushed slightly. "Well, I think I owe you an apology. This is truly wonderful. You've done a very good job."

He nodded. "Now, if you will excuse me, signorina, I must get back to the kitchen to bring out the *primera*."

"Can I ask what we're having?" she asked.

"And what kind of surprise would that be?" he winked.

She watched him walk away, thinking to herself, *Okay, so maybe he's not* completely *cheesy.*

And even if he is, maybe that's not so bad…

CHAPTER 14

❄

True to his word, Fabrizio's presentation was superb.

The *primera* of pasticcio al forno, "a traditional Christmas pasta bake," according to their host, delighted the guests. Layers of rigatoni, ground lamb, tomato sauce, and generous helpings of cheese were a welcome way to replenish after a day of sight-seeing.

The tender slices of veal and delicious roasted potatoes that comprised the *secondi* were an absolute delight, too. When Helen O'Brien raised a faint objection to eating veal, Fabrizio noted that, "little animals are the sacrificial victims of the Italian lust for meat at Christmas. It is… tradition."

One bite later, Helen's moral qualms melted away like the meat in her mouth.

So delicious was everything that no one seemed to notice just how much wine was being consumed.

This was partly Fabrizio's doing: rather than leaving a bottle of wine for the table, he insisted on pairing different wines with each course.

By the time dessert rolled around, everyone had had more than their share of delicious Barberas, Sangioveses and Vermentinos.

It was after Fabrizio brought out a delightful-looking *zuppa inglese* that things started going downhill.

The festive dessert, made of rum, jam, pastry cream, whipped cream and fruit, reminded Paddy of sherry trifle, easily his favourite dessert.

He hadn't been particularly impressed by the wines nor the *limoncello* Fabrizio had foisted upon the table, but this – this was a rare slice of home, and Paddy was simply delighted.

"Nothing beats a good trifle," he said, his mouth watering.

Patricia shot him a look. "Trifle?" she repeated, amusedly. "How... *quaint.*"

"Now, don't get me wrong," Paddy continued between mouthfuls of *zuppe*, "it's nothing compared to my Helen's here. No one does it better. But this isn't half bad at all."

"I can't say I've ever had trifle before," James mused.

Patricia nodded. "Of course you haven't, dear," she said haughtily. "It's a rather ... common dessert, no flair or artistry needed."

Helen's gaze shot up. "Really ..." she said decidedly unimpressed.

"Oh darling," Patricia insisted, "that wasn't meant to be insulting."

"Good," Helen replied flatly. "Because it certainly sounded like that."

Patricia wasn't finished. "I just think," she continued, "it speaks to a certain... *kind.*"

"Mother..." Ben interjected warily.

"No Ben," Patricia continued, holding up a hand to silence him, "I am tired of having to hold my tongue. You are asking me to be something that I simply am not. And I also resent being told that I have to pretend to think this....Italian charade... is all okay when it simply is *not.*"

Ben shook his head apologetically at Molly. "Father," he motioned towards Patricia, "couldn't you..."

James merely looked down as his wife continued on. "Ben," she said, softening as she gazed concernedly at her son, "this can't truly be what you want - a hush-hush ceremony in a tiny church in a foreign country? You are entitled to so much *more*. You are the son of a lord, and heir to an important title. One day, you will be the 16th Earl of Daventry. Our family has certain *standards* to uphold. And however pleasant this young lady," she motioned towards Molly, "might be, I simply do not believe she understands what inheriting such a title might mean.

Of course, I cannot blame her for that. Manners are taught as much as they are learned."

"Now, you hold on!" Helen exploded, shocking everyone at the table as she stood angrily. "I don't know who you think you are to insult my daughter and my family the way you have, Patricia, but this is *truly* beyond the pale. Your so-called English *title* does not bring with it the opportunity to look down your nose at *any*one's manners, at least not with the way you yourself are acting."

Helen's breathing increased in rapidity, and she felt her heart race in her chest. She glanced at her daughter, who looked on the verge of tears, and took a deep breath before continuing in a more relaxed tone.

"For Molly's sake, I am going to assume that you simply have had too much wine tonight, and it has loosened your tongue. I can be far more forgiving of an obnoxious drunk than I can the nasty person you are showing yourself to be this evening. I think we should leave now, before I say something I myself might *truly* regret. Paddy?"

Paddy looked at Molly, then to Ben, and finally stood and joined his wife.

"I – good evening," he said simply as Helen stormed off.

Molly stared at Patricia, who seemed unconcerned by their exit.

"Molly, dear," she said with a put-on smile, "I hope you know this had nothing to do with you…"

The bride-to-be looked shocked. She looked at Patricia quizzically. "Nothing… to do… with me?" she repeated.

"Of course not," Patricia shook her head. "We simply want the best for our son that's all."

Molly's jaw hit the floor. "So… what you're saying is… I'm *not* the best for Ben." She looked at her fiance, who said nothing. "How… *dare* you…!"

"See. Like mother, like daughter," Patricia muttered under her breath.

"And *you*," she exploded, turning on Ben. "That you could just *sit* there while this… *woman* insults me, insults my mother and my father while all we're here in Rome - for our wedding?"

"I – I don't—"

Molly narrowed her eyes. "You know what, Ben?" she snapped. "You can keep your titles, and your Lordship and your stuck-up parents. I can't be with someone who cares so much about a title and so little for his wife-to-be."

With that, she spun on her heel and walked off.

Caroline jumped up to chase after her – but before doing so, she turned to the Pembreys. "You're just… I can't even …" she muttered before going after her friend.

Ben sat at the table in stunned silence. His mother sipped on her limoncello, a satisfied look on her face, while his father continued to stare off into the distance. "See Ben, this isn't—"

"Mother," he said quietly, "can you *please* give it a rest for once?"

"I'm only saying…"

"Not. Now."

"All right, all right," Patricia responded. "But at some point, you're going to have to face facts, Ben: that girl is simply all wrong for us. And her family is —"

"*Mother,*" Ben interjected hotly. "That is *enough*. You have been rude, pretentious, and condescending, particularly towards the O'Briens. And now, you've ruined the one thing that has made me happier than anything ever has. I want to *marry* Molly. I'm *going* to marry Molly - here in Rome on Christmas Eve. And there is simply nothing you can say or do that's going to stop me." He stood up and angrily tossed his napkin on the table. "Molly however, might well be a different story. "

CHAPTER 15

❄

*T*ears streamed down Molly's face as she wound her way through the cobblestone streets and back alleys of the beloved city of her dreams.

The sun had set on Rome, and everywhere she looked, shops were closing up, their darkened windows displaying clothes of red and green and large, intricately decorated signs proclaiming, BUON NATALE.

It was too much to take. What had she been thinking, bringing her and Ben's families here?

Since she was a little girl, all she'd ever dreamed about was a romantic Christmas wedding in Rome.

She knew the place so well she felt almost like an honorary Roman. She knew the sites by heart, knew the history of the city and the empire that bore its name, the names of the great men and women who had made this the single most legendary Italian city in the world.

And one of the most important things she'd planned for her wedding day was bringing the guests to the Trevi Fountain after the ceremony, to carry out the famed tradition of throwing coins in the fountain.

But would any of her guests truly want to return to Rome? And more to the point, after this trip, would Molly want to?

She passed by the Pantheon, its columns illuminated by a row of Christmas trees lit up along the piazza in front.

It was beautiful and looked so magically festive in such glorious surrounds, but for once, failed to lift her spirits.

She continued walking, eventually crossing the Tiber and coming up on Vatican City.

St. Peter's Basilica glowed in the sun's fading light.

I'm usually so entranced by this, she thought glumly. *What's wrong with me?*

But she knew exactly what was wrong: Ben. Why hadn't he stood up to his parents back there? How could he let his mother say such things about her family – and to her?

She could never have imagined sitting idly by while Paddy or Helen said similar things about Ben.

How can we recover from this? she wondered as she found herself walking past the Castel Sant'Angelo.

She knew the answer to this, too: maybe they couldn't. This was *it*.

She was in her city of her dreams, at her favourite time of the year…supposedly to marry the man of her dreams, and now everything was ruined.

All because of stuck-up Patricia Pembrey and her penchant for wine and haughtiness.

Molly saw a tram coming and decided to escape for a while.

She bought a ticket and jumped randomly on the departing #19 and took a seat in the back.

She gazed longingly out the window, watching her beloved Eternal City passing by, wishing for something – anything – to give her that familiar burst of inspiration.

It wasn't forthcoming. Everywhere she seemed to look now, she saw commercialism, tourist traps, and big-city trappings.

There was no magic here anymore, she decided sadly; it was like just any another city.

The accents might be different, the language more melodic-sounding, and the skin tones a bit darker, but a city was still a city. Her parents were right; she should have just got married back home.

Married. She cringed. Was she still getting married? She loved Ben, certainly – but she simply couldn't handle his mother being the way she was. And if he wouldn't stand up to Patricia, stand up *for* his new wife, his new family, this simply was not to be.

She shook her head, and got off the tram to unfamiliar surroundings. The sign designated this area Piazza Buenos Aires, but she was pretty sure she'd never been here before.

She wasn't sure how long she'd been travelling, nor exactly where she was either. She shrugged and trudged on dejectedly.

That was when she saw it.

It wasn't quite a clock tower – there was no clock on it – but it nonetheless rang out, a bell tower dressed up in its festive finest, beautiful brown Tuscan architecture housing tresses that seemed to stretch up into the sky.

Molly walked towards the structure, entranced.

Suddenly, as the tower rose in front of her, she came upon an archway, lit up with fairy lights, a face in the centre almost gazing down upon her, beckoning her to enter. Where was this?

Balconies like something out of *Romeo and Juliet* adorned buildings that almost looked like miniature castles. Cars, apartments, trees, and green grassy areas were all smashed up against each other in a thoroughly confusing fashion.

The entire area was decorated with white fairy lights, while multi-coloured bulbs hung from the tent coverings of pop-up cafes along the street.

She heard a rhythmic beating from somewhere nearby: a drum circle, replete with locals dancing in time had apparently sprung up in a nearby park.

The winter wind blew chilly now, but no one seemed to care.

Molly turned around in full circle, in awe of what she had just stumbled upon. She closed her eyes and breathed in deeply, taking it all in. *This* was the magic of Rome she knew.

It wasn't in the historical sites or the typical trappings of the ancient city she'd shown her parents – it was *here*, in *this* place, wherever it was, with these people, obviously locals, dancing and singing and being festive. The lifeblood.

She grinned as she found herself swaying to the beat, smiles of joy now replacing tears of heartbreak and frustration.

This was *her* Rome.

CHAPTER 16

"Well, where *is* she?" Ben demanded, breathing heavily and sounding more than a little panicked, as he paced his hotel room.

"I've tried phoning her, asked around the hotel – I even asked that dopey desk clerk if she had seen her. Nothing. No one knows where Molly went."

Caroline poured a glass of water and handed it to him. "Calm down," she said soothingly. "I'm sure she'll turn up. She was really annoyed by your mum. She probably just needs to blow off some steam. This is the city of her dreams, isn't it?"

When he looked even glummer at this, Caroline put a hand on his shoulder.

"Ben," she continued, "Molly's a big girl. She can take care of herself. Look, maybe we should talk about something else, help get your mind off things."

"Like what?" he asked.

"Like, what in God's name is wrong with your parents?"

Ben shook his head disappointedly. "I don't even know where to begin. My mother can be—"

"A heinous she-witch?" Caroline offered.

"—difficult. Hell, she's difficult in the *best* of times, let alone when she's had a few…"

"But we're here for your *wedding*." Caroline pressed. "What does she have against Helen and Paddy? And what was all that rubbish about dessert - and that whole trifle thing? I love trifle myself."

Ben sighed. "It's just …" he ventured, "my mother has always had issues with 'new' money."

Caroline cocked her head. "What do you mean, 'new' money?"

"Like, money that hasn't been inherited. Self-made wealth."

"Well, Paddy's hardly *wealthy*. I mean, he and Helen are reasonably well-off, I suppose, but nothing like—"

"Me?" Ben offered.

"Well, I wasn't going to say it, but your father *is* a member of the House of Lords…"

"*He* may be, but *I* don't want to be."

Caroline threw up her arms, exasperated with Ben's naivety. "Oh come, *on*, Ben!" she exclaimed. "You of all people *know* that's not how this works. When your dad passes away, that's it: *you* become the Earl of Coventry—"

"Daventry."

"—whatever. The point is, that English nobility stuff means nothing to the likes of us. We don't do gentry in Ireland as you know. And then for your mum to go around pretending like she's… I don't know, the Queen of England or whatever, is a bit much."

"I get that," Ben nodded. "But what's that got to do with *me*? Why would Molly be mad at *me* for how my parents act? She knows I don't agree with their values *or* their attitudes."

"Because, Ben, you didn't stand up for Molly or her parents back there! You're like a turtle: when confronted, you went right back into your shell. And if I know Molly, all she wanted was to hear you put your parents in their place."

"But I did," Ben insisted. "After you all left, I lit into them. Told them they'd better get used to the idea of Molly being around, because I'm *going* to marry her."

"Great," Caroline told him, "but does *she* know that?"

"She knows me," he replied. "She should know that about me."

"Molly's not a psychic, Ben," Caroline told him. "All she saw was you kowtowing to your mother's nastiness - and with only a day to go till your wedding. I'd imagine *that*, more than anything, is what set her off."

Ben slumped down in a chair. "I just don't know what to do Caroline," he said sadly. "If the wedding is called off —"

"That," she insisted, "won't happen." She grabbed her coat and headed towards the door. "Look," she told him, "I'll head out and see if I can find her, talk her round. You just stay there, and keep in touch."

Ben nodded glumly, and Caroline went back out to the hallway … where she collided straight with none other than Fabrizio.

CHAPTER 17

"Signorina Caroline," he said happily, "I am so happy to find you. Everyone left so quickly…"

She stared at him impatiently, waiting for him to explain what he was doing outside her room.

It was then that she noticed the clothing bag hung over his arm. "I bring good news: your dress has arrived. The wedding is saved!"

Caroline chuckled ironically as Fabrizio handed the bag to her. "Well," she said, "thanks anyway, but we're no longer sure at this point if there's actually going to *be* a wedding."

"What do you mean?" he asked, looking shocked.

She sighed. "Well," she explained, "everybody left because there was a big row over dinner between Ben's parents and Molly's, and it ended with Molly walking out on Ben."

"Oh no," he replied concernedly. "So where is she now?"

"That's the thing," Caroline said. "I'm heading out now to try and find her. She took off, and no one seems to know where she is."

"And you are going to, what, walk around *Roma* after dark calling out her name until you find her?"

Caroline shrugged. "She can't have gone far," she replied.

Fabrizio shook his head. "Of course she can. There are trains, buses, trams, taxis – she could be halfway to *Napoli* by now."

Caroline's face fell. "Oh God, Fabrizio," she said, panic rising in her voice, "you don't think she would do that, do you?"

"I do not know," he answered. "She is your friend, after all. You know her best."

Caroline nodded. "Right, right," she said. "Okay, let's see... where would she go?"

"Perhaps something related to the wedding?" Fabrizio ventured. "Maybe the church or to the *Fontana di Trevi* to think."

"At this point, I think the wedding is the last thing she wants to think about. You didn't see her, Fabrizio. She was very upset. She ran off before I even had the chance to to talk her."

Fabrizio nodded. "Okay, I have an idea. Go, leave your dress in your room, and meet me downstairs in a few minutes. We will drive in my car to a few places I know. Perhaps we will be lucky."

Caroline stared at him again – only this time, it was in admiration. "Fabrizio, that's very kind of you... I'm..."

"I know," he said, flashing her his increasingly charming smile. "I will see you downstairs."

CHAPTER 18

❄

A few minutes later, she stood outside the hotel, craning her neck to see where Fabrizio might be. Several cars passed by, but there was no indication any of them was being driven by the handsome Italian.

Her attention was struck moments later by a gorgeous yellow Lamborghini, sleek and stylish and very cool.

Boy, she thought to herself, *nice to have the money to afford one of those babies*.

The Lamborghini turned into the hotel turnabout, and the horn honked towards her. She squinted to see the driver.

It was Fabrizio. "Of *course*," she murmured.

He opened the door for her – opening it not out but *up*, which made her stand back.

"Come," he motioned.

The interior of the car was even more luxurious than she'd imagined. Gorgeous cream and black leather seats, a smooth, crisp dash, top-of-the-line stereo system... it was almost too much, and she said so.

"What," she teased, "you couldn't do well enough with a *moderately* expensive car? You have to go with the one that costs as much as a house?"

He smiled. "My job," he explained, "causes me to have to drive quite a bit. I like… style when I do so."

"And you can afford this?"

"I can afford many things."

"How is that possible?" She herself had worked at a hotel before. Even at a luxury one like the Hotel Marliconi.

"The hotel at which you are staying," he said matter-of-factly, "is my main source of income."

"There's no way you can afford a Lamborghini on an event specialist's salary."

He looked over at her quizzically. "*Signora*," he said, "I am many things, but I am no event specialist."

"What are you talking about?" she asked, frowning. "Molly has been working with you for months now."

Fabrizio shook his head. "No," he said, "Molly was working with our event specialist, yes, but he is no longer employed with us. I fired him last week."

"What do you mean, *you* fired him? Are you his manager or something?"

"You mean… the Pembreys did not tell you?"

"Ben's parents? What did they not tell me, exactly?"

"The Hotel Marliconi," he said. "It is my hotel."

Caroline felt a shock ripple through her entire body. "Wait – *your* hotel? So that would make you…"

He looked at her and once again flashed his smile. "Fabrizio Marliconi. At your service."

CHAPTER 19

"Wait, wait, wait," Caroline stammered as the car sped off. "This doesn't make any sense. Why would the owner of a luxury hotel be helping out a tiny wedding party like ours?"

"Lady Pembrey," he responded, "is an old family friend. Her mother and mine went to the same university in England. Cambridge. She asked me to step in to help with the wedding."

Caroline sat there in stunned silence. There was no way – there was simply no *way* that that horrible, vile, bigoted woman had stepped in and saved the day.

After all the complaining, the negativity and those awful things she'd said to the O'Briens... could Patricia really not be as terrible as everyone had thought?

A little while later, her thoughts were interrupted by the car jerking to a sudden stop.

"There," Fabrizio called out, pointing to a girl dancing in the middle of a nearby side street.

It was Molly.

Caroline jumped out of the car and ran straight over to her best friend. "Molly Rose O'Brien," she called out. "What on earth do you think you're doing?"

Molly just smiled, looking almost giddy.

"Caroline!" she cooed. "Oh, I'm so glad you're here. How did you – " She stopped when she saw Fabrizio standing by his car.

"Long story," Caroline said curtly. "Where have you been? We had no idea where you'd gone. Ben's been worried sick about you – literally."

Molly squeezed Caroline's hand in hers as they walked back towards Fabrizio's car. "I went exploring," she explained. "I hopped on a tram, got off completely randomly, and I kind of just stumbled upon this place. I have no idea where we are, but – Caroline, isn't it wonderful? *This* is what Rome is all about - this was the city I wanted you to see."

Molly was beaming with an enthusiasm Caroline hadn't seen since their arrival.

She took a look around her for the first time. She had to admit, this area, wherever they were, had a certain authentic charm to it, possessing more of a true Italian feel to it than other more heavily commercialised areas of the city.

"Fabrizio," she asked when they returned to the car, "where exactly are we?"

"Il Quartiere Coppedè," he said. "The Coppedè district. It is well-known for being more... erm... I am not sure of the English word... *svariato*... than any other district in Roma."

"It's wonderful," Molly said dreamily. "But now I think maybe it's time for me to get back."

"To your groom I hope?" Fabrizio inquired.

Molly nodded. "Yes, I suppose so." She turned to Caroline. "Is there any way I can have Ben's parents banned from the ceremony?"

Caroline squeezed her friend's hand again. "I don't think so love," she smiled. "But, listen... just leave everything to me. They'll be on their best behaviour, I promise."

"Fabrizio held open the car door. "After you, ladies," he said.

When they reached the hotel, Molly gave Caroline another hug. "Listen," she said, "I'm going to talk to Ben. I think we have some things to work out."

"You've only got a few hours left 'til your wedding, remember?"

Caroline said. "Do talk to him. Explain it all, but don't forget that you love him – and he loves you."

Molly waved to Fabrizio as she walked away.

"Thanks for the lift," she called.

"My pleasure," he smiled, waving back.

ONCE MOLLY WAS GONE, Caroline went over to the Italian and kissed him on the cheek.

"You might just have saved the day, Fabrizio," she whispered. "Thank you for your help."

She turned to walk away, but he grabbed her arm and pulled her back towards him.

"*Signorina*," he said, his dark eyes boring intensely into hers. "Caroline. I do these things for you because I find you fascinating. I do not normally meet women like you," he continued.

Caroline trembled slightly despite herself. "Women like me?" she scoffed shakily. "You hardly know me."

"Few women are willing to speak their minds the way you do," he told her. "You are fearless and brave. You will tell people what you think whether they want to hear it or not. I... admire that."

With that, he took her face in his large, olive-skinned hands, and brushed her hair off her face.

A moment passed between them that felt to Caroline like an eternity.

"I'm telling you, Fabrizio," she said quickly, "I'm not—"

She didn't get the opportunity to finish, because she suddenly found his face against hers, her lips locked with his.

It was the kind of kiss that made a person weak in the knees, long and serious, blissful and playful – and when it was over, left an impression.

One hell of an impression.

Caroline's eyes were still closed when he broke away. "Fabrizio—" she murmured, momentarily awestruck.

"You see, *signorina*?" he asked.

Caroline opened her eyes, realising what had just happened, and shook her head. "No," she insisted quietly.

"No?"

"No," she repeated. "No, no, *no*. I'm – I'm *so* not doing – this can't – " She began to back away from him.

"Caroline," he pleaded, more intently.

"No, Fabrizio, look, thank you for helping me find Molly, but I – I have to – to go." She walked backwards away from him unsteadily, almost in a daze. "I'm – I'm sorry. I— "

Caroline didn't say another word, but instead, turned her back on him and picked up speed until she was almost running to the lift, her mind racing.

Oh God, she thought, *What in the world have I just done?*

CHAPTER 20

❄

*B*en was watching *Sky News* – Italy's Finance Minister was caught up in some sort of scandalous affair – when a knock came at his door.

He jumped out of bed, knocking over a less-than-sturdy nightstand (and taking down a lamp with it) in the process.

He cursed mildly over his stubbed toe and hobbled over to the door to reveal an absolute shock.

"Mother …" he said, irritably.

Patricia held her expression neutral, but he noted a slight smudge in her usually impeccably applied mascara. She'd been crying.

"Ben darling," she greeted, her voice wavering ever-so-slightly, "may I come in?"

He didn't answer, but left the door open and headed back into the room. Patricia followed, swallowing hard.

"I'd offer you a drink," Ben said coldly, "but I'm pretty certain you've already had quite enough."

She chuckled a little. "I suppose I should've stopped after that first bottle of wine."

"Mother, I don't give a damn how much wine you drank," he scolded her. "What you did – the way you acted – it was—"

"—unforgivable," she finished for him, nodding. "I know, dear. I know. I was only..."

"You were *only* thinking about yourself," he snapped. Patricia stayed silent and looked to the ground. "Is there something you needed?" he asked.

She shook her head. "I just – I want you to under—" she stifled a small heave in her chest before continuing, "—to understand all that comes with being the Earl of Daventry. Because it won't be—"

"Oh for God's sake, mother!" Ben yelled. "I don't care about being the Earl of Daventry, or the rank, or the title, or any of that. I care about *Molly!*"

He ran his fingers through his hair and paced a bit around the room. "Do you know what Caroline is doing now?" he demanded. Patricia shook her head. "She's wandering around the streets of Rome, hoping that maybe, somehow, she'll run into Molly, or Molly will answer her phone. And the reason I'm not out there with her is I'm afraid that seeing *me* will only make things worse. And you know what I have to thank for that? The damned Lord and Lady Pembrey! You, and your stuck-up, closed-minded, pretentious nonsense that makes you think that because you married Father, you're somehow entitled to better treatment than your so-called social inferiors."

At this, Patricia broke. She knew her son was right; he had every right and every reason to be upset with her. But more than anything else, she also knew *she* was right.

"Ben," she said, choking back a sob, "I know the title means nothing to you. But it doesn't mean nothing to everyone. In fact, it means a great deal. It imparts status and power – not for me – I grew up without it, obviously – but for your children. The only time I've ever invoked the title has been to help *you*."

Ben looked her in the eye, his blazing fiercely. "I never *asked* for that, Mother," he said darkly.

"You never *had* to," she insisted. "You are my *son*. Perhaps... perhaps when you have children of your own, you'll understand."

"If I have children," he said, "it's going to be with Molly. I only hope she can forgive me for not standing up to you sooner."

"Oh Ben," Patricia remarked, "I'm not concerned with whether or not you have children with Molly or – or – bloody Princess Beatrice!"

Ben arched an eyebrow. "Wha— why would I ever have children with— what?"

Patricia shook her head. "Never mind. The *point*, my dear, is that you can marry whomever you want – but you must choose carefully, because what you stand to inherit affects not only you but your children and your children's children." She fumbled with her fingers a bit before continuing, obviously searching for the right words to convey her feelings. "Do you remember Digadoo?"

"Digadoo?" Ben chuckled. "Sounds like a really awful kids' TV show."

"Digadoo," Patricia explained, "was your imaginary pony. When you were about three, you were absolutely *obsessed* with ponies, and you said you wanted one. When your father and I told you you'd have to wait 'til you were older, you invented this pony of your own, Digadoo. He was your friend, your confidante – and apparently, he could fly, too."

"Right."

"You and Digadoo were the best of friends for about a year. You'd do *everything* together. You even had me set a place at the dinner table every night for him."

"So whatever happened to him?'" Ben asked.

"Well, after about a year or so, we realised that you were still serious about this pony, so we got you riding lessons at the club."

"I remember *that*," he said. "But I don't remember Digadoo."

"That's because you don't need to, darling," Patricia said. "Digadoo faded into your memory the way imaginary friends are supposed to, and got replaced by reality. And the reality we were able to provide you with was far better than any fantasy you might have had."

"I don't recall the horse being able to fly," Ben said softly.

"No, but do you recall the fun you had?"

He nodded. "But that's hardly the point, Mother," he elaborated. "Money, wealth, power – they're all fine and well, but you can't buy happiness. And I can't remember, but I presume I was very happy with

Digadoo."

Patricia shrugged. "You may have been," she admitted, "but you were three. You would have been happy with a bowl of custard and a few ladyfingers. Children can't appreciate what their parents can offer them. It's for the parents to provide the opportunities. And the Earlship provides more opportunities, opens more doors, than you can possibly imagine."

"That may be, Mother," Ben agreed, "but that doesn't excuse how you spoke to the O'Briens. And it doesn't excuse how you treated Molly. She's a wonderful person, mother. If you'd only get past your own ludicrous biases, you'd see that."

"She might be," Patricia replied. "She could be the loveliest girl who's ever lived. But I just don't know that the... the societal *manners* she and her parents have shown is compatible with giving your children, my grandchildren, the very best of lives."

"God, Mother!" Ben complained. "This isn't a Jane Austen novel. Manners and discipline and polite society? It's all nonsense. To say nothing of the fact that none of that gentry stuff even exists in Ireland. The only thing that's important is how we treat each other. That's what all the sermons at all the masses we attended when I was a boy said. *Do unto others* and all that. It doesn't matter if Molly wanted to get married in a foreign city, or that her parents tell saucy in-jokes. They are good people. They are kind people. And they deserve far better than how you've treated them." Incensed afresh, Ben rose and opened the door. "I think it's best if you leave now."

"Ben," she pleaded, panic overtaking her face, "I wish you would only try to understand. I'm not against Molly or her parents. I simply want what's best for you."

"What's best for me, Mother," he responded flatly, "is to be happy. And the only way that's going to happen is if Molly comes back tonight, safe and sound, and we get married in this city tomorrow. You and Father can come or not come to the ceremony – that's entirely up to you – but if Molly will still have me, we're getting married tomorrow."

Patricia nodded curtly and left the room without saying another word.

BEN CLOSED the door behind her and collapsed against the door. He knew his mother cared – the fact that she'd remembered an imaginary friend he'd forgotten like Digadoo was proof of that – but her haughtiness and closed-mindedness were simply unforgivable.

He was startled to attention rather quickly by a brusque rapping on the door. He stood, straightened his shirt, and began opening the door. Patricia, it appeared, had more to say. "Okay, look," he began, "I need you to hear me loud and clear: what you think at this point is imma— *oh.*"

It wasn't his mother standing in the doorway. Instead, it was a vision from heaven itself, an angel sent to guide him home. It was Molly, and she was grinning lopsidedly at her fiancee.

"Hey there, handsome," she said in her best American drawl. "Wanna get hitched?"

CHAPTER 21

❄

Ben took Molly into his arms and kissed her. "Where on earth have you been?" he asked. "I'm so sorry."

Molly smiled. "I went looking for something," she said. "I needed – I don't know – I needed to remember that Rome was the same city I knew and loved, I needed it to calm and heal me in the way it always did. And I needed to think."

"About my mother?" Ben asked warily. "Look, I need you to know – whatever she thinks, you are the woman I—"

Molly was shaking her head rapidly. "No, no, no," she insisted. "Not about your mum. About *me*." She took a deep breath before continuing. "Ben, I've been unfair to you," she began.

"No, you—"

"Please," she insisted, "let me get this out." She straightened her dress in front of her and continued, her voice barely above a whisper. "I've been very unfair to you and everyone. I wanted this wedding in Italy at Christmas. I pushed ahead with it despite what our families - both our parents wanted. And I tried to force my dream, my perfect vision of Rome on everyone.

And before you say anything, I know we both agreed on this, and that at the time it suited *both* of us. But if I'm being honest, you've given me everything I've wanted, while I haven't really given much back."

"That's not true," Ben argued. "Molly, you've been more than fair. Putting up with Mother – and Father – isn't even the half of it. Everything's seems to have gone wrong since we got here, and—"

"It's all gone wrong *because* of me, trying to make everything perfect. And when I walked out on dinner—"

"—which you had every right to do…"

"Perhaps," Molly admitted. "But it was still poor form. And after all your parents have done …"

A confused look overtook Ben's face. "What are you talking about?" he asked.

"It's okay," she said patiently. "Caroline told me all about what your mum and dad did. About how the wedding planner I hired messed everything up, and how Fabrizio is the owner of the hotel…"

"He's *what?*" Ben gasped.

Molly titled her head curiously. "Wait…" she said, putting two and two together. "You didn't know?"

"Know what?"

"That your mum asked for Fabrizio's help because she's old friends with his mum."

Ben sat down, mystified. "I – I honestly had no idea," he murmured. He looked up at Molly. "Mother was just in here. I read her the riot act because of how she'd acted. I… I had no idea she'd done that." He shook his head, recalling the conversation. "But that still doesn't excuse what she said to you and your folks."

"No, it doesn't," Molly agreed. "But Ben, whatever your mum said while she was drinking, I don't know if that means she actually *believes* it. She just wants the best for you, I suppose."

"*You* are the best for me," he said, standing and taking her in his arms.

"So then, you do still want to marry me?" she asked.

"Only if you still want to marry me," he said, adding, "and marry *into* my family."

Molly half-smiled. "I think I can make do," she mused. "Besides, we'll only have to see them occasionally. Every other Christmas or so."

Ben nodded. "If that, even," he said. "We could always move somewhere they'd never come, like—"

"—Naples?" Molly joked.

Ben laughed and kissed her. "I love you, Signorina O'Brien," he said, his heart filling up.

"And I love you, Lord Pembrey," she teased.

"Don't call me that," he insisted.

"I think I will actually," she said, smiling and holding him close.

CHAPTER 22

Helen stood in her room, staring out the window at the glorious Roman skyline lit up against the darkness.

Behind her, Paddy sat on a chair, his laptop open in front of him and his ear glued to his mobile phone.

It seemed yet another shipment was running late, and rather than trusting that everything would be taken care of, as the others had been, he seemed to think he could will the packages to their destinations in time for Christmas by sheer thought.

"No, Felicity," Paddy said, irritation rising in his voice. "N-no— no — look, just get it done, all right? Now, where are we with the Jefferson Electronics account?" He typed a few notes on his computer, continuing back-and-forth with his assistant over the other end of the phone.

Helen had heard enough. "Paddy," she called soothingly, turning back to him. "We have barely hours until our daughter's wedding. Don't you think you can give the phone a rest? Can't someone else handle it?"

Paddy covered the receiver with his hand. "What?" he asked her, squinting towards her form. "What did you say, love?"

"Nothing," Helen sighed. "Nothing at all." She resumed looking out the window. Why couldn't she get him to put down the phone for more than a few minutes at a time? He hadn't always been this way. Only when DHL had taken over the business did his penchant for working constantly become an issue.

Here they were in one of the most beautiful cities in the word two days before Christmas, their daughter's relationship was in crisis, and all he could think about was computer part deliveries.

Helen stared across at the Vatican and St Peter's Basilica, silently wishing for a miracle.

CHAPTER 23

In the room next door, things were only slightly less frosty. "I simply don't know what more to say to him," Patricia told her husband.

"Perhaps you shouldn't say anything," he counselled her. "Ben's a grown man. He needs to make his own choices, questionable though we may think them."

"But James," she whined insistently, "the O'Briens are... so..."

"Oh, they're all right, Patricia," he scolded her. "Paddy is a decent sort, and Helen is quite charming."

"But they're so... so..."

"Ordinary?"

"Yes!" Patricia exclaimed. "How can Ben settle for that when he can do so much better?"

"Do you even know your son?" James asked her. "He's far more comfortable with them than he ever was with us. He skipped out on Cambridge for Dublin, for God's sake. Let's let him make his own decisions. And I won't have any more of these hostilities. You will go and apologise to Molly and her parents."

"You can't be serious."

"Of course I'm serious," he said sternly. "This wedding is going to happen whether we want it to or not, Patricia, and I would prefer that we make the best of it, wouldn't you?"

Patricia sighed. "You're right, of course," she said resignedly. "All right. Tomorrow, over breakfast... I will... apologise."

"You know why I adore you, my dear?"

"Why's that?"

"Because you have more sense than any woman I've ever known."

"Tell that to your son," Patricia muttered.

"I plan to," James said, grinning and taking her into his arms.

CHAPTER 24

❄

Caroline paced around her room. What had she just done? This was exactly what she'd wanted to avoid – what she'd *tried* to avoid. Now, not only was it obvious Fabrizio was interested, but it turned out he was handsome *and* wealthy.

Good God, she thought to herself, *could I possibly be any more of a cliche?*

She was still pacing when Molly walked in, a smile plastered to her face.

"Caroline," she cooed, "I have to thank you. You've really gone above and beyond. Again." She went over to her friend, oblivious to her distress, and hugged her. She broke the embrace, however, when she noticed her face. "What's wrong?" she asked.

Caroline shook her head. "I can't even begin..." she said exasperatedly. "I'm just... I'm an idiot, that's what."

"You're not," cried Molly. "What are you talking about?"

"Oh," Caroline said, a note of sarcasm in her voice, "you have *no* idea, Mol. I've just been making, you know, fantastic decisions since I got here. Flirt with the suave Italian host? Check. Have a combative but strangely endearing relationship with him? Check. Find out he's loaded? Check. Snog him in the lobby of his hotel? Check. Make a total gobshite of myse—"

"Hang on," Molly cut in, putting her hands up in a *stop* motion. "What's all this about snogging? And are you talking about Fabrizio?"

"It's not like I even *wanted* to," Caroline said manically as if Molly hadn't interjected. "I mean, yeah, I'd thought about it a bit, but he was so – I mean, he was just *there*, but then he'd been so sweet as to help me find you, and that smile – oh, that smile – but *no*. I can't be the stupid tourist on holiday who falls for the first Italian who gives her the glad eye. I mean, he's Roman. He'll flirt with anything that moves, probably charm the pants off them, too…"

"Caroline," Molly said, putting her hands on her friend's shoulders, "Get a grip. Are you trying to tell me something happened between you and my wedding planner?"

Caroline finally snapped out of her fit and looked at her best friend. "Your wedding planner …oh my God, Molly," she said with a half-smile, "you're getting *married* tomorrow…you are still getting married tomorrow, aren't you?"

Molly nodded. "Ben and I had a chat," she said. "Though really, a lot has been my fault too. But now, back to this… what happened with Fabrizio?"

Caroline pursed her lips and let out a long puff of air.

"Well, when you left to talk to Ben," she explained, "I thanked him, and I might have kissed him on the cheek. But only friendly-like," she added quickly. "And then… he twirled me into his arms, ran his hands through my hair… and … kissed me."

Molly positively beamed. "Oh my *God*, Caroline," she cried. "That's *so* romantic."

"It's not!" Caroline retorted. "It's cheesy and obvious and – and – *stupid*! It's exactly the cliche I wanted to avoid coming here."

Molly shook her head. "Oh come *on*," she told her friend. "Don't be ridiculous. He's *very* good-looking. And for the love of God, he owns the hotel. At the very least, you'd be able to come back to Rome any time you wanted and stay for free…"

"You see?" Caroline said, a wry smile coming to her lips. "This is why I never tell you anything. You always have to go from a simple kiss to a lifelong romance."

"It worked for Ben and me."

"Did not."

"Fair point. But *seriously*, if you were ever going to take a chance on love, now's the time to do it. I mean really, what is the worst that could happen?"

That question made Caroline pause. What *was* the worst that could happen? Certainly, things could be much worse than a holiday romance with a handsome, rich Italian who owned a hotel and drove a fancy car, and at Christmastime no less.

Still...

"Honestly?" she finally replied. "I think I'd lose some respect for myself."

"Whatever for?" Molly asked, incredulous.

Caroline sighed deeply. "I'm... I'm not like you, Mol," she explained. "I don't go all passionate about things and fall head-over-heels. Not that there's anything wrong with that, but it's just not my style. And I never, ever wanted to be a cliche. I absolutely *hate* that holiday romance nonsense."

"Okay," Molly assented, "but I want you to think about this: why do you think they become cliches in the first place?"

"What?"

"All those films and books with broad-chested, impossibly handsome men on the covers... They might be sensationalised fantasy, but in the end, do you think those cliches just sort of happened, like they were just created out of thin air? No way. They were inspired by things that really happened, or that we always *wanted* to happen.

A woman gets swept off her feet by a gorgeous, rich suitor in a romantic Italian city... what in the world is wrong with you that you *wouldn't* just jump on that ride and see where it takes you?"

Caroline was dumbstruck. She hadn't really thought of it that way. It wasn't just a matter of not wanting to be a cliche, she realised – it was her own pride that she'd been riding for last few days.

Fabrizio was a fantasy of sorts: impossibly handsome, incredibly wealthy, and rather sweet. And yet, here she was, pushing him away, just so, what, she could prove a point to herself? She had to admit, that seemed really...

"Stupid," Caroline said finally.

"What's that?" Molly asked.

"*Me*," she continued. "*I'm* stupid. Molly, I've been an absolute idiot. This lovely man has been throwing himself at me, and I've pushed him away. What is wrong with me?"

Molly laughed at that. "There's nothing wrong with you, honey," she reassured her. "You're just as human as the rest of us. And sometimes, that means we do stupid things. But it's nothing that can't be fixed. You just need the opportunity."

"What kind of opportunity?"

"Well," Molly said, beaming, "I hear there's this big celebration tomorrow..."

CHAPTER 25

❄

"*Paddy?*" Helen called from the bathroom the following morning. "Love, can you bring me another towel?" She waited a few moments before calling her husband again. "Paddy? Are you there?"

Helen stepped out of the bathroom wrapped in a towel, a plume of steam trailing her. She rounded the corner into the bedroom to see where her husband was – only to find him barking orders into the phone.

Again.

"Felicity," he said sternly, "we need to – well no, I – don't make – well just go over it again then."

"*Paddy O'Brien!*" Helen thundered.

"I'm going to have to call you back," he said sheepishly into the phone before hanging it up. "Something wrong, pet?" he asked, turning to his wife.

Helen's face was red with fury. "Paddy," she said, her voice so low he had to strain to hear her, "today is your daughter's wedding day. It is a day for celebrating. For God's sake, Paddy, it's Christmas Eve! No one should even be at the office today."

"I hate to break it to you, love," Paddy replied patiently, "but today is the busiest day of the year for us. I can't just abandon them."

"Oh, you can too," she snapped. "I swear, if I see you on that phone *once* between now and the end of today, I'll break the damned phone – or your neck – or both."

"Yes, mammy," he chortled. He fixed his eyes directly on his wife. "Helen," he said, rising from his seat and approaching her, "I've never left Felicity in charge before. She's nervous, and I'm nervous, and we both just need everything to go smoothly."

"I realise that," she responded, "but the least your family can expect today is your undivided attention. Besides," she continued with a wink, "I'm going to need all the support I can get if I'm to deal with that – that – *woman*."

Paddy embraced his wife, who attempted to pull away. "Paddy, don't," she chuckled, "I'm all wet."

"I don't care," he replied. "We'll just have to be wet together, then."

"That's not *all* we can be together…" Helen said suggestively. "But for now," she added, kissing him on the nose, "I have to do my hair." With that, she returned to the bathroom mirror and turned on the hair dryer.

She left it on as she returned to the room to grab her hairbrush – only to find Paddy back on the phone again, barking orders.

Helen sighed, rolled her eyes, and went back to fixing her hair.

CHAPTER 26

❆

Down the hall, Ben was practically screaming into his own phone.

"What do you *mean*, 'I forgot my suit?' Why did you not just wear it on the plane? ... No, Mark, I don't. Just... just stop off somewhere and buy one. It is Italy after all, home of well-cut suits. Yes. Okay. Half-eleven. I'll see you there."

He hung up the phone and ran his hands through his hair. Once again, his idiot brother was throwing a monkey wrench into the best-laid plans.

How could Mark *possibly* have forgotten his suit? He was the *best man*. It was the one thing he was asked to bring. He wasn't even responsible for the rings. He – that was –

A sudden panic came to Ben's mind. *Oh God*, he thought, *what did I do with the rings?*

He first checked the room safe, but he didn't even remember using it, and sure enough, they weren't there.

Neither were they in or under the bed, in the bathroom, or on the desk.

He eyed his suitcase and, in a moment of pure hysteria, grabbed the entire case and attempted to flip it upside-down over his head.

Unfortunately, being less than coordinated on even his best day, he tripped on the suitcase table and went tumbling forward, knocking the side of his head on the edge of the cabinet and sending clothes and toiletries flying every which way.

He cursed loudly and stood, noticing a sharp pain at his temple. He went to look in the mirror for what he already presumed was there – and sure enough, a long trail of cut skin and blood streaked down the side of his face.

What a start to your wedding day...

He had just begun to clean up the blood with a washcloth and some soap when a knock came at the door. He opened it to find, much to his surprise, his father standing outside. The chipper look on James' face turned to horror when he saw his son's face – and astonishment when he saw the state of the room.

"Good Lord, Ben," James said, shocked, "what in heaven's name happened in here?"

"I – er—" his son stammered, "I couldn't find the rings. And I kind of – you know – panicked."

To his utter surprise, James burst out laughing. "Ben, old boy," he said, the sounds of his laughter echoing off the tiles in the bathroom. He was laughing so hard, he couldn't even get the next sentence out, so instead, he reached into his pocket and pulled out a small, black velvet box and opened it. Inside were two gold bands.

Ben closed his eyes in exasperation with himself. "Oh," he said slowly, "I... am such... an *idiot*..."

James shook his head and handed the box to his son. "Nonsense, my boy," he said, "you're just nervous. As you should be. Today's a big day."

"One you don't approve of," Ben said glumly.

"Now, whatever gave you that idea?"

"Oh, I don't know," Ben replied sarcastically. "How about *everything* that happened yesterday?"

"You mean, that business with your mother? Ben, your mother is the love of my life, but she and I are by no means a single mind. Believe it or not, she's really just trying to help. And she's scared. She's losing her baby boy after all."

"What? But you've still got Mark."

"Mark is… a sweet boy. But you know as well as I do, he's incomparably stupid."

Now it was Ben's turn to laugh. "He is, isn't he?"

"Absolutely," James responded. "But Ben: your mother may have her faults, but she is also immeasurably sensible. And her worry isn't so much that Molly won't be good for the title; it's that she won't be good for *you*. All we want is to see you happy."

"But don't you see? I *am* happy."

"I know, son. I know."

"So why these shenanigans then, Father?" Ben asked. "Why allow Mother to treat the O'Briens like her inferiors?"

"Your mother is going to apologise to them this morning. Most of what happened was because of the wine. Your mother's tongue was loosened, and she made some very poor choices with what was being said. I seem to remember something similar happening a few Christmases ago."

"That business with the McGanns?"

"Precisely right," James agreed. "What started it all was your mother making an ill-advised comment on Lady McGann's – erm – *ample* posterior."

"Oh God."

"You have no idea. It took six dinners between me and that insufferable Earl of Cheshunt to get things back on track. 'Your mother has a history of saying ill-timed, ill-advised things. But she isn't bad by any stretch. In fact, she quite often has a very lucid understanding of the situation. And her worry in this case is that through your association with Molly – and the O'Briens generally – you will forget about the title, and hurt your children's chances at the finest things you always had access to."

"I never *wanted* access, Father," Ben insisted.

"I know that, but that's hardly the point. Don't you want the best for your children, whenever you may have them?"

"Of course I do."

"Well, that's all we ever wanted for you, too."

Ben closed his eyes and exhaled deeply. "I know, Father. And I appreciate it – *all* of it."

"Right then," James said, ready to change the subject. "Let's get you cleaned up and ready. It's not every day a future Earl of Daventry gets married in Rome."

CHAPTER 27

"What do you think?" Molly asked Caroline as she came out of the bathroom.

Caroline clasped her hands against her face. Her best friend looked stunning beyond belief.

The dress was perfectly form-fitting, gleaming white like falling snow, with a stripe of red and green around it for a suitably festive feel.

Her silver high heeled shoes sparkled with tiny crystals, while red beads looked like holly berries expertly threaded throughout her elegant blonde chignon,.

"Molly," Caroline said, awestruck, "you look like a Christmas princess."

Behind her, a knock came at the door, which Caroline answered.

Helen walked in, grinning ear to ear. "Caroline, you look gorgeous this morning," she said – before she laid eyes on her only daughter. "Oh," she said, stopping dead in her tracks. "Oh – oh *my*… " Tears came to her eyes and she dabbed at them with a handkerchief and strode up to the younger woman. "Oh *Molly*," she said, now sobbing as she hugged her daughter. "Oh my little girl, my beautiful little girl…"

"Mum," Molly laughed through her own tears. "Stop, you're going to leave streaks on my dress."

Helen sniffled and pulled away. "Oh, I'm sorry," she said, laughing too. "I'm just… my goodness, Molly, you look so beautiful."

"I do, don't I?" Molly said immodestly and all three women laughed again.

Caroline went into the bathroom and came out with three glasses and a bottle. "Okay, girls," she giggled. "I got this downstairs earlier. It's grappa, not champagne, but same thing, I think."

Caroline poured three glasses and Helen raised a toast. "To my Molly," she said. "May your perfect winter wedding in Rome live up to all your dreams and be a delight …"

"…and may all your Christmases be white," Caroline rhymed wickedly.

The three women collapsed in a fit of laughter so cacophonous that they didn't hear the knock coming from the door, nor the creak as it opened.

Suddenly, Caroline straightened up, quickly followed by the others.

"I'm so sorry," Patricia said quietly, "the door was open a crack, and I didn't know if you could—" When her eyes caught sight of Molly, she smiled. "My word, dear," she said sincerely, "you look absolutely ravishing."

"Thanks," Molly said flatly.

"Caroline, I don't suppose…" Patricia said, motioning towards the door.

"Yeah… I'm – er – going to see if I can find some more – erm – ice," Caroline winced as she looked apologetically towards Molly and Helen. "I'll be back in a few."

Once the door was closed, Patricia inhaled deeply. "You're probably wondering why I'm here," she began.

"You could say that," said Helen coldly. "Though honestly, I'm wondering why I'd care, too."

"Right enough," Patricia conceded. "Molly, I should start with you. I was entirely out of line with what I said last night. I had far too much wine and far too loose a tongue, and I pushed my concern for Ben way, way too far. I apologise."

Molly nodded but said nothing.

"And Helen," Patricia continued, turning to the younger woman, "I—"

"Save it," she cut her off. "I don't want or need your apology."

"Mum," Molly said gently, "let her speak."

"No, love," Helen's iciness continued. "There is much I can abide, but Patricia, you aren't just a snob or a lush. You're mean-spirited. You think so much of yourself and your titles and your family, but you have no regard for those who don't share your obsession with nobility. You are conceited and self-interested, and I have no use for any of that. Particularly when it comes to the way you hurt my daughter."

Patricia swallowed her pride and pressed on. "Helen, I realise what I did. I know it's too late to take back, and I wish that I could, because it isn't something I actually believe."

"Oh it's not, is it?" Helen charged, her anger rising. "Come on, Patricia. Let's be honest here. Because of this English nobility business, you think yourself and James as being *better* than Paddy and me. You don't think Molly here is worthy of Ben. Isn't that right?"

"Do I think we're *better* than you?" Patricia repeated. "No, I don't think we're better than you, Helen. But do I think Molly is worthy of Ben? Of course not." Helen's eyes flashed, but Patricia continued, "We're being honest, here aren't we? So tell me – honestly – do you think Ben worthy of Molly?"

The words hit Helen like a stone into still water. She liked Ben; she thought him a nice boy and a fine catch, but was he *worthy* of marrying Helen's only daughter?

"No," she admitted quietly. "No, Patricia, you're right. I don't think he is, and I probably never could."

Patricia smiled warmly. "You see?" she asked, a kindred kindness in her voice neither Helen nor Molly had ever heard before. "We have at least that much in common." She eyed the bottle sitting on the table and poured three glasses quickly. "Whatever the case, dears, I would like to propose a toast: to new beginnings. May we all have the opportunity to wipe the slate clean and start today anew – as friends."

Slowly, Helen took up her glass, never taking her eyes off of Patricia. The two women clinked glasses and drank down the grappa, not noticing that Molly simply was watching them, not having her own.

"Oh *God*," Patricia winced. "That is simply *dreadful!*"

"Isn't it?" Helen laughed. "Disgusting. Ought to be outlawed."

"I need wine. Or champagne."

"Or both," Helen added.

Molly smiled. "Why don't you two go head out and find yourselves a drink then? And if you could, open the door carefully; I'm sure Caroline is right outside with her ear pressed against it."

With that, Helen and Patricia left, and to Molly's delight, they were talking.

Perhaps there was hope after all.

CHAPTER 28

❄

"You can't be serious," Helen said to Fabrizio as he led her, Caroline, Patricia, and Molly to Santa Maria, a tiny church close to the Trevi fountain, "This is a *church*?"

From the outside, it wasn't much to look at; indeed, Helen would have walked right past it on any other day, thinking it an apartment or maybe a small hotel.

But a church?

"Wait till you see it, Mum," Molly responded cheerily. "It's absolutely *perfect*."

Helen and Patricia exchanged skeptical glances – but those looks began to melt the second they stepped into the building.

The inside of Santa Maria was as far from its nondescript exterior as could possibly be.

It was certainly tiny – just a single row of wooden pews extended in front of the altar – but it was adorned in magnificent Italian opulence.

Paintings of the Virgin Mary and the crucifixion hung in ornately woven golden frames along the sides of the entrance. Renaissance-era archways held up walls reaching to the sky.

And most impressively, a large fresco, painted on the ceiling, showed the Assumption of Mary in vibrant colours that stood with even the great Sistine Chapel as a Renaissance masterpiece.

Molly had seen the church before, but to be getting married in it was beyond her wildest dreams.

"See, Mum?" she laughed at her mother's gaping mouth. "I told you this would be great."

"Well," Patricia told her, "I have to admit, Molly, that I was indeed a bit worried about this when Ben told me how tiny the church would be — oh my!"

Patricia was surprised by a man dressed all in black, standing quietly and solemnly in the back of the church next to the Advent wreath. It took her only a moment to realise he was the priest. "Beg your pardon, Father," she said apologetically.

The priest waved his hand as if to say, *don't worry about it*, and summoned the four women and their companion to him.

His face was serene, but it suddenly became quite expressive, a smile breaking out across his wide face. "*Buongiorno! Buongiorno!*" he said excitedly, "*e Buon Natale!*"

"*Buon Natale, Padre,*" Fabrizio replied. "*È tutto pronto per il matrimonio di oggi?*"

"Please, Fabrizio," the priest said happily, "For respect of our guests, let us speak in English." He went straight up to Molly. "And you, I imagine, must be our beautiful bride."

She smiled. "I am," she said happily.

"Wonderful. *Wonderful!* Well. I am Padre Giuseppe Mazzolo, but please, call me Padre Beppe."

"Padre Beppe," she cooed, "I'd like to introduce my mum Helen, my best friend Caroline, and my fiance's mother Patricia."

Padre Beppe seemed absolutely tickled. "It is so good to see you. We so rarely get to have non-local weddings here. This is very exciting for me."

"For us, too," Helen replied.

"I am certain," Padre Beppe said. "So," he continued, slapping his hands together, "We have a little sanctuary in the back where you can get prepared and so that your husband does not see you before we start. Since there is only a small congregation today, I have done away with much of the boring stuff. We will make this very *bam-bam-bam,* quick and painless, yes?"

The women laughed.

"That sounds ... perfect, Padre," Molly said, gulping a little.

"Well," Fabrizio told the group, "it seems you have everything you need here. I must go and prepare something for the groom, and then bring the men over here. I will see you ladies shortly." He turned to walk out the front of the church.

Molly nodded in her bridesmaid's direction and then jerked her head towards Fabrizio.

Caroline took her meaning. "Excuse me just one moment," she said, "There's something I need to, just really fast..." With that, she hiked up the bottom of her dress and shuffled down the aisle quickly. "Fabrizio," she called. "Wait up a second, would you?"

Fabrizio paused and turned around on the steps outside the church. Caroline joined him outside and caught her breath. "Is everything okay, *signorina*?" he asked.

Caroline took a deep breath before starting. "Look," she said, "I wanted to explain myself. About last night..."

"Ah," he said, holding up a hand, "there is no need. I realise I overstepped."

"No, Fabrizio," she said, slightly abashed. "That's not what I meant at all. I was ... I've never been very good at romance. I've always been... guarded. Especially when it comes to something spontaneous like this."

"But how could one live without spontaneity?" he asked sincerely.

Caroline shrugged. "I guess I just like to have a plan," she replied. "Or at least an exit strategy. I don't just go on flings. And I certainly don't just fall for random strange men."

"Fall for?" he repeated bemusedly.

"Yeah. That's not me. I'm not the kind to fall head-over-heels for a guy I've only just met. And yet..."

Fabrizio grinned. "And yet," he said quietly, "you find yourself... falling for me?"

Caroline looked down at her shoes, feeling stupid. "Yeah," she whispered, feeling her face go hot like she was a teenager.

Fabrizio placed his index finger under her chin and lifted her head up to face him. "Caroline," he said, "I do not know where this path will lead us. But I do know one thing: if I did not at least follow the path as far as I can, I would regret it the rest of my life. Is this what you feel?"

She nodded.

"Then perhaps we should take the journey together," Fabrizio said. And with that, he leaned in and kissed her.

After what seemed like an eternity (but more likely was only a few seconds), he broke away. "I am very sorry," he said, "but I really do have to go. But I will return soon. And afterwards we can spend a bit more time together, yes?"

"I'd like that," Caroline smiled. "But yeah, go. Go get the groom."

Fabrizio nodded and went off as Caroline returned to the church a huge smile on her face.

Inside the sanctuary, Molly cast her a furtive glance. "So...?" she inquired.

Caroline shrugged. "So... what, Mol?"

"Oh come *on!*" Molly nearly exploded. "What's the story with your Italian gigolo?"

Caroline only smiled in response.

CHAPTER 29

An hour later, Ben stood outside the church with the other men – including, finally, his errant brother Mark.

"Ready to do this, big brother?" he asked, a glint in his eye.

Ben, visibly nervous, nodded tentatively and wiped the sweat from his palms onto his suit pants. "I could use a drink," he said.

James laughed. "So could I, son," his father said, "but there'll be plenty of time for that soon enough. Shall we head in? Paddy?" He turned to the bride's father.

"—and I don't care if they have to work 'til all hours of the morning, Felicity," Paddy spat into the phone, "I want that delivery there before their kids come down for Christmas morning." He held up a finger to ask the others to wait a moment. "No— No— Yes. Yes. All right, just heading off for Molly's wedding now, I'll call again later."

He hung up the phone to find all four of the other men with exasperated expressions. "Sorry, lads," he apologised, "couldn't be helped. Christmas and all."

"Okay then," Fabrizio said at last, "I think we are all ready then. Shall we?" He motioned towards the door, holding it open as the men went in.

Ben, Mark, and James took their places in front of the altar, while Paddy stayed back to await his daughter.

Molly surprised him by coming in behind him, unnoticed. His eyes fell to her dress first, then her face, and he found himself overcome with emotion.

"My God, Molly," he said, "You are a vision. I—" He wiped away a tear streaming down his cheek.

She collapsed in his arms. "Oh Daddy," she sniffed.

"I know, love," he said, patting her back. "I love you, Mol. More than anything in this world. And all this …" he gestured to the church and the beautiful Italian surroundings "you were right, this is perfect."

Molly wiped the tears from her eyes. "Okay," she said, straightening her dress. "Are you ready?"

"No," he replied honestly. "Are you?"

She nodded slowly. "Yeah," she said, sniffling away another sob. "Yeah, I am. Let's do this."

"Rightio," Paddy replied. He offered her his elbow, and, arm-in-arm, he and Molly began the procession up the aisle of Santa Maria.

CHAPTER 30

❄

The priest called the service together and blessed them. "We are gathered here," he began, "on this nativity of the Lord's birth, to celebrate that special union between Ben and Molly. The readings today will focus on God's love, but we must not forget that love from on high is manifested so well in these two wonderful young people."

Molly and Ben smiled at each other as the priest continued the ceremony in Italian, as arranged.

They continued smiling through the readings, and even through the homily (though what the priest was saying barely registered for their guests).

Following the declaration of consent, Molly held her breath as they prepared their vows.

Ben went first, watching Molly intently, never breaking his gaze as he took her hand in his and spoke in perfect Italian: "I, Ben, take you Molly ..."

Molly felt weak. Ben had been so good about all this, so determined to make this the perfect Italian Christmas wedding for her – and she felt she was going to break down at any moment.

She swallowed hard before beginning. "I take you, Ben, to be my husband .."

Ben smiled from ear to ear as the priest requested the rings, reassuring Molly that everything was going to be okay. She felt filled up, her heart rising as James handed Ben the rings.

Without warning, she heard a *clink! clink! clink!*, the sound of metal rolling down the steps of the altar and into the aisle. Ben groaned and Mark began to laugh.

He had dropped the rings.

He ran down the aisle after them, muttering to himself as he did. Molly couldn't help but laugh aloud. Whatever the case, whatever came next, *this* was her husband, the man she loved so dearly. He was strong, and he was brave – and sometimes, he was a complete klutz.

After finally catching the rings, Ben rushed back up to the altar. "Sorry," he lamented.

Padre Beppe laughed. "You would be amazed at how often that happens," he reassured.

"Really?" Ben asked, heartened.

"No," the priest quipped. "It has never happened before. Not once."

Ben groaned, but everyone else laughed.

"Okay, now, where were we?" Padre Beppe asked. "Ah yes… Ben, please place the ring on Molly's finger – carefully this time – and repeat after me …"

There were several more prayers in Italian, but Ben and Molly were in such a daze that they barely noticed anything until the priest announced, "Ben, you may now kiss the bride."

Ben took his new wife in his arms and gazed at her lovingly. He mouthed, *We did it*, and she nodded tearfully.

He then kissed her with a passion she'd never known before. She enveloped him, wrapping her arms around him. As they finally broke the kiss, he looked her in the eyes again.

"I love you, Molly," he said.

"I love you too," she replied before adding with a mischievous smile, "Lord Pembrey."

CHAPTER 31

A little while later, the wedding party were out on the streets of Rome, everyone beaming at them.

"Okay," Molly called out to them, "time to make a wish."

Fabrizio nodded. "Does everyone have coins with them?" he asked the group. "I have some cents here if needed."

"Not sure Mark has any cents,'" Ben joked.

"That's a really awful joke," his brother mocked him.

"About as awful as your suit," Ben noted, appraising the royal blue and white pinstripes of Mark's jacket, which he clearly hadn't picked up in the Piazza de Spagna. "Did you think you were up for a role as a backup dancer for Lady Gaga or something?"

"That's funny," Mark jibed back, "as I assumed you were yourself going to be a guest star on *Boring Old Married Guys*."

As they rounded the corner, not far from the church to the beautiful baroque structure that was the Fontana di Trevi, they were surprised to find the area relatively quiet.

"It's because it is Christmas Eve," Fabrizio explained. "Not as many tourists now, and locals stay home. You have a perfect opportunity."

"Okay," Molly announced excitedly, "Now, according to legend, if you want to return to Rome, you have to throw a coin with your right hand over your left shoulder. Ready?"

The group turned their backs to the fountain, coins in hand. Just as they were getting ready to toss them in, however, Paddy's phone rang.

He reached into his pocket to answer it. "Hello?" he asked. "Oh, hiya, Felicity…"

Helen scowled and set her jaw. "That's it," she grunted. "I've had it." She grabbed the phone from him and said into the receiver, "Felicity, stop calling and go home. Happy Christmas."

She then took her husband's phone in her right hand and promptly tossed it over her left shoulder and into the fountain.

"Helen!" Paddy exploded. "That's my *phone*!"

"It *was* your phone, love," she said tenderly.

"But – but – I *needed* that!"

"And we need *you*, Paddy. It's time to give up the damned phone calls. It's Molly's wedding day. And it's Christmas!" Seeing the look of consternation on his face, she softened even more. "Tell you what, love: if we get back in a few days and the business is gone, I'll make you a trifle."

Paddy stared hard at her – and then a resigned smile spread across his face. "I'm sorry I've been ignoring you, love. I've been under an awful lot of stress lately…"

"I know pet," she replied. "But it's time to let it go. We're in this beautiful city on our daughter's wedding day - on Christmas Eve. And I don't know about you but I have every intention of coming back here. "

She reached for her husband and pulled his face in for a kiss.

"*AHEM!*" Molly cleared her throat loudly to catch her parent's attention. "Now, if you two lovebirds don't mind …?"

"Go ahead honey," her mother replied, smiling.

"Okay," Molly said again. "One – two – three!"

Eight pennies flew through the air in perfect unison, and clinked against the stone edifice before falling into the water.

Ben grabbed Molly by the hand and kissed her. Helen wrapped herself around Paddy, as Patricia and James grasped hands.

Fabrizio enveloped Caroline in a passionate embrace, while poor Mark just stood by, embarrassingly kicking at a stone on the ground.

Suddenly, as they all stood there, little white flakes began to appear

– at first just a dusting falling softly, then more and more until they were pouring out of the sky.

"Snow in Rome?" Molly gasped delightedly. "But how...?"

Ben just smiled. "Merry Christmas, darling," he said to her. Seeing the confused look on her face, he continued, "I talked to Fabrizio, and he called in a favour from a friend who runs a ski resort up north. I wanted to make sure your dream Christmas wedding was perfect in every way."

Sure enough as Molly looked around, she spotted the snow machine a few yards away tucked behind a Fiat, shooting snow into the late evening sky.

"It's... it's perfect, Ben," she cried, hugging him close.

"All right, everybody," Fabrizio called out, "I think we are ready to head back to the hotel. In about ninety minutes, we'll begin dinner on the terrazza. I have reserved it specially just for you. I look forward to seeing you all there."

As the others made their way back to the hotel, Caroline hung back a minute. She nudged Fabrizio with her elbow. "You've really played a blinder on this, Fabrizio," she complimented. "I don't know how we could ever thank you."

He arched an eyebrow. "*I* know how you could," he said.

"How?"

"Come back to me, Caroline."

"What?"

He kissed her, a kiss full of meaning and promise. "I do not want this to be, as you said, just a 'fling,'" he explained. "I enjoy your company. I enjoy everything about you, Caroline. I want to enjoy you more. I want the legend of the Fontana di Trevi to work its magic and bring you back to me."

Her eyes widened. "I just... I don't know, Fabrizio. We've only just met—"

"—so let's continue meeting!" he said excitedly. "I do not make this offer lightly, Caroline. I make it only because I want to see more of you and..."

"...and see where this is going," she finished for him. "No, I get it. I do. And…" She watched her best friend and new husband walking away. Molly and Ben looked so happy, so contented, so perfect together. "Oh, what the hell," she said. "I don't know, maybe it's the romance of Italy, or the snow on Christmas Eve…"

Caroline pulled her handsome Italian down by the collar and kissed him passionately.

Sometimes, being part of a cliche was a very good thing.

ALSO BY MELISSA HILL

Escape to Italy Series
Escape to the Islands Series
Caribbean Escape Series

AVAILABLE NOW

Antigua sands

HOLLY GREENE

AVAILABLE NOW

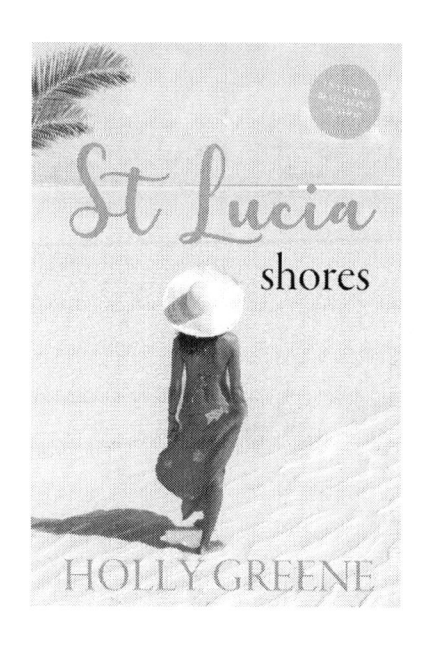

CHRISTMAS AT THE HEARTBREAK CAFE

CHAPTER 1

*E*lla Harris shuffled down the empty Lakeview Main Street at breakneck speed.

At sixty-two, she was still the same speed-walker as when much younger, and as she shot through the early crisp winter air, twinkling lights decorating the windows and roofs still-lit from the night before, flew past in a blur of reds, white and greens.

But Ella had no time to enjoy this sparkling festive display on the first day of December. Instead, she had one thing on her mind: getting to her café on time. Nicknamed The Heartbreak Cafe by the locals for reasons that no-one could no longer quite remember, it was the perfect gathering place for all sorts of world-weary Lakeview residents and tourists looking for a warm drink and an even warmer welcome.

The popular tourist village, twenty minutes-drive from Dublin, was centred round a broad oxbow lake from which it took its name. The lake, surrounded by low-hanging beech and willow trees, wound its way around the centre, and a small humpback stone bridge joined all sides of the township together.

The cobbled streets and ornate lanterns on Main Street, as well as the beautiful one-hundred-year-old artisan cottages decorated with hanging floral baskets, had resulted in the village being designated heritage status by the Irish Tourist Board, and the chocolate-box look and feel was intentionally well preserved.

Ella's café was situated in a small two-storey building with an enviable position right at the edge of the lake and on the corner where Main Street began. Early in their marriage, Ella and her husband took over the running of the café from her father-in-law, and she spent nearly every waking moment since then ensuring that his legacy—and that of her dearly departed husband Gregory—lived on through good food, hot coffee, and warm conversation.

The interior hadn't changed much over the years — it was still a warm cosy room with parquet oak flooring, shelves full of dried flowers and old country-style knick-knacks, along with haphazard seating and mismatched tables, one of which was an antique Singer sewing table.

In front of the kitchen and serving area was a long granite countertop, where various solo customers typically nursed their coffees and pastries atop a row of stools. Alongside this was a glass display case filled with a selection of freshly baked goods; muffins, doughnuts, carrot cake, brownies and cream puffs for the sweet-toothed, and pies, sausage rolls and Italian breads for the more savoury-orientated.

From early morning the place was flooded with families, friends, and neighbours, all there to grab a bite to eat—and to gossip. Ella thrived on the commotion and excitement, and the community had embraced her: she had become a figurehead in the town and a confidant to anyone who came in looking for a bit of conversation with their coffee.

But her job was never easy. The early morning start meant that Ella was up at 5am to make the mile-long trek from her home on the other side of town, across the humpback stone bridge to the café's kitchen.

This morning, she was running atypically late. Late—it was such an unfamiliar word. She hadn't slept late in nearly twenty years. She was gripped with an unsettling feeling of panic as she checked her watch.

6:15. *Damn,* she thought to herself.

This was going to be tight. She could certainly get the coffee started, and set her chef Colm's baked breakfast favourites out on display, but would she have time to get the tables set and fried breakfasts prepped before her first customer arrived? Breakfast choices at the café typically ranged from yoghurt, muesli and bagels, to the Full Irish heart attack of fried sausages, mushrooms, eggs bacon and hash browns, complete with locally produced black pudding.

Ella turned her quick walk into a half-jog. It was tight, because many of her early-morning regulars were residents commuting to work in Dublin so she'd better pick up the pace.

She was speeding around the corner by the edge of the walkway to the lake when she felt her right shoe slip from underneath her. She grabbed for the silver tinsel hanging from the nearby lamppost when her left foot turned the other way and her back moved in reverse in an almost pained slow motion. She swirled in an almost elegant three-quarter turn and was suddenly staring skyward, her back on the ground.

Ouch.

She inched herself off the ground and quickly looked around her, stunned and a little embarrassed.

Thank goodness, she thought, seeing no other early morning walkers around. Using her hands for support and leverage, she pushed herself upright and on to her feet. As soon as she was able to lean her body weight to her right side, she let out a horrible yelp. Her ankle had failed her. She briefly cursed her love of old-fashioned Mary Jane heels and her neglectful landlord who always "forgot" to salt the path in frosty weather.

With her pride a bit battered, she hopped on one foot the rest of the way to the café.

CHAPTER 2

As she opened the side entrance, she wondered what she should do now. Colm wasn't due in until later this morning, so she had no other choice but to close for the morning—maybe even longer. She certainly couldn't arrange breakfast and run the place all by herself.

As she sat in the back of the café's darkened kitchen with her ankle elevated on a nearby chair, she teared up at the thought of having to call a taxi to bring herself to the hospital. Ella prided herself for being independent and for never asking for help. Now she had to, and the thought of it was both disheartening and frightening.

Just as she began to fall into a pit of despair, she heard a knock on the front door of the café. "We're closed, sorry!" she cried loudly at the stranger. The knocking suddenly stopped and she heard heavy footsteps quickly moving away from the front door.

She let out a sigh of relief as she dropped her bad leg to the ground and used her arms and good leg to anchor her to stand again. She slowly made her way to where she left her handbag and as she rummaged through it for her mobile phone, the knocking started up again. This time, it was at the back door. The knock was forceful and urgent.

"Ella! Are you in there? Are you all right?" The voice was gruff, yet had a tinge of obvious concern, and she instantly recognised who was calling for her. That distinct, gravelly voice belonged to her most loyal customer, Joseph Evans. The owner of Lakeview riding school and stables, Joseph had been visiting the café every Monday since he was the new person in town almost thirty years before, about the same time as Ella and Gregory took over the café. Even though he lived a little way outside the village, he still stopped in faithfully every morning for a blueberry scone and a cup of coffee.

"Joseph? Is that you? Give me a second." Ella dropped the handbag on the table, quickly smoothed her hands over her tightly braided hair, and realigned her dress. With all her might, she managed to use the tables and counter space to limp towards the back door.

As she opened the door, she caught a familiar earthy smell from the man towering over her—fresh pine trees and grass. His grey hair almost sparkled as gently falling snow touched the strands. Joseph had yet to lose the rugged good looks that had made him quite the catch in Lakeview for many years. Yet he'd never married.

"You sounded flustered," he said gently as she opened the door. "You're never flustered."

"Oh," she said, blushing slightly, "it's—um—"

"What happened?" he asked. "Baking accident? Tell me it wasn't the scones..." The lighthearted humour in his voice made her forget why he was here.

She shook her head bashfully. "It's nothing," she replied, shaking her head. "I just slid on the ice out front. You would think that Paul would have salted the paths, but you know how cheap he is," she added, referring to her landlord, a wealthy banker married to a local girl, who owned the properties housing over half the local businesses on Main Street.

"Ella," Joseph insisted, "it's obviously *not* nothing. You're hurt. Why didn't you call an ambulance?"

"An ambulance?" she asked, attempting to smile. "I don't need an ambulance. I was just going to call a taxi to come pick me up and bring me to Jim Kelly to see if he'd put a bandage on it. It's *not* that big a deal. I mean, I can still walk..."

"Not a big deal?" he said sardonically, looking down at her leg. "You can't even put any weight on it. I'm sure Dr Kelly will agree and send you straight to A&E."

"But I can," she insisted.

"Prove it," he challenged her.

Ella slowly lowered her foot, steadied her leg, and leaned to the side. The pain instantly shot through her body as she let out a loud squeal and stumbled forward. Joseph grabbed her arm as she nearly tumbled into his chest. Obviously, her pride had once again got the best of her.

"Okay, yeah," he said, holding her up and shaking his head. "I'm taking you to the hospital myself. You can pay me back in scones and coffee when you're back on your feet."

Ella reluctantly nodded. Joseph helped her find a seat and quickly ran out the back door to retrieve his Land Rover. As she waited, she made a list of all the things she would need to do to get the café opened by this afternoon.

Maybe she could just serve drinks instead of food today. That would keep her off her feet. Or perhaps she should serve food, considering that Monday was always her most profitable day. And she knew that she had to alert the waiting staff one way or another, so she quickly jotted down a note to her chef Colm and a small crew that explained why she wouldn't be in this morning.

She trusted Colm to handle the staff in her absence. He had, after all, worked for her since he was an awkward teenage boy nearly fifteen years ago.

The lights of Joseph's truck suddenly flooded the kitchen's back window and Joseph raced inside. "Okay," he said, a braced look on his face, "I know it's not the best plan, but I need to get you into the jeep, so I'm going to have to pick you up."

"No," she said, blushing again. "I'm like a sack of spuds."

"You have a better idea?" he asked.

"Crane?" she joked.

Joseph smiled and shook his head. "I'm not taking 'No' for an answer," he insisted. Without another word, he reached for Ella's arms and gently stood her up out of the chair. Then with one quick and steady motion, he picked her up. He even grabbed her handbag as he carried her out the threshold of the cafe and into his humming vehicle.

THE DRIVE to the hospital was beautiful and breathtaking. Rarely had Ella taken the moment to look around at the beauty of her home town. But as the snow fell sparingly on the windshield and the old fashioned street lamps glittered in the darkness, Ella felt a fondness for Lakeview that she had not felt in years.

Christmas here had always been a beautiful and special time growing up.

The ice skating on the frozen lake, the hot chocolate, and the town's festive parades.

As a teenager, her future father-in-law's café would transform into a gathering place as the then much smaller community came together and celebrated the festive season.

There was a jolly Santa Claus, plenty of mince pies, homemade mulled wine, and general joviality through the streets. At the end of the night, local musicians would play a combination of traditional Irish and Christmas music—the kind that made you fall in love all over again, and she remembered dancing cheek to cheek with Gregory, her soon-to-be husband.

"Your ankle must not be hurting you much," Joseph proclaimed.

"Hmmm?" Ella broke out of her sentimental memories to acknowledge him.

"You're smiling." He winked at her as he took his eyes off the road momentarily.

"Oh, I was just remembering those old Christmas parties on Main Street and how special they were. Were you around for those?"

"I was for the last couple, I believe. They were great. Always loved that mulled wine—especially the stronger version that came out after the children left." He laughed heartily at the thought. "Why don't we throw them anymore? I'm sure the village would love to have something like that again."

"Gregory used to drive them mostly. That all stopped after he died." Her voice dropped to a whisper. She hadn't said her husband's name out loud in years.

"Oh, I'm sorr—"

"Don't be. Once he passed away, his father and I didn't have it in us to take on the organising of it. Those were the days though." She looked off into the distance hoping to spot something she couldn't quite put her finger on.

"So, why not now?" He asked, breaking a short silence.

"Why not now what?"

"Why not think about another Christmas party now?" He looked at her earnestly.

Excitement glimmered in his dark brown eyes. His wide, mischievous grin was unavoidable. "By my reckoning, the café is coming up to thirty years in business with you at the helm. Good enough reason to celebrate."

"Ah, I'm way too old for that. I would need so much help, and I can't—"

"Can't imagine asking for help?" Joseph rolled his eyes. "When are you going to understand that Lakeview loves you, Ella? They love the café and they adore *you*. I'm pretty sure that everybody, including myself would love to get involved. Just think about it, okay?"

Ella sank back into the jeep's heated seats. She had to admit the idea of throwing an old-fashioned party was very tempting, especially given the year that was in it.

Joseph was right; she had indeed been in business in Lakeview for thirty years and it would be a lovely way to show some gratitude to the community for their support over that time.

But if she were going to do this and do it right, she would have to ask for help. She could do that, surely. Just like Joseph said, there wasn't a soul in Lakeview that Ella couldn't turn to.

It was all about finding the right people.

. . .

As the two pulled up to the hospital's Emergency Room doors, Joseph idled the jeep in the entryway. He swung around to Ella's passenger side door and offered his arm to her. As he lifted her effortlessly out of the seat, she sighed.

"You know what, Joseph. I'm going to do it. I am going to organise a thank you Christmas party for my customers this year. You're right, it's would be amazing. But I'm going to need your help with one particular task."

"What's that?" He asked as he carried her like a child into the ER waiting room.

"Oh, you'll see soon enough. First, I need to find the rest of my help." Ella smiled brightly as the thought of all that she needed to do and prepare danced in her head.

She always did love a challenge.

CHAPTER 3

Ruth Seymour sped through the village like a madwoman. Limbs of trees flew past her car window in a fury of pine green and icy white. Music blared from her SUV's speakers as she loudly sung along, belting each and every high note she possibly could.

Driving was Ruth's therapy. Ever since she gave up her LA actress career and returned to live in Lakeview almost two years before, she found she needed more and more to be in the driver's seat. Speeding along the tree-lined roads and gravel pathways of the back way routes around her hometown was a stark contrast from her old stomping grounds of Los Angeles.

She enjoyed being home once again and the freedom and relative anonymity that came with small town life. It was all Ruth could do to keep from bursting with happiness as she took pin tight corners and rolled her windows down to feel the crisp and clean wintry air on her face and hair.

Luckily for her, the lack of a major police presence and complete absence of photographers made it easy for her to indulge in her vice without much care or worry. One time she'd been pulled over for speeding on the road to Dublin, and the cop let her go once he recognised her as the glamorous star of the popular US TV show *Glamazons*.

But that was a couple of years ago, and these days Ruth was no longer quite as famous or indeed glamorous.

She slowed the car as the outskirts of the village loomed, houses grew closer together and she neared the old secondary school.

Just driving past, she was flooded with memories of her former Lakeview school days. She remembered her very first dramatic solo, a musical piece in Latin. Her singing received a standing ovation and requests that she perform at village weddings and funerals for years to come. And then there was her first play. As a mere second-year, she had landed the lead role in *Evita*. It was challenging at first as she struggled to learn all of the songs and cues, but she would never forget the crowd rising to their feet in applause as she hit the final big note in "Don't Cry for Me Argentina."

Then of course, she could never forget the day she met Charlie Mellon.

She remembered how he sauntered past her in the school's hallway. She was surrounded by her gaggle of friends—a group that never left her side. Older and devastatingly handsome, with a leather jacket and a confident smile, Ruth was immediately smitten and determined to make him hers.

A few days later, she found him standing outside a classroom waiting for the bell to ring. Taking a deep breath in, she casually strolled up to him, flashed her most radiant smile, and asked if he could help her with her Maths homework. "It would be such a help," she practically begged. "I can't seem to get through this by myself."

He just stared at her for several seconds, studying her face with such a quizzical look.

He offered his hand to her—a formality so rare in school boys that reminded her of old romance movies. Ruth practically swooned. As they made plans for their study sessions, he never once took his eyes off of her. Unlike the rest of the boys who couldn't ever dare to look her in the eye, his unassuming confidence made her feel shy again. Her face reddened, her palms sweat, and her heart raced.

They spent the next few months studying together without any romantic overtures. Sometimes Ruth would lean into him as she turned the page, but he never returned the affection. Only once did he touch her hand as they both grabbed for a pencil at the same time.

Ruth was about to give up on Charlie ever making a move until their final week before the Christmas break. It was a few short days away from the holidays and Ruth was becoming more and more anxious. As she went to meet him in the secluded study area of the town's library, she braced herself for another session of serious Charlie. But he wasn't at their usual table. Instead, a handwritten note was left on the chair:

Ruth,

I THOUGHT WE COULD HAVE A CHANGE OF PACE FOR TODAY. I'M SICK OF THE LIBRARY. MEET ME AT ELLA'S CAFÉ WHEN YOU GET THIS. FOOD'S ON ME.

— CHARLIE.

She grabbed her schoolbag and ran through the town square onto Main Street towards the café, The Heartbreak Cafe some of the older girls called it. Hopefully nothing like heartbreak awaited Ruth there today.

Through the window, she could see Charlie sitting at the granite counter, chatting casually with the owner, Ella. She strolled in confidently and took a seat next to him, waving a friendly hello to Ella, who smiled knowingly and made herself scarce.

"Well, this is a lovely change from the library,' Ruth smiled. 'What made you think of this?"

"I just felt like something sweet. Ella makes the best muffins in the universe. Have you tried them?"

"No, believe it or not I've actually have never been here before. It's really cool though." She studied the olde-worlde decor. It wasn't exactly her style, but it had a real charm complete with cosy details. The wall's pink and green accents reminded her of the movie sets for technicolor musicals. The mix matched china teacups were even out of date in a way that was comforting. It was almost like she had stepped into her grandmother's front room.

"I'll order you something. How about tea, a muffin, and a piece of Twix cake? My mate, Colm works here at weekends, and he has some secret recipe he's been bugging us all about. Ella finally let him sell it, so it must be good."

Ruth nodded in agreement and Charlie casually rattled off the order to Ella. Without much time to change the subject, the café owner was back again with two muffins from the back. As she placed them down in front of them, she winked at Ruth as if she knew what was going on. Ruth blushed for the second time in her life.

In the middle of sips and bites, Charlie broke the silence, "So, I don't think you really need to cram anymore Maths. You're going to do fine on the test."

"Easy for you to say. You know it all. I've never met someone as brilliant as you are. You should do something like programme a space launch. The world needs more of you."

"Nothing that elaborate. I want to be a mechanic actually. I love figuring out how things work."

"A mechanic? That's amazing." Ruth flirtatiously sipped her coffee, all the while keeping her eyes locked on his, though she privately thought that he was aiming a little low. A boring old mechanic when he could easily be some kind of high-ranking engineer in Dublin, or London even.

When she suggested as much, he smiled. "Well, as much as the money might be nice, I'll probably just stay here in Lakeview. Nothing too glamorous like you have in mind for yourself."

"Like I have in mind?"

"Yeah, I'm imagining you in New York—a big Broadway star or something. Give it ten years and your name will be everywhere."

Ruth smiled at this. It wasn't hard for anyone to guess that she had her eyes on something bigger and brighter than Lakeview, yet no one ever said it so confidently to her.

"Yes. I want to be a star. Doing what I'm not sure. But I plan on having my name in lights somehow. Maybe an Oscar or a Grammy, even." She grinned from ear to ear.

"Speaking of which, I have a gift for you. I figured that since we have seen each other twice a week for the last couple of months, I should get you something for Christmas. Open it."

He handed her a flat gift box wrapped in red tissue and a white bow. Her name was neatly printed on a tag. Ruth's heart skipped a beat as she gently tore the paper. She didn't want to seem too eager. As she opened the box, she began to tear up. Inside was a framed piece of sheet music. It was the score to "Don't Cry for Me Argentina."

"Last year, I saw you in the play. Your voice was beautiful. I had never heard anything like that in my entire life." He stared at her with his grey piercing eyes waiting for a response, but all Ruth could do was to just gently rub her hands on the gold, metal frame. Tears fell onto the glass.

Before she knew it, she had stood up, reached up towards Charlie Mellon's face, and kissed him. It was soft and gentle, but her mouth lingered on his until he wrapped his arm around her waist and his other around the back of her head. The café's stereo played the old Dean Martin Christmas hit, "I've Got My Love to Keep Me Warm."

IT WAS Charlie and Ruth's first kiss, but it certainly wouldn't be their last. They were together for the remainder of their time in secondary school and afterwards. Then afterwards he went to work in his family's car dealership, and before long Ruth was bound for Dublin for an audition for a soap opera produced by the Irish TV station. With a heavy heart they said their goodbyes, and promised in earnest to keep in touch.

Twelve years later, and Ruth could still feel the pain of those final moments together. A first love was always the hardest to let go of, but luckily for Ruth, she got a second chance. While Charlie remained in Lakeview eventually growing the dealership and taking over, Ruth had grown in the soap opera world and moved to LA full time.

After a few bit parts in movies, she became a regular star in *Glamazons*. But after a brief ill-advised affair with her co-star Troy, she found out she was pregnant and returned home to figure out what to do next.

Despite her problems, she and Charlie managed to reunite and when little Scarlett was born a few months later, Charlie was by Ruth's side. Troy had refused to visit or even acknowledge the birth of his daughter, whereas Charlie jumped in and assisted Ruth with the first few weeks of feedings, nappy changes, and bath times. At this point she had quit LA and moved back to Lakeview. Life, it seemed had other, more important plans for her.

Scarlett had just turned twelve months when Charlie proposed. She was already walking and that night she occasionally stopped, looked at Charlie, and stumbled into his arms for a hug or a quick snuggle before she was back at it again. After several moments of this, Charlie took her aside, and whispered something in her ear. She toddled into the kitchen where Ruth was reading over a script and tugged at her hand.

"What is it sweetie?" Ruth asked following her daughter into the living room. Charlie had moved off of the couch and onto his knee. In his hands were two rings. One was made from candy and the other was a diamond that shone so bright it glimmered from several feet away.

"Ruth and Scarlett—I cannot imagine my life without the two of you. I need you both home with me here in Lakeview. Will you two marry me?" Little Scarlett held her mother's hand, looking up at her for permission to go and take the sweet.

"Oh my goodness, YES!" Ruth squealed as she ran into Charlie's arms and Scarlett followed right behind her, grabbing the sweet as she hugged them both.

Now, as Ruth pulled into the Lakeside parking area near the Heartbreak Café, she took a moment to think about how different her life was now. No longer was she living in a swanky LA townhouse or hobnobbing with Hollywood celebrities. She rarely had signed one autograph since moving in with Charlie to his house just outside the village. But she was happy—she truly was.

Except for one little problem.

Ruth walked into the café and spotted *her*. Sitting at the counter chatting with Ella was a woman dressed in black from head to toe. Her hair was piled into a neat, old fashioned bun at the top of her head, and she sipped her tea with her pinky finger out as if she were way more important than she was. Charlie's mother, Ita.

Ruth gritted her teeth. She was not going to let this woman ruin her much needed morning latte. She walked in confidently, strolled to a table on the other side of the room, and faced away from her. Her face flushed in annoyance as she could feel Ita staring daggers at her back.

Ella using a cane, slowly walked to her table, "Ruth, love! What can I get you?"

"Oh Ella! I heard about your ankle. You poor thing. Why aren't you sitting in the back resting and letting Colm take over?"

"Too much to do! And it's only a sprain. I'll be back at it in a week or two. Did you hear about my bringing back the old Christmas party? You, Charlie, and Scarlett will come, yes?"

"A Christmas party! Here in Lakeview? We will certainly be there, Ella. Is there anything I can do to help you prepare?"

"Actually now that you say it, I am in need of a singer. A party wouldn't be any good without a singsong. And everyone in Lakeview just loves to hear you sing. You'd just need to do some Christmas favourites and a few ballads."

"Ha, not a chance," Ita piped up from her seat at the counter. "It wouldn't be good enough for Ms. Hollywood unless you plan on inviting the paparazzi and maybe Elvis. Isn't that right, Ruth dear?"

Ruth shuttered in embarrassment and anger. She was used to her mother-in-law's snide comments about her former life as a TV star, but it stung nonetheless. She knew that Ita was furious that Charlie choose to marry her and adopt Scarlett instead of finding his own, baggage-free wife here in town. Never mind that Charlie was Scarlett's father through and through. To Ita, Ruth was just some tramp that trapped her beloved son into raising a child that was not his.

"Ella, I would be honoured," she smiled. When is the party?"

"On the evening of December 22, just in time for Christmas. We'll have a big celebration; food, mulled wine, Santa and hopefully carriage rides around the lake for the kids if Daniel can arrange it, so please bring little Scarlett along too."

"I'll be there, I promise. But in the meantime," she smiled apologetically. "I'm starving and in a bit of a rush. I have to pick up Scarlett from creche in a half hour for a playdate. Can I get a latte and a pain au chocolat to take away?"

"Certainly, pet." Ella hobbled off, leaving Ita and Ruth to both stew in their collective corners of the café.

Maybe Ruth agreeing to take part in something like this party might help Ita see that she loved Charlie and had every intention of staying in Lakeview, and then in turn might cause her to treat Scarlett as her granddaughter instead of a complete stranger. Ruth knew it really hurt Charlie that his mother still wouldn't acknowledge Ruth and Scarlett as family, even after all this time.

She sighed. At this point, she wasn't sure how anything could repair their relationship.

Taking out her Prada purse to pay for the food, her eyes rested on the Hollywood script in her bag that had arrived from her agent only that morning.

The fact that Ruth was of late considering a return to work in Tinseltown, certainly wouldn't improve matters.

CHAPTER 4

Heidi Clancy was running late. After spending a very pleasant morning in Dublin getting her hair and nails done, she was stuck behind the slow moving trucks of the old timber yard just outside the village.

Currently, her car, a brand new black BMW, was idling behind a large red semi carrying at least a dozen of unruly pine trunks. It took everything in Heidi's power not to honk her horn, but she resisted out of fear of breaking her nails.

Behind her outward impatience was a smidgen of satisfaction though. While being late was always a social sin, being late to an occasion like the Lakeview Mum's Club did have its benefits. Heidi knew that her late entrance to Cynthia Roland's house, in which they were holding today's gathering, would be fawned over, with the crowd of women asking her about traffic and her morning.

Everyone would rise to make a fuss of her gorgeous daughter Amelia, grab her box of 'homemade' cupcakes, and remark at her brand new DVF coat. Attention would be all hers and Heidi certainly knew how to milk it.

But most importantly, her absence would have everyone talking. The girls couldn't resist an opportunity to gossip about the village's wealthiest woman.

Well, maybe the second richest woman in Lakeview. Ever since that soap star moved back home a few years back, it was all that the town's gossip crowd could chat about. If they were not whispering about Ruth Seymour's scandalous affair with her co star, they were discussing how much her Los Angeles townhouse must have sold for.

Heidi did not mind the competition one bit. It gave her an excuse to step up her game. She had already laid out plans to redecorate the living room of their palatial home on the Dublin Road, and add on separate living quarters for their live-in nanny.

Of course her bank manager husband Paul certainly could also not resist her when she asked to borrow his credit card for a day at the salon because hers was already maxed-out. Whatever Heidi wanted, Heidi got, and she was never afraid to ask for more.

Finally past the literal log jam of timber trucks, Heidi put her pedal to the floor. She still had to pop by the house to pick up little Amelia and the nanny, and she also had to make it to Ella's Cafe to pick up some of Colm's special cupcakes. She had to hurry if she wanted to make a fashionably late entrance and avoid being outright rude.

Luckily for her, Miriam and Amelia were already waiting for her in the porch. Miriam had a pained look on her face that Heidi shrugged off with a couple of insincere apologies and promises to let her know when she would be late in the future. Amelia, on the other hand, was as pleasant as ever. At only two years, she had a glow and a smile that never failed to put a smile on Heidi's face. As expected, she was a natural at motherhood and she found it hard to believe that after all the related fuss of her sister Cara's wedding, whereupon a heavily pregnant Heidi had to travel to St Lucia to watch her sister walk down the aisle, that she'd still managed to retain a level head and good spirits for the remainder of her pregnancy.

Though in truth, she and her sister had a much better relationship these days, and while Heidi and her sister-in-law Kim still like to engage in an occasional war of words, they too had managed a truce of sorts, made easier by the fact Amelia and Kim's son Jago, were the same age.

With Miriam in the back of the car entertaining Amelia, Heidi was soon back on the road. As she parked directly onto double yellow lines directly outside Ella's café (her husband owned the building so she was entitled), her phone began to ring.

Looking at the caller ID, she sighed. It was her sister-in-law from the other side of the family, Gemma, Paul's youngest sibling. She was what Heidi called a 'Mummy Martyr.' She spent her time at the club complaining about how hard it was to raise her twins and spent hours counting pennies and avoiding a much needed facial. It was so tiring to Heidi—so much so that she routinely ignored Gemma's calls. Today would not be an exception.

Heidi raced inside the café to meet Ella at the counter. Her Lucy Choi heels clinked loudly on the wooden floor enough that the noise caught the attention of the rest of the customers.

"Hello Ella, do you have my order ready? I'm running 40 minutes late already."

"Of course I do. We never forget your orders." Ella answered, a bit wounded.

"Thank you soooo much!" Heidi flashed her ultra-bright white smile at the older woman and quickly handed her Paul's platinum credit card.

"Now that I have you, when you get a chance, with all the frost we're getting lately, can you please ask Paul to salt the paths out front? I twisted my ankle the other day and am on crutches for the next month. I understand he's busy but he really should get someone to do that if he can't come to do it himself." Ella was gently scolding Heidi, but Heidi was too busy checking her reflection in the display glass casing.

"Oh, yeah. I will as soon as I see him," she replied, absent-mindedly.

'Um...sorry Heidi, but the card has been declined,' Ella said then, looking apologetic, and she immediately jumped to attention.

"What? But that's impossible! I just used it this morning and — " She rummaged in her wallet for some cash.

"Not to worry, sure you can sort me out some other time...." Waving the incident away, Ella smiled and handed her back the card.

"Are you sure? It's just I don't usually carry cash and — "

Flustered, Heidi felt her cheeks redden. This could *not* be happening. She hadn't gone too crazy in the city this morning had she? Yes, she'd been stocking up on Christmas presents (to say nothing of her own wardrobe) but it was a platinum card for goodness sake, the limit must be sky high. If there even was a limit ...

Heidi couldn't understand it. "Thank you. I'll pop back later when I've been to a cashpoint. *Au revoir!*" she called as she flipped her hair and strutted towards the door with the cupcake box in her free arm.

"OK, let's roll guys - Mum's Club time!" She proclaimed as she belted herself in, checked her lipstick and backed out of the space, the incident with the credit card already forgotten.

CHAPTER 5

❄

Cynthia Roland's house was next door to her sister-in-law's. Nestled in a modest estate, the house looked exactly like all the other boring others. Besides the amount of cars in the driveway and the sign on the front lawn, Heidi wouldn't have even begun to know which house she was headed towards.

As she parked the car, she noticed the women subtly staring at her from the window. *This* was exactly the entrance Heidi had wanted. She confidently strolled in carrying the cupcakes with Miriam and Amelia about ten feet behind.

"Cynthia, darling. You look fabulous as always!" she crowed at the sight of the pale, meek woman answering the door.

"Not as good as you, I'm afraid." Her friend's insincere smile did nothing to faze Heidi as she was greeted by a gaggle of women all ready and eager to make note of her presence.

"Let me take that from you!"

"Oh! Look at your jacket! Is it new?"

"Who did your hair? It looks perfect."

"You shouldn't have gone to the trouble of baking all these, Heidi! It's too kind of you."

"How is Paul? I hear you bought another building in town recently."

"Your nails are the most perfect shade. I wish I was bold enough to wear that colour."

As the compliments rolled in, Heidi effortlessly swivelled back and forth to give each woman her answer and a polite peck on the cheek.

All except Gemma. While the rest of the Mum's Club had greeted her at the door, her sister-in-law had remained in her chair by the fireplace. She was staring daggers at Heidi, but her look significantly softened as she spotted Miriam and Amelia walking through the door.

"Miriam, let me take Amelia from you. I never get enough time with her when I visit. And you must be exhausted from taking care of her all by yourself day in and day out." Gemma proclaimed loudly so that each of the other mums would hear her. The women moved from Heidi and began to swoon loudly over Amelia. While Gemma's barb should have ruffled Heidi, it only boosted up her self-importance that much more.

After the cordial greetings and compliments were sufficiently dispensed, Heidi led the gang back into the living room. Taking her place at the front of the room, she watched as Amelia gingerly toddled towards the other children to play with the plethora of toys assembled.

"So, what was your day like Heidi?" asked a woman she vaguely recognised but couldn't be bothered to remember her name.

"Oh... the usual. I went to Dublin to get my nails done at the BT Nail Bar and while there I dropped an absolute fortune on the second floor. Then I went to have my hair done at Hair Box, before picking up Paul's suits from the dry cleaner, and I barely managed to get in a light workout before heading out earlier. It's been such a busy day already!"

"If only I could manage to get to the gym." sighed another woman Heidi avoided.

"It's all about priorities, really. You can do it if you set your mind to it." She smiled at her own encouragement.

"You mean, you could set your mind to it if you had plenty of money and a live-in nanny, and a cleaner, don't you?" The women giggled as Gemma snarked. "You have to admit that you have it lucky with Paul's money paying for everything. You don't have to lift a finger."

"I suppose, but he does work hard, and we have the same worries as everyone else. I just don't talk about them non-stop." Heidi felt a bit defensive at the insinuation that her life was easy.

"Not all of us marry for money. Some of us do so for love." Gemma's comments came across as a slap in the face. While Heidi had known that her sister-in-law harboured resentment towards her, she had never heard her express it so openly or in such a public space before. She could do nothing but look down at her shoes. Which of course was no great hardship.

"Did you girls hear about Ella's big Christmas party? I remember those from when I was a little girl." Cynthia interjected, breaking the awkward silence that had fallen after Heidi and Gemma's sparring.

"Really? A party? Here in Lakeview?" asked one of the other mothers whose baby was currently drooling contentedly in her arms.

Heidi was intrigued. Any social occasion piqued her interest, especially if it gave her a chance to do a little good old fashioned showing off.

"Yes. The village Christmas parties used to be great fun. Free food, free drinks, music, lots going on for the kids. The whole town would turn out." Cynthia practically beamed at the memory.

"Where on earth is Ella hosting it? She certainly cannot fit the entire village in that tiny café."

Heidi thought Gemma had an excellent point and it got her thinking.

"I'm not sure actually. I remember they used to have people back to the house, but after her husband died, I doubt she would want to have anything there."

"I know where it'll be." Heidi interjected, deciding. "Our house. Ours is the only one big enough to hold the village anyway. We already have our own marquee and I'm working with a party coordinator now about where to place everything, but I am thinking red and green linen with poinsettia centre pieces accented with mistletoe, of course..."

The last bit was a bald-faced lie, but she was sure Ella Harris would only jump at the chance to save herself the bother of holding a messy gathering at the café.

Gemma kept her eyes squarely on Heidi as she continued to ramble off her imagined plans for the café Christmas party. She suspected instantly that Heidi was lying, but she held her tongue.

As the women chatted excitedly about the party, Heidi excused herself to the bathroom. As she snuck upstairs she quietly dialled Ella's number.

"This is Ella speaking." Ella's soft voice momentarily soothed Heidi. "Hello?"

"Ella, this is Heidi. I just heard that you were throwing a Christmas party for the whole village to celebrate your thirtieth year in business! Is that true?" Heidi couldn't come across as too eager.

"Oh, hello Heidi." Ella said in a significantly lower tone, her voice losing her friendly chirp. "That's right, I am throwing a Christmas party on December 22nd. You, Paul, and Amelia are certainly invited."

"That's great! Do you have a location in mind?" Heidi asked innocently.

"Well naturally I was thinking the café and -"

Heidi cut her off, ready to bite, "No, no, no. The café is way too small. I insist that your party be at our home. As your landlord, Paul would be only too delighted to allow you to do so for free. We will arrange the marquee, the tables, the heating, everything. Guests can use our bathrooms and your staff can set up in our kitchen. It will be more than enough room for the town."

The silence that followed was almost deafening. If Ella said no, she wouldn't know what to do. "And naturally we'll arrange to have someone in for the clean-up afterwards. Honestly, do you really want your café to be subjected to such upheaval, especially so close to Christmas?"

"I suppose you have a point and it looks like there'll be a lot of people…" Ella trailed off, Heidi's words obviously hitting home. "Are you sure Paul is on board with this?"

"Yes, we insist!" Heidi said as loudly as she could without potentially drawing attention to herself.

"All right then. How about you pop back in soon, and we'll discuss it."

"It's a plan. Chat with you soon, Ella."

Heidi hung up her phone, tucked it back into her trouser pocket, and strolled confidently back into the living room. Her smile was as bold as ever as she practically burst in anticipation.

Not only would she be hosting the most talked-about Lakeview party in years, she would be doing it in her own gorgeous house in front of the whole town.

Heidi lived for opportunities like these.

CHAPTER 6

*E*lla had spent the following week listening to Heidi's plans for what she proclaimed to be the "The Lakeview social outing of the century!"

Reluctant at first to let go of some of the reins to someone as disconnected from the essence of the community as Heidi (despite being born and bred here and the daughter of one of Ella's closest friends) she had nevertheless been impressed with just how devoted Heidi seemed to be. Truth be told she was actually a little relieved to have someone deal with the finer details other than food and music.

During the first meeting, Betty Clancy's youngest rambled on about tableware choices (pin tuck, red silk, extra long runners, etc.) while pouring through sample books from party planning companies. The joy she seemed to take from hosting this party was infectious as Ella grew more and more excited for the big day to arrive.

They ended the meeting agreeing on invitation layouts and the best way to distribute them. Debbie from Amazing Days Design, owner of the local stationery designer business, would be asked to design a specially commissioned invite incorporating Christmas and the café's thirty-year anniversary celebrations. Heidi would also ask her to create matching fliers for Ella to hang in the café and to distribute around to make sure everyone in the village knew about the party.

It seemed as if no stone would be left unturned when it came to this 'collaboration'.

THE SECOND MEETING felt vastly different by comparison. Heidi had been distracted and, dare Ella say, a bit dishevelled for her usually high standards?

Her nail polish was a little chipped, her hair appeared uncoiffed, and she looked as though she hadn't been sleeping very well.

Did this have something to do with the declined credit card from before? Ella wondered.

Despite herself, she felt a little sorry for Heidi. It had to be hard to keep up appearances all the time. While Ella couldn't care less about things like jewellery, Mummy clubs, or professional garden maintenance, she did understand that Heidi's self-created reputation was constantly at stake when she stepped out in public.

Nonetheless, Heidi ploughed through the meeting with few breaks for chit-chat. She made a couple of notes about changes she had made, and occasionally snuck in a remark about the price of items like lighting or the silk napkins. Ella could easily pick up that Heidi seemed to be avoiding a much bigger topic, but Ella wouldn't be the one to bring it up.

Instead, Ella had spent the meeting mentally planning out the menu. There would be café favourites from down through the years, mince pies as well as cupcakes decorated as Christmas presents, cookies in the shape of toys, traditional Irish Christmas fruitcake and pudding, and a mulled wine recipe that would make her father-in-law proud. Then in the evening, as the party wound down and music began, they would bring out mini burners so that the children and hungry adults could roast marshmallows to dip in chocolate.

While Heidi ended their second meeting with a long face, Ella felt practically euphoric. The thought of all the cooking ahead of her didn't break her spirit. Instead, it gave her life and purpose that she had not felt in years. She couldn't help but rush into the kitchen to chat with Colm about her plans.

Before she could make it to the back of the café, one of her staff members handed her the post that had come in earlier that morning. Mainly junk, she quickly sorted through it with fine eye for bills and important notes.

But a letter from the estate agent who handled her lease quickly caught her eye. The letter, official and to the point felt heavy in her hands and a feeling of dread came over her as she read:

Dear Tenant,

We regret to inform you that following a repossession order in favour of Allied Trust Bank in Wicklow, the property located on 34 Main Street, Lakeview will be ending its lease agreement with Ella's Cafe as of January 1 in the new year. We ask for your cooperation at this time.

CHAPTER 7

❄

A repossession order....

Ella's hands shook and tremored as she dropped the letter to the ground. Her lively, pink face drained of colour, and she forcefully held back panic as she attempted to maintain a sense of calm in front of her staff and customers.

Quickly taking her cane, Ella departed for her small office in the corner of the kitchen. She couldn't hold her anger in anymore as she forcefully slammed her door not caring if Colm or the other staff heard her. She needed a moment to think and to re-read in private and she did not want to be interrupted.

Ella had been aware of her lease changing hands over the years. Just two years before, she had been forced to make almost double her old rent when Heidi's husband took over. Now, despite the fact that Ella always paid her rent on time, it seemed like Paul had defaulted on the mortgage and the bank wanted to take the property back. It was an unimaginable, crushing blow.

She didn't quite understand. When he had taken over the building, she simply received a letter informing her of the change and where she should send her monthly payments. Why couldn't the bank just take her lease over? Why was she being put out? Unless a repossession order meant the bank was planning to sell....

Her mind raced in terror. Perhaps she could afford to buy the building herself, but the thought of the property price made her abandon that idea as quickly as it had come.

While Ella had managed to scrimp and save over the years, she never had much left over except to pay for her own mortgage and utility bills. A building like this in such a prime location would have to be on the market for way more than she could ever afford.

The party suddenly came back to the forefront of her mind. Momentarily, she had forgotten all about Heidi's planning books, and her insistence that the café celebrations be at her Lakeview mini-palace. Did she not know what her husband was up to? That he had been taking Ella's money but hadn't been keeping up repayments on the property?

She thought again about the declined credit card and wondered if there were serious financial problems behind all these largesse displays. Or worse, Ella wondered now, did Heidi know all along that Ella was going to be thrown out, and wanted to take pity on her by hosting the party? And was this why she seemed so distracted and evasive at the meeting today?

Tears began to flow from her eyes as she began to rummage through her desk drawers.

Grabbing a dusty brown folder from the bottom of a neglected shelf, she quickly pulled out a large stack of pictures. She had avoided looking at these images for so long, but now the pictures of her husband, her father-in-law, and former staff of the café down through the years were an immediate comfort to her. She flipped through the pictures of customers sitting at the same tables still in use today, ordering tea and coffee from the counter.

In one particularly striking picture, Ella saw her husband as a teenager mopping the very room she herself was in now. In the photo, Gregory's hair spiked and curled in a carefree way like his wide, toothy smile. His white shirt and black work pants were filthy, a trait she would later nag him about, yet he would never allow her to buy him new clothing unless they were completely destroyed.

Seeing her husband in these images calmed her, if only temporarily.

"What would you do, Gregory?" she whispered into the void, in hopes that an answer would come as easily to her.

The last photo in the stack was of the café, her beautiful sanctuary, lit up at Christmas time. The walls were full of sparkly tinsel, and holly and ivy decorated the display cases. In the centre of the photo stood the staff; her husband, probably at about twenty years old at the time, stood dead centre wearing a silly Santa's cap. Behind him, she spotted a much younger version of herself wearing a velvet dress and a joyous smile.

She remembered that day. It was Christmas Eve, and the staff were just about to leave to prepare for the town Christmas party. As they left, Gregory insisted on staying behind just a little while longer with Ella. He dimmed the lights as the last person left and spun on his heels. Then he turned towards Ella and walked towards her with an ease that made her knees shake.

She had been working at the café for a few months and had developed such a crush on the owner's son. His boisterous laugh, his ease with strangers, and his devotion to his family had made him quite the catch. Despite seeing each other almost every day, they hadn't spoken very often. When he had asked for her to stay behind, she really couldn't imagine what it would be for. But now, as he approached her, he did not have to say a word. Instead, he looked at her straight in the eye and swept a piece of chestnut hair from her forehead to behind her ear.

"Ella Ryan, I want to kiss you. Will you let me?" His question was so earnest, so sincere. It was passionate without being forceful. Ella had never been kissed before, but she nodded, speechless. He tipped her chin back and leaned his head to hers. His lips gently brushed her forehead first, and then her cheek, and finally her own mouth. The sensation knocked her breath away. And even now, all these years later, she found herself stunned, touching her lips as if that first kiss had happened to her right here and now.

Her answer to her earlier question became clear. Ella knew what she had to do. While she may not be able to save the Heartbreak Café from closing, she would be able to keep her promise to thank the town for their custom, and to celebrate her husband's memory.

She would not let all those great memories fade into the darkness with the rest of her business. She would instead throw the best Christmas party she could.

Steadfast and focused, she brushed her tears from her eyes, stored the eviction letter in her desk drawer, before heading out to the kitchen to find Colm and the crew.

Ella wasn't about to let another moment go to waste when there was so much to be done.

CHAPTER 8

❄

A phone began to ring loudly in Ruth's ears. She stirred but didn't roll over. She could guess who it was and why they were calling. She looked at the digital clock next to her reading 4:07 in bright red digits sighed, and picked up the receiver. But turns out it wasn't her agent, it was one of the locals looking for Charlie.

"Hello?" she heard him say brightly as she passed him the receiver. Even at this early hour, he was commanding and alive, unlike Ruth, who could barely peel her eyes open. "I can get there in about fifteen minutes. And don't panic I'll organise a courtesy car in the meantime."

As he hung up, Ruth mustered enough energy to roll over and face Charlie as he quickly threw on some jeans and a flannel shirt.

"Who was that, hon?" She could barely make out the words, but she was curious and genuinely wanted to know what was so important that it would rouse her husband from his bed at this unreasonable hour.

"Luke. His car is giving trouble and he needs to be in Rosslare to get the morning boat." A more recent addition to the community, Luke worked for months on end on Atlantic oil rigs so he wouldn't want to miss the ferry to his next destination.

"Say hi to Tara for me if she's awake," she mumbled blearily, referring to Luke's girlfriend who ran a life-coaching clinic from their house.

Giving up her LA lifestyle had necessitated lots of adjustments for Ruth and in the early days, and Tara had been a godsend. They were now no longer client/coach but good friends.

"Will do. I might just drop him down to the ferry port altogether rather than having to mess around with paperwork for a courtesy car, especially as he'll be gone for months."

She smiled. "You're a saint, do you know that? What would this town do without you?" She meant every word. Charlie was beloved by everyone—the local hero always went out of his way to make sure everyone in Lakeview was taken care of. She couldn't help but be in awe of his dedication.

"I'll see you later then. I'll try to drop back in the afternoon, if I can. I'm going to go give Scarlett a kiss, grab an apple, and let you get back to your beauty sleep." With that, he swooped down, kissed her softly on the forehead, and went across the hall to Scarlett's room.

Ruth lay in bed as she heard her husband's quick footsteps move from the bedroom, down the stairs to the kitchen, and out to the garage. When she confirmed that the car had left and the garage was shut, she quickly threw off her covers and headed downstairs to the living room where she had left her handbag and the script.

Mailed to her from her agent a few days before, Ruth had had little time to study it properly with Charlie being in and out of the house and Scarlett demanding more and more of her time. Now with the promise of some alone time, she could finally read and assess.

All she knew about the untitled movie was that her agent had called it "once in a lifetime opportunity." It was her chance to work with some of the biggest names in Hollywood, including a director who was well-known for working with former TV actors and making them stars. His last two movies had won Academy Awards. In Ruth's hands now was a script for his next big film, and they were practically giving her the lead role without even an audition.

Ruth dived right in. The movie centred around a young female factory worker who falls in love with the doomed foreman. It was a complete page turner as Ruth hung on every word and every direction written. When the characters fell in love, she did too. And when her potential part died, she burst into tears as if watching the scene come to life.

She was only brought back to reality when Scarlett appeared at the top of the stairs ready to start her day. It was now 7am and Ruth was back to reality.

"Hey there, sunshine! How was your night? Did you sleep well?"

"Mummy, where's Dad?" Ruth's heart melted whenever Scarlett called Charlie "dad."

"He went to work. He's had to go and save someone, but you will see him later. Right now, let's get you breakfast and then ready for creche. What do you think?" Ruth hopped upstairs, leaving the script and note from the agent still sitting on the couch to be further read and dissected later.

BY 8AM, Ruth and Scarlett had made it to creche just in time. While Ruth hated leaving her daughter there in the mornings, she hoped it would be the best place for her to socialise. Her daughter had opportunities to run around, meet children her own age, and to learn from the preschool curriculum. The creche itself cared for almost every child in the town under the age of five, so it was also an opportunity for Ruth to run into the other mothers.

Today, there were some different faces in the entryway.

"Good morning Ruth! How is Scarlett? I heard Charlie was out early this morning on a call." The owner, Mrs. Lane, approached her politely.

"Yes. He was. It was an early morning for both Scarlett and I, so don't be surprised if she is a bit cranky." Ruth watched from the parent's viewing window as Scarlett settled in to her routine.

"No worries about that. I'm sure nap time will help. Scarlett has a new classmate joining her today. Have you met Heidi? Heidi, this is Ruth Seymour. Her daughter Scarlett will be in class with Amelia."

"I don't believe I have had the pleasure," cooed the soft voice of Heidi. "It's so nice to finally meet you. I have heard all about you. Of course you're practically a legend around here!"

"Thank you, I suppose. But I'm just another Lakeview mum these days, and happy to be. Your husband owns this building, doesn't he?"

"Well, um, yes. I mean I um, think so...Honestly he owns so much of this town I can't keep track," Heidi's voice was tense. "Anyway I must invite you to the café Christmas party. You'll come?"

Ruth was thrown by the subject change (and indeed this woman's involvement), but quickly caught up. "Yes, Ella asked me to sing actually. I'm really looking forward to it. I have already memorised several songs and am rehearsing tomorrow with Nicky."

"That's wonderful! I don't know if you caught the address, but the party is actually being hosted at our house. So feel free to let me know if you have any questions about the event. It is, after all, going to be the party of the year!" As she said the words *party of the year*, Ruth could hear the strain and the nervousness in her tone. It was if Heidi was trying to convince herself that everything was going to be as great as she had made it sound.

"I'm certainly looking for — " Ruth stopped short as she noticed Heidi's attention was no longer focused on her. Instead, the other woman's eyes continually darted back and forth towards the front door where other mothers were gathering. She looked as though she was on the run and needed a place to hide.

"I'm sorry, but I need to go check on my daughter. I'll see you at the party, then?" Heidi's voice was rushed and forced. She didn't even attempt to smile or lift her gaze at Ruth. Instead, she kept her focus on that door and the steady stream of women and children entering and exiting.

"Yes, see you there." With that, Ruth watched as Heidi ducked into the classroom and out of eyesight.

As predicted, she was not alone for long.

Within seconds of Heidi's hasty departure, Ruth was being fussed over by the group of Lakeview mums. Some she knew from school, like Nina and of course her next-door neighbour Gemma, but others were usually a blur to her. All of them knew Ruth though, her husband, and her reputation. There was always incessant chatter about their favourite episodes, handsome co-actors, and award show gossip. Ruth attempted to keep up most of the time, but these ladies seemed to know more about her old life than she did.

These discussions merely highlighted how far away from that life she was now. Growing up, dreaming of becoming a star, it was all she ever wanted—to be recognised, admired, and fawned over.

But now that she was back in Lakeview, it felt less significant. A part of her yearned to still be in Hollywood so that she could be more than just a retired actress.

AFTER TANGLING with the creche mothers, Ruth needed a pick me up, and Ella's coffee and breakfast pastries were the only cure she could think of to get over her Hollywood homesick blues. But Ruth had learnt her lesson last time. Before she entered the café, she quickly surveyed it from her car for any signs of her mother-in-law. If Ita was inside, she'd have to do without. Luckily for her, there was no sign.

In fact, there wasn't a single soul in the café—a first for that hour of the morning that Ruth could recall. Tables were empty, and counter stools appeared to not have been used since the day before. The staff was at a minimum. If there were tumbleweeds in Lakeview, they would have stopped here.

Ruth seated herself at the counter while she waited for someone to appear. From the back, Ella quietly approached her. Unlike her usual, bubbly self, she seemed aloof and almost pensive. It was a bit disarming given that part of the café's enduring appeal was Ella's bright smile and hospitality.

"Hello Ruth. What can I get for you?" Her voice was soft and meek and Ruth could sense that she was tense and listless. Maybe the party arrangements were taking their toll on her, or more likely, perhaps Queen Bee Heidi was taking her toll?

"Just a skinny latte and a Danish, if you have them." Ruth eyed the surprisingly sparse display counter.

"I'll check. In the meantime, I'm letting every customer know that December 21st will be our last day."

"What?" Ruth was hugely taken aback. This news was totally out of left field. Ella's café was a village institution. There was no way she wasn't doing enough business to keep the place afloat. "Ella what on earth's happened? Why are you closing? Is there anything I can do?"

"Ah no, pet. It's just time for me to...ah... retire. This café has been my life for too long. I'm letting it go now."

"Isn't there someone who could take over for you and keep this place alive? Surely Colm would jump at the chance?" Ruth felt herself intruding but she was still in shock from the news itself.

"No, pet. He has his own plans. Anyway, let me go and get you that Danish."

Ruth sat at the empty counter looking at her hands. Well, this certainly explained the absence of townspeople at the café. If news of Ella's sad retirement was spreading, they were likely avoiding the place to let the woman go out in peace.

It was strange though to think of the word 'retirement' where Ella was concerned. To Ruth's limited knowledge, her family all lived away. Yes, she had all her stray animals but what would she do if she retired? Why would she sacrifice doing something that she loved so much to just make do with a bunch of cats and dogs?

The word 'sacrifice' echoed through Ruth's mind and instantly reminded her of that script sitting on the couch, and the decision that she herself would soon need to make.

Ruth had never been one to settle for anything but her dreams. So why now when Scarlett was old enough was she still sacrificing her career? Her mind raced with regret and dare she say it, remorse for all the things she herself had given up.

Ella reappeared with the coffee and the Danish.

"You look like you have something on your mind, honey." She broke the silence between the two as she passed Ruth the white plate and red cup.

"I was just thinking about retirement. It must have been a hard decision, but you're probably feeling good about it too?"

"Sometimes you have to make the hard decisions. Life is full of them. But once you know what your gut is saying, you have to just go for it. Head first. Even if it hurts or feels helpless, when it is time, it is time."

Ruth studied Ella's face. Her eyes had those soft, wave-like wrinkles around her eyes, and her hands were cracked—most likely from washing dishes and serving customers for over thirty years. This woman had devoted her life to her work, the work that she loved. While Ella Harris may have seemed broken, passion still radiated off of her in waves.

"You know what, I think I am going to take these to go," Ruth told her. "I have some calls to make, and I probably should get at it." She quickly grabbed her wallet and her coat from the back of her chair. She paid Ella and darted outside onto Main Street, her coffee spilling carelessly as she sped to her parked car.

She knew what she had to do.

Hollywood was once again calling and Ruth needed to decide once and for all whether or not she would answer.

CHAPTER 9

"I've been laid off."

Heidi stared at Paul across the kitchen table. "What do you mean you got laid off? When? Is this a joke, like that thing with the credit card? If it is, it isn't very funny, and I do not appreciate being teased."

Her husband just stared at his plate in silence. "Oh Paul," she lamented, trying to think back to anything that could have pointed to this coming. Was it the regional manager's visit that he had obsessed about? Maybe it was the closures of other branches throughout the city. Paul had talked constantly about how all these huge changes in the banking industry following the credit crash would eventually mean lay-offs and redundancies.

"They just didn't need me anymore," he said stoically. "I don't think there was anything I could have done or said." He seemed resolved but uncharacteristically quiet. She barely recognised the man who was so often full of life and laughter.

"How could they not need you? You're an area manager. You've been at that bank since you were twenty-one. This is ridiculous, Paul. It really is."

"There's more." His voice lowered and his head still pointed downward as he avoided eye contact with her. He reminded Heidi of a scolded dog, or one who knew that he was about to get in trouble. "We're in a lot of debt."

"We will just have to find you a new job of course," she continued, as if he hadn't spoken. "Our savings will hold us over until you find another, better paying position." Her voice changed to optimism. She needed to believe it, for her own sake.

"That's the thing Heidi, there are no savings. We used our savings money to buy all the rental properties, but it seems I leveraged them too high to make all the repayments and … bottom line is the bank is repossessing everything." He met her gaze. "And I mean everything."

"Repossessing what? The rental properties?" His silence led her to a stark realisation. "The house, this house? No, Paul! Not our home! Amelia has lived here since birth. We have raised her here. We have made a home here. I will not part with this place."

"Honey, I'm sorry. I really am. But I have been looking at the numbers for a while now, and if we want to hold onto this place, we have to make serious cuts — and fast. Miriam has to go. The renovations are off. We're going to have to think about selling a car or two in the meantime just to make the next repayment. I've been trying to keep things going for as long as I could by using rental income from the investment properties to pay off this place, but with the layoff …I'm not sure what to do now."

"You can't be serious!" She panicked. This house was her crowning glory. It was everything she had ever wanted. Now that, along with their entire lives, was under threat. And all the rental properties in the village, their hometown to be repossessed? She couldn't stand it.

"Listen," he said tentatively, "one of my old golfing buddies has been interested in this place for years. When I was let go, he approached me and asked me about it again. Maybe we should consider selling. The equity would hold us over for a while at least."

"Paul, no, please! Think of Amelia. We cannot do this to her. We cannot do this to *us*. We have to make things work without selling the house." She pleaded with him, her voice breaking as tears pooled in her eyes.

"Like I said, I've tried everything and there is nothing else we can do. We're behind on all the rentals and if we can't make the mortgage repayment, which we won't be able to with none of us working, the house will eventually have to be sold anyway. We have to let Miriam go straight away too. If we don't get a handle on things soon, we will not be able to stay on top of our bills for much more than two or three weeks with my redundancy package." His voice was firm. This was it. He needed to tell Heidi that. He needed to make her know that this was the only way.

"I just don't understand." As she sat, wordless in their beautiful kitchen, her husband gently kissed the top of her forehead, brushed the hair out of her face, and turned to leave.

"I know you don't." His resolve melted into what Heidi could only describe as guilt. It looked like it was overwhelming him. "I am sorry that I cannot make this perfect for you sweetheart. All that I have ever wanted was to give you and Amelia the world, and I have failed you. I am never going to stop being sorry about this. But you have to know that if there was any other way, I would have found it. It just … is what it is."

"Okay." Her voice quivered as she struggled to find an answer for his world-rocking confession. But Heidi really had no other words for him. She had no way to express the feelings she had without making it worse for him. This was going to have to be her battle. It would be too much to make Paul feel more guilt he didn't deserve.

With her one worded response, she was alone.

Paul quietly left for his study, closing the grand french doors behind him. She listened to his soft and slow footsteps as he walked to his leather lounge chair, a chair that had belonged to his father years before. He turned on the room's 40 inch flatscreen television, lowered the volume, and faded into the background.

Upstairs, Amelia was already in bed asleep. The long day of creche and then play with the nanny had worn her out, and she quickly fell asleep soon after Paul had come home from work. For the first time since her daughter was born, Heidi was grateful for the silence. While she had spent every moment thankful for the laughter, the shrieks, the cries, and even the occasional tantrum, having this moment alone to process everything was a gift.

Heidi got up to clear her and Paul's plates and dishes. As she passed the patio doors, the view of her back garden came into view. All those past barbecue and garden party memories, with Paul on the grill, Amelia in her arms, and friends and family gathered around her came flooding back like a cruel joke.

This was not the time to be nostalgic or attached, Heidi decided. This was her reality. This was her life. She had to accept it one way or another. Paul knew what he was talking about, and if he said the house might have to be sold, then it might have to be sold. There was no use trying to solve it.

The helplessness broke her down. It crumbled her heart and dulled her mind. She went about housework mindlessly. She picked up Amelia's toys from the living room, cleaned the kitchen countertops, and tried to hum along to a song on her radio as she prepared her clothing and accessories for tomorrow.

Tomorrow, she told herself, channeling Scarlett O'Hara, one of her favourite movie heroines, *I will awake from this nightmare. I just have to get through tonight. Tomorrow will be better and brighter. Tomorrow will be all right.*

CHAPTER 10

When Heidi awoke at six the following morning, Paul was already gone. It was a familiar sight. She rarely woke up to him still being home unless it was a rare day off or he was sick. He had always strived to be first in the office long before his subordinates arrived.

His absence when she awoke gave Heidi a bit of a jolt. *Maybe last night really* didn't *happen*, she thought to herself. She sprang out of bed, grabbed her robe, and headed to the bathroom in hopes of starting her day on the right foot.

When she came out and began to get dressed, the familiar voice of her husband coming from the hallway creeped in through the half open door. "I am so sorry Miriam. We never wanted this to happen. We never even saw it coming."

"I understand, Paul. I really do."

"As soon as we can hire you back, we will. We just don't know when that will be."

"I will really miss Amelia." Heidi could hear Miriam fighting back a sob as she said her charge's name out loud.

"Please feel free to stay in the house as long as you need to." *Or at least for as long as we're allowed to keep it*, Heidi thought mournfully.

"That's not necessary but thank you. I can stay with my sister until I find myself another placement. Would you be comfortable with writing me a recommendation?"

"Certainly. If there is anything else you need, just let Heidi or I know."

"How is she doing? Is she taking the news okay?" Heidi yearned to run down the stairs and hug Miriam. How lovely that instead of focusing on her ending job, she seemed to genuinely care about how Heidi was handling the big news. She wished she had appreciated her more.

"Not well, I'm afraid." Paul's voice had become a whisper as if he suspected Heidi could hear him. "She cried in her sleep last night. I knew it was going to be tough, but I could never imagine it would break her this much."

"I am sure she will recover soon. Heidi is strong-willed but always manages to land on her feet. Don't count her out."

"Thanks, Miriam. Again, if you need anything..." his voiced trailed off as they moved from the downstairs living room into a different part of the house.

Reality again hit her like a ton of bricks. This was her new life. No nanny. No cleaner. No manicures. No trips to Dublin to high-end stores. Heidi made a mental list of everything she would need to get done immediately from cancelling her next hair appointment to rescheduling the Lakeview Mum's Club meeting. She would also have to return the Christmas gifts she had purchased—the watch and ties for Paul and the endless amount of clothing and toys for Amelia. And all of her new clothes of course, including the beautiful Dolce & Gabbana dress she'd planned to wear at the café Christmas party.

The thought of Christmas without gifts or maybe even a home rattled her to the core. Being bankrupt was not how she had envisioned it. Luckily, Amelia would still be young enough to forget this Christmas. Years from now she wouldn't remember the lack of a tree or the missing presents. She would forget about the un-RSVP'd parties.

Ella's party came again to Heidi's mind. Amidst all this new stress, she had forgotten about her lies to the other mothers about her hosting it and her meetings with Ella where she had discussed decorative choices and how everything would be staged. All of that seemed like a million years ago now.

But suddenly, it dawned on her: Paul had been talking about the rental properties being repossessed. One of those properties was the very building in which the café was leased. The thought racing through her mind, Heidi hurtled down the stairs and into her husband's study. He sat at his imposing, wooden desk looking over his stacks of paperwork. As she entered, he barely looked up at her or acknowledged her presence. "Paul!" she cried breathlessly. "Are you closing down the café?"

"What? What are you talking about?" He studied her quizzically. She had never asked about his business in the past and rarely showed interest in the properties he picked up or the stocks he chose, other than to boast about them of course.

"The properties the bank want to take. Is one of them The Heartbreak Café?"

"The *what*?" he asked, still wildly confused.

"You know, Ella's place," she clarified. "Is it part of the repossession order?"

Paul looked down at his paperwork and shuffled through a pile. At the bottom of the stack, he pulled out a cream coloured, official looking envelope and handed it to her.

"Yes, Heidi. The café building is being repossessed. I'm sorry."

CHAPTER 11

The days after receiving the eviction notice were the hardest ever for Ella.

In the midst of attempting to plan the party with little help from a now absent Heidi, she also had to mourn the loss of her business privately. She could not bare to break the bad news to her staff, all of whom were depending on her to get them through the expensive Christmas period. She would have to keep the news to herself until she could find an appropriate moment to tell the others.

So Ella made a plan. While her staff discussed prepared the menus for the Christmas party and served their regular customers, Ella continued to plant the idea that she was nearing retirement. That way, she would feel less of a failure and more like this time was coming anyway. She had hoped the idea of retirement would be a softer blow than forceful closure. At least it was then in her power and not at the hands of some banker.

It started with an innocent lie to Colm as they started the baking of hundreds of snowman shaped shortbread cookies that would be offered at the party.

"I'll tell you one thing: I will not miss *this*," she commented.

"Miss what?" Colm didn't even look up from his work.

"Ah, you know," she said, pointing towards the ovens. "The hassle of baking the same thing over and over again, day after day. When I retire, I plan on having others bake me goodies." She attempted to make herself sound exasperated at the thought.

In truth, she loved the process. She relished in combining ingredients, preheating the oven, the scent of slowly baking food, and the occasional taste of fresh batter. It reminded her of her first days in the old kitchen with her father-in-law in charge of teaching her the ins and outs of bakery goods. It reminded her of her husband and his insistence that he try the first of everything she baked.

As hard as it was for her to lie to her staff, it was even harder to talk to some of her favourite customers. One by one, she would casually mention it. It started with her friend Ita who was a notorious gossip. She knew that if Ita caught on to her retirement, the rest of the town would be in talks of it for the rest of the week.

"Ita," she'd casually interjected as she poured her another cup of coffee, "Do you know of anyone around here who works with people in finding post-retirement activities?"

"Here in Lakeview?" Ita's wheels were slowly churning, Ella could tell by the gleam in her eye and the annoying urgency in her voice. "Other than golfing, I doubt it. The way we treat our senior citizens these da—"

"No I'm not interested in golf. Maybe volunteering or something like that. In any case I need to do something to entertain myself once I finish up here."

"I suppose so..." Ita was looking at her, the wheels in her head slowly turning and her voice now had a shake as if she was given a secret key. No doubt she was making a mental note of who in the town to break the news first.

As Ita left in her haste, Ella realised that this was the beginning of the end. This was how her "retirement" started. That word stung the more and more she thought of it. Her father-in-law would have never retired. Her husband would have put his foot down at the thought. She attempted to cough back the disappointment and anger at herself. But this was her only option, wasn't it?

. . .

COME NOON, the café had emptied. The place was uncharacteristically quiet for lunchtime. The only customers so far this morning had been Ruth, a few passing tourists, and a couple of the local teenagers sneaking out of school for a lunch run. She went in back to help Colm to prepare afternoon pastries, yet she had a feeling that the rest of the day would also be atypically quiet.

Her ruse must have done the trick. Of course the word had spread like wildfire. Ita wouldn't be able to resist telling everyone she ran into. No doubt she had stopped into Rich Rags, the boutique up the road, the hair salon, and several houses of her friends and neighbours.

By now, she estimated that at least half of the village had received some word that Ella was retiring.

In the quiet and the calm, she went out back to her office beside the kitchen as Colm quietly chatted and went about their day none the wiser. She should start packing things up, she told herself, but she instead decided to sort through the stacks of invoices and bills, time sheets and staff notes, and the couple of random menu mockups she had begun to compose for January.

She began to tear through the pile like a madwoman on a mission. Her rubbish bin filled up quickly with the bits of pieces she found disposable. Within minutes, her tiny workstation had become completely clear of the familiar and comforting clutter.

All that was left to do was to make a moving to-do list. There would be equipment to sell, things to move and staff to let go. It all felt so overwhelming and daunting, yet she knew she couldn't ignore it for long. Christmas was less than two weeks away and then she would have only another few days throughout the holiday period to get the place clear and empty for the café's end.

As her list began to add up, a knock came at the door. It was urgent, forceful, and familiar. Colm typically let himself in, but this person insisted on knocking. Whipping her eyes and clearing her mascara from her face, she replied "Come in." She kept her back facing the door. She would hate for anyone to see the mess she looked.

"Ella, when were you going to tell me?" The voice was firm, yet soothing. Ella swivelled in her desk chair, meeting Joseph's eyes.

Without speaking a word, she stared at him for a few seconds, maybe even minutes.

He looked tired and worn. She couldn't imagine how she appeared in that moment to him.

As time passed, she attempted to speak but was wordless in her response. She couldn't do more than to stare in his icy pools of blue irises and to study the way his greying hair shone in the desk light. Goodness he was a handsome man.

He waited though. He kept his hands firm on the doorknob as if he would need to make a retreat at any second. He too couldn't help but survey Ella and the way that she looked small and wounded. Her cast still on, her body bent over the desk, her pile of paperwork carelessly tossed in the black bin next to her. He wanted nothing more than to kneel down next to her and to hold her hand.

"Joseph. I'm so sorry." She began to sob. Her voice quaked and rattled. She had forgotten to tell him. She had forgotten that her old friend and most loyal customer should know first. Not that he needed to, but she had wanted to tell him. She had wanted to tell Joseph everything.

With her cries, he moved next to her, gently placing his one arm on the top of her heaving back as the other grabbed the chair next to her. He sat down quickly, facing her directly. His hand casually rubbed her shoulders and her neck.

"Ella, Ella. Please, please stop crying. Let's just talk. Just tell me what you are thinking, what you are doing?"

"What I am doing? I am not doing anything!" Her outburst took him aback. He had never seen her act this way. He felt as if he should spring into action, yet she was giving him no direction.

"But, I heard you were retiring and closing down the café. Is that true? If it is, it's okay…. it's exciting. A big step but you would probably lo—"

"No, Joseph, I'm not retiring. I'm being evicted." Ella hadn't planned on telling anyone the truth, yet here she was confessing all to Joseph. Maybe it was the way he touched her tenderly or how he faced her head on. She couldn't help herself as she went on to explain how she received the estate agent's letter, and had no other option but clear out. How she had lied to Ita and Colm to soften the blow on everyone.

"Why couldn't you tell everyone the truth? Maybe it would help you keep the café?"

"I just couldn't. Look at me. I don't ask for help. I *give* help. For thirty years I have helped people in this town find jobs, mind their children, sort through their marriage problems, take in their abandoned animals. Yet I wouldn't dream of asking a thing of anyone. Gregory would have never let me ask for help. He always said 'Our problems are our problems.'" Until she had said it, she had forgotten that her husband had always lived by the unwritten rules that those who stepped into the café were allowed to share their problems while those working in it would keep theirs private. It kept up a mystique and the charm.

"You cannot live your life like that. I know that you want to keep this café. I know that you would never, ever retire—much less to go take up *golfing*."

He was right of course—but that didn't change her resolve. "This is how it is, Joseph. This is how it has to be. It breaks my heart to have to close but I have no choice. The Heartbreak Café is finally living up to its nickname." Just as he was so certain that he knew her well enough to keep her from retiring, Ella was certain of what she had to do.

"Come on. Let's just talk this through. You could talk to the estate agent, find out if the bank might let you stay on as a sitting tenant or something. We can come up with a plan." His genuine want to help was admirable, but Ella knew better.

She shook her head. "There is no 'we' in this Joseph. This is *my* café, and *I* will decide how I want this to end." She looked away from him, not daring to meet his gaze, which she knew would be wounded by her stalwart rejections. "I'm sorry, but I need to be leaving now. The afternoon crowd should be coming through and I am a bit short-staffed." She slowly stood, her weight leaning onto her stick. He stood too, towering over her.

"I'm sorry Ella. I didn't mean to imply anything. I just want to help you. I want to make sure that you are okay and that this is what you really want."

"What I really want is to get out there and serve my customers while I still have any. Are you staying?" She couldn't help but to offer some hospitality for his troubles, but by the way he looked at her, she could sense that Joseph was hurt by her refusal to allow him interject himself in her affairs.

"No. I'd better get back to work myself. I will see you tomorrow though. And the next day. And the next. I will be here till the very end or until you ask me to leave."

He stared down at her as he placed his hand on her cheek. He rubbed his rough thumb over where her face had turned a glowing pink. Using the tip of his finger, he brushed a tear from the tip of her eye. And without a word more, Joseph opened the door, and walked back out to the café floor.

Ella stood in the dark corner of her office touching the place where his hand had been. She hadn't been touched there by anyone else in years. It was so personal and intimate that it took her several moments to recover. But in those passing seconds, she realised something else deep and real.

For the first time in decades, she thought she might be falling in love.

CHAPTER 12

※

That afternoon things did pick up substantially at the café. A busload of tourists arrived, and a steady stream of locals came through to give their personal opinions to Ella regarding her retirement.

"We will so miss you and your amazing quiches!"

"Will you stay in town?"

"Will Colm be taking over the café? He'd be great, but I don't know if he has your business sense."

"Who is going to take care of the catering for our parties?"

The last comment came from the village queen bee herself, Cynthia Roland. Since she was a young child, Cynthia had basically taken over the place with her know-it-all smirks and her insistence that she know everything about everyone. In comparison, Cynthia made Ita's gossipy and judgemental tendencies look like child's play.

Today, she was joined by the group of women who called themselves the Lakeview Mum's Club, but whom Ella had more often heard referred to as 'The Mummy Martyrs'. Flanked at both sides of Cynthia, they travelled in packs with their strollers and baby carriers. Each carried a designer nappy bag in their designated colour, a fresh bottle or dummy and a nasty attitude.

Time had not changed much from when these women were in

school and their accessories were backpacks, makeup cases, and an unsuspecting boyfriend from the football team. Now all married to successful men working in Dublin, the girls had no other purpose than to rule Lakeview with an iron fist. They dictated everything from what hairstyle was de rigueur at the beauty salon, which drink was in vogue, and which boutique was a must to visit for the latest fashions.

Dare to contradict them or refuse to play nice to their demands, and there would be consequences. Their refusal to shop in certain places in the village had closed several new business down. Ella knew it was a delicate balance, so she either played along or avoided them altogether. The drama, in her opinion, was way beneath her.

But today, there was no other staff to take their order or to set up high chairs for their crying, snotty children. It was all on Ella to make sure their needs were met to their impeccable standards.

She seated the group in the front section of tables closest to the window but more importantly far enough away from the other customers. The women preferred it this way. They could chat loudly while watching and judging the townspeople pass by the windows. Their children, on the other hand, could be supervised by Ella as she worked the counter and checked out customers from the front.

"It's such as shame about this place. It was always so … what is the word, um … charming." Deirdre piped up first, ignoring the fussy baby to her right as he attempted to grab at the ketchup bottle next to him.

"I agree, but what can you do to stop progress?" Emer was practically salivating at the thought of a coffee giant moving in. "I'm hopeful that we'll finally get that Starbucks this place desperately needs."

"Well I for one, will be glad to get an upgrade," Cynthia agreed. "This town needs to get with the times. No more run-down takeaways or discount grocers." She wrinkled her nose. "With the closing of this place, I can see the whole Main Street changing for the better." Of course, Cynthia had to own the idea that what the place needed was big businesses putting out what had been in place for years before her time as queen bee.

"Hear, hear!" Emer laughed loudly as she agreed with Cynthia's proclamation. The whole group cackled together as they discussed popular chains that should replace some of the older shops on the street.

Not a single stone was left unturned, or any business left unscathed as Deirdre even took notes on the girl's opinions as if she was the acting secretary of a select town meeting.

AFTER SEVERAL MINUTES, Ella headed over to take their orders. As she passed by the door, a hooded figure entered quietly with eyes focused straight ahead. The two collided, with Ella stumbling a bit. The other person caught her, giving Ella a chance to realise who she had run into.

"Oh I'm sorry Heidi! I didn't see you coming in." Ella hadn't recognised her either with her face concealed in an oversized sweatshirt that almost certainly belonged to her husband. From what she could tell, she was makeup free and her hair had been hastily gathered in a messy bun at the top of her head.

"Are you OK?" Heidi whispered towards Ella with her head deliberately turned away from the window, but Ella wasn't quite sure if she was referring to their brief collision or the fact that her husband's financial carelessness was putting her out of business.

"I'm fine. Just getting used to this cane. Why don't you take a seat wherever you can find one, and I'll bring you a fresh cup of coffee."

"Thanks Ella." Heidi quickly shuffled herself to the back of the room, finally settling on a place near the end of the counter. Her back was turned from the window as she studied a menu.

Ella made her way to the girls' table with pen and paper ready for their orders, but the girls were too distracted by the new entry to pay her any heed.

"Is that who I think it is? Gemma, is that her?" Emer ducked in towards the table's centre with her finger pointed directly at Heidi's back.

"I'm not sure. It's hard to tell without the nanny following her every move." Gemma whispered.

"Who does she think she is? That girl has no class." Cynthia refused to keep her voice down like the rest of them. She said it loud enough for everyone in the surrounding area to hear. "You think that her husband going bankrupt would make her a humbler person. Yet it seems as if her money was the only thing forcing her to play nice." All but one of the women nodded solemnly at Cynthia's seemingly deft observation.

"I heard they never had all the money they claimed to in the first place.The reason Paul was fired from the bank was because Heidi had put them into so much debt with her spending."

"That's not true, Deirdre. It's because Paul was caught stealing money, probably so that Heidi could spend, spend, spend on that spoiled little brat of hers!" Emer was going straight for the jugular.

"Gemma, is it true that they have already sold the house?" Cynthia sat up straight at the thought of fresh news to add to Heidi's tales of woe.

"Not yet. Paul says they're still trying to hold on to it."

"But if they have to sell the house where will they move to? Certainly not to our estate, I hope." Deirdre sounded absolutely frightened at the prospect of a bankrupt family moving in across the road.

"No, but I think they are looking for something smaller, maybe an apartment."

"AN *APARTMENT.*" Cynthia laughed maniacally at the thought of Heidi downgrading to a tiny apartment. The rest of the girls joined in, their laughter overtaking the conversations of the other diners that were not already eavesdropping in. All but Heidi had turned to pay attention to what the women had to say.

"I think that is enough, Cynthia." Ella made her presence known as she tapped the well-coiffed woman on the shoulder.

"Excuse me?" Cynthia seemed genuinely shocked to hear of anyone interrupting her conversation.

"I *said*, I think that is enough. I am politely asking you to keep your voices down so as not to disturb the other diners. We all just want to enjoy our food in peace." Ella stared daggers at the rest of the women. She was one hundred percent serious about her command.

"Well, oh dear. It looks as if we have disturbed the rest of the customers, what few you have." Her voice oozed with sarcasm and disregard. "OK, we promise that we will keep our voices down, Ella." She batted her eyes innocently at the café owner. The rest of the women snickered loudly.

"Cynthia Roland, I have known you since you were a small child, and while I have refused to step in before, I am saying this now—you are no longer welcome in this establishment. If you cannot respect my wishes or the lives of the other, respectable customers, then you will not be served here. Do I make myself clear?"

The girls stared wordless at Ella. One of their babies began to cry, but the mums continued to ignore her. All eyes were placed squarely on Ella and back at Cynthia. The rest of the café seemed to have leaned in to see what would happen next. You could hear a pin drop.

"Well, ladies, it looks like we will take our business elsewhere. This café has lost all charm and appeal to me anyway. Perhaps it is good that this place be gutted and replaced by something more civilised."

Ella burst in anger. "You four wouldn't know civilised if it slapped you in the face. I recommend that you leave now before I call Colm out here to escort you and your ill-behaved cohort out this door."

With that, she turned, picked up the coffee pot, and began to serve the rest of the customers who had sat in silence—some with their mouths gaping at the sight of her scolding the women.

THE GROUP LEFT without another word, slamming the door behind them. Ella watched from the corner of her eye as they struggled with their pushchairs and their fussy, irritable children. In front of the café window they remained, each loudly debating about what had just happened. Cynthia, in a rage, fled first away from the group and Julia followed suite, running to keep up with her. Emer hesitated, but eventually followed at a quick step.

Gemma stayed behind. With her toddler in her arms, she glanced back into the café as if she wanted to come back inside. Yet, after a few seconds of hesitation, she picked up her nappy bag from the ground and headed towards the lakeside car park where the women had parked their identical cars. Her head hung low as she disappeared out of Ella's sight.

The café remained silent for several minutes. All were looking to Ella to make a move or to say something else. In the air was a mix of fear, respect, and wonder.

Ella hated it. She had never kicked anyone out of her café before, and now with her final weeks upon her, she had made the place inhospitable. But while she wanted to feel ashamed at how childishly she handled the situation, she couldn't help but give herself a pat on the back for standing up to the bullish women. After all, what harm could they do to her now?

She began to circle throughout the café. At each table, she greeted those she had yet to say hello to and listened respectfully as each gave their regards about her retirement. Instead of impatiently answering, she instead chose to give hugs, free coffee, and kind smiles to those who seemed genuinely shaken by the loss of her business. This was the side of the village that she had loved and adored all these years.

As she reached the end of the tables, she could not help but notice that Heidi remained at the counter. One of the waiting staff had served her a cup of tea and a ham sandwich. Yet, she had barely touched her food or her drink. Instead, she kept her eyes towards the back of the room, away from the rest of the prying town that had overheard what the others had said about her and her husband.

Ella took a deep breath. While the last thing she wanted to do was chat with Heidi, she knew that she couldn't just ignore her for any longer. She could not avoid the situation.

Circling the counter, she placed herself directly in front of Heidi's stony gaze. She could instantly tell that the younger woman had been crying. Her eyes were muddy and her face had streaks from where the tears had flowed. Ella handed her several napkins to which she silently dabbed at her cheeks.

"Heidi, I think it's about time you and I talked about what's going on with our party."

CHAPTER 13

Heidi had heard almost every word uttered by her 'friends', but it was nothing compared to what she had been through.

For several days, talk had spread like wildfire throughout the village of her husband's job loss and their bankruptcy. Vultures had practically lined up to take shots at the formerly affluent family that was now reduced to pieces.

While Heidi had done her best to avoid the crowds, the gazers, and the gossip (and even her own family) it followed her everywhere. Whether she was dropping her daughter off at creche or picking up detergent from the local corner shop, there was always someone whispering in a corner about what had happened to them.

Even poor Amelia wasn't immune. Just yesterday, she had asked Heidi why daddy was at home in the afternoon. When Heidi explained that Paul was trying to get a new job and that this was a little 'holiday' for the three of them, Heidi's two year old began to use the word *fired* as if it was just something she knew had happened. Nothing was more heartbreaking than realising your toddler had to be a witness to other's insensitivities. Heidi couldn't take it anymore, so she took Amelia out, away from prying eyes and cruel mouths. Amelia's new childminder was Paul, who looked after her as he sent out CVs and made phone calls to old business associates.

Meanwhile, Heidi had taken it upon herself to handle everything else in order to shield Paul from some of the village talk. She picked up boxes from the hardware shop, sold her beloved clothes and shoes at a designer exchange in Dublin, and occasionally stopped in for groceries at Tesco. She listened to the rumours, the backhanded comments, and the laughs just so she could try and protect the two people she loved from being exposed.

But what had happened at Ella's just now was beyond compare. While most locals attempted to hide their contempt for Heidi and her family's situation, these women, including Paul's own sister, seemed to be openly rejoicing at their terrible situation. It made Heidi sick to think that just a week or two ago, she was sitting in their homes, playing with their children, feeding them snacks and goodies. Heidi was once apart of that group of women, and now she was abandoned and smeared as if their history never mattered.

However, as much as Heidi wanted to be mad at the rest of her former friends, she had realised early on that much of the town's maliciousness was perhaps her own doing. For all of these years she had cultivated this character, this facade, of a woman who had everything she could ever ask or desire for. She put herself on a lone pedestal for all those to admire. Who wouldn't blame these people for looking down on her when she faltered and failed? Who could stop them for feeling no remorse for the person who refused to share their good fortune and wealth but instead kept to their mansion on the hill?

Heidi had even gone so far as to lie and cheat her way there, and Ella was her most recent victim. She shouldn't have presumed to host the Christmas party at her house, especially now that there may no longer even be a house.

Now, face to face with Ella herself for the first time since word was out about her family's affairs, she felt the swell of regret and remorse for her actions. Here was a woman who just defended her honour to a group of customers who practically ran this town, yet Heidi had nothing to show her gratitude. She had nothing to give the one woman who had the nerve to put an end to the cruel comments and incessant laughter.

She was barely paying attention when Ella came over and gently touched her elbow. "We can go in back to my office if you want to get out of here."

Heidi could see that Ella was also upset, but she instantly realised that this woman actually felt bad enough for her to offer some more kindness. She sighed and nodded as she blew her nose into a napkin. Removing her hood, she followed Ella to the back of the kitchen where Colm and the other staff worked. The mood around her was sombre, but occasionally, someone cracked a joke, and the group would laugh together. It felt like family; it felt like a home.

Ella unlocked the office door, turned on the lamp in the corner, and pulled her desk chair next to the only empty one. The office was all wooden, almost like a den. No doubt that this office once belonged to Ella's husband. It had that feel of a man's touch. The vintage, worn desk had to be original as well. Ella had obviously wanted to keep as much of her family as she could in this place.

Heidi had realised that she had not known much about Ella's situation. She had heard several years ago that the café had once belonged to Ella's father-in-law and when he passed away, she and her husband had kept it going. However, Ella's husband died several years later, leaving her all alone to run the place. Heidi had never confirmed this, and was not about to broach the subject now, but she felt the guilt of not knowing this woman who had given her so much hospitality and loyalty better than what she had. And now her husband's financial mismanagement was about to take it all away from her. Just when she was about to celebrate her thirtieth year in business.

"Well, I think we are going to need to make some changes to our plans for the Christmas party in light of both our new circumstances, don't you?" Ella began, obviously wanting to be in control. It was a complete change from their other meetings when Ella would sit back and listen to Heidi ramble on about her opinions and choices.

"Yes," Heidi mustered. "I think that'll be necessary."

"Let's start with the basics—venue first. I think we are going to have to move the party here to the café. Space isn't a concern and seeing how today is going, I am thinking that some may be avoiding the party altogether. Not that it will be much of a loss to us…" She winked at Heidi. Even in this awkward situation, Ella was there with a bit of a joke and some charm to boot. "But the good news is, and I suspect you have heard, I will be retiring at the end of this month and will be closing the café for good." She emphasised the word "retiring" enough so that Heidi quickly caught on. "I will need to get rid of the furniture, the counter, and much of the decor and kitchen items in anticipation. With that, there will be much more space available for folks to mingle and chat."

Heidi nodded in agreement. She couldn't help but wonder why Ella wasn't angry at her for the café shutting down. Surely she knew her family was behind the end of the place?

"So while I am moving the party to the café, I still need you Heidi. I need help coordinating the music, the decorations, and the food. I will also need someone to help spread the word about the changes to the invitations. Can you do this? I mean, do you still *want* to do this?"

"Yes, I do. Of course I want to help you. I want to make this party the best this café has seen in years." She was earnest in her response, because she knew she owed it to Ella to make this party exactly as she had wanted. If that meant putting herself out there to the rest of the town, Heidi would be happy to take whatever flack may come her way from the busybodies and the judgemental gossips. This she would do in service of Ella.

"Well, Colm has planned the menu, we have already started baking, and now I will just need help deciding on decor. You're the best at this. What do you think?"

Heidi was taken aback by Ella and her kindness in still letting her be involved in the party, considering. But she was more than grateful to be of any kind of help. It was the very least she could do.

"Well, we're not having much of a Christmas this year, so I can certainly bring our house decorations. I have string lights, ornaments, trees of all shapes and sizes, tinsel, Santas—table decorations, you name it, I probably have it."

"Great. I think that would be lovely and I will leave it up to your taste to decorate. I should be mostly all moved-out by the twenty-first …" Heidi noticed the slight break in her voice as she said this and her heart ached for the woman, "so you will have all day on the eve before the party to put your touches. Would that work for you?"

Heidi was speechless. Ella had given her back some of her dignity and pride. She was happy to help for as long as she would let her. "Given the size of the room, I say we limit the music to just a keyboard and a singer. I hear that you asked Ruth to sing?"

"I think that would be an excellent idea. A band would be too loud and imposing here." Ella lit up at the thought of a more intimate affair, just as her husband and father-in-law had intended all those years ago.

The two continued to go through their mental to-do lists. Ella had taken out a notepad to make notes about their decisions as the two plotted and chatted about everything from keeping Ita Mellon away from the mulled wine to how they could best space out the guests' arrival so it wouldn't get too crowded.

"What about the Santa? You said we were going to organise a Santa to drop in at the end of the night." Ella's face dropped a bit, but Heidi could not sense why. Was this another sore spot?

"Well, I had a friend who was going to play Santa, but I am not sure if he is up to it anymore."

"Who is it? I can check with him myself if you would like."

"No, no don't worry about that. I will talk to him. If not, there just won't be a Santa at the party, but that's okay." Ella's voice was tinged with different kind of regret that Heidi couldn't quite understand. But she resisted prying more. The old Heidi would demand to know why this person would be so flaky about such a huge responsibility. The new Heidi wanted to respect Ella's personal life as she had respected her own.

With that, the two women stood, finished with their party planning. They both looked at each other for several seconds until Heidi made the move. She stepped closer to Ella and placed her arms around her in a hug. Warmth radiated off the older woman and onto Heidi. Eventually, Ella reciprocated, holding her gently with the arm not holding on to the cane.

"Thank you, Ella," Heidi said, her voice trembling. She felt herself move into a hug with Ella, almost as if her body had a mind of its own. "Thank you for everything. I'm so sorry for what has happened. Paul was stupid and neither of us ever imagined…"

"Forget it, please," Ella interjected quickly, obviously not wanting to talk about it.

Taking her cue, Heidi turned to leave. She began to put up her hood, but then stopped. Instead, as she reached the door back to the café, she took a deep breath, shook out her limbs, and tipped her chin towards the sky.

She was ready to face whatever was out there for the first time in days. She was ready to face the music once and for all. And Heidi realised something else.

She would ensure that Ella's Christmas party would be the best celebration the village had ever seen.

CHAPTER 14

❄

"Charlie, can you bring down my hairbrush with you? I forgot to pack it in my carry-on." Ruth was panicking about her flight to LA. After hundreds of flights, one would think she would be used to travelling by now, but she still felt the same jitters as she did on her first plane ride out of Dublin, decades ago. She still felt as though she would forget something important or neglect to do something she should have before she boarded. Travelling alone was not for Ruth.

In the past, she would be with an assistant, her agent, or one of the crew from her TV show. She loved having someone to chat with, help her put her bags in the overhead storage units, and lament about the awful airline service. But today, she was flying solo.

Scarlett would stay behind with Charlie for the first time. He seemed just as nervous as Ruth about the situation, but with creche to keep her occupied and Ita invited over for dinner, Charlie seemed to have every base covered. Ruth had even left a list of dos and don'ts for his reference. Now, all that was left was for her to say goodbye.

As her husband stomped down the stairs, hairbrush in one hand, and Scarlett in his other arm, he looked just as upset as he was when Ruth explained why she wanted to look at returning to Hollywood.

"This is my dream, Charlie. This is my *career*. I cannot pass up this opportunity. Anyway, it's just a quick reading and a meeting, and then dinner with the director and casting agent. I owe it to myself to just hear them out. Who knows, they may not even offer me the movie."

Her eyes searched his for a positive answer, but Charlie had made it clear that he wasn't crazy about the idea. When Ruth had given up Hollywood last time it was a conscious decision between the two of them. It wasn't made lightly or without reservations. They had spent countless hours reassuring each other that Ruth would be happy without the cameras and the flashbulbs.

But things had moved on. This was her opportunity, her last shot at this. In a year or two, she would be too old, too forgotten by Hollywood standards to make a go of it if she chose to. He felt that it would be unfair of him to demand that she stay. He would not watch as she grew tired, frustrated, and resentful.

So Charlie handed Ruth her hairbrush and watched as she got into the front seat of the car. Before she drove away, he leaned into the open window and whispered, "I love you. I love you. I love you. Be safe. Have fun, and remember to call us when you get in. See you in a couple of days."

Ruth flashed a brilliant smile at him, threw her arms around his neck through the open window, and kissed his gruff face. Blowing kisses at a dozing Scarlett, she said her first goodbye since she had made the decision to move back home to Lakeview. It was heartbreakingly painful, yet there was a resounding assurance that this was the right thing to do for everyone involved.

As she drove through Main Street and headed out towards the motorway, Ruth watched as the decorated artisan homes twinkled in the early morning glow. The snow that had been steadily falling the past few hours cast a bright halo over the treetops and on the black, tiled roofs. Several people were heading out their doors to begin their day, head off to work, or fetch the morning paper and breakfast.

At the airport, Ruth waited as the machine printed her ticket. Economy. It was all that she could afford these days with only Charlie's income and her lack of one. She had not flown economy in years. It was about a ten hour flight to LA, and she prayed that she would have a good, quiet seat mate to help ease through the journey. After all, there was nothing worse than being seated next to a chatty or obnoxious passenger.

She was more than relieved when she found out that she was in a row all by herself, giving her the peace and quiet she longed for. While she tried to doze, she found it hard to not feel the plane give and take or worry about the landing gear. Without an assistant to talk to, she couldn't be reassured.

To distract herself from her own voice in her head, she instead reviewed the lines from the script. She marked up the white pages with character notes, phrasing suggestions, and reminders or inflections. She whispered lines and recited some of the bigger monologues by memory. She had spent the last couple of days practicing with Charlie and bouncing off ideas with him. Even Scarlett became a captive audience as her mum worked on her body movements and cues.

Thinking of the family she left behind, her heart ached immensely. By now, Scarlett would have fully woken up and Charlie would be on his way to creche. He had taken afternoons off from the dealership so that he could watch their daughter full time. And he had planned out their afternoons with activities both would enjoy. He even talked about pulling her from creche early so that they could spend time at the aquarium in nearby Bray.

His excitement and enthusiasm for caring for Scarlett was all that Ruth needed to hear. While she tried not to count her chickens, she imagined what life would be like for the family if she did get the role. The movie would be at least 4 months' worth of work and filming both in LA and on location. Then there would be the intermittent press tours, premiers, and receptions that would come a year or so later. With all that may happen, Ruth would either have to bring Scarlett on the road while Charlie stayed behind or he would have to become a solo dad while she worked. Either way, no option sounded appealing which is why Ruth refused to bring up the possibility. She would cross that bridge when it came.

For now, she needed to focus on nailing this reading. While it wasn't exactly an audition, the casting agent and director wanted to test her out with a potential leading man on camera. It was a nerve-racking experience despite Ruth being a pro at this sort of thing. She counted at least forty failed screen tests in her time as an actress, and that didn't even begin to touch the number of cold auditions she had been on.

But she was resilient and moved on from each rejection. This time, however was different. This could potentially be her last screen test, her last meeting with a director, her last mailed script offer. This was her final shot to make it happen. Ruth was not about to let it just slip away this time.

She was ready.

The flight passed quickly as Ruth worked tirelessly to memorise and ingrain the words on the page. As she waited for her hired car in LAX, she felt the warm breeze of California once again and felt completely at ease.

Something about being back where the sun always shined made her journey feel complete and right. She smiled as she realised that today was going to be a great day.

CHAPTER 15

❄

The car dropped her off at the hotel first so that she could freshen up and change into more Hollywood appropriate attire.

Instead of the fitted shirts and denim skinny jeans she had practically lived in since moving back to Lakeview, she shimmied into a short, flared black skirt and a lacy black top.

Picking out her most daring red lipstick, she carefully applied her makeup and slipped into a pair of four-inch patent-leather heels. For the first time in a long time, she felt glam again.

She arrived at the casting agency's office with a good half hour to spare. Yet, she was greeted immediately by a caravan of never ending industry faces she had vaguely remembered or recognised, from producers to lighting experts. All seemed eager to meet her and ready to work. The atmosphere was electric as she couldn't help but feel like the star she used to be.

"Ruth, we're ready for you." The casting director peeked into the waiting area and waited as Ruth gathered her items and her script. The room was brightly lit with a white backdrop. Two cameras, one dead centre and the other off to her left as a profile, pointed at her stool. In the darkness sat four people. Immediately, she recognised the director, one of the producers, and the casting agent. The other was concealed, but she assumed it would be the leading male she would read with.

"Ruth! How good to finally meet you in person. You're as gorgeous as ever! How is life outside of Hollywood treating you?" The director, Jeff, was unexpectedly cordial. Typically directors sat in silence and the casting agent would do all the talking. She was utterly taken aback by this dynamic shift.

"It's, it's, well it's great thanks. I'm very happy."

"Well, we are very happy to have you back," the casting agent said in a bright, cheery voice. Already, Ruth was getting a great vibe from the set. "We would like you to read the monologue on page 63. Let's start at the second line down. I will read for the mother. Are you ready?"

Ruth flipped to the page, quickly scanned the acting directions she had given herself, and smiled. She had this.

"What would make you happy Annie? Would leaving the factory make you happy? Would marrying George? What do you want? What do you want!"

Ruth took a deep breath, stared directly into the camera and began:

"I want nothing more than what we all deserve. I don't want to work at the factory making peanuts an hour for nothing to show. I don't want to marry George or start a family with him. He's not for me. This life isn't for me. This is your life, mama. This is your dream and your factory. I don't belong here. Don't you see? I belong somewhere where the air doesn't fill my lungs with smoke and smog, or my prospects are a man without money and another man without ambition."

As she said the last word, she knew that she had nailed it. The silence that lingered after she finished was telling. The smile on Jeff's face was promising. The claps from the casting agent was a rare feat. She oozed confidence as she recited the next three selections from memory, nailing every cue and inflection that she had practiced.

"Thank you Ruth. That was phenomenal. We would like to test you with the male lead now. We just need an idea of how you two would work on screen now, if there's still any chemistry between the two of you. Troy? Are you ready?"

A voice in the darkness broke as her leading male appeared. "Are you, Ruth?"

Ruth sat motionless, unable to speak as Troy, her ex co-star and Scarlett's birth father, sat down beside her.

CHAPTER 16

Charlie and Scarlett spent their day in a state of bliss. With this being the first time getting his daughter all to himself, he couldn't bear to leave her at creche. Instead, the two had spent their day messing around the snow at the park by the lake, and at home playing doctor with her large collection of stuffed animals.

As she finally laid down for a nap after an action-filled day, Charlie began to prepare dinner. He knew this was an important night for his family. His mother had yet to spend more than a second inside this house since Ruth had moved in. Ita refused to acknowledge Scarlett, and she had rarely called Charlie on the house number. Instead, she only interacted with him on his mobile phone, or when he was either at work or making a trip to see her personally.

Her blatant attempt at freezing his family out had irritated Charlie, but he understood, to an extent, the issue Ita had with their situation. For some reason she had always disliked Ruth. As a teenager, she actively tried to persuade him to not get involved with her, even when they were just studying. She instead would attempt to set him up with one of the gaggle of her friend's daughters. Each failed to catch his interest and served to infuriate and frustrate his mother more so.

Ita's rage grew when she heard of their rekindled relationship, her pregnancy by another man and Charlie's acceptance of it. When she received the call from him about their engagement, she hung up without a word, too upset to say anything kind. Charlie had genuinely been hurt, but knew that it would take time and love. He would prove to his mother that Ruth was the only woman for him and that Scarlett was his daughter in all but blood.

Tonight would be the night that it all came together, at least he hoped so. It had taken some persuading to get her to come, but with Ruth out of the picture for the next two days, Ita couldn't deny any pleads for her company.

The doorbell rang at exactly 6pm. She was always on time, a trait that she had passed down to Charlie.

"Mum! Welcome! Come in, come in." He assisted her in taking off her coat and hung it in the hallway. Without a word, she surveyed their home. While not the largest in the village, it was modest, modern and tastefully decorated with art work Ruth had moved from her old place in LA. Every bit of the house had Ruth's touch and character. Charlie loved it.

"Scarlett, come say hello to your grandmother." The little girl walked uneasily towards Charlie, gripping his pant leg and hiding behind his arms. She was always cautious around strangers and Ita was certainly an unfamiliar face.

For her part, Ita just looked down at Scarlett and whispered a brief greeting. She then walked off into the dining room where she sat waiting for Charlie to follow.

"How have you been, mum? I haven't heard from you in a while." He smiled at her from the other end of the table. Scarlett sat in his lap, playing with a plastic zoo animal.

"I have been doing well. I repainted your old bedroom and purchased a new sofa bed for it. I decided there wasn't much use in keeping it as a bedroom."

"No, of course not. Where did you ge—"

"Where is Miss Ruth exactly?" she interrupted him, obviously wanting to get right to the point.

"She flew back to LA on an errand," he explained patiently, sensing a trap. "She'll be back in a couple of days."

"LA?" Ita said disdainfully. "Really? And what errand is so important that she could just leave her child in the care of someone who isn't a parent?"

"Mum," he said, his voice rising, "I *am* Scarlett's parent. I adopted her. My name is on her paperwork. I *am* her father."

"Don't be stupid, Charlie," Ita countered. "You know what I mean."

"I don't think I do, mum," Charlie said through gritted teeth. "What exactly are you saying?"

Ita pounced. "That child is not yours," she said haughtily. "She is not your flesh and blood; she's someone else's—probably someone as irresponsible and flighty as Ruth. But where's he? Where's *she*? You're here taking care of Scarlett while her mother gallivants around Hollywood and her *real* father is God knows where. *She is not your child.*" A sense of satisfaction washed over Ita as she let that out.

"Who said she was there for work?"

"She's *obviously* up to something—a film or a TV show or something. Either way, it cannot lead to anything good but Ruth getting everything that she wants."

"And what exactly do you think Ruth wants?"

Ita smiled disdainfully. "To dump her daughter on some unsuspecting, moony-eyed idiot like you. She knows you mean money and security and she just wants to latch on like she always has. Don't you see Charlie? You are her ticket out of here and back into the limelight."

Charlie stared at his mother, utterly disgusted by the woman sitting in front of him. He put down Scarlett and allowed her to walk away to the living room where a children's cartoon played softly. "You don't know her, mum," he said, quietly seething, "and you obviously do not know me."

"Oh I know Madam Ruth well enough," she replied. "And I know her kind. She's always been selfish and self-involved, and she will only bring pain to our lives."

"*My* life, mom," he said, his voice beginning to rise again. "There is no 'our lives,' not where Scarlett is concerned. You don't get to manage me anymore. What happens between Ruth, Scarlett, and me is none of your business."

"Where my son is involved, it's *always* my business."

He stared at her icily and shook his head. "Not anymore," he reiterated, stabbing a finger her direction. "I am tired of you talking badly about Ruth when you haven't even given her a chance. And for you to say that about Scarlett—that's my *daughter*—your *grand*daughter. I—" He slowed down, his voice shaking. "No. I'm finished. You need to leave."

"Charlie—" she said, her voice far softer now.

"Now."

"You're not serious," she said as Charlie got up from the table and headed for the door. He opened it, ushering her out. Ita got up and looked him over one more time. "I have no idea what to say to you anymore."

"I think enough has been said," he said coldly, his eyes locked on his mother's wrinkled painted face.

"Will I be seeing you at Christmas?"

"Will you be welcoming my entire family or just me?" he shot back. "If the answer is just me, then I think you know the answer."

"Oh, hello!" A sweet, unexpected voice broke through the anger radiating off the mother and son. Both Ita and Charlie turned to face the uninvited guest standing at the door. "I was just about to ring the bell. It looks like I have perfect timing!" A smiling Heidi stood at the doorway, handbag in one hand and a clipboard in the other.

"What are you doing here?" Ita was on the attack. Her voice was ready to rip into her next victim.

"Well, I was hoping to talk to Charlie and Ruth, but I can kill two birds with one stone. Do you mind if I come in? It's starting to snow again."

"No, you may not." Ita had completely taken over.

"*Excuse* me, mother," Charlie said testily. "Heidi, please come in. My mother was just leaving." Ita glanced at Charlie, and then at Heidi. With an audible huff, she walked out of the door, narrowly missing bumping into Heidi's shoulder.

Heidi smiled awkwardly at the dishevelled man in front of her as they stood in the doorway. Both had known each other for years.

"I suppose I should explain why I am bothering you at dinner," she sighed. "I'm sure you know that Ella, the owner of café is retiring—but that's not exactly the whole story …."

Charlie had heard the rumours that Ella was closing down, but had not heard the part about her being forcefully evicted until earlier that day when out and about around town. The news rattled him. Ella had always been so kind and supportive to everyone in this village. But in addition to hearing about Ella's retirement, the rumour mill was on high about Heidi's husband and their financial situation.

"OK but I don't understand …"

"Charlie you and I both know that Ella isn't retiring, at least not of her own volition. And I think I might have found a way to ensure that she doesn't need to. But I need some help. Do you mind if I come in?"

CHAPTER 17

❄

Half an hour later Heidi turned to leave, a considerable spring in her step. After spending a solid day going door to door and facing rejection after rejection, Charlie guessed that having someone like him on the case would certainly help ease her burden. He was intrigued by her idea but wasn't sure if it had legs. Well, he'd ask around certainly. Anything to help save poor Ella from a sorry fate.

Heidi grabbed several elaborately decorated Christmas cards from her clipboard. "Here, I am having everyone who contributes to sign a card for her. I already have a growing list of donors and if you could take another .… If you need more, just call me."

"Sure. I can't promise anything but …"

"You have no idea how much this means for the town, Charlie. I hope we can do this. Ella deserves it. Anyway, I'll be out of your way. Say hello to Ruth for me and I look forward to hearing her perform next week."

Charlie closed the door behind her. Scarlett had been blissfully unaware of everything that had transpired as she entertained herself with her zoo animal collection and the cartoons on the television.

Once she had been fed and the dinner dishes had been cleared and cleaned, Charlie began to notice just how quiet the house had been. Ruth had always been the life of the place. Dinners with her were full of songs and finger puppets. She often chased Scarlett around the house pretending to be the friendly tickle monster. The shrieks of joy between the two were what kept Charlie going every day. But in Ruth's absence, Charlie tried to remember just how life was before he became a dad and a husband.

He retrieved his mobile phone from his coat pocket. No calls from Ruth. She would have arrived hours ago, but he figured she was either too nervous or distracted to remember to call.

Two hours later, the phone remained silent. Scarlett had been put to bed hours ago, and the house was both dark and silent. Charlie sat up reading a book from Ruth's collection, occasionally glancing down at his phone to be sure he hadn't missed her. It was just as silent.

Swallowing his pride, he made the first call to her. And then a second one an hour later. Then a text: "Are you all right?" It remained marked unread and went unanswered.

He reassured himself that he shouldn't worry. She was fine. He knew it. She was simply at her meeting and had her phone off. Maybe she even forgot it and left it at the hotel. She was constantly forgetting her phone. This probably wasn't an exception.

But in the depth of the night with the hours ticking by, all Charlie could do was think about what his mother had suggested. Perhaps this life wasn't for Ruth after all.

Maybe she was made for important meetings with directors and agents and not for the provincial life he could give her.

Was this the end or the beginning?

CHAPTER 18

❄

The cold nipped at Heidi's face as she exited her car. She grabbed her clipboard, the envelope, and the Christmas cards as she hurried to the door. This was her third attempt at this house, but she wasn't about to take no for an answer.

She rang once. No answer. She rang again. Nothing. Lights were on in the house, so she did what she had done at two others: she used the internet and her growing number of community friends to find the house phone number and call it. She could hear the phone ring from inside and then someone quickly walk or run to grab it.

"Hello," she began in her cheeriest, most ingratiating voice, "This is Heidi. As I know you are in, I would really appreciate it if you could open your door for me. Thank you!" She hung up her phone and waited.

An older woman peered out as the door cracked a mere inch, enough for the woman to stick her head out. "For the third time," she scowled disdainfully, "we are not interested."

The woman's obstinance only enraged Heidi further. "Mrs McGrath," she pressed, "I understand that you said no the last time. But since we last spoke, I have learned from some very reliable sources that you patron the café for breakfast on a regular basis. You cannot make me believe that when Ella closes up shop for good that you will not miss her or her wonderful Irish fry-ups." Eric McGrath's mother squinted her beady eyes at Heidi, clearly both impressed and irritated at her salesmanship. "I'm are not asking for much. I just ask that you give what you can. It could be ten euro, twenty—whatever you can contribute. Your money will go directly to paying off the outstanding liabilities. Nobody but the bank will touch a cent of it."

Heidi then smiled at the woman who had only allowed her head to show. Without a word, Maeve turned, leaving the door partially open. Heidi didn't dare to take a step inside. Moments passed, but when she returned she handed Heidi a cheque that was more generous than she'd expected. Without a word, Heidi handed her the Christmas card to sign and left with a loud thank you.

Back in her car, she took out her notepad. With the McGrath's donation, she, with the help and time of Charlie, had raised quite a lot of money.

Based on the outstanding liabilities though, it would take a lot more than that to bring the arrears back into credit and make the bank lift the repossession order.

That number sank in. With only a week left until the party, the full amount seemed impossible. Heidi had hit up every single house in the village and had even ventured to nearby communities for help. Her persistence had paid off. Just like Maeve McGrath, most households gave in to Heidi's requests on the second or third try.

She used tactics like spying on frequent customers and having her mother Betty and sister in law Kim track down others for the cause, and Conor Dempsey, a popular local businessman (and another part of Heidi's family of sorts), tap up some of his corporate golf buddy clients. Her network had pulled off a miracle, yet they were still short for what was needed.

Still, Heidi couldn't help but feel satisfied. For the first time in her life, she had accomplished something on her own. And even more so, the community had actually turned itself around on her. While she was not looking to change her own reputation, she could feel that she was respected and taken more seriously than she was when word of Paul's job loss hit.

Her only problem was just that—Paul had little idea what she was up to when she left for the day. Heidi had promised she was out job searching, but she hadn't even attempted to find work. She was too busy focusing on this one task.

Heidi pulled out a map of the village. Little marks denoted homes, businesses, and the names of the owners. She had made a big "X" through the mark when a family had donated. And she highlighted those she had yet to go to or who had refused her. She was glad to cross the McGrath house of the list. It would be the last of this row to hold out on a donation. Even that itself was a major accomplishment that could not be ignored.

But there was no time to settle. With so little time left, Heidi had to practically double her outreach. Using her index finger, she searched and scanned the map for any other Lakeview homes or business that she may have missed.

In the western corner, a little way outside town she found the riding stables. Of course! The place was brimming with regulars to Ella's café, and the owner, Joseph Evans, was forever holding up the counter in there. In her eagerness to grab all of the donors from the village itself, she had completely forgotten about this potential goldmine.

Heidi sped out of the centre and headed up the hill towards the stables, situated in a woody area outside Lakeview. As she entered a small reception just in front of the old stone building, a young woman greeted her with a reserved smile. "How can I help you?"

"I am looking for Mr Evans," she explained, batting her eyes serenely in an attempt to look both innocent and appealing. "Would he happen to be in?"

"He is, but I am afraid Joseph is busy. Can I ask what this is in reference to?"

"I'm here about the café. I am a friend of the owner, Ella and am in the process of—"

A tall, grey haired man suddenly appeared in a doorway nearby. He looked at Heidi with concern.

"I'm sorry Nina, I thought I heard something about the café. I can take over from here." He gestured Heidi to join him in his small office. Quickly, he gathered up the maps and papers that littered the office chairs and desk. She sat in the first empty one she could find.

"Mr. Evans, it is great to meet you. I am Heidi Clancy, and as I said, I am here about the Heartbreak Café. As you may have heard Ella, the owner, is planning on closing the restaurant after Christmas. While she is saying that she is retiring, the real reason is that her building is being repossessed. But I believe that the Heartbreak Café can and must be saved. It is a vital part of our community and culture, and I am sure that your customers and staff—all frequent café patrons—can and will agree. At this time, I have raised a substantial amount of money to clear the arrears and stave off the repossession order, but it is not yet enough. And that is why I am here."

Heidi paused, waiting for the man to say something. Instead, he just stared at her with his hands cupped in front of his mouth, concealing his emotions.

"I understand that times are hard and that you may not be able to give much, but if you are able, I am accepting donations which will be used to pay off the arrears."

Again, Heidi waited, but the man just looked directly at her.

"So would you be willing to contribute something to help save the café?" She had exasperated her entire sales pitch. Yet this man just sat there as if he was a stone gargoyle passing judgement.

"What was your name again?"

"Heidi Clancy.

"Can I ask you a question, Ms. Clancy? Do you happen to know the owner of the building—the person who is responsible for evicting Ella from the café she has run for almost thirty years?"

Heidi sank in her chair. She sighed. She had imagined this happening several times, yet no one had yet to ask her about her conflict of interest. And now, she was found out. While she had every intentions of saving the café and none at all for improving her family's financial situation, she knew how this had to look to someone in the know.

"Yes, I do. And yes Paul Clarke is my husband, but please allow me to explain..."

"I am not sure there is much explaining that can be done here. Despite Ella's dutiful payment of rent, your husband is underwater on the property. And here you are, trying to get the community to chip in and pay your debts for you. While I have never seen this kind of scheme before, I have to admit it's a good one. You almost had me believe that this *was* charity." Joseph's eyes burned bright in anger. He leaned forward, practically hovering over his desk.

"I know how this appears. I do. But please believe me when I say that this have nothing to do with my family's situation. My husband lost his job at the bank...he'd got behind on the repayments of some of portfolio... I had no idea how awful the situation was or that other people would be affected. Please believe me. I am here because Ella is my friend, and I believe that she deserves to keep the café. She has been good to me. She has defended me when no other would even glance at me. She has become my friend, and I cannot imagine this town without her or the café. This is why I am here, if you want to know the truth. I am here to make this right."

Heidi's voice was firm, yet sincere. While she knew there was little chance in him believing her, she had to try to explain her side of the story. At this point, she did not care what he thought about her.

"Does Ella know that you are doing this?"

"No. At least, I don't think so. Every donor I have found so far has been told not to say anything, because I don't know if we'll have enough..."

"And how much exactly have you raised?"

She momentarily let her guard down and let her pride shine through. "Approximately a quarter of the outstanding arrears in little under a week."

Joseph nodded, clearly impressed by her accomplishment. "And how much more do you need to stave off the repossession order?"

Heidi held her breath as she whispered the number to him.

"And does your husband know that you are doing this?"

"No. This is my cause, not his."

After a very long pause, Joseph spoke. "I'm sorry, I think I understand why you are doing it and I admire that. But I very much doubt that you can achieve what you need to in such a short space of time."

Heidi sighed. He was right of course. She supposed that deep down she'd realised that all along. But she'd still felt she needed to do *something*. Be it out of pride, guilt or god forbid the goodness of her heart.

"However as I said, I admire your ambition and clearly you are a determined lady." Then he paused his eyes twinkling. "But I wonder if you could use some of that same determination to do something for me…"

CHAPTER 19

❄

"Paul? Can you bring down all the boxes labelled 'Christmas Indoor Lighting?'" Heidi shouted loudly at her husband who was currently rummaging around in their attic. "Oh. And grab that blue bucket of baubles underneath the box of summer clothes."

She impatiently watched as her husband brought box after box down from the attic. Each one was full to the brim with holiday decorations they had planned to donate or leave behind now that a move from their beloved house was all but finalised.

Exhausted, Paul looked at her as if she was crazy and then when she'd finally finished her list of requests, he retreated to his study.

She did not blame him for not understanding why she was still so heavily involved in the café Christmas party. After all, their entire lives were now in boxes and her going through some of the most useless ones seemed pointless considering the coming and goings of their life.

They'd decided to sell the house to Paul's interested friend and use any profit from the sale to pay off some of the outstanding debt, which was also where much of Paul's redundancy package was going.

The sale was going through at the moment and after Christmas, the family were moving in with Heidi's parents until they found something else, perhaps something small to rent.

Betty and Mick had been insistent, although Heidi had nearly died of shame having to admit to her folks and the entire Clancy family the full extent of her and Paul's situation.

But to be fair, her siblings and in-laws were wonderful, Kim even going as far to offer Heidi a job in her beauty products company. "Clearly you're a born saleswoman," her sister in law had joked, referring to Heidi's efforts thus far at raising money for the café, "and I could really do with another rep for the Dublin area."

Though it still broke Heidi's heart to see her beloved home sold out from beneath her, she knew that there were worse things in life.

So first thing in the New Year, the family would be completely moved out and Heidi would be going out to work for the first time in her thirty-odd year life.

Now, seeing the brown boxes all taped up with labels like 'sell ASAP' or 'from Amelia's nursery' depressed her to the core. While she had begun to accept a lifestyle that wasn't all glitz and glamour, going cold turkey with her savings had been traumatic enough. Yet she knew she would get over it in time, with the help of family, friends, and a new purpose.

But with the café Christmas party less than twenty-four hours away, Heidi couldn't help but feel a bit out of sorts. She truly had no idea how her family would survive all these changes. She had hoped that Paul would quickly find a job in his old industry, but he'd had no luck securing interviews or even meetings with former colleagues.

Instead, he had spent hours upon hours in his office working on business plans for his remaining investments. While she was doing her utmost to put Ella's building back in the black, he was content working on something of his own.

He seemed to actually enjoy the hands-on aspect of managing the properties, instead of from afar, which was what had got him in to trouble in the first place. At dinner several nights ago, he'd even casually mentioned something about perhaps trying to do something in rental property maintenance. While he managed to keep his optimism at bay, Heidi could feel hope coming back to him.

It seemed that both Heidi and Paul had new roles to fill now, but while Paul had kept her up to date on his plans, she neglected to fill him in on her stint as a small business activist and fundraising mogul.

She wasn't sure how he would take it. Her saving the café was ultimately at his expense, and she didn't know how he would feel if she knew she'd been basically asking the entire community for a handout to pay back his financial misadventures.

It would be a blow to any man's ego.

Early on, she had made a plan to keep her actions a secret. Firstly, she had all correspondence from the bank regarding the building forwarded to her, and she had been keeping the local estate agent up to date on her efforts so he wouldn't unexpectedly sell the property without her knowledge.

All this and still she wasn't sure that it would be enough to save Ella's business. Especially given Joseph Evan's request last week.

Yet she had come so far, and she was not about to give up just yet. With one day until the party, she just needed to hold Paul off for twenty-four more hours by keeping him out of town (where someone might mention Heidi's door to door soliciting) and more importantly away from the party preparations. The truth was she didn't know if Paul would go to the party at all.

She knew he wasn't much in the mood for celebrating and she guessed that the last thing he wanted was to face the community in the wake of his financial disgrace.

After Heidi had finished loading the car, she began to make her retreat. "Okay, I got what I needed," she called back to her husband, "and I'm taking Amelia to the café with me. We'll be back around eight. Do you need me to grab anything while I'm in town?"

Paul peeked his head out of the office as Heidi zipped up Amelia's coat. "Actually, I was thinking about going down with you. I'd like to talk to Ella ... maybe try to explain. And I'm sure you all will need help with decorating the place."

"No, no we're totally fine! Ella's son is there and Colm too - that's more than enough people to help with the decorating." She tried her best not to snipe at him or to look him directly in the eyes. "Anyway, this is for Ella's big night and I'm not sure now is the best time. It might only drag her down."

"Oh, OK. You're right of course. For what it's worth, tell her I'm sorry anyway, OK?"

"Sure. I'll give you a full report when I get back." She kissed Paul, scooped up Amelia, and headed out the garage door. She briefly turned to smile and wave after seating her daughter in her carseat.

Paul still watched, somewhat dazedly from the doorway and she felt sorry for him having to hide away from everyone during such a big community gathering.

Heidi gulped, realising that tomorrow night she was just about to do the opposite of hiding away. The whole village would be at the party, and some of them would be whispering, pointing and looking down their noses at her.

Yet, she realised taking heart, as she drove over the stone bridge and towards the café, snow gently falling around them, that there would be many others, including Ella that would empathise with her family's woes and go out of their way to include in the celebrations.

She was one of Lakeview's own after all.

CHAPTER 20

❄

*E*lla waited for Heidi in her completely empty café.

In all her life, she had never seen the place without the signature picture frames on the wall, old Singer table in the corner, or the cherry red bar stools at the counter. Colm and the staff had done much of the work for her, allowing her to supervise from a chair in the corner.

After the furniture was gone, the few folding tables and chairs Heidi had borrowed from the community hall had arrived, just as Joseph walked through the door.

As he had promised, Joseph still visited Ella at the café every single day. Today would be no exception as he helped her son Dan and the remaining staff unfold and unbox the supplies, and even supervised the laying out of the empty trays to be filled tomorrow.

The place buzzed with both anticipation and sadness. Tomorrow would sadly be the last time her staff gathered here, and Ella was not about to waste it. She had already begun to hand out cards with heartfelt thanks and letters of recommendation to those she knew would want to move on quickly. There were hugs and memories shared while old and new joked and sang cheery Christmas carols to help keep spirits up.

Whenever she felt herself get emotional, Ella reminded herself that this party was exactly how her father-in-law and husband would have wanted things to end.

This ode to her loved ones was not only her way of getting closure but also a way to honour the community in this village that made this café what it was—a Lakeview institution. Therefore, everything would be perfect—from the mulled wine to the last mince pie. She wouldn't take anything less.

Just as she began to supervise the kitchen cleanup crew, Heidi walked in holding Amelia's hand and a large blue bucket in the other.

"Perfect weather for a Christmas party, isn't it?" Her cheeks were bright pink from the chill in the air, but her eyes were lit up with energy. It was a complete change from the run-down, beat up Heidi that came into her café barely two weeks prior.

"Let me help you with that Heidi," Joseph grabbed the heavy container from her arms and set it down in the corner.

"I didn't know you two knew each other?" Ella couldn't imagine where Heidi could have met Joseph.

"Oh, I know Joseph from ….when one time Paul and I were thinking about getting Amelia a pony. He gave us great advice." She was totally floundering with her lies, but she couldn't give away anything. Either way, it didn't seem as if Ella was paying too much attention. Her gaze was set on Amelia in her cute festive outfit.

"Would you like to help me taste some Christmas cookies pet? I think there are some Santa ones with your name on them." Amelia giggled excitedly as she rushed to Ella's side. They disappeared in the back, leaving Joseph and Ella alone to sort through the decorations and supplies.

As the two leaned down to untangle the ropes of lighting, Joseph whispered, "Are we all set for tomorrow?"

"Yes, I have everything prepared. Just be ready at eight sharp. Santa is supposed to arrive at that time, which I think it would be just the right moment."

He nodded in agreement, and the two set off on their decorating.

. . .

BY THE TIME the group had finished, the café was completely illuminated by large, white bulbs that arched from the wooden ceilings. Garlands of silver red and gold intertwined along the wall lamps, and a medium sized picture-postcard fir tree, adorned with Heidi's finest designer decorations, sat in the far corner where a keyboard, microphone, and Santa's chair would be set up.

As the last twinkling bauble was hung with care, Ella reappeared with Amelia in hand.

"So pwetty!" Amelia ran to the centre of the room, excitedly jumping and spinning under the sparkling lights and the shadow of the tree.

Ella was similarly entranced. "Oh it looks beautiful Heidi, you've done an amazing job." She took the younger woman's hand. "Thank you, I mean that. I know you and Paul will both go on to better things."

"No, thank you." Heidi was overcome with emotion and gratitude for this lovely woman who by rights should hate her guts. "Come on, Amelia," she sniffed. "We better get going if we want to get a good night's sleep. I have a feeling that a very special visitor might be here tomorrow and we want to get our beauty rest for it." She turned again to face Ella and Joseph. "See you tomorrow at around four OK? Ruth and Nicky will be in at five to set up the music. And the party will officially begin at six. I think that gives us just enough time to get everything ready. But if you need anything else, just let me know!"

She quickly grabbed her empty containers and Amelia's coat before taking off, leaving only Joseph and Ella in the café. It was almost silent save for the Dean Martin festive classics CD playing softly in the background.

For a long moment, the two stared at each other, unsure of what to say.

Joseph went first. "Yes, the place indeed looks beautiful. It reminds me of how it all used to be." He looked around the café noting just how so much and so little had managed to change since he first moved to the village.

"It does," Ella said, blushing. She couldn't seem to feel anything but uncomfortable in Joseph's presence now, especially given her recent realisation. "It really does." She sighed and turned towards him. "Listen," she began apologetically, "I wanted to talk to you. I've been meaning to apologise for the way I acted the day I told you about the eviction."

Joseph shook his head. "Let's not talk about this tonight," he reassured her. "Let's focus on what is happening here and now."

"What's happening here and now?" Ella looked up into his eyes that now practically danced beneath the twinkling lights.

"Us." Joseph leaned down, gently kissed her forehead, and then slowly walked towards the door. She remained motionless, too stunned to speak. "See you tomorrow, Ella."

Ella stood standing alone in the centre of the room for a very long time after that.

It was as if her whole life had flashed back and then forward with one innocent kiss.

It reminded her of what she had and what she had lost.

Yet in the silence of the empty café, she couldn't help but wonder if this was what she actually had wanted all along.

CHAPTER 21

"Charlie? *Charlie!* Are you ready? We are *so late*. Ella is going to kill me."

Ruth darted down the stairs while pinning her hair into a tight bun. She grabbed her black velvet Louboutin heels and quickly tossed them on.

"Charlie!" she yelled again. "Let's go!" She hated to be late, and at ten minutes to five, she feared that she would have no time to warm up her vocal cords or to practice with the keyboard player.

"Go on ahead without us if you like," Charlie replied. "We'll take the van." His voice wasn't rushed; in fact, it was perfectly even. His lack of urgency irritated Ruth—not because he refused to be ready in time, but because he had been acting like this since she got back from LA.

She could still feel his coldness as she'd walked through the door from the airport, bags still in hand. Scarlett had run to greet her with a hug and to ask if she had brought anything back for her, but Charlie remained in the kitchen pretending to be preoccupied with dinner. When she found him, he walked up to her, rubbed her shoulders, and kissed her cheek—hardly the effusive welcome she had pictured.

The next few days were more of the same. Charlie had thrown himself into his work by volunteering to pick up an entire week's worth of daytime sales shifts and be night-time mechanic on call duty.

When Ruth did see him, he practically ignored her and instead focused on Scarlett, or another part of the house, like the broken step or the frosty path out front.

Ruth had so much to tell him about her trip, the reading, and her meeting, yet he never gave her the chance to fully talk about it. When she announced that she had been offered the part, he interrupted her, changed the subject completely, and then excused himself to prepare for work. She never got to explain herself or the situation.

And with the way their relationship was going, she was afraid that whatever was going on in Charlie's mind would eventually boil over. She just hoped it wouldn't be tonight. Tonight she would be returning to her roots. She wasn't just going to be Charlie Mellon's wife or the girl that used to be in that TV show. No, instead, she was stepping out as someone entirely different. And she planned to announce it during her set.

Before heading out the door, Ruth checked herself in the mirror one last time. Her red satin dress looked fabulous on her lightly tanned skin. She smiled at herself while repeating *"This is going to be a great night!"* over and over again in her head. She just wished she believed her own mantra.

Ruth sped towards the café, eager to try to make it at least within ten minutes of when she said she would. She parked her car and straightening her low-cut figure-hugging dress, quickly ran inside.

Once through the door, she gasped. The café that she had known and loved all these years had been completely transformed by the dimmed lights and the glittering tinsel. A tree straight out of a magazine spread stood at the very back of the room. A musician in a suit and tie, Colm's partner Nicky, waited next to it, checking his watch.

"What. Are. You. Doing. Here." The direct, pointed voice cut through Ruth like a knife. She spun on her heel to face it.

"Ita, hello. How are you doing?" She plastered on a fake smile, wide enough that her teeth showed like an animal ready for a fight.

"What am I doing here? I am Ella's friend, a loyal member of this community. I have every right to be here." The contempt in her mother in law's voice was dripping and Ruth could tell by the way Ita sauntered slowly and feebly over to her that she had already been drinking the mulled wine.

"Ella asked me to perform tonight, so I am here and happy to help."

"And how much did you demand to be paid?"

"Excuse me?" Ruth wasn't completely sure where she was going with that.

"Don't play stupid with me, madam. I know that you would do just about anything for money." Ita's voice echoed around the nearly empty room, yet Ruth could spot some of the volunteer staff's gaze directly pointed at two, watching and waiting for what would happen next.

"I'm sorry, but I need to speak with Nicky now so I can warm up and be ready for when the party begins." It was all Ruth could do to compose herself. She walked away from Ita, leaving her standing alone in the centre of the room clutching her glass of mulled wine and grinning ear to ear.

By the way she was smiling, Ruth could tell that Ita felt like she had won.

She distracted herself with her music partner's notes. He handed her a stack of sheet music and played a bit of every song to give her an idea of what key would begin each one. He then assisted her by playing a couple of vocal warmups. Ruth was ready, but she had yet to spot Ella for further direction.

While Nicky went outside to take a phone call, Ruth ran to the back in hopes of finding the hostess there. Unsuccessful, she found a different volunteer placing cookies on the trays. He pointed her to the closed office door in the far corner of the kitchen.

Ruth knocked and let herself in. Inside, Ella sat in tears, her head in her hands, Heidi kneeling alongside her.

"I'm so sorry," Ruth blushed, mortified. "I should have waited for you to tell me to come in." She looked over at Heidi, who had already exhausted a box of tissues.

"Nonsense," Ella insisted, collecting herself. "Come on in. I'm just a little emotional today. I thought I would be ready to say goodbye, but here I am, blubbering like a baby."

Ruth took a seat next to the older woman and reached over to pat her on the back of her deep jade velvet dress. "It's all right," she said consolingly, "I completely understand. I mean, you're losing a part of you that you never thought you could give up. That's tough."

"She's right," Heidi said, wiping her own eyes. "This place has been yours for so many years, and…" She trailed off and shook her head, composing herself. "But today is a new day Ella. It's not an end; it's a beginning."

Ruth thought this was a little bit rich coming from Heidi Clancy, considering. She'd heard about her fundraising exploits and wasn't entirely sure how to feel about them. Yet she seemed genuinely concerned for Ella now.

"You're both right," Ella smiled. "I just thought I had come to terms with it by now. I don't know. I suppose it's silly but I've never been one to give up on a desperate case. My cats and dogs will tell you that."

Ruth smiled and handed her a fresh tissue from her clutch. She patted her shoulder reassuringly. "No one would ever think that you're silly," she said.

"Yes, you mean everything to this town. *Every*thing. You'll see tonight." Heidi winked at Ruth, who had no idea what to decipher from that. Had her fundraising come good after all? She couldn't see how…

"Come on. It's almost six, and I already saw a line outside waiting for you to open the doors," Heidi urged Ella. "Let's go out there and throw the best damn Christmas party this place has ever seen."

Ella nodded, smiled, and dabbed her eyes. She used a small pocket mirror to check the rest of her makeup and then boldly opened the door. "Colm," she said, "are we ready?"

"'We are sweetheart," he said, smiling. "Are you?"

Ella dabbed her eyes one more time and straightened her dress. "Yes," she replied, smiling through her tears.

It was time to say goodbye.

CHAPTER 22

❄

A few volunteers gathered to the front of the café as people began to stream in, each batting the light snow off of their shoes and coats before entering.

Ella welcomed them all with a warm hug, and Heidi passed out mince pies and glasses of mulled wine. The guests then dispersed around the room, each stopping to look at the old photos from down through the years that Ella had put on display.

Love and friendship filled the small space within minutes. It was beyond Ella's wildest expectations. Every corner was packed with customers—friends. Everyone had kind words to say about the café—a moment or a memory they wanted to reminisce about.

When Paul tentatively arrived with Amelia a few minutes later, he spotted Heidi and waved at her from across the crowded room. She smiled back, proud that he had in the end decided to show his face, but her face quickly fell as she spotted the Lakeview Mum's Club following closely behind.

Cynthia was in the lead (of course) and her husband towing ten steps behind as if he was dragged on a leash. Deirdre and Emer quickly followed, obviously perturbed at the lack of space in the tight room. Paul's sister Gemma and her husband entered last, clearly looking out of place and unwilling to join in.

Heidi held in her breath as she made her way to the entrance. She gave Amelia a hug and kissed Paul. She then faced the women. "Hello ladies," she said in the kindest tone she could muster. "Welcome to the party. Here are your tickets for the kids' carriage ride. They have a time on them but if you need to exchange for an earlier time, feel free to swap with someone."

To the surprise of no one—least of all Heidi—Cynthia took the opportunity to be catty. "I never took you for a horsey organiser, Heidi," she crowed sarcastically, "but then again, I never believed you when you said you were hosting this party in the first place. Tell me, is Ella paying you for this or are you just hoping to network yourself for a job as a stable girl?" The three laughed at Cynthia's 'wit' while their husbands slipped away.

Heidi ignored them. Impressing or entertaining these women was no longer on her agenda. Instead, she whispered a hello to Gemma and offered to hang her coat.

"I heard you were doing some *fundraising*," Cynthia called at her as she walked away. Paul put down his drink and looked interested. "You stopped at every house but mine. I wonder why that is? Is it because you knew I wouldn't help you, or was it because you knew that I knew exactly what you were up to?" Cynthia had been waiting for this moment, Heidi could feel it. Every word she said was calculated and said at a rate that was slow and deliberate.

"I'm sorry, what's all this?" Paul asked, looking searchingly at Heidi.

"That's right," Gemma sneered. "I know that while you have been pretending to raise money for Ella, all along, you have been raising the money for your husband. If you were able to save this place, your husband's debt on it would be paid or, or is there another scheme you are working on? Con-artists like you always seem to have something up their sleeves."

Half of the party had now turned to watch. Christmas carols playing softly over the loudspeaker were practically the only other sounds. Heidi scanned the room for Ella, but she was nowhere to be seen. She was most likely in the back, preparing to refill the drinks bowl or gathering up more food.

"Heidi, what is going on?" Paul looked at her sternly.

She tried to explain quickly. "Honey, I was just helping Ella. I owed it to her, so I helped her out by raising money to try and pay back the arrears."

"Raising money from this community to pay our debts? Why? Why would you do that? You know what this looks like, surely?" His anger was growing as faces burned a hole into the couple.

Taking a deep breath, Heidi took her husband's hand and turned and faced the onlookers. "I didn't try to do this for Paul or myself," she told the crowd. "I tried because Ella is the one person in this village that deserves our love and respect. She doesn't deserve to be evicted. I know what Paul did was wrong." She faced her husband directly. "But he didn't mean …we never meant for this to happen." Her voice was passionate, pleading. "I never meant to swindle or deceive anyone. I just wanted what was best for Ella."

"I believe you, Heidi." Ruth's voice reached over the tops of everyone's head.

"I believe you too," Colm chorused and Ella's staff also followed, joining Ruth as they made their way to Heidi.

"A true Clancy woman never lets anything go without a fight." Kim, Heidi's sister in law, suddenly appeared from nowhere and stood beside her, along with her brother Ben and the rest of the Clancy family.

"I believe you too," Her other sister-in-law piped in quietly. Cynthia and the girls shot Paul's sister Gemma a look that permanently sealed her fate in the group.

Similar agreeable mumbles began to pop up around the café, as Lakeview friends and neighbours gathered around Heidi to shield her from the dreaded Mummy Martyrs.

Some shook her hand, one of her mother's and Ella's mutual friends gave her a bear hug, and thanked her for her efforts.

Despite herself, Heidi swelled with pride.

. . .

SEEING SOMEONE OUTSIDE, Ruth ran to the back of the room as she spotted Ella entering, party platter in hand. "Merry Christmas, everyone," she called out huskily over the microphone. "While we know it's not the big night just yet, I heard that a very special visitor is making his way to Lakeview a couple of days early. Let's give a big round of applause for the man himself, Santa Claus!"

On cue, in walked a very convincing Santa Claus complete with long white beard, red velvet suit and black boots. He greeted each child as he made his way to the back of the room. Children gathered around him all ready to tell him their holiday wish lists.

Ella watched from the kitchen, smiling at the joy and happiness that came with her Santa Claus. As she put down the platter, Heidi approached her in a hurry, looking panicked.

"Ella, Ella. The carriage is here, but there's some kind of problem. I think there's something wrong with one of the horses."

CHAPTER 23

❄

*E*lla looked at Heidi quizzically. She had no idea what could be wrong with the horses and if there was, what she could do about it.

Obviously Joseph was otherwise engaged in Santa duties, but if there was an issue with one of the animals, someone would have surely told him in advance.

She put down the platter and grabbed her coat and a hat from the kitchen.

"Did they say what was wrong?"

"No. But it sounded bad."

"Of all things to go wrong, horses shouldn't be one of them."

As Ella made her way through the back door of the kitchen, she could hear Santa make an announcement over the speaker, yet there was no time to hear what exactly what was being said.

"Ho! Ho! Ho!" he called out jovially. "Before I begin, I have a very special present for someone here tonight. While I know it is cold and snowing, I hope you can all join me outside in the car park where my carriage awaits."

Santa led the group of partygoers outside, each curiously following behind in clusters of families and neighbours.

Ella was already outside trying to talk to Eric, one of Joseph's staff.

"What do you mean you can't let the kids ride in the carriages? That's exactly what they're for, didn't Joseph tell you! This is for the town, Eric." She pleaded with him, but he just smiled and shook his head. Heidi stood next to her, not a peep out of her.

"Is there a problem here?" Santa tapped Ella on her shoulder and she turned in shock to see practically the entire village, now gathered outside the café. She took a couple of steps back in shock.

"Just a little snag with the carriage rides, Jos…erm, Santa. We'll get it sorted out in no time. How about we go back inside?" She began to walk towards the door to the kitchen, yet no one moved. Everyone just watched her, and they were smiling.

"Ella, my dear girl," Joseph said with a wink, "How about you sit up in this carriage. Santa has a special present for you." Ella nervously took his hand as he hoisted her up in the old-fashioned open-top carriage's back seat, placing her walking cane in her lap. He stood on the step, elevated in front of the crowd.

"As you may have heard, this is to be our last night in Ella's beloved Heartbreak Cafe, for it is closing soon. When I first heard this, I was extremely upset. It was my favourite place to stop on my Christmas rounds. That is when Heidi suggested she help me out. While my Elves can build toys and wrap presents, it cannot make everything in the workshop." He grinned and Ella chuckled nervously at the crowd. Oh, so it was a going away present, how lovely. She guessed a bunch of roses or a box of chocolates or something.

"See, Santa knows that Ella hasn't been a good girl exactly. She told a little white lie to make us all feel better about her departure. It seems as though she didn't really want to retire, but had to because of reasons beyond her control. So with a little bit of Christmas magic and a whole lot of help from almost everyone in Lakeview, let me present Ella with a very special Christmas gift. Heidi?"

He moved out of the way as Heidi hopped into the carriage in the seat across from Ella. She quietly handed her an envelope and Ella's hands shook as she opened it.

Heidi's eyes were wet. "We couldn't bear to let you leave, Ella. We love you. The whole community loves you."

As she perused the envelope's contents, Ella's breath hitched audibly. Her jaw dropped and tears began to stream down her cheeks and onto her coat. Inside was another letter from the estate agent, this time announcing that the repossession order on the building had been lifted, and she was free to continue trading.

"How? When?" Her voice was shaking.

"Everyone chipped in to help pay off the arrears. Some gave a couple of euro, some gave hundreds. But we did it, Ella. We saved the café."

Heidi had too begun to cry and laugh all at the same time as Ella flung herself towards her for a huge, grateful hug.

How on earth? And Heidi Clancy of all people….

CHAPTER 24

❄

*A*fter several overwhelming minutes, she turned to face the crowd, "This is too much. How will I ever repay you all?"

"More muffins! Free coffee!" a voice in the crowd cried, as laughter erupted.

Ella stood up, balancing herself on Heidi's arm. She felt that she did need to say more. Her gratitude was overflowing.

"When I first met my husband and his family all those years ago, I was just another Lakeview girl. I loved this village. Every bit of it. From the neighbours who always had a kind word to say, to the way that the hair salon always knew when you were due for a trim. But my favourite place in the world was this café. It was where I met my husband Gregory, where we shared our first kiss, and where I last said goodbye to him the night he passed on from a heart attack." She looked down at her hands, choking back tears, and then ploughed on. "It's the place where all of our kids took their first steps, where they learned to talk, and definitely where they picked up a sweet tooth!" She looked up and waved at her smiling eldest son Dan, near the front.

"When I was left alone to run this café, I wasn't sure I could do it. I wasn't sure I could keep retain the same environment that you have all grown to love. But every day, customers would arrive. Every day, you ordered your cups of tea, your Irish breakfasts, your ham sandwiches.

And even when it was so hard to just get through another day alone, there was always someone there with a smile and a friendly hello. One night, I swore to myself and to my family's memory that I would keep this place alive in their spirit. I would make it the place they had dreamed it to be. Thanks to devoted staff members like Colm, Nina and the gang, it has been. But still, I never knew how much this place meant to me until I thought I was going to have to leave it. Today, you have given me back my home, my family, and my heart. There is no better Christmas gift than that. Thank you all. Thank you so much."

The crowd clapped as whistles and hollers were cried out. Ella sat down, waving at the friendly and familiar faces that blew her kisses and nodded happily.

Heidi stood again to speak, her voice shaking from the emotion of the moment. "Now, I think it is time for the first carriage ride around the lake! You all have your tickets, so be sure to meet here or miss out. Ella and Santa, will you do the honour of leading the first group?"

Joseph laughed as he got in the carriage next to Ella. He pulled the blanket up to his lap and waved at the crowd as he shouted his promises to the children to be back shortly for visits.

Heidi stepped out of the carriage as Ella grabbed her hand, "You, my dear, are something else."

Heidi smiled at her, more grateful for a friend than ever. She leaned over and whispered into Ella's ear. As Heidi caught her up, she looked at in shock. Heidi continued giving her more and more details on the situation. When she was finished, Ella smiled brightly and turned to Santa, her hand grasping his.

"Eric," Heidi called to the driver of the carriage, "I think we're ready now!"

The carriage sped off as Heidi stayed behind. She organised the next group by having them line up in families or groups of six. As they boarded, she took their ticket and waved them off, their sleds and horses making tracks in the snow. Kim was right. She was a good organiser.

The rest of the crowd began to disperse back inside. Heidi could hear Ruth and the pianist begin to perform.

"I am so proud of you." Paul wrapped his arms around her. She spun around to face him. His face was bright and cheery for the first time in weeks.

"I am so sorry I didn't tell you. I wanted to, but I didn't know how you would react."

"It's okay. It really is."

"No it isn't. I should have told you. I shouldn't have risked your reputation like that. You're my husband and you deserved to know and at least have a say in what I was doing. I am finished with lying. From now on, I am going to be one hundred percent honest with you, no matter what." She waited for him to begin scolding her, to agree with what she was saying.

"What you did here tonight and this week was amazing. While I am not happy that you lied, I am more thrilled that you are who you are, and that I am married to you. This is a side of you I have never seen. It's like falling in love with a completely new person." He laughed.

"Merry Christmas, honey," she whispered .

"Merry Christmas to you too sweetheart. Now let's go inside! I'm freezing, and Amelia is being watched by Kim. We'd better go and save her before her aunt starts giving her mulled wine."

Paul winked at Heidi, took her hand, and led her back into the party.

CHAPTER 25

❄

Inside the café, Ruth was just getting started. She was leading the entire crowd in carols and old Christmas favourites that everyone knew or could catch on to. Children excitedly ran through the gathering as the adults joined arms and sang along with neighbours and loved ones.

The music and jubilant atmosphere was infectious.

Ruth looked out at the crowd as she crooned into the microphone. It seemed like everyone was here in this tiny space—everyone but Charlie and Scarlett. She'd hoped she had missed them, that they were perhaps hiding in the kitchen waiting for her set to finish or maybe running behind in hopes of missing the crowd. But as time passed, the only member of her family that remained in the room was Ita.

It was hard not to spot her. Out of all the happy faces, hers was the most solemn. Dressed head to toe in mourning black, she sat at the front table just staring at Ruth. That fight they had earlier obviously wasn't done. And as Ruth's first set neared its break, she tried to plan an exit strategy to avoid any and all contact with this woman.

As the last song played, Ruth gave her, "We'll be back shortly! Enjoy the mulled wine responsibly" joke and turned to face Nicky, pretending to converse in order to avoid speaking with anyone else. While she did this, she grabbed her phone and sent a text message:

"Charlie! Where are you? What is going on? My first set just ended and your mother is here. Please come soon with Scarlett."

As she hit send, Ita, now sloppily drunk, approached her. *"Weshoultak,"* she said, slurring.

"Excuse me?" Ruth said, an eyebrow raised.

Ita composed herself and tried again. "We should talk," she responded.

"I'm just gonna go grab a bottle of water," Ruth explained, "and then we can talk if I have time before I go on again."

"No!" Ita shouted loudly at the back of Ruth's head as she walked away. "I want to talk to you *now*."

Ruth spun on her heel and walked off towards the kitchen, Ita on her heels. Cornered in the kitchen, Ruth had no choice but to confront her mother-in-law. "What do you want, Ita?" Ruth whispered low but stern hoping that she wouldn't draw anymore attention.

"You couldn't stay away, could you?" Ita said loudly. "I knew from the moment he met you—I knew that you were going to be trouble for the both of us. But then, you left and everything was back to normal. He got on with his life and got over you. But that wasn't good enough for you, was it? You had to come crawling back."

"I don't know what you are talking about."

"Yes you do! Stop lying! *This* was your plan all along. But I never imagined that you would be so trashy as to bring a baby into this mess. Was this your plan? Get knocked up from some random, rich actor for guaranteed payouts and then trap good old Charlie for extra support?"

"You nutcase!" Ruth exploded "How dare you! Yes, it was a mistake —getting pregnant, I mean—but Scarlett was never part of any plot. I love my daughter, and because of that I have never taken a single red cent from her father."

"Really? Then why were you in LA then? I read that you were spotted around town with him!" The accusation came out of the blue, completely unexpected.

"What are you implying, Ita? That I am cheating on Charlie, that I am getting back together with Scarlett's birth father—the man who abandoned his own daughter?"

"I wouldn't put it past a slut like you." She pointed her finger square in Ruth's chest emphasising the words, "like you."

"You know what, Ita?" Ruth said, grabbing her finger. "What I was doing is none of your business." She continued angrily. "For your information, I *did* see Troy while I was in LA, but it was completely unplanned. I had no idea that he was going to be there. Our time together was limited to reading at the casting agency's office and then at dinner that night with the director."

"So you admit it!" Ita declared triumphantly. "You're moving back there. You're leaving Charlie to care for your daughter while you galavant around Hollywood."

"Ita," Ruth said, disgust coming over her face. "You are so ignorant, it's not even funny. I turned down the damn role! I want nothing to do with it. When I saw who my co-star was, I knew I was not going to take the part. Plus, I would never, ever want to leave my daughter and husband behind. They are my family—something I value, but you obviously don't. And this is my home, too. I *live* here Ita—here, in Lakeview. If you have an issue with that, then that's your problem. I love your son, every bit of him and I always have. I love him because he fills my life with love and happiness, because he is a good father for Scarlett, and because he's going to be a great dad for the children we will have together. I love him because he has always supported and loved me. I cannot trade him in for a career or a chance with someone who let me down enough already! Charlie is *the whole reason* for all of it. Everything else is just window-dressing. I love your son. The only thing that blows my mind is how such a sweet, caring, wonderful man came from such a hateful, spiteful parent."

With that, Ruth marched off, her words echoing in her own ears. As she made her way back into the dining room, someone touched her arm and led her towards the corner of the room.

"Charlie! You scared me. Where have you been?"

"Listening to you." He pulled her to him tightly, leaning his body into hers. "I am so sorry for how I acted. When you left and I didn't hear from you that night, I let my mother get into my head. I let her convince me that you had this all planned, and that you were leaving me."

"Honey, I would never leave you. Ever. You and Scarlett are my life forever and always."

"But what about your career? What if Lakeview isn't good enough for you again?"

She sighed. Now seemed the best time to tell him the news that she had been keeping to herself. "I have some news about that, actually. I wanted to wait to tell you after the party… But I decided that I need to do something to give back to this community. So, I took some of my savings and took over one of Paul's properties. You know, the old pub off the square?"

"A pub?" Charlie looked at her, unsure if he should be mortified or if he should let her continue.

"No. I thought that maybe I could turn it into a stage school. It has all the right bones for it, and looks like it would be fairly easy to transform. I wanted to tell you. I really did, but I wasn't sure how to." She waited for a response, but he remained speechless, his face free from any expression or emotion.

"I am going to turn it into a stage school and maybe a theatre. It would be free to participate and the shows would raise money for different causes. To keep costs down, we can even host events there during the off season like small wedding ceremonies or town event meetings or something. It could really be something special. Are you mad? You should be. I should have told you."

"You are amazing," he smiled down at her, completely flabbergasted at this woman and her crazy notions. "Of course I will support you. This idea sounds amazing. But let's talk about it tomorrow. Tonight is your night."

He took her hand and led her back into the crowd, just in time to watch Ita walk out the door in a huff. Her attempt at slamming the door was completely masked by the roar of the crowd as Ruth took the mic once again.

"This song, I dedicate to my husband, the man of my life forever and always." Ruth turned to Nicky and began to sing one of her favourite Christmas ballads 'Have Yourself a Merry Little Christmas.'

And as she sang the lyric, about all troubles being out of sight, she looked directly at Charlie who had picked up Scarlett from the group of children and begun to dance.

CHAPTER 26

❄

The carriage bounced up and down and rattled to and fro. But while the ride around the lake was rocky, Ella didn't mind. She was too preoccupied with watching the houses and businesses of the community pass her by. The snow was falling softly as it covered the trees with a light dusting in front of them.

After several minutes of silence, she moved her hand out from under Santa and turned to face him. She tugged at his beard a bit and pulled off his hat. She knew all along that Joseph would make the perfect Santa Claus.

"Can I ask you a question?"

"Is it how I manage to fit all those presents in my sled?" he chuckled.

"No. I want to ask you why."

"Why what?"

"Why did you give Heidi the rest of the money? It's just too much. I don't know if I can accept it, Joseph."

"Well, I refuse to take it back, so there is no use in telling me you don't want my contribution." He smiled at her.

"Please, let's just make this a loan. I will pay you back, every penny with interest."

"And I wont accept a cent."

"Be serious, Joseph. I know this is a lot of money we are talking about. There is no way you just had it lying around to give to a friend like me and my lowly little café."

He stared at her long and hard, unsure of how to proceed. Sighing, he said, "You are not my friend."

"What?"

"Ella, I love you. I have loved you for nearly two decades now, but I have never had the courage to say it, never found the right moment to tell you. I'm not trying to use this money, this gift, to buy your affection and you don't have to say it back to me if you do not mean it. You're under no obligation. But that money is money I have been saving to start a family of my own. It just never happened for me, but now, I know what I want. I want you. I want to be part of *your* family. And I want to help keep this café alive and going."

She looked at him, studied his face, and searched for an answer. Every bit of her was screaming to say something, but she could only smile and hold his hand. Eventually, she leaned down and nuzzled into the wide expanse of his shoulders. His coat still smelling of pine trees and Christmas.

"If I am going to accept this money, I want you to make me a promise."

"Yeah, and what is that?"

"You will be a partner. And," she held up a hand to silence the protest she knew was coming, "I will not take *no* for an answer. We will be partners in the business—you and me."

"It doesn't seem like I have much of a choice, does it?" he chuckled, kissing the top of her forehead as they snuggled closer together. They passed the rest of the ride in silence, but it was also full with hope and promise that for these two people past the prime of their lives, each day from hereon would be more meaningful with the other in it.

"Here we are, Ella," Eric McGrath said as he pulled the carriage to a halt in front of the back door. Already a second group had lined up with Heidi giving out instructions and taking tickets. As they approached, Joseph quickly repositioned his beard and fixed his red hat on top of his head.

Ella led the way as the couple entered the party once more. When Ruth spotted the two, she quickly finished her song and ushered Ella to the stage.

Ella lowered the microphone and spoke, "Now is my favourite time of the evening. For all the boys and girls out there, Santa is here to visit! We will be taking pictures and he'll be listening to all of your wish lists. Parents, you can enjoy the famous Heartbreak Café Christmas mulled wine while your children are waiting." She winked. "And it looks like it's going to be a long queue!"

The crowd burst into applause and shouts of glee as everyone moved to either the Santa line or the food and drinks queue. Ruth began to sing some more.

While everyone was preoccupied, Ella snuck back out to her little office. She again searched her desk for the brown envelope of pictures. While most of them she had put on display, she had kept one to herself —the black and white photo of herself and her husband on the night of their first kiss.

She looked at their faces, so young and full of optimism of the life they had ahead of them. Gregory especially looked as if he could Lakeview and easily the world. It was that smile. She grinned at the thought of him. Running her fingers over the thick paper, she put her lips to the photograph and placed it back in the envelope. She knew in her heart that he would be delighted for her.

It was then that she heard the music start the first few notes of an old familiar song that she remembered fondly dancing to with her Gregory. She headed outside, past the well-wishers and in search of Joseph. Unfortunately, she could not find him anywhere. All of the children had finished their turns sitting on Santa's lap and were preoccupied with the lollipops he had given them. The parents were still hovering over the mulled wine. The rest of the crowd danced in the centre of the room.

That is when she spotted him—Santa suit and all. Walking back to her office, she grabbed her coat and met him in the front. "Joseph Evans," she chided. "What are you doing out here? Come back inside."

Joseph turned to face her, shovel in hand. "If you want me to be a co-owner of this café," he called, "you have to let me keep you safe. First order of business is keeping the paths clear and free of snow and frost. I wouldn't want anyone fall—"

Before he could say another word, Ella walked towards him, grabbed the white trim collar, and pulled him in for a long, slow kiss.

Such an embrace was the first in a very long time for both of them, but she knew that they would learn and love together.

It was a kiss filled with promise and meaning, a sign of love that had been growing for forever.

And as the snow fell gently around them and festive music played in the background, it was, Ella thought to herself, the first of many, many more to come.

NEW NOW FROM MELISSA

THE BEAUTIFUL LITTLE THINGS - EXCERPT

The magic was missing...

Romy Moore sat at the window chair in her late mother's study and looked out over the nearby woods and forestry trails, appreciating why her mum had always found this spot so peaceful.

The trees wore a light dusting of white, the family home's elevated position in the Dublin Mountains ensuring they always got a bit of proper snow in winter, as opposed to the typically damper stuff on lower ground.

Fittingly beautiful for the season, but also serving merely to highlight the fact that everything felt so... wrong.

Romy's world was so out of kilter now that it should be howling gales and driving rain out, not Christmas-card perfection. It made everything even more desperately hollow and painful, and now she understood why some people found this time of year so difficult. The forced festive gaiety, the crippling sense of nostalgia and the idea that everything was supposed to be so bloody *wonderful*. When all she wanted to do right then was pull the covers over her head like it was just another day, a normal day, and she didn't have to pretend to be OK, to try to cheer up and put a brave face on for anyone else's sake.

And most of all, not to have to lie to herself that this time of year, to say nothing of *life*, could ever be the same without her mother.

Romy turned back to the desk and opened up a drawer, seeking a tissue. She found an already open packet of Kleenex and paused a little, reflecting that her mum would've likely used the one just before it, oblivious to the fact that her youngest would be needing the next to grieve her passing.

She wiped her eyes and then blew her nose into the tissue, looking idly through bits and pieces scattered across the desk before coming across a prettily patterned notebook beneath some letters.

Opening the cover, she saw her mother's familiar neat handwriting swirl into focus, achingly comforting, and as she began to read the opening words on the page, Romy quickly realised it was one of her journals.

Her mother loved to write and had kept a journal for as long as Romy could remember – ever the traditionalist at heart, despite her sister Joanna's grand attempt a couple of years back to move her into the twenty-first century with the gift of an iPad.

Feeling like an interloper for even daring to read – these were her mother's private thoughts, after all – she couldn't help but be drawn in, desperate to feel close to her once more.

If you are reading this, then for certain I am no longer with you.

In body at least.

Indeed, it is hard for me to be writing this now, from a place where I am still full of the joys, having just watched you all depart our very last family Christmas together.

While this year's gathering was, in a word . . . eventful, it gives me such joy that all ended happily – just as I'd hoped.

I wish I could imagine how your lives have been since – and, admittedly, I have tried – but when I attempt to imagine any scenarios that have transpired in the interim, I tend to go down a rabbit hole and overwhelm myself.

I cannot control what will happen. Just as I cannot see the future, I have no way of knowing how any of you will handle my passing.

The only thing I can do from this vantage point right this minute is provide my thoughts, my words, and perhaps a little bit of motherly advice.

I'm trying to picture you all together this time next year without me – and truth be told, I struggle with the concept because it feels so foreign.

So bear with me, as I seek to find the words and comb the recesses of my mind for any wisdom or reminders that might be useful as you navigate the festive period without me.

Firstly, it's OK to feel sad . . . but not forever.

And please do not let grief colour the first Christmas where I am absent. Whatever you do, don't allow sorrow to serve as the backdrop.

Because, oh my darlings, it is still the absolute best time of year and as you know has always been my favourite.

So please, for my sake, celebrate this Christmas as if I was still here?

Because I will be, in my own way – in all the little festive traditions we have followed over the years, and recipes and rituals that have become our family's staples.

Yes, of course this will be a Christmas like no other.

But that doesn't mean it has to be a terrible one.

It was like . . . a gift, Romy thought, a lump in her throat; though obviously not for her alone.

Because of course her mother would have understood that the family's first holiday period without her would be impossibly difficult.

Though she couldn't possibly have known just how scattered and broken they'd all become since her passing.

But maybe . . . Romy thought, sitting up straight as an idea struck her, and her mind raced as she flicked through the pages, desperate to read more of her mother's wisdom, or any pointers that might help endure her absence.

Maybe this was *exactly* what was needed to mend things – something to gather up all the little broken pieces that were this family now, and help put them back together?

As Romy continued reading, something akin to hope blossomed within her for the first time all year, as she realised that this was the miracle she'd been searching for.

Thank you, Mum. I think I know what to do . . .

While this family might be sinking beneath the surface at the moment, perhaps, with a little guidance, there was hope for them yet.

END OF EXCERPT.

THE BEAUTIFUL LITTLE THINGS - is out now in paperback, ebook and audio.

ABOUT THE AUTHOR

International #1 and USA Today bestselling author Melissa Hill lives in County Wicklow, Ireland.

Her page-turning emotional stories of family, friendship and romance have been translated into 25 different languages and are regular chart-toppers internationally.

A Reese Witherspoon x Hello Sunshine adaptation of her worldwide bestseller SOMETHING FROM TIFFANY'S is filming now for release in 2022.

THE CHARM BRACELET aired in 2020 as a holiday movie A Little Christmas Charm. A GIFT TO REMEMBER (and a sequel) was also adapted for screen by Hallmark Channel and multiple other titles by Melissa are currently in development for film and TV.

Visit her website at
www.melissahill.info
Or get in touch via social media links below.

Printed in Great Britain
by Amazon